PUFFIN BOOKS

DOCTOR DOLITTLE AND THE SECRET LAKE

Long before the time of this story, when Doctor Dolittle was running his post office in Africa, he had a letter from an old turtle called Mudface, who lived, as you may remember, in the Secret Lake of Junganyika. Mudface was so old that he had been alive in the days of the Flood, and as he was suffering from gout brought on by the damp climate, the Doctor had arranged for the birds to drop stones and pebbles in the lake to make a nice dry island for him to live on.

So it was a nasty surprise for the Doctor, and Mudface's other friends, when Cheapside the cockney sparrow returned from a trip to Africa with the news that half the island had collapsed and buried Mudface in an earthquake. Of course, amphibious reptiles can stay under water and go without food for a long time, but the Doctor said, 'I don't know whether I can be of any real help to my old friend Mudface. But I feel that at least I ought to go down there and see what I can do.'

Polynesia said, 'I quite agree with you, Doctor. Of course we ought to go back to the Secret Lake – not only on the turtle's account, but to get the story of the Flood again.

DOCTOR DOLITTLE and THE SECRET LAKE

ILLUSTRATED BY THE AUTHOR

BY HUGH LOFTING

PUFFIN BOOKS

Puffin Books, Penguin Books Ltd, Harmondsworth, Middlesex, England
Penguin Books, 625 Madison Avenue, New York, New York 10022, U.S.A.
Penguin Books Australia Ltd, Ringwood, Victoria, Australia
Penguin Books Canada Ltd, 2801 John Street, Markham, Ontario, Canada L3R 1B4
Penguin Books (N.Z.) Ltd, 182–190 Wairau Road, Auckland 10, New Zealand

—

First published by Jonathan Cape 1949
Published in Puffin Books 1969
Reprinted 1973, 1974, 1975, 1977, 1981

—

Set, printed and bound in Great Britain by
Cox & Wyman Ltd, Reading
Set in Linotype Pilgrim

For my son Christopher

CONTENTS

PART ONE

I

THE SEEDS FROM THE MOON

I WAS writing at my office-table, in Doctor Dolittle's house; and it was about nine o'clock in the morning.

Polynesia the parrot sat at the window, looking out into the garden. She was humming a sailor song to herself as she watched the tree-boughs sway in the wind. Suddenly, with a squawk, the song stopped.

'Tommy,' said she, 'there's that good-for-nothing Matthew Mugg coming in at the gate.'

'Oh, splendid!' I cried, getting up from my desk. 'I'll go and let him in. The cats'-meat-man hasn't been around to see us in ages.'

'Oh, he's been in jail again, I suppose – as usual,' muttered the parrot. – 'Been *borrowing* a few rabbits or pheasants from Squire Jenkins' place. – The lazy poacher! I'm going out into the pantry to get a drink.'

I hurried to open the big front door. Matthew Mugg stood, smiling, on the steps.

'Why, Tommy Stubbins!' he cried. 'I declare you grow a foot taller every time I meet you.'

'You shouldn't stay away so long, Matthew,' said I. 'Come in. It's good to see you.'

'Thank you, Tommy. Hope I ain't interruptin' your work.'

'No, Matthew. The Doctor will be glad you've come too. Let's go into my study. And then I'll find him and tell him you're here.'

'*Your* study!' said Matthew, following me down the

passage. 'You mean to say you got an office of your own now?'

'Well,' I said, 'it's really the Doctor's old waiting-room. But he lets me use it as an office – gives him more peace, to write alone. Here it is: what do you think of it?'

I opened the door off the hall and let him in. The cats'-meat-man gasped.

'My word, Tommy, but it's helegant! What a lovely office! And all to yourself too. This must make you feel awful grown up. My, but you're a lucky boy!"

'Yes,' I said – 'very lucky, Matthew.'

'I'll bet your ma and pa are proud. At your age, to be

secretary to the great Doctor John Dolittle! Getting all your schooling pleasant-like. No teacher running after you with a stick. And here's your office; with a desk, and ink-pots, and books and microscope and – everything! I suppose you can talk the animal languages as good as the Doctor now.'

'Ah, no,' I laughed – 'not as well as the Doctor. I don't think anyone will ever do that. But let me go and tell him you're here, Matthew. I know he wants to see you.'

'No, hold on a minute, Tommy. Don't bother him just yet. I want to have a word with you first – just you and me – if you don't mind.'

'Why, certainly, Matthew,' said I. 'Sit down, won't you?'

I closed the door while the cats'-meat-man settled himself in an armchair.

'Now,' I said, 'we won't be disturbed here – for a while at least. What was it, Matthew?'

He leaned forward, glancing over his shoulder as though afraid someone else would hear.

'Well – ' he began. Then he laughed. 'Funny, ain't it? I just can't seem to help talkin' in whispers when I get speakin' of your voyage to the Moon with the Doctor. Sort of habit I got into – when we was so afraid of them news-papermen comin' around, trying to find out things.'

'Yes,' I said, 'I don't wonder at that.'

'You remember last time I saw you, Tommy? The Doc-tor was busy on them melon-seeds he brought back from the Moon. Trying to grow vegetables, he was, to keep a man alive for ever. You remember?'

'Yes, Matthew, he was.'

'And that's what I wanted to talk to you about. How's he getting on with that everlasting-life business? Seemed a kind of balmy notion to me.'

'It's hard to say, Matthew. Although I help him all I can, you know, I believe the Doctor is beginning to get a bit dis-couraged. This climate here in England is very different from the climate we found in the Moon. And while we have used the conservatory and the hot-houses in the garden trying to copy the moon climate, we have not had any great success so far. You know the Doctor, Matthew; he never grumbles or complains; but I'm afraid he's growing discouraged just the same. Polynesia thinks so too.'

The cats'-meat-man shook his head.

'Well, Tommy, if that parrot thinks that John Dolittle is down-hearted, you can be sure he is. What do you suppose the Doctor is going to do now?'

'I'm not sure, Matthew; I never pester him. He hates to be hustled. That's what interested him about lengthening life – the way it is on the Moon. He wanted to feel that he had all the time in the world for all the things he wants to do – without this hustling and bustling, as he calls it.'

'Do you think, maybe, he'll be going on a voyage, Tommy?'

'I don't know, Matthew. He'll tell us when he's ready to. That at least is sure.'

'It's a long time since he went on one. Let's see – how long is it?'

'Quite a while,' I answered. 'But let me go and try to find him. You wait here. I'll be back in a minute.'

I was pretty certain that the Doctor would be in his study – at that hour of the morning he usually was. But today he wasn't. Then I started to hunt for Polynesia the parrot; for I felt sure she could tell me where the Doctor was. But I could not find Polynesia either. So I supposed the Doctor must have gone for a walk.

When I came back and told Matthew, the cats'-meat-man said he would not wait now for John Dolittle's return. He had some business to attend to in Puddleby; but he would try to come in again later in the day.

So I bade him good-bye for the present and went back to the work in my office.

Funny old Matthew! He was always hoping that John

14

Dolittle (of whose friendship he was so proud) would take him along on one of his voyages. He wanted to see the world and have adventures in foreign lands. But Polynesia said she was sure that all he really wanted was to keep away from the police – when he had done something he shouldn't.

2

PRINCE, THE IRISH SETTER

WITHIN the Doctor's house and garden there were a tremendous lot of things for me to do these days. But Matthew had been right when he said I was lucky. No youngster could have been busier – or happier. And certainly no one can look back upon his years of learning with more pleasure than can I, Tommy Stubbins of Puddleby-on-the-Marsh.

The schooling I got from Doctor Dolittle, through being his secretary, was not only good schooling; it was wonderful fun, thrilling and exciting for a boy, as well. I dipped into so many things which most people do not study till they are quite grown up. Astronomy; navigation; geology or the history of rocks and fossils; the science of medicine; kitchen-gardening – for both the sick and the well; all these – and a hundred more – interested me tremendously.

But one thing above all made my education most different from that of other young people: animal languages. Through this I was able to learn so much which I could not have done in any other way. The same thing had been true for the Doctor himself. Many times he had said to me: 'Stubbins, if it had not been for Polynesia – and the lessons she gave me in parrot talk years ago – I never could have learned a quarter of what I have about natural history.'

And to this I answered: 'Yes, Sir. But let's not forget that the animals are grateful to you too. Before you came along how much was known about animal-doctoring?'

There were times, though, when even I was bound to wonder whether knowing the languages of animals was *always* a good thing for us. The creatures that came to the Doctor's door with their troubles (everything from plough-horses to field-mice) took up a terrible lot of our time. But the Doctor would not turn a single one of them away.

And then, besides the doctoring work, there were many other things we did for the animals – sometimes quite peculiar things. For instance, when I got back to my office that morning I found the Doctor's dog, Jip, waiting for me. And Jip had brought a friend with him.

This friend was an Irish setter, called Prince. And he had been well named; for he was, I think, the most princely, gentlemanly dog I have ever known. Many months ago Jip had brought him to us to try and get him into the Doctor's 'Home for Crossbred Dogs.' Not that he was a cross-bred, a mongrel – indeed, no! He had in his day been a prize-winner, a blue-ribbon champion, at the shows. And though the Doctor suspected that he had run away from some rich home, Jip and Prince never told anyone where he came from. And they begged very hard that he should be made a member of the Doctor's Dog Club, which was inside the 'zoo' enclosure at the bottom of the garden.

John Dolittle was quite willing, of course. But, by the club rules, Prince couldn't be a member unless the other dogs (the club committee) said they wanted him. Well, to my great surprise, at first the committee did not want poor Prince.

You see, they were all mongrels and crossbreds them-selves; and they did not want any thoroughbreds joining *their* club. Jip got so angry with the committee he took the whole lot of them on in a free-for-all fight; and I had to get up in the middle of the night and stop the battle.

But before morning the committee gave in; and the beautiful Irish setter was made a club-member and allowed to stay with us.

Well, this morning, as I looked at the two dogs waiting in my office, I knew at once that something was wrong. In Prince's proud but friendly face there was a great sadness; while Jip just looked very disgruntled and upset. It was Jip who started the talk.

Now when I speak of 'talk' between animals and myself, you who read this must understand that I do not always mean the usual kind of talk between persons. Animal 'talk' is very different. For instance, you don't only use the mouth for speaking. Dogs use the tail, twitchings of the nose, movements of the ears, heavy breathing – all sorts of things – to make one another understand what they want. Of course the Doctor and I had no tails of our own to swing around. So we used the tails of our coats instead. Dogs are very clever; they quickly caught on to what a man meant to say when he wagged his coat-tail.

Doctor Dolittle had started learning dog talk long before I had; and I never got to be as good at it as he was. But I managed all right. After getting lessons from old Jip (and from Polynesia the parrot – who spoke English too, very well) I could make myself understood by any dog – even the German dachshund.

'Well, Tommy,' Jip began, 'Prince here doesn't want to stay with us any longer. He wants to leave.'

'Wants to leave!' I asked. 'Why? – Isn't he comfortable at the Dogs' Club?'

Poor Jip seemed almost too unhappy to go on talking. He fidgeted uneasily with his front feet. At last he said:

'No, Tommy, it's not that. But – er – he – well – er he –' Then suddenly he turned almost savagely to the other dog.

'*You* tell him, Prince,' he snapped. 'Why do you leave it to me to do all the talking for you?'

Prince had been looking out of the window into the garden. Now he started to squirm and fidget too. Presently he said:

'Well, Tommy, I – er – we brought this to you – I mean we didn't go to the Doctor about it – because we didn't want to hurt the Doctor's feelings. I have been very happy at the Dogs' Club – happier than I have ever been in my life – anywhere. But –'

The setter stopped and looked out of the window again. And I began to wonder if I would ever get to hear what the trouble was. The morning was almost gone and I had a lot of work to do.

'Come, come!' said I. 'Tell me: you say you like living at the club. Then why do you want to go away?'

Again there was a short silence. At last Prince looked straight at me and said in a low voice:

'It's the rabbits, Tommy.'

'The rabbits?' I gasped. 'You don't mean to say *they* are driving you away!'

'Yes, I do,' said the dog. 'They have made my life just unbearable.'

'But how?' I asked. 'I don't understand.'

Then suddenly speaking fast, he said:

'They're so cheeky – those wretched rabbits. You know, Tommy, that the Doctor won't allow Jip or me to *touch* them – not even to chase them. He says that every animal who lives here, in his house or his garden, is to be allowed to live in peace – even the rats in the tool-shed. The Doctor's so kind-hearted. But you should just see those rabbits! They've dug their holes right in his lawn, all over the place – ruined it. But that isn't enough. Just because John Dolittle protects them from us dogs, they try to poke fun at us. It gets worse and worse all the time. They don't even pop into their holes when I walk over the lawn now. I have to shut my eyes, so I won't see them. And the other day, as I crossed the garden with my eyes closed, I ran smack into a

tree and gave my head a terrible crack. They thought that
was a great joke and burst out laughing. One of them – his
name's Floppy, I think – he's made up a song about me. –
Something like this:

> 'Mincie, mincie, mincie!
> Look at silly Princie!
> Always walking on his toes
> While rabbits run right by his nose.
> You can't catch ME!'

'It's more than any dog could stand, Tommy. Those hor-
rible, little underground, lop-eared vermin! I believe if
they had hands they would thumb their noses at me, *me*
the grandson of "Will o' the Mist," the greatest gun dog,
the most famous prize-winning Irish setter of all time. ....
I – I'm sorry, but I've *got* to go.'

If you can imagine a dog just about to break down crying, real tears and all, then you have a picture of Prince at
that moment – and of Jip too, for that matter. I myself was
a little bit inclined to laugh at the story of the cheeky
rabbits; but seeing how serious a matter it was to the well-
bred setter who had told it, I kept a very straight face as I
said:

'Well, but Prince, why not let the Doctor speak to this
silly Floppy – or whatever his name is? Maybe that's all
that is needed to make him behave – and the rest of the
rabbits too.'

'No, Tommy,' said Prince sadly. 'I don't want to cause
trouble between the Doctor and his friends. Besides, my
nose – for a good gun dog – is getting spoiled entirely. If I
stay here much longer I won't be able to smell the difference between a rabbit and a cat on a damp wind. The only
thing for me to do is to leave.'

'But where will you go when you leave us?'

'Well, Tommy,' said Prince, 'that's part of what I came
to talk to you about. When people have lost their dogs,

don't they sometimes put a piece in the newspaper about it?'

'Oh,' said I, 'you mean an advertisement – for lost and found property, eh?'

'Yes,' said the setter, 'I suppose that's what you call it. Only this wouldn't be an advertisement for a lost dog; just for a new home for a dog. Couldn't you put a piece in the newspaper saying a thoroughbred Irish setter can be had for nothing?'

'Why, certainly, Prince, I should think so. But there's no telling what kind of a home you'll get – that way. It might not be as good as what you have here.'

'Well,' said the dog, 'can't we say in the advertisement just what kind of a home I'd like?'

'Humph!' I muttered. 'It's a new idea: a dog advertising in the newspaper for the kind of home and people *he* wants, instead of the people going round picking and choosing the dog *they* want.'

'They'll want me all right, Tommy,' said Prince. 'I'm not conceited, you know that. But after all, I do know more about the business of being a good gun dog than anyone else. And you could put this in the paper too: say that I'll be willing to teach young puppies to be good gun dogs. You know those little tykes: how they're always running in front of the guns just as the men fire – and getting their tails shot off. Yes, put that in: I'll give classes for setter-pups – so long, of course, as I am given the kind of home and treatment *I* want. – Oh, I almost forgot: I don't want any children, either, around the place – that is, not real young children.'

'Why, Prince?' I asked. 'Don't you like children?'

'Oh, yes,' said he. 'But not the very young ones – under, say, six years old. Those little boys and girls always want to play with dogs on the nursery floor. They haven't much sense – can't tell the difference between us, the live dogs, and those stuffed, woolly dogs they get for Christmas.

They're always trying to pull our eyes out and change them over. And their mothers raise no end of fuss if we even growl at the brats for it. . . . Oh, and another thing: no flea-soap – please! I don't want anyone washing me with flea-soap.'

It was hard for me not to smile at the serious look on Prince's face as he spoke. Jip, too, showed by a nod and a deep growl that he agreed with what his friend said. While Jip had never won prizes as a gun dog, as Prince had done, he was, in his own way, a better, more clever smeller even than this thoroughbred setter. He still wore around his neck the solid-gold dog-collar (with his name on it) which had been given him years ago for saving a sailor's life at sea, by tracing him to a desert island just by smell.

So, to keep them both from seeing that I was trying not to laugh, I reached for paper and a pencil on my desk and began taking notes of what Prince was telling me.

'No, Tommy,' he went on, 'most of those flea-soaps smell of carbolic – or tar. It may be very healthy and all that. But it's an awful whiff! Besides, no gun dog could tell if he's following a pheasant or a quail or a beer-barrel, so long as his own coat smells like a chemist's shop.'

'All right, Prince,' I said. 'I'll put that down too. Now is there anything else? How about cats? Do you mind if your new home has any cats?'

I was surprised when he told me, no – he had no objection to cats. As a matter of fact, I had noticed that the setter was the only dog in the Doctor's Club who seemed really friendly with Itty, the cat which John Dolittle had brought back with him from the Moon. All the other animals in the Doctor's household still kept away from her. But the gentle Prince could often be seen walking and talking with the moon cat in the garden. I sometimes wondered if he was, in his own way, a little sorry for this strange and lonely creature who had been willing and brave enough to come down to Earth with the Doctor.

So, I wrote out the advertisement to be put in the newspaper, *The Puddleby Press*. I am very sure that nothing like it ever appeared, before or since, in the whole history of advertising. It ran like this:

WANTED a good home for pedigreed Irish setter, grandson of Champion "Will o' the Mist". No money required. Dog must be free at all times, never chained up or fenced in. Good manners. Three times winner of the West Counties Trophy for the Best Sporting Dog of the Year. Willing to teach thoroughbred puppies to be good gun dogs for all kinds of game. No baths with flea-soap. Will come on trial. Strictly no small children. Home and family must be the very best. Only those with good-natured gamekeepers need apply. Write to "Prince", care of *Puddleby Press*.

3

A VISIT FROM CHEAPSIDE

NOT long after Prince's advertisement was put in the newspaper he found a good home and left us. But he made an arrangement that he would be given one week-end of holiday every month, so that he would be free to visit the Doctor, Jip and all his old friends of the club.

On the day he left to go to his new home he came into my office to thank me.

'It was very kind of you, Tommy,' he said. 'It made it much easier for me – like that. I would have hated to go straight to the Doctor saying I wanted to leave his club.'

That was the way it always was: if the animals wanted anything done, which they were afraid might hurt the Doctor's feelings, they asked me to do it for them. That same morning when I wrote the advertisement a bird, a mother chaffinch, came to see me. Would I, please, she asked, speak to the Doctor for her? With a sigh I put away the note-book I was working on. I asked the chaffinch what was the trouble.

'It's the Doctor, Tommy,' she said. 'He *will* keep feeding my children – with bird-seed – close to the nest.'

'Well,' I asked, 'what's wrong with that?'

'What's *wrong*, young man!' said the mother-bird almost angrily. 'Why, my children aren't learning to fly! Oh, yes, they'll flutter a few feet, off a bush, down to the ground to eat the seed and then back to the nest again. Their father and I just don't know what to do. *Our* children have always been such good fliers. But this lot! – They could barely fly over a barn. They're as fat as turkeys. – Stuffing their faces, instead of hunting their food. . . . Between meals they sleep all day . . . waiting for the Doctor to –'

The mother chaffinch was on the edge of tears, I could see. So before she started weeping, I quickly interrupted her.

'Why didn't you speak to the Doctor?' I asked.

'Oh, I couldn't,' she said quickly. 'The Doctor has always been so kind, I'd be afraid –'

'Ah, yes,' I said hurriedly. 'I'd forgotten. Well, I wish some of you, *once* in a while, would be afraid you might overwork me too . . . All right, I'll speak to him. I'll go and do it right away.'

But of course, while it was sometimes a nuisance, when I was especially busy, it was a thing I was very proud of: that the creatures so often brought their troubles to me – because I was the only one, besides the Doctor, who could speak their languages.

I went back to the Doctor's study. I did not find him there – but I did find, to my great surprise, Cheapside the London sparrow. He was looking at a book which lay open on the Doctor's desk. At the same time he was eating cake-crumbs from a plate the Doctor had used last night.

'Why, hulloa, Cheapside!' I cried. 'I had no idea you were in the house. How long have you been here?'

'Only just come,' he mumbled with his mouth full. 'Was awful hungry. – Good cake, that. – Tell me, Tommy, this book the Doc's been reading, what's it about?'

I looked at the top of the open page.

'It seems to be – er – a sort of very ancient history – long, long ago, you know, when people lived in caves and all that.'

'Yer don't say!' murmured the sparrow as I turned over the leaves. – 'Oh, look, there's a pitcher! – Ain't 'e a rummy-looking bloke? What's 'is name?'

'It doesn't say, Cheapside. – It's just a picture of a cave-man.'

'Well, 'e should 'ave 'ad 'is 'air cut afore 'e 'ad 'is likeness took. But tell me Tommy: what's the Doctor studying all this stuff for? I thought you said 'e was working on them moon-plants and heverlastin' life.'

'Yes,' I said – 'he was. But lately I've noticed he is doing a lot of reading on what they call *pre-historic times*. That's one of the reasons I fear he is getting discouraged over the work he has been busy on ever since we got back from the Moon.'

'Humph!' muttered Cheapside thoughtfully. – 'Pre-'is-toric times, eh? John Dolittle's got one friend anyway, what could tell 'im a lot about them days.'

'Oh, who's that?' I asked.

'Why, old Mudface the turtle,' said the sparrow. ''E could tell 'im plenty. – Claims 'e was one of the animals on the Ark with Old Man Noah. Meself, I don't believe a word of the yarn.'

'Oh, of course!' said I. 'You were on that trip to the Secret Lake to visit Mudface, with the Doctor, weren't you, Cheapside?'

'You bet I was, Tommy. The muddiest, messiest journey I ever made. The trouble with old Mudface was 'e talked too much. But if the Doc is takin' up early 'istory, Mudface could tell 'im more than any books could.'

24

'Yes,' I said. 'He brought back many note-books which he had filled with things that Mudface told him. They're all carefully stored away in the underground library, you know, Cheapside – the one I made in the garden while we were waiting for the Doctor to get back from the Moon?'

'That's right, Tommy. There must 'ave been a good twenty of them note-books. And when the turtle was finished, the Doctor got all of us birds to build 'im a new home – a sort of island we made by dropping stones into the lake where the old Mudface lived.'

'My, but that must have taken a long time, Cheapside! Even the biggest birds could not carry a very large load of stone. How deep was the lake?'

'I've no idea, Tommy. But deep enough, I can tell you. Days and days the job took us. Of course big birds – eagles and the likes of them – they could bring stones as big as bricks. Little blokes, in my class, we fetched pebbles.'

'Goodness, Cheapside, I'd have thought it would take years instead of days!'

'No. You see there was millions of us on the job. That was when the Doctor had his post-office service – you know, the Swallow Mail, as 'e called it. It seems the old turtle got a message to him, somehow, through the mail. 'E was 'avin rheumatics in 'is legs.'

'I see, Cheapside. – The usual thing: the animals bringing their ailments to John Dolittle to cure.'

'That's it, Tommy. Only this time the Doctor was brought to the patient, instead of the other way around. My, what a trip it was to get to that Secret Lake! Right into the heart of darkest Africa.'

'How big was the island you made?' I asked.

'As big around as St James's Park,' said the sparrow – 'bigger, if anything. Yes, we done a nice job, if I do say it meself. Nice and high – and flat on the top. That was to keep old Mudface dry when he wasn't swimming. Seemed to me a lot of that fancy business was wasted on a turtle. But the

Doc said nothin' was too good for an animal what had sailed on the Ark with Noah.'

'Well,' I said thoughtfully, 'it does seem kind of wonderful, when you come to think of it.'

'Maybe,' grunted Cheapside. 'But gettin' back to dear old London seemed a lot more wonderful to me. I don't know what the Doctor wrote down in all them note-books 'e filled about the Flood. The story part of it we all understood; but there was some skyentific stuff we didn't.'

'As a matter of fact, Cheapside,' said I, 'I haven't looked into those note-books, myself. I've been too busy.... But – I'm not sure yet – I think you have given me an idea. Let us go and hunt up Polynesia. – I can't find the Doctor anywhere – maybe she can tell us where he is.'

4

THE DOCTOR DISAPPEARS

I WENT to the kitchen first. And here I found most of the Doctor's regular animal family. Dab-Dab the duck was there; also Jip, Too-Too the owl, Chee-Chee the monkey, Gub-Gub the pig and Whitey the white mouse. There was perfect silence in the kitchen when I came in. But somehow I was sure that they had only just stopped talking before I opened the door – most likely when Too-Too's keen ears had heard my step coming along the passage.

Then I noticed that Polynesia was not among them. I asked Dab-Dab if she knew where the parrot was. And that seemed to break the spell, as it were; they all started talking at once. But I begged them to be quiet so that I could hear the duck's answer to my question. Then Dab-Dab poured out a long story.

The Doctor had disappeared! No one had seen him since he went to bed last night. I would not ordinarily have been upset by this news; but I had, myself, been wondering that morning what had become of him. It was now nearly noon; and usually by that hour I had seen the Doctor several times.

But, as I had told Matthew, the ever-cheerful Doctor had lately seemed discouraged about his work. I was not, however, going to let Dab-Dab or any of the others see I was upset.

I said that, after all, there was no reason why John Dolittle couldn't go for a walk by himself without having to tell everyone in his house. He might have wanted to go shopping in the town, I said – or half a dozen other things.

But Dab-Dab interrupted me by telling me something else which sounded serious. Polynesia had sent off some thrushes who lived in the garden and told them to ask all the wild birds in the country if they had seen the Doctor. The sparrows in the Market-place of Puddleby had also been told to let her know if the Doctor had been seen shopping. These birds had come back (Dab-Dab was almost in tears as she told me) and they had brought no word of the Doctor – no news, either from the town or from the country round about.

It was difficult for me, after that, to think of anything to say to comfort Dab-Dab. She was openly weeping when she ended by telling me that in all the years she had been housekeeper for the Doctor he had never done such a thing before.

Luckily, a message was brought to me at that moment that there was a mother-weasel in the surgery with a sick young one. So I whispered to Cheapside to do his best to cheer up Dab-Dab and the rest of them in the kitchen; and I hurried off to do my job as the Doctor's assistant.

Once I got to the surgery, I was kept there – very busy. There were plenty of other animal patients, besides the baby-weasel. And before I had done the whole afternoon was gone; and the long shadows of evening already stretched across the Doctor's lawn. And still John Dolittle had not shown up!

I began to wonder what I should do if this went on for some days. Ought I to go to the police in Puddleby, so they could arrange a search for him? Then I thought how foolish that sounded: set the police to hunt for John Dolittle when the birds themselves couldn't find him! And what would he say, or think, of my fussing like an old woman? He hated fuss. . . . But still, just because he had always seemed to us so calm and safe against danger, that did not mean that no harm could come to him. . . . And it was true, what Dab-Dab had said: the Doctor had never done such a thing before. Although he mixed so little with the world of people, we, the members of his household, always knew where he was – and usually what he was doing. . . . Where, and why, had he hidden himself?

While these upsetting thoughts ran through my mind I was walking across the big lawn at the back of the house. As I passed under an apple-tree I heard a voice I knew well.

'Pst! – Tommy!'

I looked up. And there on a bough above my head was Polynesia the parrot.

'He's coming, Tommy,' she whispered. – 'Down the road. He looks awful weary – as though he'd been for a long walk. Though how those stupid thrushes and larks couldn't spot him for me is more than I can tell you.'

'Anyway, thank goodness he's back,' I said. 'He had got me really worried.'

'Me too, Tommy,' said the parrot – 'me too. But don't let on. Just pretend we never had any idea he could have been in trouble.'

But news travels fast in the animal world. John Dolittle's high hat had no sooner appeared at the gate than there were squawks and squeals from the house; and all his

28

animal family spilled out of the doors and windows to greet him.

I could see at once that Polynesia was right: he did indeed look weary. Just the same, his cheerful, kindly smile spread over his face as his pets gathered about him, all chattering at once.

'Where on earth have you been, Doctor?' asked Dab-Dab.

'I was out walking on Eastmoor Heath,' he answered innocently.

'For twelve hours!' cried the housekeeper.

'Well, most of that time,' said he. 'I wasn't actually walking every moment of course. Anyway, I admit I'm pretty tired now.'

'Come into the kitchen and let me give you some tea,' said Dab-Dab. – 'Gub-Gub, Jip – and the rest of you – stop pestering the Doctor. Get out of his way so that he can walk, will you!'

'Ah, tea!' said the Doctor. 'That sounds a wonderful idea. What would I do without you, Dab-Dab? – Oh, hulloa, Stubbins! How is everything?'

'Quite all right, Doctor,' said I. 'There is only one really urgent case in the surgery – a fox with a broken leg.'

'Oh, then I'll look at it right away,' said he – 'while Dab-Dab gets the kettle boiling.'

But the motherly housekeeper would not allow any of the household to question the Doctor any more that night – much to Gub-Gub's and the white mouse's disgust. And it was not until after supper, when most of the family were in bed, that I myself learned what had happened. We were in his study, he and I. The only others with us were Cheapside and Polynesia. The Doctor was filling his pipe carefully and thoughtfully from the tobacco-jar upon his desk. In silence, the three of us waited for him to speak – quite sure that something important was coming.

5

THE END OF A DREAM

WHEN the Doctor had his pipe lighted he sat back in his chair, sent a puff of smoke towards the ceiling and said:

'Today I had to make quite an important decision. I made up my mind to stop my work not only on – er – making everlasting life possible for Man through the vegetable seeds we brought down from the Moon, but – '

Here the Doctor stopped suddenly and stared at the flame of his reading-lamp; while a smile, a sad smile of bitterness, came into his eyes for a moment. Then he went on:

'But – for the present at least – *even of lengthening* human life. . . . I'm dropping it.'

And then there was a silence. I suppose it only lasted a part of a minute. But to me it seemed endless. I glanced in turn at Polynesia and Cheapside the London sparrow. The look on their faces was very solemn. For they too knew, as well as I did, what a serious thing it was that John Dolittle had just said to us. Ever since he had come back from the Moon he had worked untiringly on this, and only this: to get the moon-seeds to grow properly in the climate of the Earth. It was to leave his time free for this that he had taught me surgery and animal medicine, so I could look after the patients who came daily to his door.

The dream he had had was a truly great one. It was to make human life in this world last practically for ever, the same as we had seen it in the Moon. He was certain that the secret was in the food they ate up there – vegetables and fruits. As the Doctor explained to me, the trouble with our world down here was *time*. People were in such a hurry. If, said he, Man knew he could live as long as he wanted, then we would stop all this crazy rushing around; this fear – which even he, the easygoing John Dolittle, had felt – would be taken from us. . . . Yes, it was a great dream.

And now, here in his quiet study, he had just told us he was giving up that dream – saying that he knew he was beaten! I had never felt so sorry for anyone in my whole life. His body, slumped in the chair, looked desperately tired. As his eyes went on staring at the lamp I wondered if he remembered we were in the room. I noticed that the pipe he had lit had gone out again. I rose quietly from my chair, struck a match and held it over his pipe-bowl.

'Oh, thank you, Stubbins, thank you!' he said, sitting up with a start.

'Tell me, Doctor,' I said as he puffed the tobacco into life again: 'What made you make up your mind to this now – I mean, why today, particularly?'

31

'Well, Stubbins,' he said. 'I got some news today. I told you I had been hoping to get Long Arrow, the Indian naturalist, to help me grow these moon-seeds we brought back. – Wonderful fellow on plants and trees, you know, Long Arrow.'

'Oh, yes, Doctor, of course. And I remember very well that years ago he got lost; and you tried to find out exactly whereabouts he was at that time. It was Miranda, the purple bird-of-paradise, who brought you the message. None of the birds could tell where he was.'

'That's right, Stubbins. I got another message from Miranda. And – well – history has repeated itself, as they say. Long Arrow once more is – is missing.'

'But you went and found him anyway before, Doctor. Maybe you could do the same again.'

The Doctor shook his head.

'That was just a freak chance, Stubbins. We couldn't expect such luck as that to happen a second time. No, I'm afraid my one last great hope – of getting the Indian's help – has faded out.'

'Did the bird-of-paradise think an accident had happened to him?' I asked fearfully.

'Well, Stubbins, who can say? That Indian used to take such awful chances with his life. A most extraordinary man: I was always nervous about him. He would take such fearful risks.'

If I had not been in such a serious mood, I would have been amused at that. John Dolittle and the Indian naturalist made a good pair. Both of them took the most hair-raising chances with their safety, without so much as batting an eyelid.

'But, Doctor,' I asked, 'did Miranda tell you nothing that would give you any hope?'

'It wasn't Miranda who brought me the news,' he answered. 'She sent her daughter, Esmeralda. That is why I did not have her come here to the house. Esmeralda's a bit young – terribly shy and all that sort of thing.'

Then, Polynesia, sitting atop the bookcase, spoke for the first time.

'How did you know she was arriving this morning, Doctor?'

'Her mother, Miranda, told a sea-bird – a gull, who was coming this way anyhow – to let me know.'

'Huh!' grunted Polynesia. 'But how was it that the wild birds around here didn't see you out walking, Doctor?'

'Well, of course I knew it might be a long job, waiting. I couldn't tell the exact time Esmeralda would arrive. And birds-of-paradise can't pop up suddenly in the English countryside without a lot of finches or sparrows crowding around and gaping. So, I just gave instructions to a pair of thrushes in my garden to go out and tell all the wild birds exactly where my meeting-place with Esmeralda was to be – and ask them all to keep away.'

'Good heavens!' groaned Polynesia. 'The mystery is solved! I should have known.'

'Is there no one else, Doctor,' I asked, 'whom you could get to help you, besides Long Arrow?'

'Oh, yes,' he said wearily. 'There are several great scientists – botanists, they're called – who have made a special study of just this thing. *Acclimatization* is the proper name for it; making seeds and trees, taken from foreign countries, grow in other lands and other climates, you know. But, my goodness, Stubbins, there would be no sense in my going to them! . . . They would only say I was cracked – crazy.'

Again a short silence fell upon the room. Then the Doctor knocked out his pipe and refilled it before he went on:

'I gave a lot of time to this – before I made up my mind. Well, it can't be helped. That time's been wasted. . . . Time, time! But something tells me to stop right now – for the present at all events. There are other things I want to work on. We'll keep the moon-seeds we have left – especially that of the long-life melon – with the greatest care. But we'll do no more work on acclimatization. From today on' (the Doctor made a little movement with his hand, like sweeping something away) 'from today on, Stubbins, I am done with it. It is finished.'

6

CHEAPSIDE AND I AGREE UPON A PLAN

IT was not often that the Doctor went to bed early. He got along with very little sleep. But that night (it could not have been later than half past nine, I believe) even while I was trying to think of some comforting answer to his last words, he got up from his desk, bade us all good night and left his study.

'Golly!' muttered Cheapside the sparrow as the door closed behind him. 'I never saw the good old Doc so down-'earted. – Swap me if I did! It takes a lot to lick 'im. Anyone can guess 'ow 'e feels, though – years' work throw'd away! Poor old Doc! Gone to bed without 'is supper.'

'Oh, we should get him away on a voyage,' said Polynesia impatiently. 'He's gone stale: that's what's mostly wrong with him. I've never known him to stick to anything the way he has to this blessed everlasting-life business. He needs a change from this beastly English climate. – And so do I. We've only had two hours of sunshine this whole month. Fog, rain, mist and drizzle. Only fit for frogs and ducks. Now in Africa –'

'But, Polynesia,' I interrupted, knowing that the old parrot was starting off on one of her long lectures about the weather of the British Isles, 'where are we going to get him to go?'

'Yes, Polly, me old chicken,' chirped Cheapside, hopping across the Doctor's table to see if he had missed any cake-crumbs, 'for me, you can 'ave your blinkin' Hafrican

34

climate – and welcome. Too 'ot – much too 'ot. Just the same, I agree with you that the old gentleman needs a change – needs it bad.'

The sparrow, while he was speaking, skipped about the table till he was in front of the open book, the book which he and I were talking of that morning. And suddenly he looked up at me and said:

'By Jove, Tommy, this might do it!'

'How do you mean?' I asked.

'Well,' chirped the sparrow, 'you wanted something that would take the Doctor on a sea voyage, to foreign lands, didn't yer?'

'Yes,' I said, 'that's true.'

'And 'is mind is still on this long-life business, ain't it? – Anyone can see that, in spite of 'is saying he's done and finished with it, eh?'

'Yes.'

'Well, like I told you this morning, Tommy, when we was lookin' at the picture of Mr Caveman 'ere. Mudface the turtle was on the Ark with Noah – or, leastways 'e says 'e was. And *that's* ancient 'istory, ain't it?'

'Certainly, Cheapside,' I said. 'Go on.'

'Old Man Noah was supposed to be 'undreds and 'undreds of years old. See? So it's my idea that you get the Doc interested in making another visit to the Secret Lake and our good friend, Mudface the turtle.'

'Oh, splendid, Cheapside!' I cried. 'Of course! Everybody lived to a great age, they tell us, in those days before the Flood. And there is at least a chance Mudface could tell the Doctor something about how they did it – what they ate and how they lived and so on. At the same time your plan would get the Doctor on a voyage – a change of scene and all that – which is what he needs *now*, above all.'

'Erzackerly, young man,' said the sparrow in a very grand tone. 'You catches on real quick – for a youngster.'

'What do *you* think of the idea, Polynesia?' I asked, turning to the parrot.

'Not bad, not bad at all – for a Cockney sparrow,' said she.

'All right, all right, you stuffed pin-cushion,' snorted Cheapside, as the feathers on his neck rose in anger. 'Don't get puttin' on airs – just because you're a couple of 'undred years old yourself. I notice some birds never get no sense, no matter 'ow long they live.'

'Now, now,' said I. 'We must get together peaceably and work this thing out.'

I looked across at the parrot again to see if she had any ideas.

'Well,' said Polynesia after thinking a moment, 'I believe that now, for once in his life, John Dolittle has money enough to take a voyage.'

'Yes,' I said, 'I think that is so.'

'Then,' the parrot went on, 'he has a whole lot of note-books which he filled on his last voyage to the Secret Lake – when he wrote down the turtle's story of the Flood. I wasn't with him on that trip, but Cheapside was.'

'That's right,' said the sparrow. – 'And you didn't miss much on that picnic, old girl. Mud, mud, mud! But the Doc wrote all day and all night. 'E said our Mr Mudface – as far as 'e could make out – was surely the last of the passengers left what sailed on the Ark. 'E said it was 'ighly skyentific stuff. 'E told us 'e never expected to write *all* of it in a regular book for ordinary folks to read, 'cause they wouldn't believe it. – And, meself, I wouldn't blame 'em neither. But the Doc, 'e says it was all waluable hinforma-tion, werry waluable. And some day 'e might make use of it. He took it all down: what Noah said; what Mrs Noah said; and what all the little Noahs said. And when the Doc ran out of note-books he got dried palm-leaves, and wrote on them instead. We 'ad that blinkin' canoe so 'eavy-loaded comin' back, I thought we was goin' to sink.'

'Tommy,' said Polynesia, 'you'd better hunt out those note-books in the morning. I don't know what work the Doctor has in mind to go after next. – You know he always has millions of things that he intends to take up – to study. He was certainly blue and miserable enough tonight. But that won't last long, you may be sure. In a day or so he'll be off on something new. You better tackle him about a second visit to Mudface before he thinks up something out of his own head. Because that something may not mean a voyage. It *may* mean his staying right here at home.'

'Very true, Polynesia,' I agreed. 'Those note-books are important. I'd better get after them without wasting any time, first thing, tomorrow. – That is, after I've spoken to the Doctor, you know – said good morning and sort of sounded him out a bit on the *idea* of a new voyage.'

'*That's* the plan, young feller,' said the parrot. 'I won't come in on the business unless he gets difficult. You try him out by yourself first. Let me know how you get on. And – good luck to you, Tommy.'

'Same 'ere, young man,' sighed Cheapside sleepily. 'We got to pull the old Doc out of this some'ow. – Never saw 'im in such a spell of the dumps.'

And with that, our little committee-meeting broke up and we all went to bed.

7

MEMORIES OF MUDFACE AND THE SECRET LAKE

THE next morning, when I came into the Doctor's study, I found him working at his desk. He glanced over his shoulder as I opened the door.

'Oh, good morning, Stubbins, good morning!' said he cheerfully enough. 'You're up earlier than usual, aren't you?' (It did my heart good to see him smile like that – after last night.)

'Good morning, Doctor,' said I. 'Yes, I suppose I am a little earlier than usual. I've – er – I've been thinking over what you said last night. And I wanted to ask you something.'

'Well?' he said, seeing me hesitate.

'Tell me, Doctor: what is the oldest creature you ever met? – I don't mean in the Moon, but the oldest earthly creature – in this world?'

'Oh, Mudface the turtle, of course,' said he, arranging the papers on his desk. 'He was on the Ark, you know, with Noah. Why did you want – ?'

He broke off suddenly. His hands became quite still

among the papers. Then he looked up at me slowly.

'*Mudface!*' he murmured. – 'Noah ... All of them ...
They lived to a great age. – Or so we are told. But there
couldn't be any doubt about that turtle – the structure of his
shell. ... I examined it myself. Thousands and thousands of
years old it must have been. .... Why, the carapace – oh, but
I'm finished with all that long-life business. I told you last
night I've wasted too much time on it already. .... Yet –'

Again he fell silent. He looked away from me to the ceiling. For a moment he stared up with a puzzled frown, while
his lips moved as though he were talking to himself. But I
managed to catch a word or two.

'It ... all so long ago. I know I took down a tremendous
lot of notes. But only zoology – some history – and archaeology. I wrote it very fast. Haven't looked at it since. I
wonder –'

And then of a sudden he looked back to me and spoke out
loud.

'What made you ask me about all this now – today, Stubbins?'

'Well, Doctor,' I said, 'of course I had heard about your
visit to Mudface and the Secret Lake; your building an
island for him and all that – although I wasn't with you on
that voyage. And I know you will not think it cheeky of me,
Sir, to – er – well, to make a suggestion – give an idea?'

'Oh, my goodness, no!' he said. 'Fire away. I'd like to
hear it.'

'You have spent years, Doctor, on trying to bring everlasting life, to the people of this world, by growing the
melons and foodstuffs of the Moon for them. But have you
yet given much time to the people in the Earth's history
who lived to a far greater age than folk do nowadays?'

'Er – no,' he answered slowly. 'In a general way that's
true, Stubbins.'

'Then, another thing,' said I: 'if you'll allow me to say so,
Sir, you have not been well. – Oh, I don't mean real sick,

Doctor – thank goodness, you are never that. But you have seemed discouraged and – er – out of sorts. That's not like you.'

'Yes, Stubbins,' he muttered, 'I'm afraid you're certainly right there. I should have chucked up the business a long while back. But, you know, I hated to throw away the time I'd already given to it. . . . Time – always time! . . . And then, besides, you never can tell. The whole history of discovery is full of cases where men have worked and slaved for years – with their families begging them to give up, take their meals regularly and live like human beings. And then! – Then, just as they are about to quit, success comes to them at last! – No, Stubbins, that's the trouble in this *research* game, as they call it: you never know. – But go on with what you are saying.'

'I think you need a change, Doctor. It isn't how hard you've been working. – You always work hard. But you've been on this one thing too long – without a real change.'

He made no answer to that – just nodded thoughtfully to show that he partly agreed with what I had said.

'How about taking a voyage, Doctor?' I asked, trying hard to steady my voice, so it would not show my excitement. 'It's a long while since you took one. And I was wondering if you would perhaps make a second visit to Mudface and the Secret Lake. At least there would be a chance that you could learn something from the turtle about long life, wouldn't there?'

'It would all depend, Stubbins, on – er – well, on two things. First, whether we could find Mudface again. – I've had no news from him, you know, in some time. – And second, I'm by no means sure that he would have noticed the sort of things that made people live to such ages as they did then – supposing of course that what we are told about their enormously long lives is true.'

'But, Doctor,' said I, 'there can be no question about the great age of the turtle himself, can there? Didn't he remember things that actually happened before the Flood?'

'True, quite true,' he said. 'But while Mudface was a very intelligent creature, it was only the history of the Flood itself I asked him to tell me. I doubt if he could give me much information – scientific information I mean – about what it was in the foods they ate, or in the way they lived, which caused their long lives.'

'Well, Doctor,' said I, 'that first trip of yours to the lake was a good long while back, wasn't it? All your note-books about it have been kept, as I told you, in the underground library I made – to protect them against fire. Suppose I get those note-books out, Doctor, and let us see if some of what you wrote won't be helpful to you in this study of how to live a long time. What do you say?'

'I can't see any harm in that, Stubbins,' he murmured after a moment's thought. . . . 'No, as you say, there isn't any reason why you shouldn't get those note-books out and let us take a look at them.'

'Very good, Doctor,' said I and quietly left the room.

Never in my whole life had I found it so hard to pretend I wasn't in a hurry! But as I walked those few steps from his desk to the door, I reminded myself of something Polynesia had said the night before. 'Remember, Tommy,' she had whispered as I went upstairs to bed, 'whatever you do, don't hustle the Doctor.'

So, I even stopped half-way to the door and went back to fetch the sandwich-plate off his desk to take to the pantry-sink. And I closed the door of his study *very* softly behind me. But the moment it was latched, I raced down the passage on tiptoe, like the wind, to find Polynesia – to tell her what the Doctor had said.

8

THE MYSTERY OF THE NOTE-BOOKS

AFTER some hunting, I found Polynesia in the pantry perched on a dripping faucet over the sink. She was trying to get a drink upside down – while she gargled Swedish swearwords through the water.

'Listen, Polynesia,' I said in a low voice. 'I've just come from the Doctor – and I spoke to him about a voyage.'

'Oh, you did, eh? Well, we can't talk here. Lift me out of this rats' shower-bath, will you? – On to your shoulder, please. . . . So. . . . Now let's go into your office – while we still have a chance to chat, without the rest of the household joining in.'

In my office I quickly told the parrot what the Doctor had said. When I had finished the old bird muttered:

'Humph! – Sounds good to me, young feller. Quite good. At least he didn't say he had work which would keep him here, in Puddleby. It will all depend on what's in those note-books. He's forgotten, you see? – And no wonder, when you think of all the things he makes notes on.'

'Yes,' I said. 'If there is anything in the books about the food they ate in those days before the Flood, then I think the Doctor might be persuaded to go back to the turtle again – to ask a few more questions.'

'Exactly,' said she. 'You go and dig out those note-books right away. But try not to let the others know – at least as long as possible. That silly pig, Gub-Gub, and the rest of them will only be pestering the poor man with questions – asking can they come on the voyage too.'

'All right, Polynesia,' I said. 'I'll keep it as quiet as I can.'

'And remember, Tommy, there's no time to lose. You know John Dolittle. He hates to be idle for a minute. If we don't watch out, he'll be off on some new tack in natural

HUGH LOFTING

history before you can turn around. And then we'll never get him away.'

So, being careful not to run into any of the other house-pets, I went and got the key to the underground library. I hardly ever came to this library alone; almost always I took Whitey the white mouse with me. That was because Whitey, quite a long time ago, had been made our Chief Librarian. Of course such a small animal as a mouse was not strong enough to move the books around by himself. He always got me to help him with the heavier work.

But the Doctor had discovered that a mouse has one thing which is very useful in taking care of books: he has *microscopic eyes*. That means that his special kind of eyesight made it possible for him to see things which neither the Doctor nor I could see at all, such as tiny insects which eat into and destroy books.

And then his tiny body was small enough to go anywhere – all around the books, as they stood on the shelves, without taking them down. And if he found any mites, or damp or even dust he would come to me about it and we would put the matter right.

He was indeed a splendid librarian. And after the Doctor bought him a little magnifying-glass of his own, so that he could even see the eggs of these tiny insects which eat paper, Whitey was tremendously proud of his job – *and* of his magnifying-glass!

Whitey also had a wonderful memory. The Doctor had, besides all his precious note-books, an enormous lot of books written by other naturalists and scientists. The most precious of these were kept in the underground library for safety. And although the white mouse could not of course read English, I only had to tell him what a book was about, when I put it into the library for the first time, and forever after he could immediately tell me where to look for it. Some years later he told me that his very keen sense of smell helped him a lot in this. If he could not tell one book from another by its title printed on the back, he could often tell it by its colour or by the way it smelt.

Today, as I put the key into the heavy lock of the library-door, I glanced back over my shoulder, wondering where he was. Little Whitey always had a trick of turning up in the most unexpected way – and the most unexpected places. He had a most enormous curiosity – just couldn't bear having anything happen without his knowing all about it.

But this morning I felt sure I had given him the slip. In the garden behind me there was no one in sight, except Polynesia in a willow-tree. Her sharp old eyes were darting about in every direction, keeping watch for me. I swung the heavy door open, stepped inside and locked it behind me.

I struck a match. On the big table in the centre of the room we always kept oil-lamps and candles. I lit the largest of the lamps. As the light glowed up, I noticed there was dust on the table – a lot of it. This, I thought, was strange because the white mouse was usually most particular about keeping the library furniture and floor – as well as the books – neat and clean.

I remembered exactly where those note-books were kept – the ones about Mudface the turtle, and the Secret Lake. It is true I had never read them, though I had always planned to. But that was not surprising. I did not get time to read much now. I lit a candle and carried it at once to the north-west corner of the room, where the note-books I wanted had always been kept.

When they had first been put in here I had, myself, wrapped and tied them in careful packages, to keep them from the damp; and these parcels had, I remembered, been put on the second shelf from the bottom, right in the corner – almost against the north wall. There had been four packages of them; and together they had taken up quite a little space.

By the light of the candle I now saw that this space on the second shelf was empty!

I knelt down on the floor and peered in, so I could see right to the back of the shelf. There was not a single note-book there. I swept the shelf with my left hand. Some crumbs of chewed-up paper fell silently on to the floor at my knees.

I didn't stop to look anywhere else in the library. I knew at once that something had happened – something serious.

I rushed to the door, turned the key and swung it open. Outside, in the brilliant sunlight, the old parrot was still perched in the willow-tree.

'Polynesia!' I cried. – 'The note-books have disappeared. They're – they're *gone*!'

9

THE WHITE MOUSE LIBRARIAN

NEITHER did the parrot bother about searching the library further after I showed her those crumbs of paper on the floor. She let fly a few swear-words and then muttered to me:

'Tommy, we've got to find him – Whitey. He's the only one who can tell us about this. Come on, boy – let's hunt him down.'

She climbed up on to my shoulder again (where she usually travelled when she was with me). I blew out the lamp and candle, locked up the library and together we started for the house.

'You know, Polynesia,' I said, as we were crossing the lawn, 'I've just remembered; it has been a long time – weeks and weeks – since our Chief Librarian has come to me about the books back there. Usually it was every few days – and nearly always about something which didn't matter a bit – just wanted to show off his importance as librarian. But now – my goodness, I can't remember – but it's simply ages since he came and asked for my help with the books.'

'Huh!' grunted the parrot. 'Didn't you smell a rat, then – or a mouse?'

'Yes, I should have done, it's true,' I said. 'But I've been so busy – especially with the surgery and the dispensary. You know how it is in early summer, when the birds have new broods that are learning to fly; and the squirrels and foxes and the rest have young ones who are always falling and getting themselves hurt?'

'Heigh ho! – Don't I know?' sighed the parrot. 'Sometimes I wonder how John Dolittle is alive today, when I think how he worked alone at the doctoring business before he had you to help him.'

'Oh, I'm glad to do it, Polynesia,' I said quickly. 'Don't think I'm not. And it's very interesting – most of it. But, after all, there are only twenty-four hours in the day, you know. The trouble is – '

'The trouble is *Time*,' the parrot interrupted. 'That's what the Doctor himself said: "Time! If we only had the time to do all the things we want to do ..." Poor man! – That's what fascinated him most, I think, about the life on the Moon. Well, here we are at the house. We had better separate now. You go in by the front-door and I'll fly round to the kitchen door. Watch it now! Don't let our librarian escape – that is, *if* he's in the house.'

We found out afterwards that our precious librarian had overheard the talk between the Doctor and me about the note-books; and the mouse knew of course that he would be in for trouble as soon as I found them missing and came to look for him.

Well, no one would think it, but it took us the rest of the day to find Whitey – or, I should say, to catch him. When a mouse (even a *white* mouse) really wants to hide himself in an old-fashioned, English country house, it is surprising how many places he can use for dodging into, or behind, to keep out of sight. What a chase he led us! He would get in the china-closet and hide behind an egg-cup. Then, after I had moved every single piece of china separately, there would suddenly be a white flash and Polynesia would yell: 'There he is!'

But he *wasn't*. He would dive through a knot-hole in the back of the closet; and two seconds later he would be in the next room, hiding under a corner of the carpet – or upstairs in my bedroom, behind the clock on the dressing-table.

By this time of course the whole household had joined in the hunt – though we had not told them yet why we were going after the little villain (nor why he was running away from us).

Gub-Gub thought the whole thing was some kind of a

new game; and while he tried very hard to be helpful, all he
succeeded in doing was getting in the way. I think I must
have tripped over that pig a good dozen times – once on the
stairs when I almost had the mouse by the tail) and I
somersaulted all the way down from the attic to the first-
floor – where I landed with a bruised elbow, two barked
shins and a crack on the head which all but stunned me.

After that we called a council of war.

'Listen, Tommy,' whispered Dab-Dab: 'we have got two
of the best mouse-catchers in the business right here with
us – a dog and an owl.'

'Why, of course!' said I – 'Jip and Too-Too.'

'Suppose the rest of us go out for a walk in the garden,'

said the duck quietly. 'I fancy Jip's nose and Too-Too's ears will very soon find out where that little devil is hiding. – But be careful, you two,' she added, turning to them, 'how you do it. The Doctor would never forgive us if the mouse got hurt. You'll have to corner him some way in a place where he can't get out. Then talk to him. Talk him into surrendering.'

'That's the idea,' I said. 'Tell him that he will only be questioned in front of the Doctor. John Dolittle will see that he isn't hurt – no matter *what* he has done. He will trust John Dolittle to look after him, even if he won't trust me. We'll be out on the front lawn, Jip. When you've cornered him, bark gently, to signal us. We won't come back till we hear you.'

So we left the two of them at it and went out into the garden. Jip told me afterwards that it was really Too-Too who ran Whitey down. He said his own sense of smell wasn't much good for that job; because the Doctor's house smelt so strong of mice anyway (from all Whitey's friends who used to visit him). Jip told me that no dog living could tell where one mouse's scent left off and another's began.

But Too-Too, with his marvellous sense of hearing, just listened at the panelling and the flooring. And Whitey couldn't even scratch his ear or polish his whiskers without the owl's knowing it – much less move from place to place. Too-Too had the patience of a mountain. And he waited, motionless – just waited.

At last Whitey, hearing no sound in the house at all, made up his mind we must have *all* gone outside. He felt hungry. Then he remembered he had left half a walnut in the coal-scuttle, beside the fireplace. On tiptoe he went to get it. But Too-Too's ears could hear a mouse walking tip-toe, as easily as you or I can hear a horse trotting on a cobble-stoned street. The owl made a sign to Jip to stand ready. The mouse's white body crept down into the deep scuttle. And then, suddenly, they jumped. With the two of them barring the only escape for the mouse – the only way out – Whitey was cornered at last.

10

HOW THE STORY OF THE FLOOD WAS LOST

WHEN I came back into the house, in answer to Jip's bark, I took Whitey in my coat pocket and went to see the Doctor. Polynesia, Jip and Cheapside came with me.

'Well, well, what's all this, Stubbins?' asked the Doctor as the dog and I, with the parrot on my shoulder, came to a stop in front of him.

I fished the white mouse out of my pocket and set him down on the desk before the Doctor.

'Whitey will have to explain to you, Sir,' said I. 'Your note-books about the Flood are missing from the library. Every single one of them is gone.'

'Good gracious!' cried the Doctor. – 'From the underground library! Is it possible? How did this happen, Whitey? You always took such good care of the books.'

'Well – er –' Whitey began. Then as he looked up at the eyes of Polynesia blazing down at him with anger, his voice trailed off and he stopped.

'Tell the truth, now,' snapped the parrot, 'you – you monstrous cheese-pirate! – Or I'll swallow you alive.'

'Gently, gently!' said the Doctor. 'Let him answer my question, Polynesia, *please*. What happened to the books, Whitey?'

'Well, it was about a month and a half ago,' the mouse began in a trembly sort of voice, 'when those Ship's Rats – you remember them, Doctor? They asked could they become members of your Rat and Mouse Club. And you said, yes, it was all right if the other members were willing. Well, soon after that, they wanted to set up housekeeping, because

Mrs Ship's Rat was going to have a whole lot of babies and they wished to make a nest.'

'And where did they want to make the nest, Whitey?' asked the Doctor quietly.

'In your potting-shed, where you keep the lawn-mower,' said the white mouse. 'But, you see, they were foreigners – from some hot country – and they always used palm-leaves – shredded out, you know – for building their nests with.'

'Oh, lumme! – I think I know what's coming,' I heard Cheapside whisper.

'Yes, yes, go on, please, Whitey,' said John Dolittle.

'So they came to me,' said the librarian, 'and asked if I knew where you had any old palm-leaves that were not being used. At first I said, no, I didn't. But then suddenly I thought of something. You remember, Doctor, when you were taking notes on Mudface's story of the Flood, you ran out of ordinary note-books; and you took dried palm-leaves and finished the story on them?'

'Yes,' said the Doctor seriously, 'I remember.'

'Well,' said the white mouse, 'I had been in charge of the library almost since it was built. And I knew that you had never once looked at those note-books you brought back from the Secret Lake. The packages had stayed in the same place on the shelves, just as Tommy had wrapped them up and put them away.'

Once more the Chief Librarian stopped while his frightened eyes glanced at the angry face of the parrot.

'So,' said Whitey in a small, scared voice, 'I thought there couldn't be any great harm if the Ship's Rats borrowed – '

'Shiver my timbers, you salty pantry-robber! roared Polynesia from my shoulder. 'Do you mean to say that you took the Doctor's note-books – notes that he had gone half-way across Africa to get – and gave them to a couple of bilge-rats to line their nest with?'

'But I didn't tell them they could take *all* the note-books,' said Whitey, almost in tears. 'It was only a week later –

after I had shown them how to get into the library through a hole I had dug for myself under the wall – that I found they had taken, not only the palm-leaf covers, but all the other note-books too, for their friends' nests, as well as their own. I hoped, even then, that some part of what the Doctor had written could be saved. But it was too late. Every single note-book had been chewed up into little tiny pieces and carried away.'

'But why didn't you come and tell me, Whitey?' I asked.

'I – I was too scared,' stuttered the mouse – 'of Polynesia.'

Then there was a silence. And I knew that everyone in the room was, like myself, waiting to hear what the Doctor would say. For a moment his fingers drummed upon the desk; and at last he murmured as though he were speaking to himself:

'It's sort of strange that we should have been talking about those notes only last night. . . . Losing them would not have mattered so much if I were sure that Mudface is still alive and I could see him again. . . . But – lately – I have begun to doubt if he *can* still be living. I asked several sea-birds to call at his home and find out how he is getting on. They have all brought me the same message: no news of the giant turtle. . . . Poor old Mudface – a wonderful character. And what things he had seen! . . . I should have attended to those note-books long ago – got them written up in proper form, so they could be published any time I wanted. . . . Now it can never be written: the History of the Flood! There is no one left who saw it happen with his own eyes from the decks of Noah's Ark – so far as we know. . . . Well, it's no use crying over spilt milk, as they say.'

Poor Whitey was weeping out loud now; and the rest of us felt pretty miserable. The Doctor seemed lost in thought. It was getting late, I knew. So I made a sign to the rest of them and we all went quietly out of the study and left John Dolittle alone.

CHEAPSIDE GOES BACK TO LONDON

IN the kitchen Dab-Dab prepared a supper for us and fixed up a tray to be taken in to the Doctor. You may be sure our talk was not very gay. Our plans and hopes for a voyage had been badly dampened, to say the least.

However, after we had had hot cocoa and something to eat, we gradually grew more cheerful. And presently Cheapside, the London sparrow, said:

'Well, Tommy me lad, what are you goin' to do now? – I mean, about gettin' the Doctor off on a trip?'

'I'm afraid I really don't know, Cheapside – with those note-books gone. It is strange; but I have never known the Doctor to forget anything so important, so completely. He tells me he hardly remembers a single word he wrote in those notes.'

'Huh! – No wonder, at the speed *he* was writing,' grunted the sparrow. 'I never saw nobody write that fast, never in all me life. What's more, *I* don't remember what the turtle told us, myself – though I was right alongside the Doctor all the time.'

'It's a terrible pity,' I said, 'that none of you who were with John Dolittle can remember any of it. If Mudface is dead, as the Doctor fears he may be, the story of the Flood will never be known now.'

'Yes, I s'pose so, Tommy,' said Cheapside thoughtfully. 'But, you know, this destroyin' the note-books *might* work just the other way.'

'How do you mean?' I asked.

'Well,' said Cheapside, putting his foot on a slice of toast while he broke a corner off it with his beak, 'we ain't got no proof yet that old Mudface *is* dead, 'ave we? And *if* it should turn out that 'e's still alive – or even that there's a fair

chance of 'is bein' alive – the Doc will be all the keener to go and have another talk with him – so 'e can spend three more weeks sittin' in the mud, listenin' to the family troubles of Mr and Mrs Noah. Tell me, Tommy, when was the last time the Doc had news of our friend Mudface?'

'I'm not exactly sure,' I said. 'As you know, the Doctor gets messages and news by bird-carriers, at all times of the year, from all over the world. Let me see: I think the last news of Mudface was brought – er – about three months back.'

'Humph!' muttered Cheapside. 'Then that would be somewhere in March, wouldn't it?'

'Er – yes,' I said. 'I think that would be right.'

'What sort of birds was they what brought these reports to the Doctor?' asked Cheapside.

'Oh,' said I, 'usually they were gulls, I think – or some of the heavier kinds of sea-birds who used to make a special trip inland to the Secret Lake, as a favour to the Doctor. And once in a while they would be waders – like the herons or the storks. But why did you want to know, Cheapside?'

The sparrow didn't answer my question: instead, he murmured:

'None of them birds you speak of is what I'd call very hintelligent, Tommy. *Storks!* – All they're good for is standin' on one leg and fishin' in a puddle, like school-boys. . . . Humph! I got an idea, young feller. Nothin' may come of it. And then again, a whole lot might come. But, first of all, I want to 'ear what Becky, my wife, thinks of it. I'm goin' back to the city right now – tonight. We're raisin' the last brood of the season, you know – cutest little youngsters you ever saw. Two of 'em can talk already Becky says they're the best-lookin' family we ever raised. But then – you know mothers – she's said the same about every family we ever 'ad. Only don't never tell 'er I told you. – And if I don't get back tonight to help her with the feeding, I'll be getting it hot.'

'All right, Cheapside,' I said, opening the kitchen window for him. 'I'm sorry you can't stay with us longer now. The Doctor has hardly seen you on this visit. And you know how he enjoys hearing the news of London. You always manage to cheer him up – and goodness knows he needs it just now!'

'Yes, Tommy, you're right. But I shan't be gone long this time – or, that is, I hadn't oughter be, if things pan out the way I 'ope they does. But I really oughter get back to poor Becky tonight, to 'elp the old girl.'

'Yes, I understand that of course,' I said. 'You are still building your nest in the same place – outside St Paul's Cathedral?'

55

'That's right, Tommy,' said the sparrow. – 'Same old spot: in Saint Edmund's left ear. 'Ave you got any of that cake left – the same as I was eatin' the crumbs of, off the Doctor's plate the other night?'

'Yes,' said Dab-Dab, 'I think I've got a little piece in the larder. Wait a moment and I'll see.'

'It don't 'ave to be a big piece,' said the sparrow. 'I'm flyin' against the wind gettin' back to London, you know. So I can't carry much. – Ah, good old Dab-Dab! That's just the very ticket – the right size.'

As Cheapside took the little ball of cake which Dab-Dab laid on the table before him he glanced up at me with a twinkle in his eye.

'This'll be a treat for the kids,' he said. – 'Kind of a surprise, you know. *Cake from John Dolittle's table!* My word! – Becky will be boastin' about this for a week to all the other sparrow-mothers round St Paul's. You never saw such happetites as this last family of ours has! They keep poor Becky and me fair worn out, fetchin' and carryin' grub for 'em all day. But they'll be ready to fly next week. Then we'll get a rest.'

'Good-bye, Cheapside,' I said. 'Don't forget to give Becky our very best regards.'

'You bet, Tommy. And don't let the Doc get down-'earted. I got an idea. And *maybe* it'll work out. You'll be seein' me again in a few days. So long, everybody!'

Then taking a firm grip on the cake between his claws, Cheapside gave a flirt of his wings and was gone through the open window, out into the night.

12

THE WORK OF A NATURALIST'S ASSISTANT

For most of the next week the Doctor's house settled down into a regular, humdrum programme – or perhaps I should say it came as near as possible to settling down in such a way. John Dolittle's household never stayed very regular for long, I fear. Perhaps that was one of the things that made it so interesting.

But if life went along more quietly than usual for those few days, I was not sorry – and neither was Polynesia. The night that Cheapside flew back to London the old parrot came into my office where I was working late. As soon as she appeared I could tell from her manner she had some-thing unusual on her mind. She flew up on my desk and silently nodded towards the open door. I knew what she meant. I got up and very quietly closed it.

I smiled as I came back and sat down.

'I don't think,' I said, 'that you need be afraid of poor Whitey trying to listen now. You certainly gave him a terrible scare.'

'Maybe,' said she. 'But I wouldn't trust that little long-nosed snooper farther than I could throw him. The trouble with him is he *has* to know everything. He has already been gabbing around, trying to find out what idea Cheapside had in mind tonight when he left us. – Luckily, there isn't much chance of his learning *that*.'

'No,' I agreed, 'there isn't. The London sparrow was a bit mysterious though, wasn't he, Polynesia? – Have you any notion, yourself, of what he had in mind?'

'That's what I came to talk to you about,' said the parrot. 'No, I don't know what it was he was hinting at. But I do know this: Cheapside may be a quarrelsome, vulgar, little guttersnipe. Yet there is one thing about him no one can deny. When he makes up his mind to a thing, he generally sees it through – gets it done. There's a streak of Cockney stubbornness in that bird. – And I like it.'

'He said he was going to talk over his idea with his wife, Becky. Do you suppose it is something about a voyage, Polynesia?'

'I couldn't say,' she murmured, shrugging up her wings. 'But I'll bet you shillings to cracker-crumbs that Becky won't make him change – if Cheapside has made up his own mind first, *before* he gets to London.'

'No,' I said. 'I think that's a pretty safe bet. . . . He's a funny character, that Cheapside.'

'Well,' said Polynesia, 'all the others of the Doctor's family – besides our wonderful librarian – are trying to guess what plan or idea the sparrow had. That silly pig, Gub-Gub, has asked me a half a dozen times tonight. And he won't believe me when I tell him *I don't know!*'

The old parrot stopped a moment with her head turned to one side. I could see that she wasn't sure, even here, that someone might not come and interrupt us – or be listening outside the door to our talk. But no sound reached us from the rest of the house; and presently she went on again:

'What I wanted to tell you, Tommy, was this: it may be that Cheapside has some plan to get the Doctor to go back to Africa – to the Secret Lake. He was with John Dolittle on the first trip, you know. And you remember he said we would see him back here in a few days' time. Now, what I want you to do is to try your best to side-track the Doctor from getting started on any new important work before Cheapside pays us another visit.'

'Well, I'll certainly try, Polynesia,' I said. 'But, as you know very well yourself, it isn't always so easy to – er – side-track the Doctor away from any plans he may make. He is worse than Cheapside in that – once his mind is made up.'

'But that is just what I mean, Tommy,' said the parrot in a low, earnest voice. 'I want you to keep him busy, so he won't be thinking out any new, big plans – just for a few days, I mean, till we hear from Cheapside again. For months now John Dolittle has left the running of the whole place to you – practically everything except the tricky surgical jobs on the animals that come to his door.'

'Er – yes,' said I. 'It is true, he has.'

'Very well, then,' said the parrot. 'There must be lots and lots of things which you want to ask him about – to get him to decide on. Just keep him busy, that's the main thing. And stick close to him all day long.'

'As a matter of fact,' I said, 'there *are* a whole heap of things I want to talk over with him – things I've put off because I knew he was busy and didn't want to be interrupted.'

'*That's* the idea, Tommy,' said she. 'Just keep him busy, deciding this and that. Cheapside will keep his word, you may be sure. He said he'd be down again in a few days. And I'll take you any bet he will.'

13

THE AFTER-SUPPER STORY HOUR

As a matter of fact, I was surprised myself at what a lot of things there were for which I needed the Doctor's help and advice, now that he had some free time to give me.

There were the moon-seeds; and, although the Doctor was closing that chapter of natural history for the present, they were the only ones in the world. He might some day want to try again. He handed them over to Polynesia (a seed-eating bird) sure that she would store them away so they would keep in good condition.

And there was the garden. You never saw such a jungle of weeds in your life! Only those beds where we had tried so patiently to make the moon-seeds grow – and the hothouses – had been looked after at all.

And this time, I think, John Dolittle really saw (after Polynesia and I had taken him round to the worse spots on purpose) that if he didn't give the garden his attention right away, there soon would be nothing of it left. While his back was turned a moment, and he examined some raspberry-canes, the parrot nodded meaningly to me; and I knew that the same thought had passed through her mind. However, I did what she had told me; I stuck close to the Doctor all day and every day.

No, Polynesia and I had no difficulty keeping the Doctor busy during the *daylight* hours. It was the evening-time, when he usually went into his study (sometimes to sit at his desk until very, very late) that worried the old parrot and me. For it was then we feared he might think up some new and important work which – once he got started on it – we could not possibly get him to leave.

However, it was Gub-Gub the pig who gave me an idea which was very helpful in this.

'My word, Tommy,' he said to me one evening as he was gathering some rhubarb to take into the house (Gub-Gub still took very good care of the vegetables). 'It is really wonderful to see the Doctor around again! It had got so we hardly saw him at all, while he was working on that old everlasting-life business – with him taking his meals and everything in his study.'

'Yes, Gub-Gub,' said I. 'It's much better this way. He was working far too hard – at his desk.'

'He paid me quite a compliment,' said Gub-Gub, rooting out a large weed with his nose, 'over the way I'd kept the tomatoes. But, you know, Tommy, there is one thing I still miss – about the Doctor and his ways.'

'Oh?' I said. 'What's that?'

'It's the stories he used to tell us around the kitchen fire after supper,' said Gub-Gub, his little eyes twinkling with memories as he looked up at me over his muddy nose. 'Ah!' he sighed. 'Those were the days, Tommy, those were the days!'

'Yes,' I agreed. 'You're right.'

But I fear I was hardly thinking of what I said. My mind was turning over the words Gub-Gub had just spoken.

'Do you realize, Tommy,' said the pig, 'the Doctor has not told us a single fireside story since he got back from the Moon? We were talking about it only yesterday, Chee-Chee, Too-Too and I. – And you remember there was a time when he told us a story every single night?'

'Well,' said I, 'listen, Gub-Gub: why don't you ask him to do the same now – now that he has more time? – And take Chee-Chee and Too-Too with you when you go and ask him.'

This the pig did. And not only Chee-Chee and Too-Too went to the Doctor, but the whole of the Dolittle household: Whitey, Jip, Dab-Dab and – of course Polynesia. Even the old lame horse in the stable came clumping across the lawn and told the Doctor (through the window of his study) that the long summer evenings in his stall were very dull: and that if the Doctor should be telling stories to the crowd after supper, he would like very much to listen outside the kitchen window, the same as the Doctor had let him do in times gone by.

Well, of course in the end the Doctor gave in. Myself, I think he was rather glad to. And so that nice old habit, which all the animals enjoyed so much, was started over again: the after-supper story-telling round the kitchen fire.

As soon as the dishes were cleared away and washed, there would be the same old scramble for seats or places. Gub-Gub (who took up more room than the rest) always made the most fuss getting seated and settled. Again the white mouse climbed to his favourite listening-spot – the corner of the mantelpiece, where he could see and hear everything. And I noticed that Itty, the moon cat, was

now always in the audience too – though often you wouldn't know it; because she would choose places where she wouldn't be seen – and, as usual, she never spoke and never moved.

14

THE STORM

I CANNOT say that John Dolittle looked better, all at once, from these changes in his way of living. But he was much cheerier; more active in body and mind; more interested in everything going on in, and around, his home.

And the days passed quickly, as they always do when people are busy and happy.

But one wet and stormy night the old parrot again came into my office. The evening story was over; and the Doctor and his family had gone to bed. I remember how the wind and rain beat furiously against the window-panes, as Polynesia strutted towards me across the floor. Then with her claws and beak she climbed up the heavy curtain, like a sailor, hand over hand. When she reached the level of the desk, where I was writing, she stepped across on to it. There she fluffed out her feathers, looked me in the eye and said:

'Tommy, I'm worried – about Cheapside. We should have heard from him by now!'

'Why, how long is it,' I asked, laying down my pen, 'since he was here last?'

'It's ten days tonight,' the parrot grunted.

'Is it really!' I cried. 'I had no idea it was as long ago as that.'

'With any other bird I don't think I'd be anxious,' she said. 'But – I told you – I've been noticing little Cheapside lately. He's very reliable. If he says he'll do a thing, he'll do it. . . . I hope to goodness nothing has happened to him.'

'Oh, well, come now, Polynesia,' said I, smiling at her worried frown, 'what could happen to him? There never was a bird in all the world better able to take care of himself than that London sparrow.'

'Accidents can happen to anybody,' the parrot muttered.

Suddenly with a sharp gust the wind and rain burst against the side of the old house, rattling the windows in their frames.

'Perhaps this storm has got you fidgety,' I said. 'I wouldn't start to worry yet.'

'I tell you, young man, accidents can happen to anybody,' she repeated slowly and clearly.

'But listen,' I argued: 'Cheapside didn't say *exactly* how

long – how many days – it would be before he visited us again, did he?'

'He said "a few days," Tommy. That means, in my seven languages, less than a week – or, not more than a week, anyhow. And besides, if he was delayed, why couldn't he have let us know? Cheapside has plenty of sparrow friends, who would have flown down here for him, to bring us a message. There are London sparrows in every corner of the world. – And a pesky nuisance they are too – sometimes.'

It took a good deal to get Polynesia upset. Although she often squabbled and argued with Cheapside, I knew she was very fond of him. What she had just said was true. And having no answer to it, I said nothing. The silence in the room was broken only by the noise of rain outside and the old Dutch clock upon the wall, ticking away the seconds, the minutes, the hours – the lifetimes of sparrows and men.

Presently I saw Too-Too the owl appear from behind a pile of books on the top shelf of my bookcase. He looked sleepy as he always did at this hour – which was his time for getting up. Polynesia's back was turned and she did not see him. No one could move more silently than Too-Too – just as no creature could hear as well as he, or see better in the dark. And suddenly, without even opening his wings, he dropped down on the desk beside the parrot, like a pudding falling out of a dish.

Poor Polynesia! With a frightened squawk, she jumped as though stuck with a pin. A string of terrible seafaring swear-words, in three foreign languages, broke out; and for a moment I thought she was going to bite the little owl's head off.

'Don't *do* that!' she screamed. 'Let a body know you're coming, if you *must* fall off the ceiling like a spider.'

'I'm very sorry, Polynesia, really I am,' said Too-Too, blinking the sleep out of his eyes. 'Something woke me up – all of a sudden.'

'Huh! – Me and Tommy talking, I suppose,' snapped the

HUGH LOFTING

parrot, still in a very bad humour from the fright she had had. 'You're no better than that snooping little cheese-thief, Whitey. You were just trying to listen in on what we were saying.'

'Not at all, Polynesia, you are mistaken,' said Too-Too quietly. 'I slept right through your chatter. The noise that woke me up came from the garden – or, at least, from outside.'

'What nonsense!' snorted the parrot. 'There is a strong wind blowing outside – and rain. You couldn't have heard anything over *that* noise. Why, it's almost a gale!'

'Pardon me,' said Too-Too wearily, 'but you are forgetting that we owls, for thousands of years, have trained ourselves to hear the sounds that other creatures make at night – the creatures we hunt for food.'

'Oh, fiddlesticks!' growled Polynesia. 'What did you hear, then?'

'The noise that woke me,' said Too-Too, 'was birds flying – battling with the wind. Even on a fairly stormy night I can tell you what kind of a bird it is – by the noise his wings make, beating the air. That is, of course, if there aren't a whole lot of different sorts mixed up together.'

I could see that Polynesia was really interested now. So, indeed, was I. I opened my mouth to ask the owl a question, but he held up a claw to me to keep silent.

Both the parrot and I stayed still, holding our breath, while Too-Too, the great Night Listener, used those wonderful ears of his.

'They're small birds,' he whispered presently. – 'And not many of them. ... Ah, now they've made it! They were trying to fly across the big lawn to the house, I guess. Saw your light, I suppose. But they were driven back three times. Now they've reached the window-sill. ... If I'm right, you'll hear from them yourself now, Tommy.'

And, sure enough, as the little owl stopped speaking, there came a signal I had often heard before: it was the tapping of a bird's bill on the glass of the window-pane.

I didn't wait then, you may be sure. I leapt to the window and pulled it open at the bottom. The papers on my desk went swirling everywhere, as wind and rain and dead leaves tore into the room. But I took no notice of my papers, nor the wet, nor my guttering lamp which was all but blown out. For I had seen two other things which the wind had swept into the house with the leaves: the bodies of two little rain-drenched birds that now lay panting on the floor. In a second I had slammed the window shut again and was kneeling on the wet carpet beside them.

They were Cheapside and his wife, Becky.

15

FIRST AID FOR SPARROWS

THE two sparrows were certainly in a very bad state. You could hardly tell them from dead birds, so still they lay there, with the water trickling across the floor from under them. The eyes of both had now closed entirely. Only the slightest moving of Cheapside's feathers showed me that he, at least, was alive. Poor Becky, his wife, was so completely still I feared she was already gone. Very gently Polynesia lifted up Cheapside's bill with her own, softly calling him by name. But the sparrow's eyes did not open; and his head fell back, sideways, as she let it go.

'Quick, Tommy,' said the parrot. 'Wake the Doctor up and bring him down here. This will be a close shave. Too-Too, you rouse up Dab-Dab and Chee-Chee. Tell 'em to build up the kitchen fire – hot. And get some flannels warmed in front of it. I'll stay with them here. Hustle now, both of you. This bird's breathing is slowing down.'

I found the Doctor reading in bed. But I only got half-way through my message before he sprang up, shot past me and was running down the stairs. Over his shoulder he called back:

'Take my bedside lamp, Stubbins, and fetch the little black bag from the surgery, please.'

It was in cases of this kind that always I most admired John Dolittle as an animals' doctor – when I felt that I myself, compared with him, would never be much better than a slow and ordinary bungler. By the time I had got his bag, he had already carried the unconscious bodies of the sparrows to the warmer air of the kitchen and laid them upon the table. Chee-Chee had piled wood upon the fire; and Dab-Dab had some flannels hung before it on chair-backs.

Then, taking them in turn, the Doctor made me hold the birds with their beaks pointing straight upward. Next, his flying fingers took a tiny teaspoon and filled it with some reddish medicine out of a bottle in the black bag. He sharpened a match-stick to a chisel-point with his penknife. And with this, very, very gently, he pried the bird's beak apart, held it so with the fingers of his left hand while he took the spoon filled with medicine in the other. Then (I noticed his hand was as steady as a rock) he dropped three drops into the throat of each sparrow. After that he laid the tiny bodies down again – upon their backs; and swiftly but carefully his fingers massaged the legs, the wings and the ribs for a moment. From the bag he now yanked out a stethoscope – a special one which he had invented for small patients; and for a second or two he listened to the heart-beat.

All of us, Polynesia, Chee-Chee, Dab-Dab, Too-Too and myself, silently watched the Doctor's face, waiting for an answer to the question we were afraid to ask. Meanwhile the storm outside – growing worse now – buffeted and slapped against the old house with a noise like cannon firing far away.

'Give me the hot flannels, please,' the Doctor said to me.

Then the little travellers were rolled up till they looked like tiny mummies. Only their heads poked out of the coverings. A chair was put upside down before the fire; and on its sloping back, with a couple of heavy bath-towels under them, Mr and Mrs Cheapside were set to dry.

'Cheapside has a good chance,' he muttered. 'But I'm by no means sure about poor Becky. We'll change the flannels every ten minutes. Must get the bodies dried out. I've never seen feathers so saturated. Usually they resist the water, you know, have a sort of oil in them. Almost any bird can fly in ordinary rain for hours and come to no harm. But against a storm, that's different. Goodness! These little fellows, they're almost like a case of drowning. Even their stomachs are all filled with water. I'd like to know why on earth they flew through this weather, to reach me tonight. They should have taken shelter some place – and come on in the morning. Didn't either of them say anything at all, Stubbins, when you let them in?'

'Not a word, Doctor. Of course the roaring of the gale, when I opened the window, made it hard to hear anything – short of a shout. And by the time I got it closed again, they had both passed out, fainted away on the floor.'

'Very peculiar,' muttered the Doctor – 'very! Give me some more hot flannels, please. It's time to change their coverings now. We must get them dry, Stubbins, we *must* get them dry.'

Well, I couldn't tell you how often we unwrapped and re-wrapped those soaked little birds. From time to time the Doctor would give them one or two drops more of the medicine, while all of us around him looked on, hoping for some sign of returning life. But still the eyelids did not open; and the sparrows' heads swayed and rolled on their necks, in a way that really frightened me.

I am quite sure that John Dolittle was afraid too that we would not be able to save them. No one, who did not know him as well as I, would have guessed this, just from watching him. As a rule, the more serious a case was, the calmer the way he treated it (except of course where tremendous speed was necessary; and then, even while he hurried, he never got anybody fussed – least of all himself).

But this long, long waiting between the many changes and so on was hard on the Doctor and on us who idly watched. Yes, waiting and *doing nothing* – because there was nothing more to be done; that was the most difficult thing of all for the Doctor and all of us.

What time it was I do not know. I had grown afraid that perhaps my own anxiety might interfere with the Doctor's tremendous calm. Anyway, I had moved away from the table, feeling worse than useless. I was looking miserably out of the window. The force of the wind and rain had not dropped. The grey of the morning was, however, showing behind the darker grey of the overcast eastern sky. I realized that the Doctor had been working on Cheapside and Becky through the whole night.

He and I had not spoken to one another for an hour.

I started thinking over what it could have been which these sparrows had flown through such a storm and danger to tell us. . . . Perhaps, now, neither we nor anyone else would ever know why they had so bravely given up their lives to reach us. . . . I, as well as Polynesia and the Doctor, had become very fond of that rowdy little Cheapside the London sparrow. Perhaps, too, I was more tired than I realized. Anyway, I felt terribly like crying.

And maybe I would have done so; but at that moment I heard John Dolittle call me by name. I swung around from the window and was back at his side like a flash.

16

THE END OF A LONG NIGHT

THE Doctor still had the tubes of the stethoscope in his ears and the fingers of his right hand lightly pressed the cone over Cheapside's heart when I came to the table. I peered up anxiously into John Dolittle's face; and at once – before anything was said – I was greatly comforted. For the expression in the Doctor's eyes was now a very different one.

'Stubbins,' he whispered, 'I do believe it's getting firmer – the heart-action, I mean – and more regular too. Move your head aside, please. I want to see the watch.'

I shifted the watch which lay upon the table, closer to him, turning it round so he could read the dial more easily.

'Yes,' he repeated, 'it's firmer. With luck we're going to pull this little fellow round all right.'

'Thank heaven for that!' I sighed. I did not dare to ask him about poor Becky.

'Get me some warm milk – quickly, please, Stubbins. Not hot, you know, just warm – and another teaspoon.'

Chee-Chee the monkey had a pile of light wood handy beside the hearth. He and I – both of us glad to have something useful to do – went to work on the fire which had been allowed to die down because the kitchen had grown overwarm. We soon blew up the dying embers into a brisk blaze. Over this I warmed some milk in a long-handled saucepan.

'Ah! That's what we want,' said the Doctor when I brought it to him at the table – 'nourishment. These birds are weak from hunger, as well as nearly drowned. Hold him for me now, Stubbins, the same as you did before.'

Then Cheapside was given three teaspoonfuls of warm milk. And both the Doctor and I noticed that, with the last one, the sparrow's throat actually made the movement of swallowing. This was the first sign of life the bird had shown; and we who stood around smiled at one another.

Next, we took poor little Becky and treated her the same way. She, however, made no movement of any kind.

But, on coming back to Cheapside again, we noticed that his eyes were opening slightly. We fed him more of the warm milk, as much as he could hold.

Soon we could see he was looking at the Doctor in a puzzled sort of way, as though he were trying to remember who he was. And at last in a very weak voice he murmured: 'Oh, it's you, Doc. – What a night, what a night!'

Then his head rolled feebly on his shoulders again and it looked for a moment as though his eyes were going to close once more. But suddenly they opened wide, he struggled weakly as if to get up and look around.

'Where –' he gasped, 'where's Becky?'

'Cheapside, please –' the Doctor began. Then he stopped; for another voice, a sparrow's voice, was speaking at his elbow. Both of us turned sharply towards the sound. *It was Becky talking!*

'Here I am, Cheapside,' said she. 'I'm all right. How are you?'

Cheapside's head fell back wearily.

'Ain't that the limit, Doc?' he murmured faintly. 'The old girl wants to know 'ow *I* am – when I thought she was a goner for sure. Queer lot, women. – Swap me pink! – Queer lot.'

And with that Cheapside went fast asleep again. Becky did the same a couple of minutes later.

'Who would have thought it?' said the Doctor in a whisper, as he put the things back in his bag. 'But Becky, to pull out of a battering such as that storm gave her! I assure you, Stubbins, that throughout the last hour it was impossible for me to hear her heart-action at all. . . . It's a wonderful thing, the will to live. . . . Well, well, thank goodness that's over!'

'They certainly looked done for, Doctor,' I said, 'when that storm blew them into the room.'

'What we must do now,' said he, 'is to let them rest and sleep. Your office will be the best place – where they won't be disturbed. We'll get a fire made up there and when the room's warm we'll move them in. Then you must go and get some rest yourself, Stubbins. It's been a long night for you. We will put Too-Too on watch and he will come and wake us as soon as we are needed. For the present there's nothing more we can do for them but to keep them warm and let them sleep.'

When at last I got upstairs to my bedroom, I think I must have fallen asleep before lying down; because I certainly don't remember undressing and getting into bed.

It was around tea-time, between four and five o'clock in the afternoon, when Polynesia awakened me (by biting me gently on the nose, as she usually did when she wished to rouse me out of a sleep).

'Oh – er – Hulloa!' I said drowsily, sitting up and rubbing my eyes. 'How are they, the sparrows?'

'Doing nicely, very nicely,' said she. 'They've had a good long sleep and they've eaten a big meal. The Doctor has not let them talk so far – although he has been awake for a couple of hours. He didn't want them tiring themselves out, you know. But soon, I think, he is going to let them tell their story. And I just came up to see if you wanted to come and listen.'

'You bet I do, Polynesia,' I cried, jumping out of bed. 'Do me a favour, will you? – Ask the Doctor not to let them start till I'm there.'

'All right,' said the parrot, making for the door. 'But you better hurry down. Dab-Dab is giving him breakfast now in your office.'

'Tell them I won't be but a minute,' said I, struggling into my clothes. 'And ask Dab-Dab to let me have some buttered toast and a cup of cocoa.'

17

THE TRAVELS OF MR AND MRS CHEAPSIDE

WHEN I got down to my office I saw at once that the sparrows' story had already begun – but only just. Cheapside and Becky were standing on my big desk. The Doctor was seated in the chair where I usually wrote.

As I slipped quietly into the room John Dolittle was speaking.

'But, Cheapside,' he was saying, 'honestly I don't believe I ever heard of anything so utterly crazy! Just the two of you to make such a trip – about four thousand miles! You know what the migrating birds do when they make a journey as long as that: great flocks string out in sight of one another – in a line ten or twenty miles long –

so they can keep in touch with the leaders. The day, in fact the exact hour, they leave for those oversea hops are set by the best weather-prophets they've got. Yet you, a couple of city birds, just flip off for *Africa* as though you were hopping across a London street. Such madness! Why, at this time of year you were liable to run into an equinoctial gale!'

'Quite right, Doc,' murmured Cheapside: 'we did run into one – on the way back. Goin' down there we stayed in sight of land all the way. But flying home to England we found a wind against us. And we came by way of the Canary Islands thinkin' we'd get out of the worst of the weather. We took a four-hour rest on the islands. But it

74

was the last part, gettin' from there to Cornwall – Jimminy! That was the worstest. We hit a north-easter what pretty near blew us inside out. Lucky for us, we picked up an old freight-ship comin' our way. We sneaked on to the stern of her, when nobody was lookin', and hid in a ventilator. And did she roll, that ship? – Crikey, I come near to gettin' seasick!'

'And will you please tell me,' asked John Dolittle in a very severe voice, 'what in the name of goodness made you take this journey at all?'

'Well, Doc,' said Cheapside, shifting his feet, 'you remember last time I was 'ere you discovered that your note-books about Mudface 'ad all got chewed up by some kind friends of Whitey's.'

'Ah!' said the Doctor. And suddenly a sparkle of new excitement was shining in his eyes as he leaned forward in his chair. (I glanced at Polynesia who nodded her head and winked at me.) 'Yes, yes,' said the Doctor, 'I remember, Cheapside – the note-books. Go on, please.'

'Well,' said the sparrow, 'I seed as how you was pretty bad upset. You was afraid the turtle might be dead. I asked a few questions of Tommy, 'ere. 'E told me it 'adn't never been proved that Mudface *was* dead. And me, I always says, no news is good news – especially when you use storks to get it. They ain't the same as London sparrows, Doc.'

'Oh, stop boasting, and get on with it!' snapped Becky.

'Anyway,' said Cheapside, 'an idea comes into me 'ead. And when I gets back to London that night, I asks Becky 'ow she'd like a trip down to Africa, as soon as our new family could fly and take care of theirselves. And – would you believe it? – The Missus, most unladylike, asks me straight out if I've gone nutty.'

'Yes, and I can't blame her,' murmured the Doctor. 'Go on, please.'

'So I says to 'er, I says, the Doc's done a lot for you and

me, old gal. Remember the time when 'e come all the way up to London to look at one of our youngsters what was sick?'

'Oh, yes,' muttered the Doctor. – 'Long ago. I'd forgotten all about it.'

'Well,' Cheapside went on, 'Becky 'adn't. You saved our little Ernie's life that time, Doc. And pretty soon I persuades the Missus. I knew the way down to Fantippo all right, 'cause I'd made the trip that time you sent for me – to 'elp you with the mail deliveries in old King Koko's country – you remember?'

'Indeed I do,' said the Doctor. 'But you made that journey at a very different time of year from this.'

'You bet, Doc – very different. Anyway, it was that same week we got the new family managin' for theirselves. Then we hops across the Channel near Dover and starts flyin' south, down the coast of France. Good weather stayed with us all the way; and in a few days we reaches Fantipsy harbour. And so –'

Then Becky broke in again.

'For pity's sake, Cheapside!' she scolded. 'The Doctor is dying to hear what happened to Mudface the turtle. You can tell him all this stuff about our trip afterwards. Give him the news, give him the news – such as it is.'

'Oh – er – humph!' said Cheapside in a disgruntled sort of way. 'Well now, 'old yer 'orses, old gal. It all 'angs together. You women ain't got no patience. You –'

And this time the Doctor interrupted (I knew he was afraid that a family row was going to break out between Mr and Mrs Cheapside). He said:

'To tell you the truth, Cheapside, I *am* terribly anxious to hear what has become of Mudface. Were you able to find out anything?'

'Er – yes and no,' said Cheapside. 'Becky and me went off as fast as we could for the Secret Lake; but we 'ad to lose some time, o' course, huntin' for food – seeds, you know.

76

Them heathens don't grow regular bird-seed in the jungle; but we found a kind of wild rice that would do.'

'Good!' said the Doctor.

'But suddenly, when we was gettin' near the lake – within about a hundred miles, I'd guess – I says to the Missus, I says, "Something's wrong here, Becky. I reckernize the country – general-like. – But this river right below us: look 'ow it is!" I says. "The stream out of the Secret Lake used to be just a little brook." You remember, Doc?'

The Doctor nodded.

'But this river we was flyin' over now was miles wide. And I says to Becky, "There's somethin' queer about this. I'd swear we're on the right track. *But the landscape's changed*. And if I'm right, this could explain a whole lot – maybe – about what's 'appened to the Doc's friend, Mr Mudface. Let's drop down to the bank and look for some birds, Becky. I want to ask a few questions about this."'

18

FINDING THE SECRET LAKE

I WAS so interested in what the London sparrow had to say that I had hardly taken my eyes off him since I came into the room. Now, as Chee-Chee the monkey quietly brought me some buttered toast and a cup of cocoa, I noticed the whole family was gathered there in my office. They had all stowed themselves in different places round the room, silently listening.

'And so,' Cheapside went on, 'down we drops a good many thousand feet, out of the cool air we'd been flyin' in, to the steamy heat of the jungle. We goes pokin' along the river-bank till we meet up with a couple of birds – some sort of a snipe, I think they was. And I asks 'em, I says: "Are we on the right road to Lake Junganyika, the

Secret Lake?" "Yes," they says. "Follow the river. You'll come right to it." "But look 'ere," I says: "I travelled over this stretch years ago – with Doctor Dolittle, M.D., no less. And the blinkin' country don't seem the same now. The stream we followed in our canoe was narrow. This river's four or five miles wide in places. Who's been monkeyin' with the landscape?"

' "Hoh," says one of the snipe, "hadn't you heard? We 'ad a big shake-up here – sort of an earthquake. The ground began trembling something terrible and big floods of water started coming down; and the river's been wide like this ever since. You'll find the Secret Lake changed quite a bit too."

' "You better ask the storks," they says. "They live right on the shore of the lake. We ain't seen Mudface in a long while."

' "Storks!" I says. "They ain't no good."

' "Oh," says the snipe, "there's a couple of old ones up at the lake what we thinks very 'ighly of around 'ere."

' "Listen," I says, "I'd just as soon ask the bulrushes for hinformation. Storks ain't got no sense. Why, they build their nests on people's chimney-pots! That shows 'ow bright *they* are. – Don't talk to me about storks. 'Ave you seen anythin' of the Great Water Snake?"

'No, they said, they 'adn't. So me and Becky left Mr and Mrs Snipe and we goes on up towards the lake. And the nearer we comes to it, the more I sees the landscape 'ad changed. There was the same mangrove swamps around, like we'd seen when you was there, Doc. But when we flies over the lake proper, it was plain to see that the open water was ever so much bigger – makin' it very 'ard for me to get me bearings and be sure just where I was.'

'I can indeed believe it,' said the Doctor. 'But tell me: could you find the island which we built for Mudface?'

'Yes,' said Cheapside, 'we found that all right. But it didn't look the same. – You understand we was now flyin' 'igh up again – so we could get a better view. At first I hardly reckernized it, Doc, as the island we 'ad built accordin' to your orders. It seemed a different shape. On the west side it looked pretty much as we 'ad left it – though of course palms and such was growin' there now. But you remember the shape you told us to make it, Doc – good and high, and flat on the top?'

'Yes, I remember that very clearly,' said the Doctor.

'Well, it was like that still on the west side, towards the sea. – And all lovely and green it looked too. But when we went around on the *farther* side I saw at once what 'ad 'appened. Half of the island wasn't there no more.'

'Great heavens!' I heard the Doctor mutter beneath his breath.

'You never saw anything like it, Doc. It looked just like a big loaf of bread what had been cut in 'alf with a knife. That earthquake sure done a neat job. It hadn't been so very long ago neither, 'cause there was a high cliff of bare gravel, where the land 'ad been cut off.'

'Yes, I understand,' said the Doctor.

'Then,' Cheapside went on, 'we flew over what was left of the island and searched it from end to end. But no trace of old Mudface could we find. 'Owever, we met some wild ducks. They was kind of snooty at first. But when we told 'em we was friends of yours, they changed their tune and got real chummy. They was there, nest-building. Then we asks 'em about Mudface – and when they 'ad seen 'im last. And they told us they'd seen 'im on the morning of the very day when the island got cut in two.'

'And whereabouts on the island *was* the turtle – I mean at the time of the earthquake?' asked the Doctor in a voice which, to me, plainly showed his excitement.

'He was at that same end of the island,' said Cheapside, shaking his head sadly. 'He was on the half that broke off and disappeared. The ducks was certain of it. Mudface had found a kind of a warm spring, what was good for 'is rheumatism, down by the water's edge on the east side of the island. The ducks said that as soon as the earth began to tremble they was scared and took to the air. But, as they flew off, they saw tons and tons of sand and gravel and mud pour down on top of the old turtle, who was wading in the warm spring with only his head out of the water. The ducks said they was afraid to come back for three days – till everything was quiet again. And when they did, half the island was gone, they said, disappeared beneath the water. And they reckoned old Mudface 'ad gone with it. . . . And – well, I reckon that's all, Doc.'

As Cheapside stopped speaking, a gloomy, short silence hung over the room. I knew that all of the listeners to the sparrow's story were – like myself – just bursting to ask questions. But no one said a word. For a moment the Doctor, with a worried frown, stared down thoughtfully at the floor. At last he looked up at Cheapside and said quietly:

'I want to thank both of you, Cheapside and Becky, for making this dangerous journey – especially at such a time of year – for my sake – and for Mudface's. Just the same, please don't do such a thing again without telling me. Imagine how I would have felt if you had lost your lives and never come back. Because, sooner or later, I would have heard of your trip, you may be sure, from your children, from the snipe or from the ducks.'

'Yes, I suppose so,' said Cheapside. 'But – well, me and Becky thought we'd take a chance. Nothin' venture, nothin' gain: that's what I says. We're – we're awful sorry, Doc. I reckon we didn't do no good.'

'Oh, I'm by no means sure of that yet,' said the Doctor quickly (and I noticed how all the animals around the room leaned forward suddenly, with a new interest, to hear his words). 'Tell me, Cheapside,' he went on, 'would you say the level of the water in the Secret Lake itself is higher now, or lower, than when you and I saw it the first time?'

'Well,' said the sparrow, 'me and Becky explored along

the lake-shore quite a way. It seemed as though the earth-quake, or whatever it was, had heaved the land up some places and let it down in others. I ain't no skyentist; but even I could see how the great rush of water – and the new wide river – had been made. – Like fillin' a soup-plate, made of rubber, and then bending and twisting it: of course the soup would run out on the table and all over the place.'

Then Becky spoke.

'Yes, but the level of the water *now* is what the Doctor wants to know about.'

Cheapside thought a moment before going on. Then he said:

'There ain't no doubt the water *did* rise a lot higher than what it was when you saw it, Doc. But I think that was only while the earthquake was going on.... It seems to me –' Again he stopped a moment in thought.

'Yes,' he cried suddenly, 'I remember now. The water *must* have fallen back to near its old level, because, when we had built the island somebody asked me how high I reckoned it would be from the water to the top. And I said it was about the same as St Paul's Cathedral. And this time when we went round to the far side where half the island had been cut away, the cliff was just about the same height. That's right, Doc: the water-level *is* about the same now as when you was there.'

'Good!' said the Doctor. 'That's the first thing. Now, did you find any birds – any living creatures, in fact – who could say they were sure that Mudface was dead?'

'Er – no, Doc,' said Cheapside in a hesitating, slow sort of voice. 'But – but them ducks, Doc? – Like I told you: they *saw* the old feller get buried under tons and tons of stuff! And, natural-like, after we'd been told the turtle had half the island on top of 'im, we – we reckoned 'e was finished.'

The Doctor's next words made even me sit up. I forgot all about the breakfast I was eating.

'No, not necessarily, Cheapside,' said John Dolittle. 'You see, most of the amphibian creatures – that is, those who live on the land *and* in the water, like turtles, frogs, crocodiles and so on – can stay a long time under water, if they want to.'

'But, Doc,' cried the sparrow, 'wouldn't he get crushed? Think what would happen to you or me if St Paul's Cathedral was to fall on us!'

'But we are not turtles, Cheapside,' said the Doctor, smiling. 'If Mudface's island had been solid rock; and the earthquake cut it in two, that would have been very different. But you remember: when we built that island, we made it out of earth and sand and stones – which the birds brought up from the seashore. The very biggest of those stones was only as large as an apple. Mudface's back is covered with a shell enormously strong and thick. Even that great load of gravel and stuff would not crush him, I feel fairly sure. More likely, it would just press him down into the mud-floor of the lake.'

The look of surprise on Cheapside's face would have been comical enough to make us laugh, if the talk had not been so serious.

'Well, swap me pink!' he said with a gasp. 'Do you mean to say, Doc, you think old Mudlark's still alive down there?'

'I think there's certainly a good chance he is,' said the Doctor.

'But if he's still living,' cried Cheapside, 'why don't 'e crawl out, back to 'is home on the island?'

'Ah, no,' said John Dolittle. 'That's something very different. He would have pulled his head and legs and tail inside his shell at once, as soon as the gravel began to rattle on it. But after half the island had slid on top of him, the weight, as you said, would be tremendous. He could not have moved after that – probably couldn't even poke his head out of his shell, much less walk around.'

82

'But what about food, Doctor?' asked the sparrow. 'It's quite a while since that earthquake; and 'e ain't 'ad a thing to eat.'

'That's true,' said the Doctor. 'But amphibian reptiles can, if necessary, go without food for a long, long time. Did you ever hear of hibernating, Cheapside?'

'Er – ain't that what the bears does, sort of holing-up for the winter?'

'That's right,' said the Doctor. 'But the turtles, when they want to hibernate, bore their way down into the mud and gravel, under water, at the bottom of a river or lake. I hope that is what has happened to our old friend – only in his case of course, he didn't go into hibernation on purpose. But, from what you tell me, it is just the same as if he had.'

'But, Doctor,' asked the sparrow, 'how is the old feller ever goin' to get out of there?'

The Doctor rose from his chair; and, standing, gazed out a moment through the window into the garden.

'Cheapside,' he said presently, 'I don't think there's any chance of his ever getting out, unless someone goes to help him.'

Again a quiet spell fell over the room. It came into my head to ask the Doctor a question myself. But I glanced over at Polynesia first. And I could see that that strange bird already knew what was in my mind; for she shook her head at me and raised her right claw to her beak, like a person motioning you to keep quiet. And soon the Doctor was speaking again.

'I wonder, Cheapside,' he said, 'if you would mind making that journey to Africa again – to Lake Junganyika – quite soon, would you?'

'Why, of course,' said the sparrow, 'of course I'd be glad to. But I'd stick to the coast-line this time, you bet. What did you want me to find out for you, Doc?'

'Oh, I didn't mean to have you go alone this trip,' said

HUGH LOFTING

John Dolittle. 'I was thinking of going down there, myself, by ship, and taking you with me. You might be very helpful as a guide and all that, you know – having found your way into the Secret Lake, after it's changed so much. I would have to borrow a canoe from King Koko of Fantippo. I don't know of course whether I can be of any real help to my old friend Mudface. But I feel that at least I ought to go down there and see what I can do.'

And then Polynesia said:

'I quite agree with you, Doctor. You remember when Long Arrow was trapped in the cave in the mountain? That looked hopeless enough. And yet you got him out. Of course we ought to go back to the Secret Lake – not only on the turtle's account, but to get the story of the Flood again, to put in your note-books.'

And then, after the parrot had joined in the talk, it seemed as though pandemonium broke loose in my office. All the animals had been bursting to say something for a long time. And now, after Polynesia had spoken, suddenly they all started asking questions, giving advice and talking at once. You never heard such a racket.

Seeing that it was impossible for me to talk to the Doctor in an uproar like that, I made a signal to Jip to clear them out of the room. And that he did very quickly, leaving only the parrot and the sparrows. But even then the noise did not entirely stop. Arguments and discussions could be heard, through the closed door, going on in the passage, on the stairs – everywhere in the house.

When at last these had somewhat died down I started to ask a question of the Doctor. But at that moment a terrible mixture of squeals and barks went rushing by under the windows. I looked out. It was Jip chasing Gub-Gub, who was galloping down the garden to carry the news to the animals in the 'zoo'. The white mouse was clinging to the pig's neck like a jockey on a race-horse.

'Hey!' yelled Gub-Gub. 'Hey! The Doctor's going on a voyage – to Africa. Hooray! . . . Hooray!'

PART TWO

I

OUR SHIP, THE *ALBATROSS*

AFTER the news was out, that the Doctor was going on a voyage, it seemed to me no time at all before we were actually there, in Africa.

But, despite the need to be on our way as quickly as possible, there was of course a tremendous lot which had to be done before we could leave. First of all, we had to get a ship. This, Polynesia took charge of. The parrot was an old sailor. When she looked at a ship, right away she could tell you a whole lot about the craft without even getting on to it. The Doctor knew he could trust her to find the boat he wanted – one which was not too large for us to handle; one which could go into shallow harbours like Fantippo.

In this we had good luck (indeed, good luck stayed with us on this voyage, not only on the trip itself, but even in the preparations we made for it). We went and saw my old friend, Joe, the mussel-man at his little hut on the river-bank near King's Bridge. And Joe had just what we wanted. He took us a short way down the river where he showed us a boat tied up to a wharf.

'Here she be, Mr Tom,' said he. 'I don't reckon I could have found a better ship nowhere for what the Doctor wants.'

She was indeed a lovely little craft. Joe had, only ten days ago, finished repainting her from stem to stern. She was named the *Albatross*. Joe took Polynesia and me aboard her. I could see the old parrot's seafaring eyes noticing everything; and, although she did not ask any questions, I could tell that she was as pleased as I was with the good ship *Albatross*

'She's a sloop, as you see, Mr Tom,' said Joe, 'but cutter-rigged. Easy to handle in any weather. Nice, roomy cabin with bunks for six. – And complete too: lamps, dinghy, dishes – she's got everything, even to her charts, nautical almanac and the rest.'

So I told the mussel-man I would bring the Doctor down to see the boat later that day or tomorrow; and we left.

'We've got to think about victualling her, next,' said Polynesia from my shoulder, as I walked towards the Market-place. 'Have you got a pencil and paper on you, Tommy?'

I had; and as we went along, the old parrot gave me lists and lists of things which, she said, we must take along on a trip like this.

'And mind you, young man,' she added, 'these are just provisions – things to eat and wear and so on, for ourselves. But besides all this, there is the stuff which the ship herself may need: oil for the lamps, extra rope and so on. But we'll take care of all that later. Old Joe says she's got everything – and maybe she has. But no good ship's master puts to sea without making sure, for himself, that his craft isn't short of anything he really needs.

Once more poor old Matthew was told that he would have to be left behind when the Doctor went abroad. He complained bitterly. His wife, Theodosia, had come secretly to the house and begged John Dolittle not to take her husband. She was sure, she said, Africa wouldn't agree with him.

'You see, Matthew,' the Doctor explained to the cats'-meat-man, 'I'm counting on you to look after so many things while I am gone. – Not only the things you have taken care of for me before, but now there's the garden, as well. I haven't half finished getting it back in proper order.

And if I were to leave it to run wild any longer, it would be just ruined by next Spring. You know the way I like it kept. And you're the only man I'd put in charge of the work. In fact, I don't know what I'd do without you – really, I don't.'

And so Matthew agreed to stay behind and act as general caretaker, gardener and zoo-keeper. It relieved the Doctor's mind tremendously.

The day after we had seen the *Albatross*, Polynesia and I took the Doctor down to look over her. He was very pleased with the ship; and the same night he and I were in his study after dinner, 'armchair-travelling', as he used to call it.

'Who else had you planned to take with you, Doctor?' I asked.

'Oh, I think all of my regular household, Stubbins; that is, if they want to come along. Too-Too, Jip, Dab-Dab, the white mouse – and then of course Chee-Chee. You remember how valuable he is in the jungle, at finding foods and all that? And besides, he's very handy aboard ship too. Quite a good little sailor. And then there's Cheapside and his wife.'

'How about Gub-Gub the pig, Doctor? I know he is expecting you to take him. He says he hopes to add a new chapter to his *Encyclopaedia of Food*. He claims he is now the best pig scientist living, as well as the most famous pig comedian.'

'Maybe so,' said the Doctor thoughtfully. 'He discovered some new kinds of wild sugar-cane on our last trip.'

'But he weighs an awful lot,' I remarked, remembering that a sloop is not a very big ship.

'Quite, quite,' said John Dolittle. 'Well, don't worry about Gub-Gub. We'll take him if we can. But better not make any promises till we see just how much space we have.'

He reached for the tobacco-jar and started to fill his pipe.

'You know, Stubbins,' said he, 'I'm quite pleased with the way this trip has fallen out – just happened, as you might say. If those rats hadn't chewed up my note-books to make their nests, we wouldn't be going on this journey, would we? Of course ... Mudface, poor old fellow! ... Even when I get there, I may find I can't do anything for him. But somehow I feel we're going to be lucky on this voyage.'

He struck a match and held it to the bowl of his pipe. Then he leant forward in his chair. I had never seen his manner show greater, keener interest.

'And if our luck stays with us,' he went on, 'and we are able to get the turtle's story of the Flood again, it will be tremendously important to science.'

'How long before the Flood was Mudface born, Doctor?' I asked.

'Ah!' said John Dolittle. 'That I can't say. Maybe he told me; maybe not. My memory isn't clear on any details, any particulars. I wrote so fast. But if I'm right about his speaking of the other animals in the world at that time, as well as the trees, the plants, the rocks and so on – you see how important it will be? Perhaps there were books written on natural history before Noah's time. But anyhow they were all swept away – lost. Don't you see how important this trip of ours may be?'

'I certainly do,' I said solemnly. 'With all the books before the Deluge destroyed, only one man can bring back the knowledge that was drowned: he who speaks the language of the animals – John Dolittle.'

At once (as he always did when someone said anything complimentary to him) he looked uncomfortable.

'Oh, goodness, Stubbins!' said he. 'We mustn't forget that there are many big *ifs* between us and success. And the biggest of them is: everything will depend on *if* I can get poor old Mudface out of the lake from under that mountain of gravel.'

89

'Yes, Doctor. But also, don't forget that you said you thought we'd be lucky this trip.'

'Ah, to be sure, to be sure!' he answered, breaking into a smile. 'And I meant it. . . . It's a funny thing: sometimes a man feels that way and sometimes he doesn't. Sounds like a lot of superstitious nonsense, doesn't it? And yet, you know, I don't think it really is. . . . Well, anyway, Stubbins, I *do* feel we're going to be lucky on this voyage.'

'How soon do you think we'll be ready to sail, Doctor?' I asked.

'Oh – er – let me see: this is Tuesday, isn't it?' he murmured. 'Well, I think Saturday would be all right, Stubbins. – And by the way, you won't forget to go and say good-bye to your mother and father, will you? They have both been awfully good about letting you stay here and help me. I'm afraid they haven't been seeing very much of you lately, eh?'

'No, Doctor,' I said, 'I'll attend to that. I'll go over and see them tomorrow night.'

'Good,' he said. 'We'll set our sailing date for next Saturday, then. But don't tell anyone the exact day, Stubbins, please. It might leak out and – you know – newspapermen and all that sort of thing . . . ?'

'No, Doctor,' I repeated. 'Not a word to anyone.'

2

GOOD-BYE TO PUDDLEBY

OUT-GOING ships always leave when the tide in the river has just turned to ebb – that is, running out towards the sea. And when we had looked up the hour of the ebb tide for that Saturday, we found it was five o'clock in the morning. Of course, as early in the day as that, practically no one was up and about. So we were able to slip away

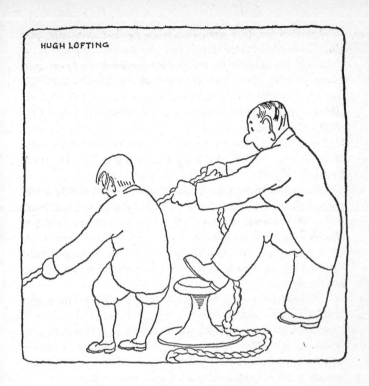

down the river, without the newspapermen (or, indeed, anybody else) seeing us or knowing we had left.

Joe the mussel-man and Matthew Mugg were the only ones at the wharf to bid us good-bye. (I always asked my parents *not* to see me off on voyages. I was afraid my mother would cry.)

The morning air was cold; and full daylight had not yet lit up the sky, as the Doctor gave the keys of the house and stable to Matthew. Then the mooring-ropes were let go and hauled aboard. The good ship *Albatross* was poled out into the current and headed downstream towards the sea. Joe stayed aboard for a short while (with his little mussel-boat trailing behind on a tow-rope). He helped the Doctor and me set one of the smaller sails. And in the misty half-light the ghostly tall shapes of warehouses on the river-banks began to slip astern of us faster and faster.

At last Joe shook the Doctor and me by the hand, got into his mussel-boat and shouted to the Doctor to cast off. John Dolittle told me to take the wheel while he undid the tow-rope.

'Good-bye!' called Joe. – 'Good-bye and good luck to yer voyage!'

I had not realized how fast we were moving. Even as we called our answering farewells to him, Joe disappeared into the mist astern of us. The Doctor took the wheel from me and asked me to find Polynesia because he wished to speak with her.

I discovered the old parrot up forward, humming a sailor song to herself as she looked over the baggage piled on the deck.

'Look at that, my lad, look at that!' said she in her severest, most seamanlike manner. 'All that gear will have to be stowed below before we get out of the river into open water. The first sea that comes over her bow will wash the whole lot overboard. – What's that? The Doctor wants to see me? All right. But get Chee-Chee to help you stow this stuff below decks. And hop to it, my lad! You haven't got much time, the way this tide is running.'

John Dolittle set Polynesia as a forward look-out, up in the fo'c'sle. Here, being right in the front or foremost part of the boat, she was able to see things ahead sooner than the Doctor at the wheel. And very helpful she was too. There were ships and barges anchored in Puddleby River – as well as buoys marking the channel of the stream. Often we would hear the old seafaring parrot roar out: 'Hard-a-port, Doctor! – Schooner off the starboard bow. – Hard-a-port!'

Then the Doctor would spin the wheel to swing us over – but not too far, lest he run the *Albatross* out of the channel, on to the mud of the river-bank. And suddenly, in the mist ahead of us, the hull of a big ship at anchor would rear up high; and it would look as though we must surely crash into her. But Polynesia's keen old eyes had seen her in time to warn the Doctor; and we would skid silently by, under her towering shadow – with only six feet of room to spare.

Speaking of the Doctor as a sea-captain, the parrot had often said: 'Yes, John Dolittle almost always does things wrong at sea – and most skippers would go grey-haired in one voyage with him. But you know, when he's managing his own boat, it doesn't seem to matter. He always gets there – where he means to go – just the same. Remember that, Tommy: you're always safe with John Dolittle.'

For the next half-hour Chee-Chee and I were kept busy carrying baggage below decks and stowing it in safe places, where it would not slam around when the sloop should start to pitch and roll. This, we knew, would begin as soon as we got out of Puddleby River into the open sea.

It was a strange collection of stuff we had brought with us. There was not much of what you would call ordinary baggage, such as trunks and the like; but there was plenty that was not ordinary. There were butterfly-nets, collecting-boxes for birds' eggs, hatching-cages for caterpillars and all sorts and kinds of other things which naturalists and explorers take with them on their travels.

All the packages were carefully labelled, telling what they had inside them. I think a stranger, reading some of these labels, would have been quite puzzled. For instance, one label read: *Moon-Seeds – Store in a dry place*. The Doctor, just before we left, had said: 'We are going to West Africa but Long Arrow might turn up anywhere. Let's take a few of those seeds along – just in case. They won't need much room.'

And there was another box, much larger, marked: *Live turtles. Keep this side up – With care!* John Dolittle knew that I did not understand turtle language at all well. And, as I was going to act as secretary this time and write down all that Mudface should tell us (*if*, of course, we succeeded in rescuing him from under the lake), the Doctor thought I ought to practise up on the language as much as I could before we got there. So he had sent Matthew Mugg up to London to buy a few turtles at a pet-shop: and I spent a couple of hours each day, learning turtle talk (with the help of the Doctor himself).

The Doctor also bought me a book on short-hand writing; and I studied that too. Because, he said, Mudface was a fast talker – though not always. The Doctor thought it would be far easier and less tiring for me to use short-hand.

Most of the rest of the baggage was of course food supply; you have to buy many things for even a few people who are going to be cut off from all shopping for several weeks at a time. And you have no idea how easy it is to forget the most important. However, with the help of Dab-Dab and Polynesia (both of whom had sailed with John Dolittle before) I can proudly say there was very little I had missed.

I did have one dreadful moment, though, as I now carried the packing-cases and barrels and parcels below deck. Cheapside and his wife Becky had been hopping around the baggage, as if hunting for something. Myself, I was too busy to talk; but presently I heard the Cockney sparrow say to his wife:

'No, Becky. It ain't 'ere. They've been and forgot it.'

'What were you looking for, Cheapside?' I asked as I heaved a small but heavy case of prunes up on to my shoulder.

'The bird-seed, of course!' said Cheapside. 'What d'yer think we'd be looking for – cigars?'

'Oh, my goodness,' I cried, 'don't tell me I forgot the *bird-seed*!'

'That's just what I am tellin' yer,' shouted the sparrow

in his most fighting manner. 'Now me and my old lady has got to live on biscuit-crumbs for three or four thousand miles. Nice kind of a first mate you are! And what 'appened to that wonderful old ship's master, Polynesia? She 'elped you make out the lists. Listen: if she 'ad you bring sunflower-seeds for parrots, and no bird-seed for sparrows, I'll pull 'er tail out for 'er. – Swap me pink if I don't!'

Cheapside's angry voice had now become so loud that it clearly reached the ears of the Doctor at the wheel. For suddenly he called out:

'It's all right, Cheapside. We have plenty of bird-seed aboard. I happened to think of it, myself, on my way to the Post Office the last time. It's in my overcoat-pocket hanging on the back of the cabin-door.'

'Oh – er – excuse me, Doc,' said the sparrow. 'I just wanted to make sure – kind of checking up on the ship's stores, like.'

And as Cheapside went below, followed by his wife, I could hear Becky scolding him.

'Of all the bad-mannered street-arabs,' she was saying, 'you're the worst! – Anyone would think you were home, the way you behave.'

3

THE DOLITTLE FAMILY AT SEA

WHEN we at last reached the mouth of the river the sun had risen upon a fair and beautiful day. The long arm of the dyke (a sort of high earth bank which marked the end of the stream) had a lighthouse on the seaward tip of it. The keeper was an old friend of ours. He waved to us from the lantern-railing, as our ship took her first plunging pitch in the swell of the open sea.

Poor Gub-Gub was lapping up a drink of water from a

bucket when the pitch came; and our ship's stern reared up so steeply and unexpectedly, the pig scientist suddenly found himself standing on his head in the pail, instead of on the deck.

Of course our sloop was small. The weather was only what regular sailors would call a swell. But I liked the way our boat handled it, the way she rode over the crests of the waves and down into the troughs between. There was something about the brave little *Albatross* (buried out of sight, she was, half the time) which gave you confidence and trust in her. The morning sun glistened on her bright new paint; she moved like something truly alive; and the tang of the salt spray on your lips made you glad to be alive with her, in this wide world of water where she seemed so much at home.

I was glad, though, that I had obeyed Polynesia and got the baggage stowed below before we passed the lighthouse, because the ship's motion now made work on the deck pretty hard. Indeed, there was plenty to keep me busy. The Doctor called to me to get Gub-Gub down below. He was afraid the pig (who was very round in shape) might get rolled right overboard. So I took him downstairs and put him to helping Dab-Dab and Chee-Chee tidy up the cabin.

Then I arranged our animal family: the sleeping quarters for each, and so on – in the way the Doctor and I had agreed upon before hand.

Gub-Gub was not the only one who had difficulty with the rolling and pitching of the ship. Mice, when they sleep, have a habit of drawing their legs in, so they look like a ball. Whitey, to begin with, wanted to sleep in the cabin with the rest of us – mostly, I think, because he was afraid that anywhere else he couldn't hear us talking and so might miss something that was being planned. Well, the first night or two he would go to sleep under my bunk; but before morning the roll of the ship would trundle him across the cabin-floor and wake him up by banging his head against the door.

So in the galley (which is what you call the kitchen aboard ship) I found an old teacup with the handle broken off. I gave it to Whitey for a nest. He lined it with ends of twine and shreds of newspaper, so it was very snug and comfortable. Then I set the cup back in the china-rack (that is where you keep your dishes at sea, so they won't slide on the floor). And for the rest of the voyage Whitey slept in peace – but Dab-Dab was very annoyed. 'What next, I'd like to know?' she snorted. 'Mice in *my* china-rack!'

'Fussy old party, ain't she?' said Cheapside who had overheard her scolding me. 'By the way, I heard the Doctor calling for you just now, Tommy.'

I found the Doctor. He wanted me to go forward with him and look at some maps in the chart-room, as it was called. This was, to me, one of the most interesting parts of the ship. It had windows or port-holes all around it. Here the charts, or maps, were kept – also the instruments which are used for finding your way at sea: the sextant, the chronometer and many more. In this little room the 'course' of the ship was worked out: that is, the direction she should go in.

My boyish imagination could always conjure up smugglers – and even pirates – who might have been captains of this ship in days gone by. And in fancy I could see them bending over the broad desk, with pistols in their belts, plotting the sloop's course to some little, uninhabited island, where they meant to bury treasure they'd stolen from other ships.

'We will hold her sou'-sou'-east, Stubbins, for the present – till we pick up Cape Finisterre,' said the Doctor as he spread out one of the maps. 'I want to check with the chart. This following wind is grand. We're making good headway. – Hope it keeps up. We'll try more canvas – more sail – on her soon.'

After we had cleared Cape Finisterre the weather got warmer and warmer, as we made our way south. At times it got a little too warm for the Doctor and myself; but Polynesia and Chee-Chee just revelled in it.

'Ah!' gurgled the old parrot, fluffing out her feathers. 'Wonderful to see the sun again! I declare if you lived in England long enough, you'd forget what sunshine looked like.'

'You got a cheek, you stuffed stocking!' snorted Cheapside. – 'Always grousing about the Henglish climate. We *like* it kind of moist there. That's what keeps our brains from dryin' up – the way yours is. *Phew!* This deck is 'ot. I'm goin' down to the cabin – before I turns into fried chicken.'

The weather certainly stayed wonderfully good and – what was still better – our northerly winds blew steadily the whole voyage. In fact everything seemed to go pleasantly and well. I do not remember any other sea trip with the Doctor where we had better or easier sailing. Even the after-supper story hour was kept up aboard ship, the same as it had been in the old house at Puddleby.

It was strange that aboard the *Albatross* the animals always asked the Doctor to tell them sea stories. And by the end of the first week John Dolittle said he had told them all he knew. But the next day Whitey the librarian, hunting through the lockers in the chart-room, came upon a nice thick book, called *Tales of the Seven Seas*. And for the rest of that peaceful journey the Doctor's family got him to read them a chapter aloud out of this, every night, translating it into animal languages as he went along.

4

THE STORMY PETREL

THE only interruption – if indeed I could call it that – to the smooth sailing and our happy voyage came towards its end. For a whole morning the Doctor had been looking at the barometer (that is the instrument for telling the weather) every ten or fifteen minutes; and I noticed he usually frowned over it. However, I was too busy to pay much attention at the time.

But presently, when the Doctor had gone down to the cabin, I noticed a bird skimming low down over the sea on the starboard side. Of course I had to watch the compass carefully (I was handling the wheel just then). But I managed to glance, every once in a while, at the bird. It was a *stormy petrel*.

In bygone days this kind of bird was supposed to be a sign of bad weather. As a matter of fact it isn't – though to be sure, it is often seen when the sky is gloomy or overcast. I have always admired the petrel (sometimes called Mother Carey's Chicken) because, hunting alone or in pairs, it seemed so safe and really at home in mid-ocean, no matter what the weather or the sea might do.

Well, to my surprise, presently this petrel came and perched upon the rail quite close to me.

'Is this Doctor Dolittle's ship?' he asked. And then, at the same moment, we both recognized one another.

'Why, it's Tommy!' he cried. – 'Grown so big no one could recognize you.'

'And you're the petrel that came and found me, after the shipwreck – on our trip to Spidermonkey Island,' I said. – 'I know you by that grey feather in your right wing. I'm awfully glad to see you again.'

'Thank you,' he said politely. 'Ever since daybreak I've

99

been hunting all over the ocean for the Doctor's ship. What I have to tell him is important. Is he awake?'

'Yes, I think so,' I said. 'I'll call him for you.' I snatched out my bos'un's whistle, which I wore on a cord round my neck, and blew a quick, sharp blast. In a moment the Doctor came trundling up on deck and ran to my side.

'Doctor,' said the petrel, 'you're sailing right into a tornado, a real bad one – ninety-mile-an-hour wind and a heavy sea. It's blowing right across your path, the way you are sailing now. You're too close to the land. Head farther out to sea and you can get behind it – but you've got to hurry, or it will pile your ship up on the coast.'

'All right,' said the Doctor. 'We're sailing due south now, with one point to westward. If I – '

'Swing her due west,' the bird interrupted quickly. – 'Due west, Doctor, hurry!'

John Dolittle took the wheel from my hands. Then with his eyes shifting from the compass to the sails, to watch their behaviour, he carefully pulled the ship's bow over till we were heading straight out into mid-ocean.

'How's that?' he said at last.

'That's fine,' said the bird. 'Hold her to that until I tell you to change. You're now running alongside the storm – coming in the opposite direction – and you're about thirty miles this side of the hurricane – but nothing to hurt you. If you had gone on and cut right across its path, I don't know what would have happened. I'm surely glad I found you in time.'

'So am I,' said the Doctor, laughing. 'And I am very grateful for your warning. I thought my barometer was dropping awfully fast. And I knew there must be bad weather brewing somewhere close to us. But I couldn't make out in what direction it was. – By the way, you said you had been searching for me. How did you know I was at sea?'

'Oh, very simple, Doctor,' said the petrel. 'Most of the

sea-birds know you by sight – at least, along these coasts. I was talking with some gulls I met; and they told me they'd seen you on a small sailing ship. But the duffers had not noticed what course you were on – just that your sloop was heading generally southward. And that *wasn't* so simple – I mean, finding you. I didn't know whether you were making for the Canary Islands or following the African coast, closer inshore. I had just flown out of the path of that same storm myself. Well, I searched the sea for a long time. And I was on my way to get some more petrels to help me hunt for you when – only by pure luck – I spied your little ship right below me.'

'Yes,' said the Doctor, suddenly serious: 'good luck has certainly been with us on this voyage – so far. Let's hope it stays. You have been most helpful. Wouldn't you like something to eat? We have some excellent sardines in the larder – real Portuguese.'

Well, in the end, the petrel stayed with us a whole day and night – and very good company he was too. He was an entirely different sort of bird from Polynesia, Too-Too, Cheapside or the rest of our friends. The stormy petrel is a citizen of the sea. And he looked it, with his sleek, long wings (indeed, when he was flying, he seemed to be all wings – with just a little hinge for a body between them, pointed at both ends). I never got tired of watching the beautiful, easy way he flew into the teeth of a high wind.

He was different too in other things: in his likes and dislikes, in his thinking – in fact, in almost everything. He was very fond of John Dolittle, who had mended one of those long wings years ago – when he had broken it flying round the rigging of an old wrecked ship, stranded on the rocks. At our after-supper story-time in the cabin the Doctor got him to tell us pieces out of his own life; and they were more thrilling than any stories of the sea which I have ever heard or read. Yet he never boasted, but spoke of the most hair-raising adventures as though they were nothing more than what a petrel must expect any day in the year.

It was quite clear that he knew a tremendous lot about sea-weather in general and of winds in particular. John Dolittle asked him many questions about winds and what caused them; and he got me to write down the petrel's answers in a notebook.

Good luck again? Who can say? Anyway, I thought, as I scribbled down the questions and answers, for me it was a mighty comfortable feeling, right now, that a stormy petrel would pop up out of nowhere and make us change our course to miss a terrible storm.

After we had sailed due west for about six hours the petrel told the Doctor the danger was passed and we could go back on our old course.

'What port are you making for, Doctor?' he asked.

'Fantippo,' said John Dolittle.

'Oh, well, you're not far off it now,' said the bird. 'Head your ship straight in for the land. – No, no, a little more east. – That's good. Hold it,' he added, when the Doctor had pulled the helm over a little farther. 'In a short while you'll come in sight of the island of No Man's Land and the entrance to Fantippo Bay. I'll be leaving you now. I must get back up north. I'm meeting a brother of mine. Is there nothing more I can do?'

'No, indeed, thank you,' said the Doctor. 'You have been most kind. I'm sorry I delayed your meeting with your brother.'

'Oh, that's all right,' said the bird. 'He'll just loaf around, fishing, till I come. We sea-folk don't bother too much about time, you know.'

The Doctor had given the wheel back to me, as soon as his eyes had noted the new course for Fantippo on the compass-card. The petrel took a little jump off the rail and spread those beautiful long wings upon the air. With no flapping or slapping, he just soared around the sloop, mak-

ing the wind lift him as he wished, till at last he skimmed over the tip of the main-mast. Then he lunged off towards the north.

'Good-bye, John Dolittle,' he called down. – 'Good-bye and good luck!'

'Good-bye, old friend,' the Doctor shouted back. – 'And the best of luck to you!'

He stood quite still at my side, his eyes watching the bird swoop over the white-capped waves till it was out of sight.

'You know, Stubbins,' he murmured at last, 'I've never wished to be anything but what I am, a doctor. Yet I believe if I *had* to change into something else, that's what I would choose to be, out of all other creatures in the world: a stormy petrel.'

Late that afternoon Too-Too, who was on look-out duty atop the mast, suddenly shouted, 'Land ahead! – Land on the starboard bow, Sir!'

And so our lucky voyage came to an end.

5

OUR WELCOME AT FANTIPPO

MOST of the Doctor's animal family had been to Fantippo before. But for me this was my first visit to that kingdom. So, as you can easily understand, I was a little excited and very interested to see what it would be like.

We had taken down the big mainsail from the sloop's mast and left only enough canvas to move us at the speed of a walk. Polynesia was now on look-out duty up in the peak of the forecastle; and the Doctor, who knew these waters to be full of rocks and sand-bars, had taken the wheel himself. I stood at his side with the telescope to my eye, watching the land grow nearer and clearer in the slanting light of the evening sun. Presently he pointed to a round lump ahead of us, on the north side of the opening to Fantippo Bay.

'That's where I had my Post Office, Stubbins,' said he: 'On a big house-boat, moored to the shore of that island.'

'I see it,' I said. – 'And the house-boat is still there. This *is* a good telescope. Why, I can even see the geraniums growing in the window-boxes.'

'You can!' he cried. 'Well, that's my old friend King Ko-ko's doing. The swallows told me that he had always kept the house-boat spic-and-span after I left – hoping, I believe, that someday I'd come back and run the Swallow Mail for him again. – What's the matter? What are you seeing now?'

'I don't know, Doctor. Strange! Seems like crowds and crowds of canoes or something. You have a look. I'll take the wheel a moment.'

The Doctor took the telescope from me and peered towards the land.

'You're right, Stubbins. – Hundreds of canoes waiting, just inside the reef. I can see the King's canoe among them too, with the flag at the stern, the royal standard. . . . Why, it almost looks as though they were waiting to welcome us. But how on earth did they know we were coming? . . . Oh, for heaven's sake! – I know what's happened: there are great flocks of gulls around the Post Office. Most likely they heard, through the petrel, that we were sailing in these waters and they gathered at my old house-boat to give us a welcome. The King must have seen them; and he probably thinks I am coming to run his mails for him again. I'm afraid he'll be disappointed. Well, anyway – from birds or kings – it *is* nice to get a welcome when you come to foreign shores. Don't you think so, Stubbins?'

'It certainly is, Doctor,' I answered. 'Just *look* at those gulls! You don't need any telescope now. See them rising over the island – like white clouds! I don't wonder the King thought there was something happening.'

'My goodness!' laughed the Doctor. 'I fancy they have sighted our ship. . . . Yes, sure enough. Here they come, flying out to meet us.'

It was indeed a sight to be remembered for a lifetime. We were still a good mile from the shore. But the air and the heavens between us and the island seemed to be filled with white wings flashing in the sun. Soon we could hear the peculiar high-pitched voices of the gulls. 'Welcome!' they called. 'Welcome, John Dolittle, welcome back to Fantippo!'

The noise they made grew into a deafening roar, as the

105

first flights of them reached our ship and circled round the masts. The air was so thick with them that, gazing up, I wondered how they managed to keep from jostling and colliding in that densely crowded space, big as it was. For I now saw, when they were closer, that this enormous army on wings had spread itself out at least a mile wide. They did not settle on the ship itself; but, like a guard of honour, formed themselves up on either side of us – leaving a wide path ahead of the *Albatross* empty and clear. They seemed to understand that they must not fly directly in front of us towards the harbour – for if they had, of course, it would have been impossible for anyone to steer his way through that fog of feathers.

It was no new thing, Polynesia told me, for the Doctor to receive welcomes by birds. But that evening I felt this was surely something that no man could ever get used to. I glanced at his smiling face behind the wheel. And I felt glad indeed that the old parrot and Cheapside had made him come; and that I, in my own way, had helped.

Any more talk was impossible for the present, with the noise that the gulls made. So John Dolittle, watching for signals from the look-outs, steered the sloop carefully through the dangerous shallows, till he at last brought her within the safety of the harbour. Chee-Chee and I were waiting, with our hands upon the anchor-cable, for him to signal us. And when at last he waved his hand, we let go. The big bow-anchor splashed into the water; the coils of rope at our feet ran out through the hawse-pipe and then suddenly went slack. We made fast to a cleat. The good ship *Albatross* swung slowly round down-wind, and then came to rest – anchored in Fantippo Bay.

As I walked towards the stern to speak to the Doctor, I noticed that the roaring chorus of sea-birds had stopped. But now another sound – though not so great – had taken its place. It was the chatter of human voices. And it came from the waiting canoes.

This crowd of little craft had stood off some distance from us, so as not to interfere with our handling of the sloop. These small boats were simply packed with people, all gaily dressed in bright-coloured clothes – all, that is, except the paddlers, whose fine black bodies wore nothing but a rag around their middle. As soon as our anchor splashed into the water a shout went up; and the whole fleet started across the bay towards us at a most surprising speed.

But though they came fast, it was no higgledy-piggledy rush. The leading paddler in one of the canoes started a song; and then all crews in all the canoes sang along with him. I now saw that this was to keep them in line, so that all the paddles should plunge into the water together. The paddles, and the canoes too, were curiously carved and painted. There seemed to be ten men or so working in each boat; and, as there were easily two hundred canoes, that made a lot of singers.

The sun had now dropped down to the sea's edge, and its red light flashed back from all the wet paddle-blades together, as the men shouted their strange but pleasing song. And the whole canoe-fleet seemed to leap forward at each powerful stroke. It was a wondrous, fascinating sight to watch.

In the centre of this crowd of canoes there was one much larger than the rest. It was more like a wide barge, with a purple awning over it to keep off the sun. Under the awning sat an enormously fat man with a crown on his head and a green lollipop in his hand. Sometimes he put the lollipop in his mouth to suck upon; and at others he held it up to his eye, to gaze through it like a quizzing-glass.

On my way to the wheel I had stopped amidships to watch the show. Now as I leant upon the rail the Doctor came up and joined me. Cheapside was with him.

'Oh, look,' cried the sparrow. 'There's old King Coconut. – Criminy giblets! 'E's fatter than ever.'

'Yes,' said the Doctor. 'And he's not likely to get any thinner, so long as he eats lollipops morning, noon and night. They were always his great weakness.'

'You're right, Doc,' said the sparrow. 'Old King Lollipop! Eatin' candy, couldn't stop. — Lumme, Doc, that's poetry, that is! Maybe I should 'ave been a writer, same as you.'

'Oh, there are plenty of writers,' said John Dolittle. 'But,' he added, smiling at the sparrow, 'there's only one Cheapside.'

'Huh! — Thank goodness for that,' said a voice behind us, and, turning around, we found that Polynesia had joined us.

'Why, you heathen, Hafrican hedgehog!' snapped Cheapside. 'For two pins I'd wring —'

But the Doctor stopped the squabble before it got really started.

'Listen, *please*,' he said. 'We will let down the rope-ladder — on this side. The canoes are making way, see — so the King's barge can come through. It looks to me as though we are going to get an official visit from His Majesty. Lend me a hand, please, with the ladder, Stubbins.'

6

THE DINNER-PARTY ON THE HOUSE-BOAT

KING KOKO'S visit of welcome to our ship turned out to be a very grand business indeed. For not only did His Majesty himself come aboard to pay his compliments, but all the important men in his kingdom came — with all their wives and all their children. I though that our able seaman, Polynesia, was going to have a fit. She and I were sitting up in the rigging. We had climbed there to get away from the crowd. Looking down, we could see that our visitors actually covered the deck from stem to stern. They were like ants on a jam-pot.

'We must get the Doctor to stop them, Tommy,' the parrot sputtered. 'We've only got six inches of free-board left; and they're still climbing up the ladder – and more yet coming out from the shore. This sloop may turn turtle and go down any minute. Shiver my timbers! I thought I'd seen everything a sailor can. But, by cracky, it seems I'm yet going to see a ship sunk by kindness! *I* can't even make the Doctor hear me, with all those fat grinning women cackling over him. Can't *you* do something to get his attention, Tommy? The water will be over the main-deck any moment.'

I cupped my hands and yelled down to John Dolittle as hard as I could. – No use. He didn't even look up. Then an idea came to me (I can't tell why it hadn't before). I snatched my bos'un's whistle from my pocket and blew on it hard and long.

That did the trick. It was a new kind of sound to the Fantippans, I suppose. Anyway, there was a sudden complete silence. John Dolittle looked up and saw me in the rigging.

'Doctor,' I cried. 'Stop the crowd. Get them off the ship. We've only six inches of free-board left. We're top-heavy. We're going to sink if – '

But the Doctor didn't wait to hear more. He said something quickly to the King at his side. His Majesty raised the sacred lollipop on high; and everyone respectfully paid attention to the royal command. He only said five or six words in a strange, clicking kind of language. But it was enough. The crowd scrambled for the canoes.

By good luck, all the port-holes down below were shut; otherwise the cabin and the hold would have been swamped. As it was, the scuppers of the main-deck were under water; and now the poor little *Albatross* leaned and listed with the rush of the visitors to one side or the other, looking for canoes with space left to take them off. In the confusion a few children fell into the sea; but they were fished out again. Nobody was hurt.

The sun had now set and it was growing dark. The King had not left the Doctor's side. As soon as Polynesia and I had climbed down out of the rigging John Dolittle introduced us. Koko had a nice merry face; and despite some rather childish habits (like his everlasting lollipop and his always wearing his crown, even in a canoe) there *was* something kingly and commanding about his great enormous figure, which even my young eyes took notice of. I liked him right away. I was surprised to find that he talked English – and well too.

'I am *deelighted* to meet you, Mr Stubbins,' said the King, bowing with difficulty from his very thick waist. 'I have just been inviting Doctor Dolittle to take dinner with me tonight, with all of his ship's company. May I trust you will honour me with your presence also?'

'Thank you, Sir – I mean, Your Majesty,' I stammered. 'If the Doctor is coming, I would like to, too.'

'Where is the dinner to be, King Koko,' the Doctor asked: 'in your palace on the edge of the town?'

'No,' said the King. 'This is a special banquet, Doctor. It will be in your old house-boat, the Post Office. Look behind you across the bay, please.'

We all turned. Then both the Doctor and I gasped at the same moment. Nearly all daylight had gone now. Only to seaward was there a faint crimson glow where the sun had set. The far shore of the bay was just a black line. Faint starlight shimmered on the silvery water; but where the sky met the shore against the island of No Man's Land the house-boat was all lit up with strings of Chinese paper-lanterns – red, green, yellow and violet. There seemed to be no end to the beautiful surprises of this strange country of Fantippo.

The King turned to me and said:

'When John Dolittle ran my Post Office for me he always had tea served to the public at four o'clock. English visitors have told me that mine was the only Post Office in the world where they got a cup of tea given them with a penny stamp. So it is only fitting and right that I should give my reception-dinner for him in the post-office house-boat. We shall expect you at seven o'clock, Doctor. It will be a grand feast.'

And gently patting his enormous stomach in happy expectation, the King walked to the ladder and went down it on to the royal barge.

Well, the dinner was a great success. A little before seven we all piled into our ship's dinghy and rowed across the bay to the gaily-lighted house-boat. Here Koko himself met us and led us to our places at a big table which was all set and ready under an awning at the stern of the boat.

Perhaps no other king in the whole world would have treated the Doctor and his strange animal family with such polite kindness and hospitality. Of course the King of Fantippo had met nearly all these animals already. And he had special foods for them which he knew they liked; and special places at the table – including a high-chair for the white mouse with tiny dishes of many sorts of cheese set before it.

Gub-Gub, who was seated next to me with a wonderful collection of vegetables and fruits in front of him, was a little nervous about his table manners.

'You know, Tommy,' he whispered, 'I had dinner with a marchioness once. That was in London – when the Doctor was putting on the Canary Opera. But this is the first time I've eaten at the table of a real king. Thank goodness the servants haven't put any spoons and forks at my place! That's what bothers me at these grand dinners: the silverware. I always use the fish-fork for the salad and the dessert-spoon for the soup. But here, look, no table-tools at all. The King has remembered I like best to pick my food up and eat it. – Very thoughtful of him. Ah, ripe mangoes! – Um-m-m!'

I must say that the animals behaved very well indeed. The only difficulty was the great number of dishes or courses. For, from the soup at the beginning to the nuts at the end, there were forty altogether! Truly King Koko was a mighty eater. The Doctor, who in the old days had often had dinner with him, had warned us all to take only a taste of each dish, so that we would have some room left inside us for the rest. His Majesty, it seemed, always got most unhappy if any of his guests stopped eating before the dinner was over. But even with the Doctor's warning, I could see that many round the table were having hard work to stay with it. And as for myself, by the time I had reached dish number twenty-four, I felt I'd surely crack down the middle if I ate another crumb.

7

THE JUNGLE-SCOUTS

THE next day the Doctor once more started to hurry things along. Those easygoing weeks while we had been at sea had given him a good change and rest; and he was now full of 'ginger and gumption' – as Polynesia called it. In the cabin at an early breakfast he said to me:

'I am anxious to lose no time in rushing on to Lake Junganyika. Mudface's life may depend on how soon we get there.'

'But I thought,' said I, 'you felt he should be safe where he is, in a sort of – er – state of hibernation.'

'True, Stubbins, quite true. And if he were a younger turtle I wouldn't worry about him. But he's old – unbelievably old. He has been sick. Everything depends on how strong he was when that earthquake happened. But he is helpless now – with those tons of gravel on top of him.'

'Have you any plan,' I asked, 'for getting him out?'

'No, Stubbins, I haven't any notion at all. I'm just hoping some idea will come to me after I look over the scene. – That's another reason why I want to get there as soon as we possibly can.'

'Yes,' said I, 'I can well understand you don't want to loaf around here. Did the King say anything last night about your running his Post Office for him again?'

'No, not a word.'

'What will you do, then, Doctor, when the King does ask you?'

'I'm not going to wait for him to ask me!' said John Dolittle. 'I'm going to ask *him* to do something for *me*, first. We have reason to return his call anyway – that's etiquette business, you know. As soon as we have finished breakfast, we will go over to his palace and get him to lend us a good canoe. And I shall want him to give us a man to stay on the sloop here while we're gone. – You understand, to take care of things, to set up her riding lights at night, so other boats won't run into her – and all that.'

Just as we were about to leave the table Polynesia and Cheapside came into the cabin. It seemed they had been having one of their arguments. The sparrow was still talking.

'And listen to me, my old Pollywog,' he ended: 'The next time you call me *Mr Cockney* I'll put you on the end of a stick and mop the decks with you. – You – flyin' dish-rag!'

'One of these days,' said the parrot thoughtfully, as she took a place on the table's edge beside me, 'I'm going to forget I'm a lady and bite that guttersnipe's head off.'

'Oh, dear,' sighed the Doctor, 'squabbling again! You know, to listen to you two, anyone would think you had never been shipmates before on a voyage. Now settle down quietly and have your breakfast, please. We have a lot to do today.'

Dab-Dab, with Chee-Chee to help her, came in bringing breakfast for the newcomers. 'And please don't crack your seeds all over the cabin,' she said to the birds. 'Chee-Chee and I are tired of sweeping up seed-shells off the floor. Crack 'em on to the table; and then they'll be cleared away with the crumbs.'

'Right you are, right you are,' said Cheapside, starting to eat. 'But it's old Pollysnoot over there what makes all the mess. Yer know, Doc,' he added as soon as the duck and monkey had started back for the galley, 'women is strange creatures. Why is it that 'ousekeepers always 'as to be so fussy? That Dab-Dab really is a wonder – when you think of all the jobs she gets done in a day. Only a short time back I was sayin' to Tommy 'ere: old Dab-Dab's more pernickety, in some ways, than your sister, Sarah Dolittle, was. Do you remember how upset she got about that crocodile you kept?'

'Ah, yes, indeed!' murmured the Doctor dreamily. 'Poor, dear Sarah! I wonder how she's getting on. – A splendid woman. But she would let the little things of life annoy her. . . . That crocodile – he came to me from a travelling circus, with a tooth-ache. Then he wanted to stay with me. So I let him. . . . Sarah said he ate the linoleum. Can you imagine it?'

'Sounds 'orrible to me,' said Cheapside with his mouth full of food. '*Linoleum* – why, even parrots wouldn't eat that!'

Polynesia pretended not to hear this last insult but went on noisily cracking her sunflower-seeds.

'You know,' said the Doctor in the same sort of far-away, remembering voice, 'Sarah simply wouldn't believe me when I told her the poor creature had promised me not to bite anyone – not even the goldfish in my garden-pond. She thought that crocodiles, when they see an arm or a leg, they just *have* to bite it – even if it is the leg of a table. . . . As a matter of fact, crocodile . . . crocodiles . . .'

The Doctor's words died away in a murmur. I had been watching him as he spoke. The look on his face had changed; and I knew, before he ended, that he was no longer thinking of what he was saying. Polynesia too stopped eating and watched him. He was now staring down at the table-cloth, his thoughts a thousand miles away.

Suddenly he looked up, all smiles.

'That's it!' he cried. 'Why didn't I think of it before? Cheapside, you're a wonder. I don't know what I'd do without you.'

Cheapside looked puzzled.

' 'Scuse me, Doc,' said the sparrow; 'but what might you be talking about?'

'Why, crocodiles, of course!' the Doctor cried. 'Here I've been badgering my brains for weeks – in fact ever since you brought me the news of that earthquake – for some way I could get Mudface up from under the floor of the lake. And then you spoke of it just now: *crocodiles!* – Polynesia, would you please find Chee-Chee and bring him down here?'

The parrot fetched the monkey; and when he was seated at the table the Doctor said:

'Now please listen carefully. You two, Chee-Chee and Polynesia, are the best jungle-scouts anyone could ask for. This country is your native land. And often in my travels you have gone ahead of me to find the way, to hunt fruits to keep us fed – and to warn us of dangers. The River Niger is not very far from us here. And on the Niger there lives a crocodile, who was once a pet of mine in Puddleby-on-the-Marsh. I brought him back to this country and left him here. He told me he was going on to the Niger, which, he says, is the finest stream for crocodiles in all Africa. Do you think you could find him for me now?'

Solemnly little Chee-Chee nodded. But Polynesia put her head on one side and said:

'Well, I *think* I'd recognize him – I surely ought to: I was with him enough at your home, Doctor. Let me see: he had a sort of a scar across his back – where the tail joins on. But those messy brutes are always so caked up with mud you couldn't tell one from the rest, if he was wearing a coat and pants. Besides, remember, Doctor, there's an awful lot of crocodiles in the Niger River.'

'Oh, please, Polynesia,' said John Dolittle quickly, 'do not think I don't know I am giving you a hard job. I am asking you to search a stream, which is thousands of miles long, for *one* animal. Of course I hope that you will be helped by asking the other crocodiles where to look for him, on what stretch of the river he was seen last – and so on.'

'Well,' said the parrot, 'can't say I was ever very good at their language – though I can talk it a little. I hate the messy creatures, myself.'

'But Chee-Chee speaks it well,' said the Doctor. 'And if you succeed – well, I can't tell you how important it may be for me – and for natural history as well.'

It was plain the parrot did not like the idea very much. She frowned and scowled a moment before she said:

'And what do you want me to do with him when – and if – we find him,' she asked: 'wrap him up in a palm-leaf and fly down here with him?'

'No, listen,' said the Doctor patiently. 'This particular crocodile has thousands and thousands of relatives living on the Niger. I want him to bring as many friends with him as he can and to meet me at the Secret Lake. I think he will be willing, on account of my fixing up his toothache long ago. Crocodiles will be the best animals of all to dig down into that mud and gravel and set the turtle free – in fact I believe they're the only ones who could do it. But we will need a lot of them. Underwater digging is hard work.'

'But will he know the way,' asked Polynesia, 'across from the Niger country to the Secret Lake?'

'Perhaps,' said the Doctor. 'The landscape has changed

somewhat since the earthquake, it's true. But to be on the safe side, I am going to ask Cheapside to go with you. He has been there only a short while back.'

That of course started another squabbling argument between the parrot and the sparrow. But I knew all along that both of them would end up by doing what the Doctor wanted.

Nor was there any time wasted in their going. That same afternoon we rowed the dinghy over to the mainland and watched them start their journey into the jungle. Of course Chee-Chee's speed of travel was slower than the birds'; but it was surprisingly fast, just the same. He did not touch the ground at all, but leapt from tree to tree in the dense tangled forest. He reminded me of a squirrel, the way he would run out to the tip of a limb and shoot himself off the end of it, to the next tree, like an arrow.

The parrot and the sparrow always waited for the monkey to catch up to them; so they had plenty of time to argue and quarrel. And even after the jungle had hidden them from our view, we could still hear them calling names at one another, back and forth, within its leafy shade.

'Ah!' said the Doctor as we turned away to go on to the King's palace. 'That's a great team. I am lucky to have such friends. What *would* I do without them?'

8

ON THE LITTLE FANTIPPO RIVER

IT was agreed that Cheapside's wife, Becky, was to travel with us because the Doctor felt we could save time on the long water-trip from Fantippo to the Secret Lake if we had a guide with us who had flown over this same stretch of country since the earthquake had happened. Also, he might wish to use Becky as a messenger between himself and the 'advance party', as he called it – that is, Chee-Chee, Polynesia and Cheapside.

So the little hen-sparrow was with us when we called at the King's palace – as were Too-Too, Jip and the white mouse. Dab-Dab and Gub-Gub had been left on the ship to wash up the breakfast dishes.

I must say that Koko behaved very well indeed when John Dolittle told him he was in a great hurry to go 'up-country' on special business. I could see from the King's face that he was very disappointed to lose his friend again so soon. The Post Office was not even spoken of at all. And as soon as the Doctor said he would need a good canoe, His Majesty sent for a man he called 'Admiral' – so we supposed this was the commander-in-chief of the Royal Navy of Fantippo. All the man wore in the way of uniform was a rag round his middle and a yachting-cap several sizes too small for him.

However, after we had thanked the King for the dinner and told him we would call on him again on our return journey, we left the palace and went back with the Admiral to the harbour.

Here we were shown a great many canoes. Most of them were beautifully carved and painted. At last the Doctor chose one of middling length which would float in very shallow water.

'It can't be too heavy, Stubbins,' he explained. 'I remember places on the way to Junganyika where the river runs over rapids and waterfalls. We have got to be able, once in a while, to lift everything and carry it around, on the banks, to the smooth water farther up. This canoe should do very nicely. Now we'll want three extra paddles – and we must arrange for a man to take care of the sloop while we're gone. Then, I think, we'll be all ready to go.'

We paddled the canoe out to the ship. The Admiral came with us. And when the Doctor had shown him over the *Albatross*, he was so pleased with her that he told the Doc-

118

tor he would be glad to live aboard her, himself, while we were away and to take good care of her.

When we had gathered all the stuff together in a pile on the ship's main-deck it certainly looked like a great deal of baggage; and we began to wonder if, after we should get it into the canoe, we would have any room left for ourselves.

However, in this the Admiral was very useful. I think he was rather proud to be helping these white friends of his King. Laying aside his beautiful yachting-cap (it was so small for him, it was always falling off his head) he set to work and stowed the baggage away for us. When he had finished there was comfortable space for the Doctor and myself to kneel, or sit, where we could paddle properly – as well as room for Gub-Gub, Jip and the others.

It was late afternoon before we had finished getting ready. But the Doctor said he would start today anyway. And so we bade the Admiral good-bye and set out.

The Doctor explained to me that the river we were going to follow was not the big one that flowed out through the reef into the ocean. A smaller stream, called the Little Fantippo River, he said, flowed into the bay on its southern side.

Besides that, the mouth of the Little Fantippo was not easy to find, where it crept out through the heavily wooded coast to join the bay.

However, Becky and Dab-Dab did some scouting ahead. And presently they found it all right and led us into it.

The mouth of the Little Fantippo was peculiar. It was so narrow and grown over you could pass it by a hundred times without guessing there was a river there at all. But once inside the mouth, we saw there was nothing 'little' about the Little Fantippo. A wide lagoon (a sort of lake) spread out before us, hidden from the bay and the ocean – calm and smooth as a mirror. We crossed this, going northward now; and soon I could see we were coming into a regular broad river. And then, little by little, it became narrower again.

It was very interesting to me to watch the jungle-covered banks of this stream draw in closer together as we paddled inland. Presently the shores were near enough for me to catch glimpses of brightly-coloured birds, parrots, macaws and others, flitting from branch to branch. Here and there beautiful orchids hung from the tree-forks. And once in a while the chatter of monkeys reached our ears from the depths of the forest, reminding me of Chee-Chee, of Polynesia, of Cheapside and the errand the Doctor had sent them on.

In those days, not much exploring had been done – beyond a few miles inland from the seashore. The stream ahead of us was now winding and turning much more, as we followed it ever onward, into the dark heart of Africa. I began to wonder what lay behind these walls of green. What was going on in these jungle-hidden lands where no white men had yet come? Truly, it was country of mystery and adventure.

Just before the last of the daylight had gone we rounded a bend and came upon a riverside village. A cleared space lay between it and the edge of the stream.

'I think, Stubbins,' said the Doctor, 'this will be a good place for us to spend the night.'

We drew in to the shore and landed. Then, while we were getting some of our baggage out of the canoe, we saw the Chief himself and other important men of the place coming down to the landing to greet us. It seemed he had recognized our canoe as one coming from Fantippo – whose king he greatly liked. The Chief made quite a speech to the Doctor, bidding him welcome to the village and inviting him to use one of the houses as his home for as long as he wished.

As a matter of fact, all of us were only too glad to sleep ashore for a change. And when we had thanked him, the

Chief sent for some porters and our baggage was quickly carried up to one of the larger houses of grass. Here we were invited to dinner, too. But the doctor was afraid of more long speeches and feasts. So he explained (mostly in sign-language) that our whole party was very, very tired from much travelling and work; and that, since we wanted to make an early start tomorrow morning, it would be best for us to prepare our own simple meal and get to bed as soon as possible.

All the villagers were disappointed (as was Gub-Gub, who had looked forward to another grand feed with forty different courses). However, the Chief bade us good night, saying he would be happy if the Doctor visited him again, on his return journey.

And after we had brewed a cup of tea and eaten a very light supper, John Dolittle and I climbed into our hammocks and pulled our mosquito-nets over us. In a very few moments we were lulled to sleep by the croaking of frogs and that strange and restful chorus of insects, birds and other creatures which makes African river-nights something to remember.

9

THE MYSTERY OF THE CROCODILES

THE next morning we were up early – even a little ahead of the sun; and again it was only a quick meal we took for breakfast. A half-hour later we had repacked the canoe and were back on the water once more, paddling northward.

'In this country, Stubbins,' said the Doctor, 'it is a good thing to start the day early – before the sun gets high and hot. You can always take a good rest around noon, when the heat is at its worst. . . . My! This paddling is hard. What a current! That's the ebb tide flowing out – and still strong. It will be easier for us once we get above the first rapids.'

After that we didn't talk much, saving our breath for the work. But about ten o'clock in the morning I asked: 'When do you think we'll hear from the advance party, Doctor?'

'It's hard to say,' he answered. 'My old crocodile friend, Jim, lives on the Niger, you know. And that river is over there, about fifty miles to the east – according to the maps. But it may be much farther; no maps have yet been made which we can trust very exactly.'

'Well, why don't we go up the Niger River, ourselves,

Doctor,' I asked – 'instead of bothering with this one?'

'The Niger would not bring us to the Secret Lake,' he said. 'There is only one stream flowing out of the lake: and that's the one we're following now, the Little Fantippo. Besides, it is more important that I should get to Mudface's island – or what's left of it – without losing any time. Our advance party can do the searching work much better than you or I could. . . . Oh, look! – Up ahead. There's the first rapids. – And a waterfall just beyond.'

While we had been talking, and I had my head turned sideways to listen to the Doctor in the stern, we had rounded another bend in the stream. Now, in front of us, I saw a straight stretch. Along this the river was so shallow that the stony bottom it raced over could be plainly seen. There were low sand-bars too, here and there. A little farther up-stream I saw a white ribbon of a waterfall. The spray rose above it like a thin mist; and faintly the distant roar of the tumbling river reached our ears.

'There should be some crocodiles on those sand-bars,' said the Doctor. – 'That's where they love to bask in the sun. If we see any, maybe they can tell us something of the advance party.'

The sun was indeed well up in the heavens by now and the heat was considerable. Presently I felt the Doctor steering us over towards the east shore.

'Take it easy now, Stubbins,' said he. – 'And keep an eye open for sudden shallows – especially for boulders and rocks.'

Paddling in the bow of that canoe, where I was, it was of course easier to watch the depths of the water for stones – and for crocodiles.

We met with no accidents – nor any sight or trace of crocodiles.

'Humph! That's strange,' the Doctor muttered. 'I felt almost certain we would have seen at least a few at such a place as this.'

Then Becky said,

'There were plenty of crocodiles here when Cheapside and I flew over, Doctor. I remember this place well. We came down at the foot of the falls up there, for a drink and a shower-bath in the spray. And I remember Cheapside pointing the creatures out to me. *I* thought they were logs, they kept so still. But there were simply hundreds of them – all over these sand-bars – then.'

'Well, quite possibly,' said John Dolittle, 'they're still back in the deeper water, waiting for the sun to get hotter or something. See if you can find the landing for a portage-trail over there, Dab-Dab, please. We have to go ashore now and carry everything around the falls.'

Dab-Dab had been over this same journey with the Doctor years ago; and she did not take long now to discover the landing-place he spoke of. But when we nosed the canoe's bow into the bank where she stood calling to us, it was so tangled and overgrown with thick bushes I was surprised she had been able to find it at all. Behind these bushes and vines there was a little cleared space. And a trail, running alongside the stream northward, could be seen.

We tied the canoe by her painter-rope to a palm-tree and unloaded the baggage on to the river-bank. Then the Doctor and I each took a load and started up the trail. Jip took one of the smaller packages in his mouth and said he would go ahead of us.

'I'm not afraid of leopards or wild animals, so long as we have you with us, Doctor,' he said. 'But these African hunters – some of 'em – have a trick of shooting a poisoned arrow at you first, and asking questions afterwards. Let me go in front – with Too-Too. We'll likely smell 'em or spot 'em before they see us.'

The upper end of the portage-trail came out on the river-shore above the falls where the water was calm and deep. Here the landing's clearing was much bigger. You could see that, in spite of the heavy jungle, this trail was in use all the year round. For, although we met no one on it today, the earth of this narrow path through the forest was worn and patted smooth by the bare feet of many native travellers who had carried their loads around the falls.

It took four trips to get all our stuff over the portage. The canoe was sort of tricky to carry. We took it upside down on our shoulders – which made it hard for the Doctor and myself to see where we were going, with our heads inside it. But Jip and the others helped guide us; and we got it safely above the falls at last.

'I think we've earned a rest, Stubbins,' said the Doctor. 'Let us have a bite to eat and then hang the hammocks between these trees in the clearing here. A couple of hours' nap, what? – But first of all: a nice cold bath in the stream?'

'That sounds the best of all – to me, Doctor,' I said. 'I don't believe I *ever* felt so hot.'

In a moment we were undressed and swimming in the river – Jip and Dab-Dab with us. (Gub-Gub decided *not* to risk the crocodiles.) We kept up-river and near the shore, though; because the Doctor feared the drag of the falls might still be strong enough to pull us over them, even here.

'You know, Stubbins,' said he, 'it's funny about those crocodiles – none of them being around. I can't make it out. – Ah, this cold water feels grand! Refreshing, eh?'

'Wonderful,' I panted. – 'Too bad we can't swim all the way to the lake, instead of paddling.'

'Yes, quite so,' he said. 'I'm satisfied, Stubbins,' the Doctor went on, 'that there are no crocodiles near these sand-bars – not now at least. But I confess I am completely puzzled.'

'I wish,' said Dab-Dab, who was paddling close behind the Doctor like a toy steamboat, 'that you'd stop talking about crocodiles while I am swimming. You make me feel that one of the brutes is going to come up right underneath me any moment and swallow me, whole.'

The Doctor laughed.

'Never fear, Dab-Dab,' he said. 'You'd see him first.'

10

THE ADVANCE PARTY

As the Doctor had foretold, we found the work of paddling far easier after we had passed the first rapids. Indeed we made very good time, seeing that we were going against the current – and how many waterfalls we had to portage around. At each of these we looked for crocodiles in the shallows and sand-bars that lay below; but as before we found none. However, at last we did come upon a few tracks which, the Doctor said, were certainly made by crocodiles' feet.

At one of our midday rests we were looking at a map. It showed the Little Fantippo – and the Niger too, the third largest river in all of Africa. According to this map, the two rivers flowed down from the north, staying pretty much the same distance apart. But at a certain point, about three hundred miles from the sea, the course of the Niger River changed; above that point it was shown flowing from the west. This place was marked on the map as the *Great South Bend*.

'You see that, Stubbins?' asked the Doctor. – 'And then this other point here, where the Little Fantippo comes nearest to the Niger? – I am holding my pencil on it. Do you see it?'

I said I did.

'Well, that will be the short cut,' said he – 'the short cut for anyone who wishes to come across from one river to the other. I wish I knew what kind of country lies between the rivers. But of course this doesn't show that.'

'You mean that is where our advance party will come

over from the Niger into this stream we're travelling on?' I asked.

'I wasn't thinking of that so much,' he said. 'Birds and monkeys can travel through almost any kind of country; it makes little difference to them. It was something else I had in mind. Anyway, we ought to be almost there by now – I mean, at that point nearest the Great South Bend. Let's see: today is Wednesday, isn't it?'

He took an old envelope out of his pocket and made a calculation in pencil on it.

'I should say we have been doing thirty miles a day,' he muttered. . . . 'Er – that will come to, er – ' for a moment I could not hear his words as he mumbled a little arithmetic.

'Why, yes,' he said at last, in a puzzled kind of way, 'we should have reached the short cut yesterday – that is, of course, unless the distances on this map are utterly crazy. . . . Too-Too, just check over my calculation here, will you, please? I may have made a mistake. Stubbins, will you glance through it too?'

I took the envelope from the Doctor; and Too-Too, the mathematical wizard, looked over my shoulder as I ran through the Doctor's reckoning. I was only half-way through the multiplication, when the owl snapped out: 'Right, Doctor – correct.'

'Humph!' said John Dolittle thoughtfully. 'Well, I wonder why we haven't seen it yet.'

'But what would there be to see, Doctor?' I asked. 'The Great Bend itself is over on the other river, the Niger, isn't it?'

'Quite so,' said he. 'But there would certainly be a path, across from one river to the other, at the shortest distance between them. Such a path is also called a portage-trail – like the short ones round the waterfalls. The trail to the Great South Bend has probably been used for hundreds of years by native traders, bringing their stuff down to the coast from up-country. . . . This *is* queer! . . . I wonder could we have paddled past it without noticing it. The jungle is still awfully thick on the banks. – Where is Becky?'

'She's just down below, at the third rapids, Doctor,' said Too-Too. 'I'll go and fetch her for you.'

But when the little hen-sparrow was brought, she said that she and Cheapside had flown over this stretch of the river at a great height. And so it would have been impossible for them to see small things on the river-bank – even a trail through the jungle. They were trying then, she told us, to spy out the Secret Lake itself.

'But listen, Doctor,' Becky added: 'why not let me and Dab-Dab fly ahead, scouting for you, while you take your mid-day rest? If the Great Bend trail is even another day's paddle farther on, we can come back and let you know before you've got the canoe repacked. There's no wind against us.'

So the Doctor let Becky and the duck go forward while we strung up our hammocks to the trees to take a rest. As we climbed into them the Doctor said:

'Dear me! What would I do without them? – I mean Becky and Dab-Dab. But you know, Stubbins, having a guide with you is sometimes not altogether a good thing.'

'Well,' I said, 'you've done so much exploring in out-landish countries it is not surprising to me that you can't remember every river and trail you've been over.'

'Ah, but I should,' said he. 'That's one of the most important things any good explorer must do: take note of everything he passes, so he'll be able to find his way back. But the trouble was that I had too good a guide on that first trip.'

'What do you mean, Doctor?' I asked.

'The Great Water Snake,' said he.

'Oh, yes,' I answered. 'I remember now: Cheapside told me about him.'

'He was perfectly marvellous,' said John Dolittle.

'Yes,' said Jip. 'Do you remember the way he used to get our canoe off the mud-banks, when we got stuck, Doctor?

– Take a turn around the bow-post with his tail and yank us into deep water, as though we weighed no more than a feather.'

The Doctor nodded, smiling to the old dog, and then went on:

'So of course, Stubbins, seeing the snake knew the streams and the swamps hereabouts so well, I'm afraid I didn't bother noticing the *way* he was taking us. There was such a lot of other things I was looking out for – birds, animals, trees and so on. Very interesting country – never been explored. That's why the animals call it the Secret Lake. They claim that its water is the actual water of the Flood – which never dried up from the swamps. You may have noticed that the map does not show the Little Fantippo River as flowing *out* of it at all. According to the map, that river begins about a hundred miles this side of the lake – which is surrounded by wide swamplands. Mud, mud, mud – miles and miles of it – with shallow water pools: and narrow streams running all through it; and the mangroves, ten feet high, sprouting and sprawling out of every square yard. Lake Junganyika, Mudface the turtle calls it. Strangest country I've ever seen, I don't wonder that it's stayed a secret lake. Why, when I was once on the shores of the Black Sea, the –'

Never before do I remember falling asleep while the Doctor was telling me of his travels; but I confess I did that day. We had been paddling hard all morning; and we had made an extra early start; so, maybe, I was particularly tired. Anyway I heard no more of what he was saying. Without any break at all his deep restful voice changed right into a dream.

I was in a sea of mud somewhere, after travelling on foot, by coach, sailing ship and canoe for months – through oceans of more mud. I was lying on my back, all tangled up with jungle vines – and a big snake was trying to yank me free by the neck. Then immediately a tremendous crocodile appeared from nowhere, grabbed hold of my boots and started to pull me the other way. At that, Cheapside popped up on to a tree-limb above me and started to laugh his silly head off.

When I opened my eyes the Doctor was standing over my hammock gently shaking me by the shoulder; and my sleepy ears heard him say:

'Stubbins, *please* wake up! Becky's back. Listen: Becky's back. And Cheapside's with her – and *all the advance party* too. Wake up, Stubbins! They've brought good news!'

II

THE TRAIL TO THE GREAT SOUTH BEND

WHEN at last I shook myself free of the dream and sat up, everybody was gathered around me – and all of them talking at once. Besides the Doctor, there were Polynesia, Chee-Chee, Jip, Cheapside, Becky, Dab-Dab, Gub-Gub, Too-Too and the white mouse. After a moment I got myself really awake.

The Doctor and I went down to the water's edge to freshen up in the cool river; but John Dolittle also wished to get me alone so we could talk in peace.

'Stubbins,' said he, as we knelt down upon a flat rock and began scooping up the water, 'our luck is holding. Polynesia tells me everything went wonderfully well. In almost the first lot of crocodiles they met, over on the Niger, there was one who knew all about me. – Had known my old pet, Jim, from the circus – was a sort of relative of his. What do you think of that – speaking of luck?'

'Oh, well,' I sputtered through the water I was throwing over my face, 'nothing very extraordinary, Doctor. The birds and the monkeys know you – throughout the whole of Africa.'

'Well, but Stubbins,' said he, 'these are reptiles. It's dif-

HUGH. LOFTING

ferent. Imagine it: just because I cured a simple toothache for that poor beast, years afterwards I come here and find I have friends – and cold-blooded, amphibian friends at that – in an African swamp! Positively astonishing! – What makes this water so muddy here?'

'I was wondering about that too,' I said.

At the place where we were kneeling there was a sort of natural basin for washing. No mud lay anywhere near; and the clean rock bottom of the river could be plainly seen – when we had first come to it. But now, as we both stared down into the water, we saw it had grown muddy. – Then it cleared again; and a moment later it was muddy once more.

'How very strange!' the Doctor murmured. – 'Well, let's get the canoe packed, Stubbins, and be on our way. Becky says the trail to the Great South Bend is only about ten miles farther up the river; so we should be able to get there before nightfall.'

There was now a feeling of excitement among all of us, as the hammocks were taken down and stowed in the canoe. Yet, after the first greeting, there was little talk – very little, seeing that we had now been joined by our advance party.

I remember that this struck me as a bit curious at the time. After all, these three, Chee-Chee, Polynesia and Cheapside, had travelled many hundreds of miles since we last saw them; and anyone would suppose they would have a lot to chat over. I noticed a rather strange look in Cheapside's eyes: as though he were trying a little too hard to make us think that a trip like that was nothing out of the ordinary for *him*. The thought went through my mind that perhaps he and Polynesia, in spite of all their arguments and squabbles, had agreed together to keep something a secret from us – a surprise.

However, I was too busy loading the canoe to attend to anything else just now.

We found the flow of the river much stronger in this stretch than it had been anywhere throughout the whole trip. One of the few times that the Doctor spoke, he told me the extra-hard current we were fighting was caused by the river being narrower and shallower here. This was one of the stretches where the trees formed a solid roof over us.

Both the Doctor and I, without knowing it, had caught some fever of hurry and were paddling harder than we had ever done in our lives. All the animals were silent – even Gub-Gub and the white mouse. In the green tunnel of that ⸻le-shaded river no sound broke the silence but the reg-⸻ *plash* of our paddles.

⸻re now that, for all our hard work, we were not

making as good a speed against this swift current as we had done most days. But, just the same, I also had a strange feeling (it sent a sort of tingle up my spine) that something very important was going to happen – and soon.

I think it was about four in the afternoon when we came around a wide curve and headed up a long straight stretch. Here the banks lay back on either side and let the full sunlight in upon our heads once more. And it went on like that all the way up the straight stretch, which must have been over a mile in length. At the far end of it some sort of commotion seemed to be going on, a tremendous splashing – whose low white line, like a bar across the river, could be plainly seen from where we were. Yet even I could tell that *this* was not made by any waterfall or rapids.

From the sudden easing of the canoe's speed, I knew that the Doctor behind me had stopped paddling. I rested too.

'What in the name of goodness is *that*?' John Dolittle gasped.

And then old Polynesia's grating voice answered:

'Crocodiles, Doctor – just crocodiles.'

She said it in a quiet, off-handish sort of way, as though telling us she thought it might rain.

'But – but,' the Doctor stammered – 'how *many*!'

'Ha!' giggled Cheapside with a cheeky chirp. – ' 'Ow many, Doc? Well, I don't reckon old Too-Too, the mathematooter, could count *them* for yer, John Dolittle. Up there is where the land trail comes across from the Niger River's Great South Bend. And when we left it, I calculated – by dead reckonin' and pigonometry – that the crocs was pouring across into the Little Fantippy here at the rate of two million an hour – this is, o' course, roughly speakin' – in round numbers.'

A second passed without anyone moving or talking. Our canoe lay perfectly still. The eyes of all of us were fixed on that strange white line across the river a mile ahead of us. Then, when the breeze changed a moment and blew into our faces, the distant sound of a mighty, hissing roar came down to us.

'Great heavens!' the Doctor murmured at last. 'No wonder the water was muddy above the last falls!'

Then suddenly he shouted like a school-boy in a football match:

'*Let's get on!* Run her up!'

Our paddles dug into the river together; and the canoe almost left the water as it leapt forward, heading for the South Bend trail.

12

GENERAL JIM

WE were nearly there when we saw one large crocodile swimming all alone towards us.

'Here comes your old circus friend to welcome you, Doc,' cried Cheapside. 'Good old Jim!'

It was a great and important meeting; and when Jim came alongside our canoe many questions were asked and answered. Myself, I could only understand, so far, a few words of the language.

Once or twice the Doctor explained to me what was being said. But, as he was in great haste, he asked old Jim to turn around and swim beside our canoe as we went on upstream.

In the books of the life of Doctor Dolittle there are a few places where I have written of certain happenings which I shall never be able to forget: scenes that are pictured so lastingly in my memory that today, years afterwards, I can see them all over again, exactly as they took place. And this, as we paddled up close to the trail-landing of the Great South Bend, was one of those pictures that was to stay in my memory for life, clear and unforgettable.

The right bank of the river rose here to quite a height.

And down this slope the crocodiles from the Niger were pouring – in a solid procession – into the Little Fantippo River. The jungle, whose heavy tangle covered all the land on either bank, had here been torn up and cleaned off by millions of clawed feet, making a wide, crowded road.

You could barely see the ground they walked on – only the creatures' backs, as close together as stitches in a carpet. But once in a while a free spot in the parade would open up; and then you saw that the earth had been trodden as smooth as a pavement.

As they reached the water's edge, this great army did not stop or hesitate a moment. They flopped into the river a hundred abreast, and headed upstream. The water all around looked as though it were boiling. I wondered how none of them got hurt, with those heavy tails slapping right and left.

Old Jim now left us and swam out to a low flat rock in the mid-stream. On to this he crawled and began directing the traffic – exactly like a policeman at a busy street-crossing. The noise of all that splashing made it hard to hear anything. We had stopped paddling; and the canoe rose and fell gently where the Doctor halted it, a hundred yards or so downstream from the trail-landing.

But as I chanced to look back a moment I saw him signal to Cheapside. And the sparrow flew on to his shoulder where he could speak right into the Doctor's ear. Then I saw John Dolittle get out a piece of paper and a pencil. I guessed what calculation he was making this time. Cheapside would be telling how many days ago this living flood had begun flowing over the trail. I saw him take his watch from his pocket and hold it in his hand while he kept an eye on the crocodiles who, row after row, came down to the edge and splashed into the water. He was trying to reckon how many of the creatures had already passed up the Little Fantippo on their way to the Secret Lake.

I glanced up the river, myself, and I saw that this

too seemed to have changed into a solid mass of reptiles. Dry-shod you could have walked from bank to bank. After about another half-hour John Dolittle sent Polynesia over to the rock in midstream with some message for old Jim.

And it was now that a strange thing happened. Jim began swinging his tail wildly from side to side. Clearly the Doctor's message was 'Enough!' For very soon I could see the swarm of beasts pouring over the trail begin to thin out – to grow less crowded. I suppose Jim's message was sent back from mouth to mouth all the way to the Niger River.

Anyway it was almost twilight when it stopped altogether. In the sudden quiet I realized that it was now possible again for us to talk. For General Jim had commanded his army to halt.

But it was Cheapside's cheeky voice which first broke that silence.

'You know, Doc,' he chirped, 'I'm beginnin' to understand your sister Sarah's notions about them crocs. You can't call 'em 'ouse-pets – really you can't. Just look what they've gone and done to that there poor jungle! – Made it look like a race-track after a ten-day rain. It's a good thing for you that old Jim didn't 'ave to bring 'is friends through your garden to get 'em to the Secret Lake.'

'Yes, indeed!' murmured Gub-Gub in a hushed, scared sort of voice. 'What *would* they have done to my tomato plants?'

'Yes – and to you too, Mr Bacon,' said Cheapside, 'if they took a fancy for a little fresh ham while Jim and the Doctor was lookin' the other way.'

As the light was now fading fast the Doctor was anxious to pitch camp. A place was found, this time on the left bank. As soon as we had the hammocks set up and a nice fire burning, the Doctor had a talk with Jim. This time either John Dolittle or Chee-Chee translated everything for me.

I had been anxious to get a good, close-up look at this famous reptile who had, quite unintentionally, so upset the

Doctor's household years ago on account of Sarah, the Doctor's sister. Well, it may be hard for you to imagine a crocodile looking friendly and quite un-dangerous, but this one did.

We gathered around the fire on which our supper was being cooked. The Doctor's own animals all knew Jim, of course, already; and none was in the least afraid of him. Not even the white mouse was scared – indeed, he kept running up and down the great beast's knobbly back, from nose to tail. Whitey's only worry was that he might miss something that was being said. And he never seemed to be certain whether it was Jim's head or Jim's tail that was doing the talking.

Meanwhile, our visitor, for his part, seemed to be greatly enjoying the attention he received at this meeting with his old friend the Doctor – answering his questions, and suggesting ideas as to how the work of setting Mudface free could best be carried out. Just the same, I could not help thinking that if any of the good people of Puddleby were to come upon us now and see John Dolittle M.D. sitting over a fire in the African jungle and talking to a crocodile, his reputation as a crazy man would surely be more firmly fixed on him than ever.

Jim told the Doctor that he had already been up to the Secret Lake, himself, as soon as Polynesia had told him what the Doctor wanted. He had taken two of his brothers with him. They had gone all around the turtle's island to make sure where to start the underwater digging. He had left his two brothers up there to wait for the coming of a good big herd of crocodiles. These would set to work, under the brothers' leadership, as soon as they arrived.

'I am very hopeful, Doctor,' said he, 'from what we saw of the lake bottom at the north end of the island, that we shall be able to dig your friend Mudface out all right. – Only it may take us a couple of days, possibly longer.'

'I am happy indeed to hear that,' the Doctor answered. 'And I find it difficult to thank you enough – not only you, but all the others who came this distance to help.'

'Oh, we were only too glad to do it,' said Jim.

'You certainly brought an awful big crowd across from the Niger,' said the Doctor, smiling.

'You know, Doctor,' said Jim, 'when you brought me back here to my homeland years ago the story how you had cured my toothache and got me away from that wretched circus, soon spread up and down the Niger – even as far as Timbuktu. Your monkey here, Chee-Chee, told me that the same thing happened when you stamped out that sickness which was killing off his people. You don't realize,

John Dolittle, how widely known you are among the wild animals of the world.'

'Well,' said the Doctor, 'with birds and monkeys, that's something else. They travel more freely – and news, I suppose, travels with them.'

Old Jim shook the mouse – who was tickling him – off his nose (much to Whitey's astonishment) and then he said:

'You'd be surprised, Doctor, how fast we can pass messages along a river – under water. It was only half a day after I sent out word that *you* needed *our* help that they began arriving. And an hour later the Great South Bend was packed so solid with crocodiles the open water of the Niger River had disappeared. Handling the traffic back there was a job, I can tell you – even when I got six big cousins of mine to help me. The overland trail was rubbed right out in no time. But your advance party went ahead of us – they could travel on land much faster than we, of course – and so the mob kept going in the right direction. But the crush was something awful, just the same.'

'My goodness!' said the Doctor. 'I had no idea you could collect so many crocodiles in so short a time.'

'The main reason for *that* Doctor,' said Jim, 'was because every single one of them was just crazy to see you.'

'Humph!' said John Dolittle thoughtfully. 'That is really a great compliment.'

'I'm afraid the others must have been terribly disappointed, Doctor,' Jim said – 'I mean those I had to send back to the Niger, when you told me that enough had gone up to the lake.'

'I'm sorry,' said the Doctor – 'very sorry that so many took the long journey for nothing.'

'Oh, well,' said Jim, 'it was a change for them anyway. Life on the Niger River gets a bit dull sometimes.'

'How far,' asked the Doctor, 'do you calculate we are from the Secret Lake here?'

'Not a great distance,' said the crocodile. 'The edge of the swamps that surround it are just around the second bend. I think we should easily reach Mudface's island tomorrow afternoon.'

By this time our supper had been prepared and eaten. And so, with the comforting picture of our journey's end at last so near, we turned in and went to sleep.

13

THE LAST LAP

NEXT day the Doctor put on another of those bursts of speed of which I have spoken before. As we passed by the trail-landing this morning it looked very different from what it had yesterday. There was not a single crocodile in sight – except old Jim, who, swimming a few yards ahead of us, acted as guide. The great wide avenue on the right bank, over which the thousands had come swarming down last evening, was now empty and deserted. It looked very strange indeed, in the bright light of the morning, clear and clean, cutting through the green jungle, up the low hill, till it disappeared from sight. I wondered how many ridges and valleys it climbed up and down before it joined the Niger so many miles away.

And now, following Jim's lead, we did not have to be watching out for those dangerous rocks and shallows. We could give all our attention to steady powerful paddling. And I knew, by the way the banks slipped by us, that we were making a far better pace than we had done before.

As our guide had told us last night, we saw, at the end of the second curve in the stream, that we were entering on the wide swamplands which surrounded Lake Junganyika. This was country such as I had never seen before. I could guess how easy it would be for a traveller to get lost here.

Gradually the Little Fantippo seemed to disappear as an

easy-to-follow waterway. And soon we found ourselves in a flat, flat world stretching out in all directions as far as the eye could see. Most of it was water. What patches of land were here never stood up more than a foot or two above the muddy slush. – They were nowhere larger than a barnyard and often as small as a foot-stool.

There seemed to be very little animal life: a few wading birds were all we saw.

As for the water, wherever you looked it lay in pools and ponds of every size and shape, joined together by a network of narrow channels and creeks. These did not seem to be coming *from*, or going *to*, anywhere – in fact, it was hard to believe they flowed at all, so still was the water. Once in a while we would reach a spot where we could see down these unmoving streams for a fair distance. But to get a longer view in this deserted swampland did not cheer you up at all: instead, it made you wonder how far the useless country went on – or if this was (as some had said) the end of the world.

But old Jim was certainly not bothered by any such notions. This puzzle of brooks and ditches never stopped our guide for a moment. He would shoot across one of these pools and disappear into a tangle of mangroves. We would follow as fast as possible. And behind a clump of bushes on the farther shore we would always find him waiting for us with a new way to get through.

Today we did not take our regular sleep at noon. We just halted by a clump of mangroves and ate our luncheon which we had made and packed at breakfast-time. When we had finished, the Doctor asked me if I was tired by the paddling. I said, no: and on we went again.

Presently I saw that the surface of the water was no longer quite smooth. Waves, very tiny but very wide, were washing towards us. With these wavelets came a breath of gentle wind which sometimes carried a thin mist. Soon the waves grew a little bigger, rocking the canoe; while the fog kept parting. One moment you saw quite a distance ahead; and the next, little indeed could be seen – even near by.

I looked over my shoulder at the Doctor. He smiled, nodding, as though he knew the question in my mind; then he pointed ahead.

Peering forward once more, I found the fog now billowing over us so thick I could see absolutely nothing at all. The next moment, magic-like, the soft wind swept it away.

But before it had time to shut down again I knew we were in the Secret Lake at last!

I have already spoken of some stretches on the Little Fantippo where that stream had flooded out so that you could not see across them. But this was different. I am sure anyone, waking up to look on this for the first time, would have sworn he was at sea.

In every direction the water stretched out to meet the dim straight line of bleak grey sky. I had the feeling now so strongly of being on a body of water which had no shores at all, that I got uneasy about our heavy-laden canoe if a storm should come up.

The clear spell lasted only a moment. But, as my eye swept around the empty circle in front of us, it stopped at one point. Almost dead ahead of us there seemed to be something sticking up above the water. I couldn't be sure. It was very far away. Perhaps it was only an odd-shaped cloud touching the lake there. . . . And then, down came more fog, blotting everything out.

But the Doctor's eyes had been as sharp as mine. 'Did you see that, Stubbins?' he cried.

'I *thought* I saw something,' I called back. 'It was away off on the horizon – right as we are headed now.'

'Well, that's it!' he shouted happily. 'That was Mudface's island. Take it easy now. Don't tire yourself out. We've had a long pull. But this is the last lap, Stubbins – the last lap!'

14

THE CITY OF MYSTERY

As John Dolittle and I settled down to an even, steady paddle-stroke to finish this open run across the lake, all the animals began to cheer up and talk. (They had barely said a word that day, so far.)

'Ah, well,' sighed Gub-Gub comfortably, 'it's a long road that has no turnip – as the saying goes.'

'You've got that wrong,' grunted Jip. 'It's a long road that has no *turning*.'

'Yes, of course,' said Gub-Gub. 'But I changed it. After

all, it's far more important that a road should have a turnip in it than a turning.'

'Tee, hee, hee!' tittered the white mouse. 'Gubby always carried a turnip with him on his travels – in case of sickness, you know.'

'Good Lord!' groaned Jip. 'I might have known. – Golly, but this fog is wet!'

'Yes,' said Cheapside who sat with hunched-up wings on the gunwale of the canoe, 'A *very* pretty climate! Grey sky, grey water, grey fog, grey mud, grey parrots, grey everything. Kind of colourful, ain't it? This is merry old Africa, me hearties. I'm just tellin' yer, for fear yer might think we'd lost our way and wandered into a public steambath.'

'Huh!' squawked Polynesia. 'And I suppose you're going to say you don't have any fog in London! Last time the Doctor and I were there the street-lamps were lit, night and day, for a whole week. – And at that, we did nothing but bump into people if we dared go outside the house. It isn't like this *all* over Africa, you ninny! This is flat swamp country; but, just the same, it is very, very high here. – So high, you practically have your head in the clouds.'

'Lumme!' muttered Cheapside, as a drop of water fell from the tip of his beak. ' "Your 'ead in the clouds!" says you. – 'Ow you do run on, old sweet'eart! Seems to me more like I got my 'ead stuck in a drain-pipe. Listen: London, at its worstest, never 'ad a climate as wet, as 'ot or as gummy as this. Go stick your 'ead back in the clouds, old Pollysponge: you're welcome to it. Gimme London any day.'

'An awful city,' said Polynesia closing her eyes in painful memory – 'just awful! Never in my life was I so glad to get away from a place.'

'Not 'alf as glad as what the Londoners was to see you go, I'll bet,' Cheapside muttered.

As for me, I hardly heard what they were saying. My attention was given to trying to see ahead through the mist. Africa, the Dark Continent, as it is called, was never more mysterious than it was here. Behind that fog you could imagine anything rising up on the horizon. You felt like an explorer crossing a sea which had never been travelled before – and that, as you went forward, even enchanted countries might appear. But the curtain of mist had not lifted again, after it had given us that one glimpse of the turtle's island.

It was almost a rule with the Doctor not to chatter while we were paddling – to save breath and strength for the work. So I was surprised to hear him join the general talk.

'You remember, Cheapside,' said he, 'that Mudface told us something about an old, old city lying beneath this lake?'

'Oh, yes, Doc,' said Cheapside, 'the most wonderful city ever built – accordin' to 'im: palaces, race-tracks, zoos and everything – belongin' to a big king. But, you know, I never believed 'is story meself. Who would ever pick a place with a climate like this 'ere to build a city?'

'Ah, but don't forget,' said the Doctor, 'the climate here may have been quite different when the city was built, from what it is now. In fact, many people believe that the Deluge, the Flood, was caused by the North and the South Poles shifting their positions. That would change climates all over the world.'

Cheapside shook the wet out of his feathers before he answered.

'Well,' said he, '*this* neck-o'-the-woods sure got a dirty deal.'

We had now been travelling on for quite a while, unable to see much – but chatting, to make up for it, of this and that. How old Jim, our guide, was keeping the right direction we had no idea.

And then suddenly (the Doctor told me afterwards it was about three o'clock in the afternoon) the fog lifted and the sun actually shone! We could hardly believe our eyes. The steamy lake was clear in every direction. The high hump of Mudface's island was now much clearer to us, though I reckoned we were still a good five miles from it. It was wonderful how cheered up I found myself, just by the sun's coming out and warming my back.

I could feel the canoe was moving faster now; and I guessed that our complete change of weather had done the same to John Dolittle as it had to me – that he was working harder on that long stern-paddle of his. And then, just as suddenly, our speed slacked off and I knew that his powerful strokes had stopped altogether. His voice sounded hushed almost to a whisper when he spoke; but I heard what he said quite plainly in that wide silent desolation of water.

'Look, Stubbins, over to starboard!'

At the Doctor's words, I shipped paddle, turning my head quickly to the right.

What I saw did not stand high out of the lake; but there could be no mistaking what it was. *It was a row of buildings!* Perhaps it would be better to say it was what was left – the ruins – of a row of buildings. It was only a short distance from us – a hundred yards, I'd judge. And as our canoe, which was still moving forward, ran silently and slowly by it, you had the feeling you were passing the waterfront, the shops and houses, of some riverside harbour.

The buildings were all of stone or brickwork. Their fronts were lined up, as though they bordered, or faced, upon a street. Yet they were not all alike by any means, either in size or style. There was no land to be seen on which they stood. They rose straight out of the lake like ghosts of the past. The wet of the fog, which had wrapped them from our sight, still glistened on their walls where the sunlight fell; and this added to their ghostly appearance. It was easy to imagine that some magician had waved a wand, only a moment before, and made this city rise out of the depths of the lake.

Some of the lower houses showed only their roofs; others,

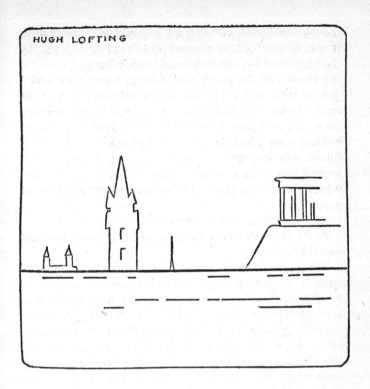

with no roof at all on them, showed a storey and a half – and the level of the water lapped gently in and out of the second-floor windows. Here and there, behind the front line, we could see pillars and pieces of wall belonging to a second row of houses.

'My goodness!' said Whitey softly. 'Why, it's a *town*! – What's it doing here?'

Indeed, that seemed a fair enough question to ask at the time. To find ourselves, in the middle of the Secret Lake, where mankind never came, suddenly facing a row of buildings – as though we were on a London street – was something hard to explain.

147

'Cheapside,' said the Doctor, 'did you see these houses when you were here a few weeks ago?'

'Yes, Doc,' said the sparrow. 'Though when *you* was here last there was nothing of the kind to be seen. – Sort of a dismal sight, ain't they? Becky and me didn't pay much attention to 'em, being anxious to get news to you of your friend Mudface. And so we forgot to speak of 'em. – Dear, dear! In a shockin' state of repair: just look at them cracks runnin' down the walls!'

'That's not surprising, Cheapside,' the Doctor murmured, 'when you think how long ago those stones were set together and carved – before the Flood, before Noah launched his Ark! ... My goodness! If, instead of becoming a naturalist, I had gone in for archaeology, what a find *this* would be!'

'What's archaeology, Doctor?' asked Gub-Gub.

'Oh – er – archaeology?' said John Dolittle. – 'Well, an archaeologist is a man who studies from ruins – such as these we see now.'

'Huh!' grunted Cheapside. 'Archaeologist or naturalist? – I'd call you a bit of both, Doc; a sort of a *Noah's-arkeeologist*. 'Ad you a notion to go over and take a look around them ruins?'

'No, no, not now,' said the Doctor quickly – 'although I'd like to. Maybe later, Cheapside. We must get on and see about Mudface. – Ah, there's another crocodile, see, talking to Jim. Perhaps he has brought some news.'

It turned out that this newcomer was one of Jim's brothers. He had been left at the island to take charge of the digging till John Dolittle himself should arrive. The brother and Jim now swam down to the stern of the canoe to give the Doctor a report.

15

AT THE TURTLE'S ISLAND

POLYNESIA guessed the Doctor would try, without losing any time, to get down under water and take a look at the old turtle. So she volunteered to go up to the island ahead of us all and find out what she could.

In about twenty minutes she was back. She had asked all the crocodiles to quit working till the Doctor should arrive; to leave the water and scramble out on to the land. This she had done, the parrot explained, so that the mud stirred up by the diggers would settle and leave the water clear.

John Dolittle was glad; but he wanted to hurry more than ever now. Until the island at last came in sight, I had had no idea how large it was. And it was hard to believe that birds alone had (at the Doctor's orders, years ago) built this great body of land, stone by stone.

Now, as we stopped in the shadow of it – our long journey ended at last – I gazed at it with great curiosity and respect. Here John Dolittle had, through his friendship with the Animal Kingdom, actually changed geography in a small way.

Jip had told me that none of the great things he had done (except, perhaps, setting up his Post Office and the Swallow Mail) had made him so popular with the creatures of all the world. This island was a monument to the Doctor's memory, Jip said, such as no kings had ever left behind them. It had taken an earthquake to disturb it; still it remained a work that men must wonder at!

As I stared up, kneeling in the canoe, at the steeply sloping sides of the island, I could well understand that what the old dog had told me was true. All animal life was important to the Doctor; but Mudface, who had known Noah, who had come through the Flood and still lived, *he* was different. When John Dolittle found him dying in the swamps of Lake Junganyika, he had made up his mind that the old turtle should have the finest home possible, on high ground.

From where I knelt I could not see the flat top of the island. Many trees had grown to a great height. Midway up the slopes, flowers bloomed in a few open places. But mostly (except upon the side where the land had broken off) the whole island was draped up to the top with heavy jungle such as we had seen on the river-shores nearer the coast.

And everywhere I looked I saw the little beady eyes of the crocodiles, who had now all crawled ashore and were resting in the undergrowth. The water was very still and clear and calm.

A sudden splash made me turn my head. The Doctor had taken off his clothes and dived overboard. For a moment I thought he was going to swim down right away to the turtle. I had no idea how deep he would have to go; and I admit I was afraid for his safety. But in a moment he bobbed up again, with his head quite close to my paddle-blade.

'Stubbins,' he said, 'you'll find a short coil of rope – underneath the grub-box, I think. Get it out and tie it in a loop for me, will you? Jim's brother is going to tow me down to Mudface. It's deep where he is – but getting towed will save my strength for looking around after I reach him.'

In a moment I got the rope out and tied it the way he said. By that time the Doctor's crocodile-guide was beside him in the water. He opened his great jaws and took the loop in his mouth like a horse's bit and reins. John Dolittle grabbed the free end. Then his tow-horse plunged downward under water. I could see the Doctor's white skin go glimmering deeper and deeper, dimmer and dimmer, as it was hauled into the lower depths of the lake. Then it disappeared altogether.

I called at once to Too-Too to get the Doctor's watch out

of his waistcoat and bring it to me. John Dolittle, I knew, was a sturdy swimmer; but I also knew that the length of time the best swimmer can stay under water has to be measured in minutes and seconds. I was taking no chances. As the little owl gave me the watch I noted the exact time, jotting it on a package near by.

'Huh!' grunted Cheapside. 'Just like the good old Doc, that. 'E no sooner harrives on the spot, after a trip of three or four thousand miles, then 'e jumps out of 'is clothes, jumps out of 'is canoe, jumps on an alligator and continues 'is journey on 'orseback under water, as you might say. 'E don't waste no time. There ain't many doctors would do that for their patients – specially if they knew they wasn't goin' to get paid nothing for the visit.'

But I was too anxious to listen to the sparrow's chatter. My eyes were on the second hand of the watch. I had now asked Polynesia to have Jim stay close to the canoe; for I intended, as soon as a minute and a half had gone by, to send him down after the Doctor . . . One minute and ten seconds – the tiny hand went jumping round the dial . . . One minute and twenty seconds . . . One minute and twenty-five seconds – my right arm rose straight up to give Jim the signal I had arranged. – And then suddenly there was a swirl in the water at the canoe's other end. The Doctor's head appeared. He was gasping for breath. He still had hold of the towing-rope. But now there were three or four crocodiles around him who seemed to be bearing him up. However, I could tell at once that he was all right, even if badly exhausted.

Polynesia called to me to come forward and make the rope fast, so that if the Doctor went unconscious he could not slip back under the water. Then the crocodile nosed the canoe across to the shore of the island. This took only a few minutes. And soon we had the canoe alongside a gravel landing where we could unload. I spread a tarpaulin and got John Dolittle to lie down and rest; meanwhile Chee-Chee slung up a hammock; and Jip scurried around and collected wood for a fire.

Presently (looking like a Red Indian chief in the blanket which I had got out of the baggage for him), John Dolittle crouched over a cheerful blaze. Polynesia, Cheapside and I waited close to him till he should have breath enough to speak.

At last, with a deep sigh, he straightened his shoulders, then turned and looked at me, smiling.

'By George, Stubbins!' said he in a low voice. 'Kind of – kind of out of training – for that sort of thing. . . . My goodness, I'm winded!'

'It's not surprising, Doctor,' I answered. 'You gave me a real scare. One minute and thirty-one seconds.'

'Hah, good old Stubbins!' he puffed. 'So you kept track of me with the watch, eh? What *would* I do without you?'

'How did you find things, Doctor? Is the turtle still alive?'

'I'm pretty sure he is,' said John Dolittle. 'It's hard to tell, though. We can't wake him up. He's fast asleep.'

'*Asleep!*' I cried. 'I don't understand.'

'Conditions,' said the Doctor. – 'Just hibernation conditions. The earthquake which buried Mudface came at the exact month of the year which is the regular time for turtles to start their hibernation – their winter sleep.'

'But, Doctor,' I said, 'do you mean he never even knew he was in any danger at all?'

'Well, Stubbins, perhaps no danger of getting killed or seriously injured, no. They are naturally a very calm race, turtles. He has buried himself before, of course, every year. But not so deep. Goodness knows how he would have got out, after his hibernation was over – if Cheapside and Becky had not come to Africa.'

There was a moment's silence. It was broken by Cheapside who had been listening thoughtfully.

'Asleep, 'is 'e? Well, swap me pink, Doc! After we makes

152

a record trip to rescue 'im, we finds the old boy takin' 'is after-dinner nap! – Criminy! That's what I'll do next time Becky starts one of 'er lectures on the duties of a good father. "Hush, my dear!" I'll say. "I feels my 'ibernation comin' on." ' (Cheapside closed his eyes, sighing noisily.) ' "*Sh!* Can't you see I'm gettin' drowsy? Bye, bye! You may call me in April – if the weather's good." '

16

THE VOICE OF THUNDER

THE Doctor told Jim he feared that, even if Mudface was awake – and trying to help lift himself – it would still be unlikely that he could be freed from the grip of that terrible mud-suction. Only after the turtle was able to use his legs to swim with, the Doctor added, would it be possible to get him to the top.

The three crocodiles had already gathered together all the other leaders and heads of families to listen to the Doctor's instructions. And a strange-looking council of war they made, crowding around Big Chief Dolittle (still wrapped in his red blanket).

'Listen, Jim,' said the Doctor: 'now that you have cleared the gravel off the *top* of the turtle, why not set a big gang to work prying *under* his lower shell – at one point only? I mean, don't let the crocodiles waste their strength working all around him at once. He's much too heavy to lift that way – tons and tons.'

'I understand, Doctor,' said Jim. 'You want us to let the water leak in under him at one place to break the mud-suction?'

'That's it exactly,' cried the Doctor. 'But for pity's sake be careful you don't crack his shell. You had better pry him up by the shoulder – a turtle's lower shell is thicker there.'

'All right,' said Jim. 'But in digging down to him, we had to make a deep hole in the floor of the lake. Now it's the same as if he were lying at the bottom of a basin – very little room for us. So I was just thinking that while I have one gang prying him up close to his head, I could set another to work behind his tail – you know, to cut away the wall of the basin.'

'A splendid idea, Jim!' cried the Doctor. 'You mean you would make a sort of down-slope ready behind him. Then, once you get his shoulders free of the suction, he would slide down backwards into the deeper water and be able to swim. For he will surely wake up as soon as he feels himself moved. – Good! Jim, you should have been an engineer. – Marvellous!'

I found that, as the Doctor's hopes rose higher, I was becoming strangely thrilled at the thought of actually seeing Mudface, the only living passenger left who had trod the decks of the Ark, the one link in all the Animal Kingdom between History and the Days Before History. After all, it was for this that we had come so far. But I never dreamed, as the Doctor finished speaking and started to put his clothes on again, that he meant to try and get the turtle free *that night*!

There was, I suppose, about two hours of daylight left. As soon as the meeting was finished, Jim gave out orders to all the leaders. Then many things seemed to start happening at once. Even with Chee-Chee's help as a translator, I couldn't keep track of it all. But later on I managed to put things together; and write them into my note-book.

First of all, a strange noise struck my ears. This was the *plop, plop – splash, splash*, as all those great beasts, in sixes and sevens, threw themselves off the land into the lake. The leaders had been ordered by Jim to divide the diggers into regular work-teams. As the Doctor had told me, it was very exhausting. So, as soon as one lot was tired out, the order would be given to change over: the weary gang would

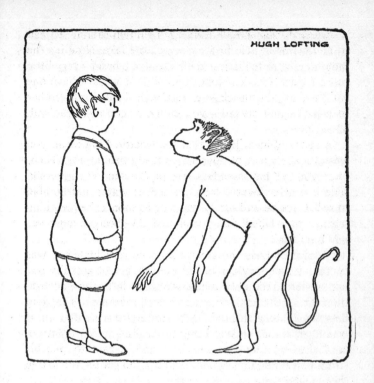

come back to rest; and a fresh lot would *plop, plop* into the water and disappear.

What was going on below of course I did not know till afterwards. But every once in a while Jim would come and tell the Doctor something; and I hoped it was good news.

After about an hour Jim and his two brothers – all three of them together – brought up some specially important information. (I knew this, because the Doctor clearly became tremendously interested; and he gave them very careful instructions to take back to the workers under water.)

It turned out that the diggers had scooped out the slope behind the turtle and were now ready to finish prying up in front to let the water under him. John Dolittle told me this was the one part of the whole job where he was afraid that the noses of all those crocodiles, heaving together, might crack or break the turtle's shell – in spite of its thickness.

The way they went about it was very clever, I thought. A dozen crocodiles, set close side by side, thrust their flat, chisel-like noses under the shoulder of the shell, as deep into the mud as they could go. Then a dozen more got up on to the tails of the first lot and bore down with all their weight.

At the first try nothing happened. And Jim's brother was all for sending word up to the Doctor for new instructions. But Jim, it seems, said, no: he didn't believe in giving up so easily. Then he sorted out the crocodiles by size; and, taking only the very largest and heaviest, he lined up another two dozen and tried again.

This time they had better success. From the way the water started to flow in under Mudface's body, Jim felt sure that the suction must soon let go. He got two more gangs of heavyweights and lined them up on the turtle's other shoulder, the right one. Then, by heaving first on one side and then on the other, he got the whole of Mudface's front part levered up a good foot out of the mud. And at last, as the water rushed in under the whole length of the turtle from head to tail, the great beast's body slid slowly down the slope prepared for it and rolled over on its back, free!

I cannot say what picture as to Mudface's size I had ever had. Cheapside had spoken of him airily, 'as big as a house' – but then I knew that the sparrow often exaggerated. I had heard the Doctor tell of the turtle's size as 'unbelievably large' or 'perfectly huge' – which could mean anything.

But when at last I saw him with my own eyes – though really I only saw parts of him that night – I thought I must be having another nightmare (like the one I'd had about the giant snake, back in the swamplands).

Twilight was coming on now. But you could still see pretty well – except where the setting sun threw the island's long shadow on the calm water. John Dolittle had finished dressing and was standing on the shore by our camp fire, staring out into wide and silent Junganyika.

Presently, in this darker shaded part of the lake, I thought I saw something come to the surface, gently breaking the calm of the water – something round and flat, like a ball just afloat. At first it seemed no bigger than a tea-tray. But as it rose, it slowly grew – larger and larger and larger still.

Close behind me I heard the Doctor give a long sigh of relief.

'Thank goodness! ... They've managed it. ... Here he comes!'

Too-Too, the night-seer, made some clicking noises with his tongue; while little Chee-Chee, always so brave in real danger, whimpered fearfully somewhere in the gloom.

It was getting harder to make things out in the fading daylight. But I could tell that this great mass out there had stopped rising and was slowly moving towards us. And, from the smoothness of its motion, I guessed it must be swimming.

'Well, well, the lucky voyage, Stubbins!' the Doctor whispered over my shoulder. – 'The lucky voyage!'

John Dolittle was never one to make a show of his feelings. (This, Polynesia had often said, was the most English thing about him.) But as the strong fingers of his right hand suddenly gripped my shoulder, they told me, better than any words, how much this successful ending to our voyage meant for him.

'He's crawling now,' I heard him say. 'You can tell his feet have touched bottom by the way he moves. – You see that? Good! Then his legs – his rheumatism, you know – can't be too bad, or he couldn't even walk that much.'

Our camp fire gave only a dim light. But I was glad we had built it well back from the water's edge; for if Mud-face was coming ashore right here, we did not want it to be in his way. Nearly all of the Doctor's animals had moved inland too, for fear of being stepped on in the half-dark.

Exactly when I first saw the turtle's head I don't know. My eyes were busy staring down into the water, watching for what might come out of it. There was a single large palm-tree quite close to me. I had noticed Chee-Chee the monkey look up at the top of this palm from time to time; and I suppose my own gaze followed his. Anyway, I suddenly saw that, besides the head of the palm-tree up there, there was something else, swaying against the sky. It was the same height as the top of the palm – and about the same size. Then, before the Doctor told me, I too moved back; I suddenly knew what it was. *It was Mudface's head!*

And, in the way we often get reminded in great moments of things unimportant and far away, I thought of a picture in the Doctor's library back home. It showed big lizards who roamed the earth thousands of years ago, nibbling the leaves from the tops of the forest.

But my dreaming thoughts were suddenly brought back. The ground beneath my feet seemed to be trembling. Was this another earthquake, I wondered? ... No. This monster, towering over us, was *speaking* to the Doctor.

How thrilled I was to find I could understand what this thunderous voice was saying! Later, when I was writing out his story of the Flood, I was to miss a word or sentence here and there; and I had to fill them in later. But this evening, when Mudface spoke his first greeting to his old friend, I caught every word of it – perfectly. My hours of study with the little turtles had not been wasted. I felt very proud, I can tell you, as I wrote down the great animal's first rumbling words in my note-book:

'Again, John Dolittle, you come in time of danger, in time of trouble – as you have always done. For this, the creatures of the land, the water and the air shall remember your name when other men, called *great*, shall be forgotten. Welcome, good friend! – Welcome once more to Lake Junganyika!'

PART THREE

I

THE HIPPOPOTAMUS FERRY-BOATS

AND now, in a very short time, the island was changed in many ways.

For one thing, before General Jim and his great army of the Niger left us, they cleared out a wide space on the high flat top. This was for the camp. They dug a good ditch around it, so that all rain-water would be drained down into the lake. Mudface's old path up to the top had disappeared with the earthquake; and the crocodiles also put that right for us. They made a new fine road from the canoe-landing at the water's edge to the camping ground where it was always dry underfoot.

Here, so much higher than the lake, the sun was often shining; and we could look down upon the tops of coloured clouds partly hiding the wide waters of Junganyika.

'Humph!' grunted Cheapside one day, as all of us were gazing down at this strange sight. 'Looks like a sea of rollin' rosy pillows, don't it? Makes me feel I ought to be flyin' around over 'em in me night-shirt, blowin' a trumpet.'

'Tee, hee, hee!' tittered the white mouse. 'Fancy Cheapside as an angel – in a *night-shirt!*'

'And why not, pray?' stormed the London sparrow. 'Angels always wears night-shirts – in pictures. It's sort of a uniform with 'em – for flyin'. I suppose you think I ain't good enough to be an angel, eh? Well, let me tell *you* somethink: I want no more sauce from you, Whitey-me-lad. – Or you'll suddenly find that smart young mice are wearing their tails shorter this season, see?'

The Doctor and I set up a tent. And the change to sleeping inside, in regular beds of dried, sweet-smelling grass – after several weeks of hammocks – was very pleasant.

And then there was the need for more food to keep us going while we listened to the story of the Flood from Mudface. We had brought only enough from the *Albatross* to last us for our trip up here, being afraid of overloading the canoe. So Polynesia and Chee-Chee set out on foraging expeditions. The parrot and monkey, native Africans, knew how, and where, to look for wild nuts, fruit, honey and roots which were good to eat.

One sort of food we did *not* have to fetch and carry. A hippopotamus and his wife called upon the Doctor, and wanted to know could they be of any help to him and his party. When they had been told about our need for food, the father hippo asked if we liked rice. The Doctor said, yes, rice was very nourishing. (It turned out that John Dolittle had treated the father, when he was a baby years ago at his Post Office, for some trouble.)

Then the hippos said they would see that we got all the wild rice we wanted. And they went off and fetched us enough to last an army for a month.

'That's done it!' grumbled Cheapside to me. 'Now old lady Dab-Dab will serve us rice-puddin' every meal for the rest of the trip. Of all the dull mush! I can stand it once or twice a year. But – oh, what's the use? Sometimes, Tommy, I think the animals are a bit *too* kind to the Doc.'

John Dolittle's main concern at first was Mudface's health. He gave him a thorough medical examination. At the end of it he told me that, all in all, he was pleased to find the great beast as well as he was.

'You know, Stubbins,' said he – 'in a way, I'm back where I was: on the study of long life. Very different from the human kind, of course. Just the same, I could write a book about Mudface's case which would make a whole lot of doctors in London open their eyes.'

'I'm sure you could,' I agreed, exchanging glances with

Polynesia who was listening to our talk. 'But you want to get the story of the Flood from him again, don't you, first?'

'Quite so, quite so,' said he. 'I was only telling you about my examination of him. I feared it might be weeks and weeks before I could let him tell his story to us. But now,' the Doctor went on, 'after looking him over, I think it will be only a matter of days, instead of weeks.'

'Oh, that's splendid, Doctor,' said I.

'In spite of his enormous age – so great we can only guess at it – I find nothing we call radically wrong. The rheumatic condition is worse, of course, I expected that. I've written out of prescription for him. Our difficulty will be to make up enough, you know. The medicine must be taken, not in teaspoonfuls, but in barrelfuls! We can get everything I'll need for this tonic in the jungle. But how to get enough. That's my problem.'

I asked why he did not speak to our hippo friends about this: and he said he intended to.

Those strange and gentle beasts (they lived almost entirely on wild rice; and Cheapside said, of course, that accounted for their having no character at all) turned out to be most helpful. Mr Hippo took the Doctor on his back and swam off with him in search of medicinal herbs. He looked a strange sight, with his high hat and all, astride that wide back – crossing the lake. Cheapside roared with laughter; and even the Doctor realized how comical he looked.

'Hippopotamus means *river-horse*,' he laughed back at us. 'They're very comfortable, plump and well padded. Too bad the Puddleby newspapermen aren't here now! Goodbye! – I'll see you later.'

And thus, as old Mudface himself had said, the creatures of the wild remembered John Dolittle and his kind deeds; they tried in every way to repay him.

All sorts of animals came to welcome him to Africa. They were all very respectful, staring at him in wonder –

as though he were something magical. A good few of them, I suspected, came just out of curiosity, or to be able to boast to their children that they had actually seen the great man himself. But there were others who turned out to be very useful to us in setting up our camp and making our work lighter in many ways.

A large band of monkeys (most of them were cousins of Chee-Chee's) travelled two or three hundred miles to visit us. When they reached the shores of the lake they could get no farther. So they called across to us in a loud chorus of howls and shrieks. Chee-Chee heard them and told the Doctor what it was. Then John Dolittle asked Mr and Mrs Hippo if they would kindly swim over and ferry the monkeys across to the island.

This was done. And I believe there must have been a good thousand of them. Every single monkey had brought a couple of bananas with him – which they knew the Doctor was especially fond of. We had not tasted any since we left Fantippo; so we had a grand feast that night. And Gub-Gub enjoyed it no end because we saved all the banana-skins for him – which he preferred to the fruit itself.

2

TURTLETOWN

WHAT the Doctor said came true: as soon as he mixed enough of the medicine and Mudface started taking it regularly, we could almost see the giant turtle getting better by the hour. John Dolittle was a great doctor – as well as a great naturalist.

This large band of monkeys who came to visit him stayed with us till we left; and it was almost unbelievable how helpful they turned out to be.

They were a bit scared of Mudface at first, of his truly tremendous size. But they quickly got over that. And as soon as they learned what the Doctor wanted, they built huts around our camping ground. I never saw such fast and clever workmen. They dug holes, using their paws to scoop out the sand. And in these holes they set posts, about as thick as your arm. Then they covered the roofs of the huts with palm-leaves – and the walls the same. They left spaces for just a door and a window.

In no time at all, it seemed, our camp (which before had been one single tent) had a cookhouse; a comfortable, roomy bunkhouse where the Doctor and I slept; a storehut in a cool place for keeping food; a surgery where the Doctor made up medicines and attended to any animals who were sick; and a big roofed shelter for Mudface himself. Altogether, it looked like a little village.

Cheapside, who was perched on my shoulder as I watched the monkeys cleaning up around the new buildings, remarked:

'Pretty nifty, eh, Tommy? Look, we got a street-cleaning department and all. We gotter give them monks credit. They're smart. It ain't everybody could put a town up for you in only a day. All we needs now is a few lamp-posts and a copper walking up and down. Yes, pretty nifty village. What'll we call it? ... Why I know! *Turtletown*, o' course!'

And still another hut was called the office. This was set well away from any of the others, so that I could write my notes without the noise of monkeys chattering near by. Also, I had made up my mind that *this time* the note-books of the story of the Flood should be kept from harm, so far as I could prevent it.

Many note-books I had already filled with things the Doctor wanted taken down on our journey here from Puddleby; and these I carefully brought from the canoe-landing and stored in a dry hole in the floor of the office.

Jip and Polynesia took it in turns to mount guard over this hut for me, night and day. And later, as each new note-book was finished, it was put away safely in the hole. I found a few large stones to cover the hole — so the note-books would be protected in case the hut should take fire.

The day after the monkeys finished Turtletown the Doctor said that Mudface should be well enough by tomorrow to tell us his History of the Deluge.

'But we must go easy with him, to begin with, Stubbins — say, half an hour or so a day — and see how it goes. Remember there are those monkey-carpenters who want to listen. So, with them all, poor Mudface is going to have a large audience to talk to. I'll give you my watch. Keep an eye on it, will you? Don't let him talk more than three-quarters of an hour the first day, eh?'

'Very good, Doctor,' I said. 'I'll signal you at forty minutes. . . . I only hope I can understand him.'

'Ah, don't worry about that,' he said with a smile. 'You can always ask us afterwards — if you get stuck, Stubbins.'

'When will we begin, Doctor?' I asked.

'Tomorrow evening, Stubbins. Mudface is always in better form at night. We'll start after supper — an early supper.'

And so, the following evening we gathered at the turtle's shelter. All the Doctor's family came: Jip the dog; Too-Too, the owl-mathematician of marvellous memory; Dab-Dab the duck; Chee-Chee, proudly at the head of all the visiting monkeys; Whitey, the inquisitive mouse who wouldn't have missed the show for anything; and Gub-Gub the pig, who was also present. Then there was Cheapside the London sparrow, and Polynesia the African parrot. These two famous quarrellers, while pretending to be bored by the turtle's story, were, I knew, far more interested than they would admit. And Becky, Cheapside's wife, she came along too.

The big crowd found places – somehow – around Mudface within the shed. (It was not much more than a roof
supported by poles.)

From this high ground you could see out in all directions. The view of lake Junganyika was extremely lovely
as the big stars came out over the quiet water and spangled
it with their silvery light.

And so I started the hardest – and perhaps the most important – job of note-taking which I had ever done in all
my experience as the Doctor's secretary.

3

DAYS OF THE DELUGE

'VERY well, then, Doctor,' said the giant turtle, 'I will tell
you the story of the Flood just as though I had never
told you any of it before. It is a good thing that we have
this second chance – since all your writings have been
lost.

'When I was a young turtle I was captured with five
others and put in a menagerie. It was a sort of zoological
gardens – owned by the great King Mashtu. May his bones
rot in the mud! Would that all memory of him might be
wiped out for ever!'

As the turtle stopped a moment and glared savagely out
across the gloomy lake, the Doctor asked:

'You sound bitter, Mudface. King Mashtu did you harm?'

'I should say he did,' growled the enormous beast – 'to
the whole world!'

The look in the turtle's eyes changed – though he still
stared out across the waters – a look of memories: sad,
fond, thrilling, all changing and mixed up.

'Out there, John Dolittle,' said he after a moment, 'in the

middle of the lake, beneath hundreds of feet of water, lie the ruins of the City of Shalba, King Mashtu's capital. Once it was the proudest, most beautiful city in the world. It had everything: a grand, royal palace for the King; lovely buildings of white marble; shops that sold anything you could wish; theatres; great libraries filled with books brought from every country on earth; an enormous circus; a racetrack; parks of flowering trees – and a zoo where wild animals were kept. And it was there, to the zoo, that I was brought when I was captured.

'The head-keeper of the zoo was a very old man. He too had been captured – taken prisoner in the wars by King Mashtu's generals. This man, in his own country, had been what is called a patriarch. And all of his family were also brought to the City of Shalba and made to work in King Mashtu's service. But the patriarch himself, for a special reason, was made head-keeper of the zoo. He was very old – for a man – six hundred years of age. His name was Noah.'

'Ah!' said the Doctor. 'I had guessed it would be Noah. But for what reason, Mudface, was he made zoo-keeper?'

'Because,' the turtle answered, 'he spoke animal languages. He was the first and only man, besides yourself, John Dolittle, who could understand animal talk. Having lived six hundred years, you see, he had plenty of time to learn.'

'Of course, of course,' said the Doctor. 'And how wonderfully well he must have learned to speak in that time!'

'No, there you're mistaken, Doctor. He could make himself understood, it is true. But he could not chat in turtle talk, for example, half as well as you can – nor even as well as Tommy, here. And as for writing down things, he *never* learned. He was not as wise and clever as he was cracked up to be. In fact often he was downright stupid – as you will see later.'

I was pleased by the turtle's praise; and I looked up to

166

smile. But Mudface was going on with his story – this time much faster. And I had to hurry on, scribbling away like mad.

'Although,' said Mudface, 'I was much smaller in those days than I am now, still I was by far the biggest and oldest of the six turtles who had been captured. And you may remember, Doctor, my kind is both sea turtle and fresh-water turtle.'

'Yes, I remember that,' said John Dolittle. 'You are the only one of your sort left in the world today. But please go on.'

'Well, they prepared a pond for us in the zoo gardens. It had no mud in it, only clean bright gravel – which we didn't like at all. We loved mud. The King and his people would come to look at us through the strong iron fence surrounding the pool. And sometimes I, the Giant Turtle as I was called, gave the visitors rides on my back – though it was as much as your life was worth if the keeper didn't watch me all the time. Because I used to spill the people off into a puddle, when I could find one, pretending it was an accident.

'We were fed by Noah. The other five turtles, even if they were unhappy, ate their food regularly. But I did not. I was separated from my wife.'

'Er, Mudface,' the Doctor interrupted. 'How is it your wife wasn't captured with you?'

'Well, you see, Doctor,' said Mudface, 'Belinda was in another part of the country visiting her relatives. – You know how women are – always getting lonesome to see a cousin or an aunt or someone's new baby. Any excuse for a change of scenery. Of course, I was glad for her sake she was still free; but I was dreadfully lonely for her. . . .' Mudface stopped a moment, sighing in memory.

'Oh, dear,' said the Doctor, 'then that is the reason Belinda is not with you now – you never saw her again?'

'Yes, indeed,' said the turtle, 'I did see her soon after my capture. I'll tell you about that as my story progresses.'

Mudface paused, wrinkling his brows. 'But her absence *now* puzzles me. She left quite suddenly a few months ago – just before the earthquake – and I haven't heard from her since. I'm worried.'

'Ain't that just like a woman, Doc?' said Cheapside. 'Galavantin'' off when 'er 'usband needs 'er most.'

'Quiet, Cheapside,' said John Dolittle. 'I'm sure Belinda will be back immediately when she hears about Mudface's trouble.'

The giant turtle raised his head and smiled at the Doctor. 'Thank you, John Dolittle,' he said. 'Perhaps I shouldn't worry. Belinda has always been able to take care of herself.' He settled his shell comfortably and went on.

'I was pretty unhappy. I moped and ate no food at all. Noah told this to the King and asked to be allowed to let me go. But Mashtu said I was the finest and the biggest of the collection; and that I would soon settle down and eat my food. But I didn't. I hated the life of the zoo. Still, as you know, turtles can go a long time without eating. And I did not die.

'All six of us spent most of the time trying to work out some plan of escape. The fence around our pond was not very high but it was too much for a turtle to climb over. I was the oldest and strongest; and the others looked to me to find them a way to liberty and freedom. And one night I thought of a clever idea for undermining the low wall, on which the iron fencing was set, and getting out underneath the fence – instead of over it. For three whole nights I worked, burrowing and scratching. At last I got one of the big square stones loose enough to pull out. Freedom was in sight!

'But we agreed to wait till the following night, so as to have plenty of darkness to get away in. The zoological gardens were large; and turtles are slow on land.

'Well, the next night came; and my five companions

168

waited breathlessly while I pulled the stone down into the pond and then made the hole large enough to climb through. All went well. We got out under the fence and started to cross the park in the dim light of a rising moon. But we had scarcely gone twenty steps when the park-gates opened to a blare of trumpets. The King himself entered with a party of friends to show them his collection of animals! With him came hundreds of guards and torch-bearers. Mashtu especially wished to show the visitors his new turtles. He made straight for our pool.

'Escape then, for such slow creatures as we, was of course impossible. We were caught at once and put back. The fencing, with its wall, was made stronger than ever, so that we shouldn't get out again.

'We were all terribly down-hearted. My grand plan had only made things worse than they were before.

'However, Noah had an assistant-keeper, little more than a boy – and he had been, like Noah, captured in the wars and brought here from some foreign land. He took pity on us turtles – out of sympathy, I suppose, for fellow-prisoners. He was our one comfort. His name was Eber. And I shall speak of him again, often.

'He had begun as a gardener – at which work he was very skilful. But later he was put under Noah, in the menagerie, as assistant-keeper.

'Eber had a kind heart; and he did his best to make our lives happier: bringing us special foods; spraying us with fresh cold water when the weather was unbearably hot; and doing anything else he could for our well-being.

'Eber had fallen in love with a beautiful young girl called Gaza. She, too, was a slave. To foreign travellers, Shalba – always boasting of her freedom – must have seemed full of slaves. Gaza, who had a truly lovely voice, used to sing for Mashtu's chief wife, who lived in a smaller palace of her own – called the Queen's Pavilion – close by the zoological gardens.

'And often in the twilight I listened to her songs of far-off lands, which reached us on the evening wind in our wretched prison-pond. Mashtu's spies discovered that Eber was meeting her secretly in the park. As a punishment, Eber was beaten most unmercifully. He could not walk for days after. King Mashtu was a cruel-hearted man.

'After a month or two had rolled by, life for me was suddenly made much brighter. Belinda, that clever wife of mine, found out where I had been taken. And she used to come at night and talk to me through the bars of the fence. You can have no idea how much this meant to me. I had begun to give up all hope – to look forward to nothing but this stupid life of prison for the rest of my days. Belinda's visits made me fearful that she might be caught; but just seeing and talking with her every night put new heart into me. She was so cheerful and so certain that we would yet escape some way, if only we'd be patient.

'Now, I had always given a good deal of study to the weather, even as a youngster. And by this time I had become quite well known among all the water creatures as a good weather-prophet. I used to foretell the rain-showers for the other turtles in our pond. You see, we looked forward to them. We like rain. It is pleasant to feel it trickling down your shell and running off the tip of your nose – exceedingly refreshing in hot climates. And on account of my being able to tell when it was going to rain, the weather became the favourite thing for us to talk about. – It is hard to find much to chat over when you are fenced in a pond only fifty feet across. And Noah himself, who often used to listen to us, got the habit of talking of the weather, too. And so it was handed down, as the favourite thing to talk about, for thousands of years.

'Well, one day a gale sprang up towards evening. The trees of the park bent down before it like lily-stalks; and big gravel stones blew along the walks just as if they were dust. The other turtles gathered around me, asking what I thought of it. I looked up at the sky and saw a whirlpool of angry black clouds spinning, twisting and crossing the heavens. It was different from anything I had ever seen.

' "Cousins," I said, turning to the other turtles, "it will rain before night."

' "Good!" said they. "It is uncomfortably hot."

'Suddenly a terrific crash of thunder seemed to split the air; and the clouds came right down low, wrapping themselves about the trees.

' "My friends," said I, "it will be a great, great rain."

' "Good!" they said. "The water in our pond needs changing badly."

'Then, with a roar, the heavens seemed to open; and a great flash of lightning spat earthward, ripping a stout oak-tree, which stood near our fence, clean in two, from fork to roots. Suddenly I wondered was Eber in safety.

' "Turtles," I said, "somehow I'm sure the time of our escape is close at hand. This will be the greatest of great rains. These Men are but weak creatures in some things. Many will be killed. They can stand only so much rain; while we turtles love it. In ten days from tonight the water in this pool will rise above the fence, freeing us to swim where we will."

' "Good!" said they. "Long have we suffered in slavery. Welcome, rain! How sweet will be the mud-banks of liberty!"

'Now, *that* rain began falling in a peculiar way. It started on a Friday – no, it was a Monday – no, now wait a second. . . . Let me see, it was – '

The listening Cheapside (I had thought he was asleep) opened one eye and muttered,

'Let's hope it wasn't an Easter Monday – spoil the holiday. There ain't nothin' worse than a wet Bank Holiday. Come on, old Muddypuss, make up yer mind. It's past bedtime.'

171

'Anyway,' whispered Dab-Dab the duck, 'there's no one can argue with him. That's one thing sure.'

'Well,' the turtle went on, 'whatever day of the week it was, the rain began in the forenoon; and it began very gently. At first my friends were very disappointed. And they thought I must be mistaken as a weather-prophet – that it was going to be only an ordinary shower.

' "Wait!" I said to them angrily. "Have I ever foretold the weather wrong for you? This rain will last for forty days, beginning light but growing heavy. After the first ten days, as I have promised, you will be free. But at the end of the forty days King Mashtu, the proud, and his City of Shalba shall be no more. The earth will be covered in water. For this, brother turtles, *this is the Deluge*."

' "Good!" said they again. "What could be more delightful than a deluge? – A lovely flood! It is high time these Men who have enslaved us should be washed away. In a world of water, we, the slow walkers and swift swimmers, will be the great ones of the Earth."

'To this for a moment I said nothing. My mind had strayed away from them and their chatter.

'At last, my voice sounding strangely serious even to my own ears, I answered:

' "Perhaps . . . perhaps."

'I was thinking – of Eber . . .'

4

THE ELEPHANTS' MARCH

REMEMBERING, suddenly, what the Doctor had told me about keeping an eye on the time, I grabbed his watch out of my pocket, as Mudface stopped a moment. My goodness! The turtle had been talking a whole half-hour longer than John Dolittle had said he should – to begin with. I made a signal to the Doctor that, for tonight, our time was up. He rose from his seat at once.

'Thank you, Mudface,' said he. 'There are a million questions already I would like to ask you about those times. But you must take a dose of your medicine now and get to bed. We will look forward – if you will be so kind – to hearing more of your story tomorrow night.'

'You can bet on that,' said Cheapside sleepily. 'We're going to be listenin' to *that* old chap's yarn for months yet.'

As the Doctor and I prepared to leave for our bunk-house a few doors farther up the main street of Turtle-town, Mudface started humming a tune. The sound – though not unpleasant to the ear – was so unbelievably powerful that the earth shook beneath us. The Doctor paused at the door.

'Pardon me,' said he. 'But what is that tune?'

'It is the "Elephants' March",' said the turtle. 'It was always played in Shalba, on circus days, for the elephants' procession on their way to the show. I learnt it by heart; it's become a habit for me to hum it as I'm going to bed.'

'Very interesting indeed,' said John Dolittle. 'I've always been keen about music myself. But never in my wildest dreams did I expect to hear a march that was written before the Flood. You must teach it to me sometime. We will write it out – the score, I mean. Good-night, Mudface.'

As we started off down the street, the pavement still trembled to the humming from the big shelter we had left.

'As I believe I remarked before,' said Cheapside, who was perched on the Doctor's shoulder, 'a voice like old Mud-pan's is kind of wasted in this gawd-forsaken swamp. He ought to get a job as fog-horn on an ocean rock some-where. Ships could hear 'im twenty miles away.'

'Tee, hee, hee!' tittered the white mouse from my left pocket.

'What an experience, what a story!' muttered the Doctor, his mind still full of the Deluge.

Once in our snug bunk-house – terribly tired – I was soon asleep. Never had I written so fast. My right hand was so cramped I wondered if I'd ever be able to straighten it again. And all night long, though I never woke once, dreams kept flitting through my mind – and always about the same person. . . . In my sleep, like Mudface, I was thinking of Eber.

5

FIREWORKS FOR THE KING'S BIRTHDAY

THE next evening Mudface seemed to be feeling better still. Waiting for us to settle down, he looked fresher. And his voice sounded keener and less tired when he spoke.

'Then,' said he, 'we turtles, for the present, just sat behind our prison-bars and waited as before. But our mood was different. For instead of thinking dreary thoughts, we were dreaming great dreams. Where would we go when, for the first time in so long, big voyagings were made easy? Each of us of course had a different plan in his heart as to what he would do first, with his new freedom.

'How clearly I remember it! It was King Mashtu's birthday, that Friday – or whatever day it was – and a public holiday. There had been shows going on at the circus ever since midday; and the royal elephants had paraded to that march I hummed last night. – Though the music sounded very sour, with the band's instruments all wet.

'The day's celebrations were to end with a display of fireworks in the Royal Zoological Park. Through the fencing around our pond we watched them getting ready for this grand finish. The wind had now eased off, though the rain still fell evenly. A deathly calm hung over the twilit park, the sort of calm that can turn a steady rain into a cyclone.

'With a most unmusical blare from wet trumpets, the King entered the park and gave orders for the fireworks to begin. The darkness, with the overcast sky, was now almost complete; and lanterns of coloured paper had been lighted and hung in the trees. But they did not stay lighted long.

'Oh, how we chuckled in our prison-pond as the rain suddenly grew heavier! The last of the lanterns flickered out. And when the men tried to light the fireworks, not a single one of them would go off. *How* we chuckled!'

Mudface leant down to moisten his throat from a calabash near by filled with muddy lake-water. (He always liked his drinking water muddy.) And while he was at this I scribbled away in the note-book more furiously than ever; for he was talking fast again and I had fallen behind.

'The magicians,' he went on presently, 'and the astrologers of the court looked up at the black, starless sky; and said the rain was a bad omen. They did not recommend that his Majesty go on with the celebrations tonight. The King, trying to take the matter lightly, then gave orders to put off the fireworks and merry-making till tomorrow. He turned and left by the same gate through which he had entered. But I noticed that on passing through it he signalled to the trumpeters to stop their blowing. This could be easily understood; for the poor drenched men were now blowing nothing but water out of their trumpets instead of music. We could just see the dim forms of Mashtu and his family, as they entered the lighted palace in the distance.

' "Cousins," said I to my fellow-prisoners, "King Mashtu enters his palace for the last time. Never again will he leave dry-shod."

'Beneath the now heavier rain the crowd which had gathered for the fireworks scattered to their homes and the park was soon left empty. In our pond we frisked and frolicked and splashed water at one another, like kittens at tag. Even I so far forgot my dignity and age as to join in the fun. Throughout the whole night it rained, heavier and heavier; and all night we played on, celebrating Mashtu's wettest birthday.

'Well, after that date we did not see the sun again for forty days. Next morning, when dawn came, it was merely a murky light, little better than twilight – and it was still raining. A few brave citizens came out with umbrellas, to see if the jollifications were going on as the King had promised. But all they found was mud. The Royal Palace was closed. The people hurried back home again.

'Late that afternoon my wife came to see me, walking carefully across the park behind the cover of the trees, lest she be seen. When she was within hearing I shouted to her.

' "There's no need to keep yourself hidden now. No one will bother you any more. This is the Deluge!"

' "As soon as the park is flooded deep enough," I said, "we are going to swim out over the top of this fencing. See, the water of our pond has already risen two inches in the night."

'My poor wife, who had already suffered much worry through our separation, was very happy. But she could not believe that our prison-days were really over.

' "Are you quite sure, my dear," she said, "that enough rain will fall to float you out?" – You know, Doctor, women will never believe anything till they see it.

' "Am I sure!" I cried, astonished. "Listen, Belinda: have I, as a weather-prophet, ever led you wrong? In nine days I will join you on the other side of this wretched fence or my name's not Mudface."

'I could see I had taken a load off her mind. Her mood too changed. And suddenly all seven of us, out of sheer recklessness, turned and shouted towards the King's palace as hard as we could.

' "Hooray! – Happy Birthday, Mashtu!"

'But no one came out to bid us be still.

'Now, when I had foretold our freedom in ten days' time I had calculated on a growing fall of rain each day. And I was right. The next morning the level of the water in our pool had risen another three inches. And we could see that many parts of the park now lay wholly under water. The day after that – it was a Sunday – or I think it was. – No, maybe – '

'Oh, never mind the day of the week!' Dab-Dab snapped. 'Just tell us what happened; don't bother about what day it was.'

'I don't believe he *knows* the days of the week,' muttered Too-Too.

'Well, you can't never tell,' said Cheapside, as the turtle still tried to remember. 'Maybe in those days they had two Sundays every week, one at each end, like. You can't never tell. They was a church-going lot, them antedelvulians.'

'The next day,' said the turtle presently, 'Belinda, who had gone into the city to find out how things were getting along, came back to us in a great state of excitement.

' "What do you think, Mudface?" she said. "Just outside the town, where the old race-track was, there's a man trying to build an enormous boat. – And all sorts of animals, hundreds of them, are standing around watching him!"

' "What does the man look like?" I asked.

' "He seems terribly old," said she. "But – listen: he can *speak to the animals in their own languages!*"

' "Why, that's Noah," I said, "our head zoo-keeper. I suppose he guesses this is no ordinary rain – that a flood is coming – and he's making a ship to save himself in."

'Well,' (old Mudface looked out over the lake, and something like a smile played around his grim mouth) 'the great hour arrived at last – on the tenth day, as I had said it would. The water-level in our pool had kept on creeping up and up till at last I could put my front claws on the top of the railing. Then with a mighty heave I pulled myself over the fence into freedom! Belinda and I embraced one another; and both of us wept tears of joy into the flooded park.

'I knew the other turtles would be all right now; so, partly swimming and partly walking, I led Belinda towards the main gate. I wanted to see the sights – and especially Noah's ship. Of course by this time water covered most of the park. Only the heads of the trees stood up out of it. As we passed the King's palace we saw people leaving by the windows in beds or rafts or anything that would float. Farther on we saw that the river which ran through Shalba was now a mad roaring torrent. The stone bridge near the Silk Market had been swept away like a piece of paper.

178

Indeed, only the higher ground in the city could be seen at all – thus it was not easy to tell whereabouts in the town you were. And the people were leaving even these higher places and making off for the mountains.

'These mountains stood about two miles from the city. And everyone thought that if he could only reach them he would be safe.

'Everyone, I ought to say, except the patriarch Noah. My wife, after we had swum and scrabbled around sight-seeing, guided me to where she had seen Noah building a ship. This was on a high flat piece of land at the western end of the city. It had been a race-track. It was now used as a timber-yard.

'I have often thought that many more people would have been saved from the Flood if they had only realized, at the start of the forty days' rain, that they must take to strong boats, prepared to live in them a long time. But everyone thought that any minute the rain would stop. So all they did, when the ground-floors of their homes became flooded, was to go upstairs and wait at the top windows. And by the time they saw that the water was going to rise right over their roofs, it was too late to build boats of any kind.

'But Noah must have known somehow – or guessed – what was going to happen. Perhaps he heard me promising the forty days' rain.

'Anyway, reaching the old race-track, we found him with a tape and rule in his hands, measuring beams of timber. His thumb, which he had hit with a hammer, was done up in a dirty rag. He looked very wet, unhappy and upset. He hadn't done much boat-building yet; all he seemed to be doing for the present was measuring – just measuring miserably in the rain. I heard him mutter to himself over and over again the same thing: "A hundred cubits by fifty by thirty." And every time he said it he looked more puzzled than ever.

'He had his three sons Ham, Shem and Japheth with
him, the son's wives – and his own wife. But none of
them seemed to be helping him much. The men were
quarrelling about who had lost the hammer; and the women were arguing over who should have the best room
on the boat when it was finished.

'And all the while the water kept rising around them.
The flat island, on which they worked, kept growing
smaller. And Noah kept on measuring – and muttering – in
the rain.'

6

NOAH'S ARK AND THE GREAT WAVE

'LISTEN, Mudface,' said the Doctor, the following evening: 'before you begin tonight may I ask you something?'

'Of course, John Dolittle,' said the turtle. 'I'll be glad to answer your questions any time – if I can.'

'Well,' said the Doctor, 'couldn't you tell us a few things about what the world was like *before* the Flood?'

'What sort of things, Doctor?'

'Well,' said John Dolittle, 'for instance, how did King Mashtu become so great that his palaces had foreign slaves brought from every corner of the Earth? How were these slaves transported? What was the most important trade or business of the people who lived in King Mashtu's kingdom; and – er – oh, a thousand things about the music and art of that strange civilization.'

In silence Mudface thought a moment before he answered.

'Suppose, Doctor, you first let me get further on with the story of the Deluge and what followed it. I'm sure you will find many of your questions answered as I go along.'

'Certainly,' said the Doctor. 'Please begin.'

'Now, at either end of this old race-track,' Mudface went on, 'two crowds of different animals stood around waiting. They were waiting, we guessed, for the ship to be finished and ready. It was, we learned later, called the *Ark*. – Just as well, because it couldn't be called a ship: the *Stable* would have been a better name. These waiting creatures were wet, but patient and quiet. All except the cats – you know, Doctor – tigers, leopards, panthers and beasts like that. Their behaviour was *not* good – cats don't like getting wet. They were snapping at the other animals and pushing everyone out of the way – so as to be ready to rush for the driest places on the Ark as soon as Noah gave the word.

'Directly the patriarch Noah caught sight of my wife and myself he said: "Ah, turtles!" Then he read down a long damp paper which he brought out from a pocket of his gown, containing instructions about the Ark. – I've no idea where he got it from. Presently he ticked off a name in the list. "Go and stand over there," he ordered us. "I have no turtles as yet." '

'Pardon me, Mudface,' said the Doctor. 'But did they have regular paper then – in Shalba?'

'Oh, yes indeed,' said the turtle. 'They had everything – or so it seemed to me.'

'Make a note of that, Stubbins, please – *paper*.'

'Very good, Doctor,' said I, jotting it down.

'Excuse the interruption,' said John Dolittle. 'Go on, Mudface – if you will, please.'

' "We don't want to go into your Ark," I said to Noah. "We turtles can swim. We *like* deluges."

' "Don't argue with me," he said angrily, going back to his measuring. "You're down on the passenger-list and you'll have to come. . . . Let me see: a hundred cubits by fifty by thirty. – It's that window that . . ." '

'Shiver my timbers!' muttered Polynesia, the sailor. " 'A hundred by fifty by thirty"; sounds like a barrel to me.'

'Yes,' groaned Cheapside – 'and mark you, only *one* window is mentioned – for all them people and animals. – *Phew!* Ain't you glad you wasn't at sea then, old Polly-patriarch?'

'So,' said Mudface, 'Belinda and I started walking towards the north end of the race-track to join the crowd of waiting animals.

' "No, not there," Noah shouted after us. "That's the end for the clean beasts. It says I'm to keep them separate. You creep. You belong to the *unclean* beasts. – Up this other end. Hurry along!"

'I was furious. "What do you mean: *unclean beasts*?" I asked the old man. "I'm as clean as you are."

'As a matter of fact, the patriarch did look frightfully bedraggled and messy after ten days of measuring in the rain.

' "Oh don't argue with him," Belinda whispered. "Let him get on building the ship – or all these animals who can't swim will be drowned before he has it finished."

'I did as she said. But as I moved off, I couldn't help firing a last shot at Noah over my shoulder.

' "Listen," I called: "we turtles *live* in water, washing all the time. You're a fine one to talk! *Your* beard has mashed potatoes in it – yes, and prune-stones as well!"

'I was never so angry in my life.'

Mudface hesitated a second, as though to calm himself down before going on with his story.

'Now, the citizens of Shalba – or what was left of the poor wretches – had all by this time gone off to the mountains. We could see them from the race-track, herding like sheep here and there on the slopes, gradually being driven higher and higher. It was lucky for Noah that they forgot about the high flat land of the race-track, or he would have certainly been mobbed by folk, clamouring for a place on the Ark. And of course the citizens, once they were on the mountains, could not come back. Because now, between us and them, there was a lake ten miles long.

'Well, for days and days my wife and I stood among the other waiting animals at the south end of the race-track – wondering why, if we were unclean animals, anyone was bothering to save us at all. Every hour the rain grew fiercer – so fierce that if there ever was any difference between *clean* and *unclean* beasts nobody could tell it after a wash like that.

'The middle of the race-track – where the ship-building gave room – was piled high with bales of hay, sacks of corn, peanuts and such-like, to feed the animals. No cover had been spread over this fodder; and of course most of it was already soaked and water-logged.

'The workers at last realized that something should be done about this – that the ship's main-deck must be finished in a hurry to protect all that food from being spoiled. They stopped quarrelling about the tools and set to shipbuilding with a will. By the end of the thirtieth day the Ark began to look like a real boat.

'And a very good thing it was, too. For the downpour had been getting worse and worse – so that Noah's family could scarcely see one another through the curtain of rain. Although the ground was not yet under water, the mud was terrific. Then, to add to the mess, Noah said the Ark had to be tarred – inside and out – before it put to sea. It was in his instructions, he said, and must be done.

'The old man was awfully particular about those instructions. And when he wasn't getting in the men's way, measuring, he was studying that piece of paper.

'Then they got barrels of tar and started messing up the Ark inside and out. Before long they had the tar all mixed up in the mud under their feet; they had it on the tools; they had it all over their hands and faces. And the wives couldn't tell one husband from another.

'At last, on the night of the thirty-eighth day of rain, everything was in readiness. And after Noah had read his instructions for the last time, he folded the paper up and put it in his pocket. There was a long heavy gang-plank leading up to a door in the ship's side. And standing at the head of this plank, Noah faced the animals gathered in the race-track and shouted (the falling rain was real noisy now): "All aboard! Unclean beasts for'ard; clean beasts aft; and my family amidships."

'Then all the animals rushed to get into the Ark. And Noah was knocked right off the gang-plank into the mud by two big deer who got there first. Some time was lost before things were straightened out. And Noah and his

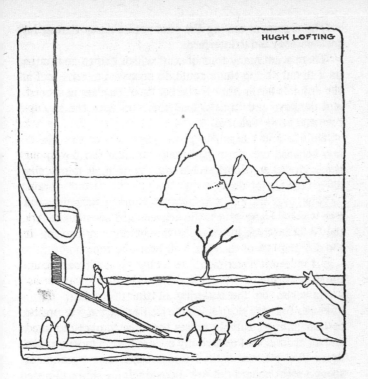

sons made the animals walk in, two by two, in a proper orderly manner. It took hours and hours to get them all in this way. And just as the last tail was disappearing through the Ark's door, Noah remembered the fodder!

'Then a terrible argument broke out among the sons, Ham, Shem and Japheth. It seems Noah had told them to be sure and remind him about the fodder before the animal-passengers were let into the Ark; and now each one of his sons was saying it wasn't *his* fault. And it came out in the argument that every one of those young men had passed on the reminding-job to one of the others. Then of course each had proceeded to forget all about the fodder, which was still out there in the wet.

'The argument among the sons got so nasty that at last their parents had to interfere.

'There were many tons of stuff which had to be brought in. The only thing Noah could do now was to fetch out all the animals again (that is the beasts of burden, like horses and donkeys and camels) load them up with the hay and corn and bring it aboard.

'Belinda and I began to grow nervous over this last delay, because the storm had really become terrible by this time. However, unbelievable though it may seem, they did get the big job done.

'Now, ever since that first clap of thunder, when the oak-tree was lightning-struck, the heavens had been quiet. True, they'd been darkly, gloomily threatening, of course; but the droning hiss of the rain, as it beat into the puddly earth – as if indeed it never meant to let up – was the only sound the storm made.

'However, on the morning of the thirty-ninth day – after our first dry sleep since the Deluge started – we awoke to hear strange, rumbly noises beneath us, over our heads and all around us. I opened my eyes and for a moment wondered where I was – till I remembered that we had just spent a night aboard the Ark. I could tell the ship still rested in the mud, because she was not rocking like a ship at sea. But what was all this rumbling racket? I at once left our quarters down below and hurried up on deck to see what was happening.

'Well, the whole race-track had almost entirely disappeared under water. You could see only the earth – or mud – just close around the Ark. Far away to the eastward I could see the upper parts of the mountains. Here the towns-folk yet clung and clustered – though they were fewer than before.

'Our ship's gang-plank had been drawn up. But old Noah was still standing outside on the last strip of ground which wasn't flooded. He was watching, like me, those miserable

people on the mountain-tops. Tears were trickling down the patriarch's dirty face. His tremendous work was finished; and all he had to do now was to wait till the waters lifted the Ark up and floated her away.

'One of his son's wives stuck her head out of the door, scolding him. She asked, didn't he know enough to come in out of the rain? – He was old enough in all conscience, she added. But Noah, weeping and watching the last of the folk on the mountains, did not even seem to hear her.

'Again I began to think of Eber, the slave who had been so kind to us. – And Gaza: what of her? I had not seen her in months and months.

187

'As for the other people of Shalba, to tell you the truth, I did not worry very much. *They* had certainly never bothered themselves about me. To them, wild animals were just something to eat; to be made to work; or looked at in menageries. Why should I– like the weeping Noah – care, now that they were being swept away to make room for other creatures? But Eber! – I had been really fond of that boy. And, as I watched those wretched folk huddling on their last mountain-refuge, I wondered only how Eber had fared. Had he been saved? . . . And, as I watched, a strange thing happened.

'Suddenly behind the mountain, a long way off, the waters – which now stretched out in nearly every direction to the skyline, like a sea – seemed to rise up as a wall and rush towards us. It was a huge wave, as wide as the world – and growing higher and higher as it came nearer.

'At that, Noah cried out to his daughter-in-law:

' "Heaven help King Mashtu's people now! See, the ocean herself has broken bounds and is running abroad like a wild thing."

'Then the rumbling noise which had been rising steadily since it first woke me, grew into a terrible roar. I sometimes wonder if the spilling over of the seas did something inside the mountains – made the volcanoes' fires explode, maybe – and earthquakes under the water. Anyway, the next thing I knew, the whole Earth was heaving and rolling about in the most terrifying way. I glanced again towards the mountains.

'And they were gone! The sea stretched flat and unbroken now, right around the world. Not a spot of land was in sight. What had happened to them I did not know. They had disappeared like magic. For Eber my heart went sick.

'But the great wave of the ocean was now roaring on towards the race-track and ourselves – quite near. Noah's wife came and joined the other women. They all screamed to the old man to come in and fasten up the door.

' "So be it," he said. And he stepped into the Ark.'

7

THE FLOATING TREE

ON the morrow we gathered again in the twilit shed. The turtle went on:

'Even while Ham, Shem and all of them were frantically barring up the door inside with strong beams, the walls of the ocean struck us. It lifted our clumsy boat high in the air, like a cork. And then down, down a great hill of water – which seemed to have no end – we were swept along, spinning and turning – down, down, down. It looked as though the ocean were shifting – as indeed it was, I believe – from one side of the world to the other. For hours we sped on down this rushing cataract of water. And I began to wonder if, and where, we'd ever stop.

'It was the last floundering agony of our Mother Earth in the grip of the Deluge. After that – when calm came – the world was water so far as we could see or know.'

In a solemn silence Mudface hesitated. Then he moved slowly to the edge of his shelter and craned his neck outside, as though to see better over the misty lake far below.

'You see that stump, John Dolittle,' he asked, pointing with a muddy claw – 'the one jutting out from the shore, where the mangroves make a sort of cape? Well, that is the very spot where Noah stood, his hand still upon the door-sill of the Ark, watching the great sea-wave sweep towards us. That is where we started from – started upon a long and wearisome voyage.

'For then began long days of idleness for us, the animal passengers. We all felt dizzy in the head from the spinning and pitching; and I even heard that Noah's wife had been a trifle seasick. However, the sun *did* come out – a sort of a sun, and the sea eventually calmed – to a sort of a calm. The coming of this calm was taken as a good sign by all – and Mrs Noah sat up and drank a cup of beef-tea.

'But oh, time hung heavy on our hands. To amuse ourselves the best we could do was guessing – guessing how long it would take the water to dry up off the land.

'As for the course we followed, I don't believe Noah himself had much idea of where we were or where we were going. We were just drifting. Nevertheless, a weak wind began presently to blow; and the Ark moved slowly before it under some makeshift sails which Shem rigged up on the main deck.

'However, if we were bored, for Noah and his family it was a very busy time. Feeding all those animals and keeping the ship clean was an enormous job. The three sons were hard at it all day, carrying and sweeping. Some of the animals got ill with the rolling of the ship and Noah had to doctor them.

'Of Noah's sons, Shem seemed the most sensible; so he was worked hardest. Ham was very lazy; and most of the day he spent playing tunes on a whistle down in the hold. One day he played the "Elephant's March". And the two elephants thought that the circus was beginning. They started parading up and down the main deck, upsetting and smashing things in all directions. After that, Ham's mother took the whistle from him and threw it overboard.

'The elephants gave a lot of trouble – though they didn't mean to at all. They were so enormously big; and they ate such a lot. The Ark was a big boat, it's true; but when you have elephants for passengers – even just a pair – you need room for them, for their fodder and for their drinking water. Quite early in the voyage their food supply ran low; and the amount they were given at each meal had to be cut down. One day the bull-elephant fainted from hunger. He fell against his stable-partition and smashed it flat.

And it took all of Noah's family, with Mrs Elephant and two hippos, to get him up on his feet again.

'On the first Thursday after we started I was looking over the side of the ship. Suddenly I noticed something a little distance away. The waters, smooth enough, moved gently under a firm wind.

'Presently this thing I was watching rolled in the swell of the sea; and I saw it was a large uprooted tree. On it there was a man's body. The breeze brought it closer to the Ark's side. And then I could see there were two bodies on it: a man and a girl. Their eyes were closed. But something told me they were not just sleeping. They were dead or unconscious. The man had an ugly cut across the back of his neck. And the only thing which kept them at all upon that floating tree was that their arms and legs were so tangled up in the roots they just couldn't slip off.

'I was about to move away and go down to dinner, when the tree pitched and turned again. With the motion, the man's head rolled backward on his shoulders. And then, for the first time, I could see his face. It was Eber, the slave who had been so kind to us during our imprisonment!

'At first, thinking he was dead, I was very sad. He was the only man in the whole world that I had wanted saved from the Deluge. And now he had been drowned! ... It seemed so unfair.

'But, while I still watched the little waves gently lapping across his body, I saw his eyelids move – only a flutter; and his lips parted, though no sound came from them. Still, that was enough to tell me that at least he was yet alive.

'With a whoop of joy I bolted down below to find Noah, upsetting a pair of guinea-pigs who were playing some game on the stairs. On my way, I met Belinda; and I told her in a few hurried words what I had seen. Then the two of us started to run through the ship in search of Noah.

'We found the patriarch at dinner with his family.

' "Listen, Noah!" I cried, rushing up to him, breathless. "There's a man out there – in the water – floating on a tree. He's drowning – only half-conscious. It's Eber! You remember? – Your helper in the zoo. Come upstairs and save him – quick!"

'But, to our great surprise, Noah did not jump up and rush to the rescue. Instead, he chewed away till his mouth was empty – he was eating potatoes. Then he turned to me and said:

' "I've no authority to save him." Then he got that old paper out of his pocket. "What name did you say?" he asked.

' "Eber," I said impatiently – "Eber, your assistant."

' "I'm sorry," said he, reading the list on the paper. "But his name is not down here. There's nothing I can do."

'And he handed his plate to his wife for a second helping of potatoes.

'Then I think I went a little mad.

' "Look here!" I almost screamed at him. "Do you mean to tell me you're going to let that boy drown just because it isn't in your instructions to save him?"

' "I can do nothing," he repeated. "That's what it says: *Only the righteous shall be saved.*' I must obey the orders given me. – Ham, take your elbows off the table."

'I thought I would choke, I was so angry.

' "And is it your idea," I spluttered, "that you and your stuffy old family are the only righteous people on the Earth – the only ones worth saving? If that's how you've read your orders, then you've read them wrong, Noah. You've read them cross-eyed with stupid conceit. That boy Eber is just as righteous as you and all your family. If you will not save him, then I and my wife will leave the Ark this minute. For we would be ashamed to stay on it while such a man as Eber is dying out there."

'In answer, the old man said nothing – just went on munching potatoes.

'Then I turned to my wife.

' "Come," I said. "Let us leave the Ark to this self-righteous family and try to rescue that boy by ourselves. And if heaven is on our side we'll win, Belinda. For Gaza, too, is out there upon the floating tree. – Gaza, the Queen's singing-girl. Eber snatched her from the Flood – even while it threatened his own life. Come! Who knows? If they're both alive, that boy who was kind to us in our captivity may some day start a world and a people of his own." '

8

IN MID-OCEAN MUDFACE LEAVES THE ARK

'THEN, our noses in the air, Belinda and I walked out of Noah's dining-saloon and up the stairs to the main deck. With no hesitation we scrambled up the rail and dived straight into the sea. A crazy thing perhaps. But I have never been sorry for it – though we paid dearly enough later for our boldness. It took one hundred and fifty days – five whole months – for the Earth to show again after the Deluge.

'Eber himself was made of wonderful stuff. And it was he in the end – rather than Belinda and I – who saved Gaza. Any ordinary man would have died in the first week from exhaustion. But that boy, in his life as a slave, had grown hard and wiry.

'When we reached those two upon the floating tree they were in terrible shape. Their lips and tongues were swollen from sunburn and thirst. They lay upon that log like dead folk. Things didn't look hopeful at all. We saw at once that the tree was dreadfully low in the water and could not float much longer.

'So, first of all, Belinda and I untangled them from among the roots. Then each of us took one of them on our backs; and we swam off looking for something better to put them on. There was plenty of stuff still floating around – all manner of things, the wreckage of a lost world.

'After about an hour of hard swimming – you have no idea what a job it is for a turtle to keep his shell above water with the weight of a man on his back – we found something that would do. It was the roof of a small house, floating complete – just as it had been lifted off its walls by the Flood. And it was big enough to carry us all.

'Indeed it turned out to be almost as good as a ship. The

slope of the roof was gentle and flattish. Belinda and I climbed right up on to it with our burdens.

'There we laid the boy and girl down side by side. My, but they looked terrible! Eber's eyelids had not even moved again since that first flutter. Both he and Gaza were unconscious all the time.

'When we had got our breath, we two turtles talked over what we'd better do with these almost-dead humans. Neither of us had much idea of how to set about such a job – with people, that is; with turtles we could have been far more helpful. Anyway, we patted them and rubbed them gently with wet seaweed. But nothing seemed any use.

195

'We were both dreadfully discouraged. For it began to look as though we'd failed in our task; and these two poor youngsters were going to die before our eyes after all. My wife stood watching them gloomily a moment; and then she said:

' "Husband, I reckon it's food they want. This is the tenth day that they've been drifting on the ocean. It's not likely they've had a single thing to eat in all that time – except the bark or roots of that tree. See, Mudface, how thin and pinched the girl's cheeks are. It's food they need. I'm certain."

' "Ah, food!" said I. "That's easier said than found." And I gazed miserably all around the flat ocean trying to spy a single thing afloat that could be eaten by a man. . . . Nothing! – but driftwood and the wreckage of houses.

' "We haven't even fresh water," I said, almost weeping, "to let them drink."

'Then, suddenly, an idea came to me.

' "Listen, Belinda," I said. "It is no use our trying to find men's food in water. Men are land-creatures, remember. Fish would be our only chance – and all fish have run from the anger of the Flood and taken refuge in the deepest oceans. We've only one hope of getting food or drink for them."

' "And what is that?" she asked.

' "To swim down *under* the water," I answered, "till we come upon a city or town; and there to search among the houses of Men till we find Men's food."

' "I think you're crazy," said she. "Cities don't grow like pebbles on the beach. How do you think you'll find a town under this sea that covers the Earth? Why, we don't even know what side of the world we're on! We may be a thousand miles from any of the drowned lands where Men ever lived."

' "Perhaps, Belinda," said I. "Yet I'm going to try."

'I went to the edge of the raft to dive off.

' "Wait a minute," my wife called out. "I don't think there is any hope at all. But if you *should* find houses of Men, go down into the lowest room, the one underneath the ground – and bring wine. It is kept in bottles or jars; and it's always stored *below* the house. Wine is what Men use in case of sickness. When the Flood was first getting bad in Shalba, I saw many families trying to rescue their wine from beneath the ground. Of course, Mudface, bring any other food you can find. But be sure and bring that: *wine*. It is red in colour; and it grows in bottles, remember. – And listen: don't go off too far and get lost. If a storm should come up it may be more than I can manage, alone, to keep these two people from rolling off the raft."

' "All right, Belinda," I said. "And in the meantime you can busy yourself rigging up some sort of tent over Eber and the girl – there are still plenty of leafy boughs floating around. That girl's skin is all cracking open from the sun. Good-bye, my dear!"

'Then I dived into the water and disappeared.'

9

BELINDA'S BROTHER

'WELL, to begin with, I swam straight downward for nearly an hour. And at the end of that time I seemed no nearer the bottom than I was when I started. I was surely over low land or the bed of an old ocean.

'So I stopped swimming downward and took a new direction by the sun – which I could still dimly see far, far above me. Then I started off in a straight line westward: hunting for mountains; looking for a town; searching for a bottle of wine beneath the waters of the Flood – for Eber my friend.

'For another hour I kept on, swimming level. I began to

fear perhaps Belinda had been right – and I was on a fool's
errand – when I met another turtle. I spied him long before
he saw me. He was paddling away in a southerly direction,
at the same level as I was. What good luck – I said to myself – that the first living creature I meet in this puzzling,
underwater world turns out to be one of my own people,
a turtle! I hastened to overtake him.

'On coming nearer – would you believe it? – I recognized
an old friend; it was a relative of my wife's – her favourite brother, in fact – a splendid fellow.

'As soon as we had exchanged greetings, I told him what
I was after.

' "Well," said he, "if it's mountainous country you want,

you had better take me along. I've just left some quite high hills to the north of here. – Not what you'd call mountains exactly, but perhaps farther behind them we'll find a real range. . . . Isn't it splendid weather we're having – just the stuff for turtles? Quite new, all this water. I haven't had such a splendid swim in weeks. No traffic at all. I hope it keeps up. Was on my way to the Turtles' Meeting – a sort of convention, you know. I heard it's being held about a hundred miles from here. Our people are going to talk over what's to be done by all the water-folk, now that there's so little land anywhere. Important business! But I'll gladly turn back and lead you to the hilly ground I left – though it's still covered over, you understand. . . . How's Belinda?''

'He always had been a cheerful sort. And you've no idea how his chatty company cheered me up. My wife called him Wag – sort of a nickname.

'So off we went together. And, sure enough, after we'd travelled about half an hour we ran right into the face of a steep cliff. We crawled up this; and found ourselves on the top of a sort of rolling plain. We swam on farther; and soon we noticed that the ground was growing steeper. We were sure we were coming to real mountains.

'It was very strange to see, around these parts, land-trees still growing under water – and wide meadowy slopes where deer had once fed. Of course in the river-beds much damage had been done – great holes in the banks, big enough to put a large house in. Here, in the first fury of the Flood, the streams had torn out trees by the roots and swirled them down the hillsides, before beginnings of a calm had come to the tormented Earth.

'Soon I saw the tops of the mountains whose foothills we'd been exploring. I clambered up one of these to the peak. And there standing with my feet on a rock pinnacle (from which eagles had looked out in past times, no doubt) I found that by stretching up my neck I could just poke my nose out into the air. Only six feet of water covered the top of that mountain! It was a strange feeling to look over a flooded world with my feet on *land*.

' "Within a few days," I said to Wag, "this mountain-top will show above the Deluge."

' "What a pity!" said he.

' "Oh, I don't know," I answered. "It's sort of dreary, all this wet desolation. I know it's grand for us water-animals. But somehow I'll be glad to see the land-creatures around again. – Besides, the scenery was better the way it was, too."

'Now of course, where the water was so shallow the light was much brighter.

' "Listen, Wag," said I. "We mustn't waste any time in hunting up a town or a village where we can find food. I'm awfully worried about that boy. Suppose we separate and search in two directions at once. You go east and I'll go west. And let's meet here again in half an hour."

'Well, on that first trip we had no luck. We met again as planned; and because night was not far off we agreed to give up the hunt till next day. We lay down where we were on the mountain-top to sleep.'

'Pardon me,' the Doctor interrupted. 'You slept on the rock, eh? But you have often spoken of how much you like mud. Tell me: can turtles see in the mud?'

'No,' said the great creature – 'at least very little. While moving or travelling in mud you find your way by bumping instead of seeing. When you meet anything, and you want to be sure what it is, you bump it. Then you know.'

'Ha!' murmured Cheapside. 'There you 'ave the sixth sense, Doc, what you naturalists is always talking about: hearing, tasting, touching, smelling, seeing – and bumping. – Glad I don't have to travel under the mud. . . . I wonder how you tell the time.'

'One of the *senses you* haven't got, Cheapside,' snapped

his wife, Becky, 'is *common* sense. For pity's sake hold your tongue and let the turtle get along with his story!'

'Thank you, Mudface,' said the Doctor. 'Please go on.'

'I ain't worried about his *going* on,' whispered Cheapside – 'Question is: when is 'e goin' to *stop*? Old Mud-pie has been drooling longer than usual tonight, seems like.'

'Well of course, John Dolittle,' said the turtle, 'our eyes are always very good and far-seeing. But in exploring a whole country for houses, when we had to work in a hurry, we needed the best light we could get. That's why I had come to the high mountain levels, where the shallower water would let more of the sunshine through.

'Early next morning Wag said to me, "Let's go off to the other end of this mountain-range. I fear we're not going to have much luck around here."

'I agreed. And together we set off, keeping along the top of the ridge, so we could find our way back. We had gone about ten miles when suddenly we came to a deep gap in the mountains – a sort of saddle. Across on the other side of this we could dimly see the ridge and the line of peaks going on into the distance.

'Wag wanted to swim across this gap at the level we now stood at – to save distance and time. But I said: "No. It will take us longer, I agree, to go down into this saddle and crawl up the other side. But I have a feeling that if we swim over it we may miss something. Let's explore it on foot."

'And it was lucky we did – or Eber might have died before I got back to him; and the later history of the world would have been different.'

10

WINE BENEATH THE SEA

'AFTER we had gone down the slope of this gap a little distance I spied something whitish in the gloom below. It looked tremendously long and snaky; and, as far as I could make out, it wound its way still lower, towards the very foot of the mountains – where it faded into the dark of the deeper water. When we had climbed down to it we found it flat and hard. It was about twelve feet wide.

' "What on earth is this?" asked Wag.

' "This," I said, "is called a road – sort of a trail. Men, when they travel, don't go straight across country, like we do – through swamps and everything. They have to have a track prepared for them, along which they drive in carts, or walk."

'By the edge of the road there stood a square, chiselled stone with some letters on it.

' "And this stone," I said, "is a milestone. I wish I could read those letters – then I could tell how far we have to go. We will follow this road; and it will lead us to a town. This highway has been made to cross the mountain-range at the lowest point – through this saddle, see? My, but I'm glad we came down into this gap on foot instead of swimming across it! How stupid of us! We could have saved ourselves the trouble of looking for towns on the top of the ridge. Let us hurry, Wag. Eber and the girl are starving for food."

'So off we tramped, side by side, along the broad road leading downward, towards a valley. And as it took us lower and lower, the light grew dimmer and dimmer. Presently the country began to flatten out into what looked

more like real farming land. By counting the milestones,
we knew how far we had come – but, alas, not how far we
had to go!

'Just as we were passing out of sight of the mountains
we'd left, we came upon something strange. It was an out-
post or a sentry station. This was to mark the line between
one kingdom and another. We had no idea what kingdoms
they had been: but clearly the lands of one king had run
up to the foot of the mountains. And there, before the
Flood, soldiers had been posted to guard the borders of his
kingdom. The men's spears and helmets, reddening with
rust, were stacked against the little shelter-hut beside the
road. Near the hut there was a well. And its wooden bucket,

tied at the end of a rope, now stood straight upright, floating at anchor a hundred feet above our heads. Wag laughed outright at the sight of it.

' "The big rain certainly turned things upside down all right," said he. And he was all for biting the rope in two, just for the fun of seeing the bucket shoot up to the surface of the ocean. But I made him leave it and hurry on. I had no idea what time it was – being unable down here to see the sun. I was afraid night might come on and force us to rest again till the following day. So on we went.

'After we passed the fifth milestone we suddenly stumbled upon an axe lying in the middle of the road.

' "That's a good sign," I said. "A town or a village is probably not far off now."

'And I was right. Near the sixth milestone we came to the outskirts of a town – at first no more than a few houses, set wide apart, here and there on either side of the road. – Heavens! You could scarcely call them houses any more. Roofless they were, most of them; while some had had their walls undermined by rushing water and were now just piles of bricks and mortar.

'However, we pried and searched each one of them in turn, hunting for that precious bottle of wine. Such rubbish and wreckage we dug through! The first building was a blacksmith's shop; and the smith's tools lay around the anvil, where he had dropped them to flee for his life. There was no food here.

'Of course, getting into the cellars of some of the houses in our hunt for wine was often impossible, on account of the big stones that blocked the cellar-stairs. But the homes became more plentiful as we went on; and I was tremendously excited and hopeful. I hustled Wag along at such a pace from door to door, the poor fellow had to swim half the time to keep up with my longer legs.

'At last, when we had reached a sort of town-square or market, we saw a large brick house, complete and almost

HUGH LOFTING

undamaged. Over the door hung a sign with the picture of a bottle on it.

' "If I'm not mistaken," I said to my brother-in-law, "this is a wine shop. And if we can make our way into it, I believe our search is ended."

'We found the doors and all the windows locked. How to get in? That was going to be a problem. But at last Wag thought of the chimney. – He was no fool. By swimming up on to the roof, we were able to scramble our way down a dirty, sooty chimney; and we came out, by the fireplace, into the large main room of the house. Here we found bottles in plenty. But they had all been opened and the wine washed out of them long ago.

'Then we went down into the cellar, where, to our great delight, we saw rows and rows of more bottles stacked up neatly against the walls. These had their corks still firmly fastened in them. Down here the light was awfully bad – the cellar having only one small window, high up in the west wall. So, to make sure these bottles were not empty too, we smashed one against the stone floor. And Wag whooped with joy as the ruby wine flowed out and mingled with the water all about us. It got in our noses and made us awful dizzy – so that for a while we could barely make our way around.

' "Ah, at last, at last!" I hiccoughed to Wag. "Now let's each of us take two bottles and get out of here – while we can still stand up."

'Just as we were about to leave – by the chimney again – I remembered that, besides the wine, I ought to take something for my friends to eat. So once more we hunted through the flooded rooms looking for food of a solid kind.

'In a cupboard we came upon some loaves of bread. But these were ruined by the water and fell to pieces as soon as we touched them. However, in the same closet, on the top shelf, Wag found a basket of apples, three unopened coconuts and a whole cheese. There were some old sacks lying in a corner of the cellar. We put some of the fruit, the cheese and two bottles of wine into a couple of these bags.

'It wasn't easy, scrabbling back up the chimney, dragging those loads clutched in our mouths. But at last we managed it; and came out on to the roof. I mumbled to Wag through a mouth full of sacking,

' "Your sister said I'd never do it. Won't *she* be surprised? Let's go! It's quite a while since I left her – and we might yet be too late to save that brave boy's life. Swim your best now, Wag – *swim!*" '

11

EBER SAVES GAZA'S LIFE

'THE journey back to the raft, in spite of the loads we dragged, did not take as long as the outward trip. I had been careful to watch and remember every change of direction I'd made since I left Belinda. And when Wag and I bobbed up to the surface of the water I at once looked at the sun. It was still fairly high; so there would be some hours yet before darkness. I took a bearing on it and led my brother-in-law off in a straight line for where I reckoned the raft to be.

'Up here, on the top, it was a great change to feel the comforting hot sun on our shells, instead of the numbing cold which had chilled us in the lower depths. Putting our best foot forward, we churned along merrily to make good time.

'At last, afar off on the rim of the sea, we spied a black speck which I felt sure must be the raft. We sighted it at this long range because Belinda, while I'd been gone, had built a fine roof of leaves and boughs to shade the girl from the sun; and this, upstanding like the mast of a ship, could be seen from quite a distance.

'As soon as I'd come within hearing, I called to my wife, "Have they opened their eyes yet?"

' "No," she answered.

' "Are they still breathing?" I yelled.

' "Yes. – But that's about all."

'Indeed it was a close thing. When Wag and I dragged our burdens up on to that raft those two people were as near dead as anyone could be. I immediately got a bottle of wine out of my sack. And then we found the cork so tight in the neck that we couldn't budge it. Both Belinda and I were almost weeping from rage and impatience as we struggled with it. Why on earth had these silly men-creatures invented such a crazy way to seal their wine?

'But the good Wag again came to the rescue. "Give it to me," he said sharply.

'I handed it over. And in a flash he'd bitten the head right off the bottle and was spitting the broken glass out into the sea. Then, while my wife gently prised open Eber's clenched teeth with her front claws, I poured the gurgling wine into the boy's throat.

'It acted like magic. In a moment his hands began to open and shut. Then his head started rolling slowly from side to side. And presently he opened his eyes. They were blue in colour – like the sea when the sun is shining. But a great fear showed in them, as he gazed round into the faces of us who had rescued him from death.

'I was puzzled by this – at the time. Yet I suppose it was natural enough. We were not of his kind. And awakening from a long wet sleep to find three giant turtles bending over him (Wag, who had a trickle of blood running from his mouth, where the broken glass had cut him a little, looked especially tough) Eber must, no doubt, have gotten something of a shock. And remember, the boy had already been through all the terrors of the Deluge.

'But presently I could see, from a changing expression in the lad's eyes, that he half recognized me. For, ever so slightly, he smiled up into my face. And, though you may hardly believe it, John Dolittle, that smile brought me one of the greatest thrills I'd felt since before I'd lost my freedom in King Mashtu's zoo.

'I had paid back a debt.

'Presently the boy closed his eyes and seemed to sleep again.

' "Let him rest now, husband," said Belinda. "We have the girl, too, to look after. Bring the bottle over here and I'll see if I can open her mouth without hurting these cracked lips."

' "Wait!" cried my brother-in-law. "Don't you two realize what you're doing? Eber was your friend, Mudface. That's different. But who is this woman? If you save her too, she'll marry the boy and raise a family. We'll have the Earth overrun with Men again. Zoos for animals and all that; while now the Earth belongs to us, the water-creatures – as it should do. Why bother with the girl?"

' "Brother," I answered, "the boy would be lonely in a world all to himself, with no others of his own kind – just as you or I would be. I doubt if he would want to live, if we let her die. For Eber – for my friend's sake – she *must* be saved."

'And, bending over Gaza, Belinda and I set to work.

'Bringing the woman to her senses was a much harder job than reviving the man. We found that on her the wine didn't seem to do any good at all. After we had worked over her for a full half-hour – and she still lay like a lifeless thing – Belinda and I became very discouraged.

' "I'm afraid," said my wife, frowning, "that with her, Mudface, we are too late."

' "You think she is already dead?" I asked fearfully.

' "Yes," whispered Belinda. "Her flesh is growing cold. She is not as strong as the man. It is no use pouring more wine into her. See, she does not swallow it."

' "Alas," I said, "that it should be so! I feel sorrier for Eber than I do for her. . . . Well, if she is dead, then let us roll her quietly into the ocean – before the boy wakes up again and sees us do it."

'So, with heavy hearts, my wife and I began to push her towards the edge of the raft.

'But just as we were about to thrust her body into the water, I felt something clutch the shoulder of my shell from behind. With a guilty start, I turned my head. It was Eber. His eyes were staring wildly from his exhausted, haggard face; his left hand gripped me; while his arm reached out over my back towards the girl.

' "What is it?" I asked Belinda. "What does he want?"

' "He's trying to stop us from burying her in the sea,"
said my wife. "Maybe he thinks she is not dead yet. Stand
aside and let us see what he will do."

'We drew Gaza's body back from the roof's edge and
laid it at his feet. Over it Eber knelt; and, while big tears
welled up in his blood-shot eyes, he bent and listened at
her heart. Then suddenly with frantic efforts he tried to
roll her over, face downward. The task was too much for
his weakened strength – and we helped him. Next, he
pressed her back and sides, then he worked her arms up and
down.

'He seemed to know a lot more about what to do with

half-drowned humans than we did; for when, in answer to his signals, we turned her face-upward again, we could see that she was now plainly breathing – though with a gurgling sound in her throat.

'Presently Eber pointed to the bottle. And this time after we trickled the wine into her mouth, she gulped and swallowed it.

'And then – thank goodness! – she too opened her eyes.

'At that the lad gave a great cry of joy. Suddenly he fainted from exhaustion, fell down beside the woman and lay still.'

12

THE SIGN IN THE SKY

'AND, a moment later, we knew that Eber and the girl were sound asleep. Belinda and I breathed a sigh of thankfulness.

' "They will both live," said my wife, turning away. "Let us get out the fruit and cheese you brought and prepare it against the time when they awake."

' "Well," muttered my brother-in-law, opening the second sack, "it seems all wrong to me. However – just as you say, Belinda. But remember, if you're sorry for this later, don't say I didn't warn you. – *Don't say I didn't warn you!*"

' "And where," my wife asked of him, "did you pop up from, Wag? I've been too busy with this job even to give you a single word of greeting. – Gracious, what a home to welcome you to! – But it's good to have you with us, brother. For we're in need of cheerful company. Tell me: how is it you and Mudface returned together?"

' "Oh," said Wag airily, "we ran into one another – by chance, you know. Your husband was hunting for mountains; and he took me along – just for the trip."

'Wag was never one to boast.

' "Don't you believe him, Belinda," said I. "He was tremendously useful to me. It was he who led me to the country where we found the wine. I don't know what I could have done without him." '

'Hah!' whispered Cheapside the sparrow. 'That's what the Doctor's always sayin': "what *would* I do without you?" ... Funny, how people is always wondering what they'd do without you – when you're useful: and when you ain't, they're wonderin' what they'll do *with* you.'

'That's not surprising – in your case,' murmured Becky wearily.

'Cockney chatterbox!' snapped Polynesia the parrot. 'I'd hate to tell you what I would like to do with you – if you don't keep quiet.'

'Tee, hee, hee!' tittered the white mouse.

'Ho, indeed!' said Cheapside, turning upon Polynesia and bristling up for a fight. 'Becky was talkin' to *me*. But of course *you* have to shove yer hooked nose in, interfering between 'usband and wife. Breakin' up 'omes and the like – you – you flyin' carpet, you! Why, for two pins I'd –'

'Now, now!' said the Doctor quickly. 'Stop the squabbling, *please*! Isn't it bad enough to have me interrupting with questions all the time, without you birds starting a fight? Settle down, settle down for pity's sake and let's hear the rest of Mudface's story.'

'Okay, Doc,' said Cheapside wearily. 'But I do wish old Fuddymuddy would lay off for the night. I'm gettin' sleepy.'

'By the way, Mudface,' said the Doctor. 'Some time back you spoke of Noah eating potatoes on the Ark. In our histories, potatoes were not known on this side of the world till long after the Flood. Sir Walter Raleigh is said to have brought them back with him from the Americas. I meant to ask you about it, when you told us of Noah eating them; but I forgot. I won't stop your story for that question at this time. But remind me to ask you later on. Please go ahead now – whenever you are ready.'

'And so,' the turtle went on, 'I moved down to the other

end of the raft to help Wag get out the food which Belinda had asked for. But I had hardly turned my back when she suddenly cried out, "Look, *look*!"

'I swung round and found her pointing at the western skyline. And there, just peeping out of the waters, was a mountain-top!

'A drowned world was at last arising from the Flood!

'That mountain-peak was a long way off and very little of it showed as yet; but the setting sun behind made it stand out sharp and clear. I turned once more to help Wag – facing eastward now. And in that quarter, where a slight shower was falling, I saw a rainbow. Two great, gaily-coloured arches, one within the other, curved across the sky, dazzlingly bright.

'The gorgeous beauty of that double rainbow fairly took your breath away; and I could not take my eyes off it. I felt my wife move up close to me, her shell touching mine. And together, in solemn silence, we gazed at this glory of the heavens – till it began to grow dim in the twilight of coming night.

' "It is a sign, husband," whispered Belinda, "a sign of better things and brighter days to come – with this first showing of the drying land."

' "Maybe so," said I. "Anyway, my dear, I'm glad we saved those youngsters. For, come what may, at least we've made a good start – in whatever new world is being born tonight."

'Then the rainbow faded out, as the sun behind us slipped gently into the sea.'

13

A NEW LANGUAGE IS BORN

'WHEN, next day, dawn broke over a sunlit sea, the tip of the mountain, which Belinda had sighted, showed much plainer – and larger. My wife and I took to the water and pulled the raft close to it. Then Eber and Gaza got out on to the land at last.

'They were both of course still very weak and exhausted. The mountain-top had nothing on it whatever to eat. It was all bare rock. But firm land of any kind was better for them than the raft, which had often pitched and swung terribly in the swell of the ocean.

'In a day or so the fruit and cheese which we had got for them was nearly gone – since the two, as soon as their appetites came back, needed more food. So I made many trips again to the village of the wine shop, away down in the drowned valley, to get more supplies. And besides food, I brought up blankets for them which, when dried, kept off the cold night winds. I got tools, too, to make things with – axes and the like.'

'Excuse me,' the Doctor interrupted again. 'But how did you communicate with Eber? – What I mean is: he couldn't talk your language, could he? How did you manage about that?'

'No,' said the turtle. 'At first it was very difficult. Belinda and I had to do a lot of guessing over what things he needed. Besides, Eber could not even talk the girl's language. This surprised us; for we had supposed that all men used the same talk – the way we turtles do, all over the world. But, you will remember that these two young people, although they had met in Shalba, were not born there. They were both slaves; they had been brought to Mashtu's court from different lands, as prisoners of war: Eber, the clever gardener and Gaza, the beautiful singer. And neither one spoke the other's language.

'Now, as I have said, everything in Shalba was very grand – away ahead of all other countries – for the free people, that is: the Shalbians themselves. Especially education. After paper was invented – instead of that old clumsy business of writing on bricks – all who were free people learned to read and write.

'Besides the main library in the Square of Victory, there were many smaller branch libraries all about the city; and book-stores and magazine-stands on every street-corner. Millions of books were printed every year. Myself, I think there were far too many books. Everyone spent his time loafing around, reading. And – still worse – if they weren't *reading* books, they were *writing* them. Everybody seemed to think he just had to write a book. Goodness only knows why! So you see the Shalbians had plenty to read; and if anyone wasn't well educated, it was his own fault.

'But now, with the drowning of the world, all this printed stuff was swept away, every bit of it – except a few story books which were taken on to the Ark by Ham, the lazy one. But even these were later eaten up by the goats, when their regular food ran low. – You know, Doctor, goats don't seem to care *what* they eat.

'Sometimes I think that was perhaps the only good thing the Deluge did: sweeping away all the books. Because if it hadn't, the authors, who made their living by writing books, would surely have had to go out of business – into plough-ing or something – since there would have been nothing left to write about when the Flood was over.

'But for those who were slaves it was very different, of course. They had to do honest real work – and plenty of it. For them there was no time to learn reading and writing. All they had was the spoken language they were born with.

'And when Eber and Gaza found themselves rescued to-gether on our raft, a new language was made. Up to that

215

time, just making love as they had done in the Royal Park, well, *that* of course has always been something that needed no *real* language at all. Folks in love get along simply with "*Goo, goo!*" and such stuff; but now these two had to talk really – sensibly.

'At first it was a puzzle for them. They began by picking up things and saying a sound. And that sound would be whatever their mothers had taught them when they were little. Eber would pick up, for instance, an apple; and say to the girl, "*Boo-boo?*" Then Gaza would shake her head and say, "*Bah-bah.*" So in the end they would mix the two sounds and call it a *boo-bah*. And in that way boobah became the word for apple in their new language.

'By this time dear old Wag had gone off and left us – because he suddenly remembered he had a wife and family of his own somewhere, who probably needed looking after. So then there were only Belinda and I to listen to this new language which Eber and Gaza were building up together, word by word. We were tremendously interested. And of course we could not help but learn it too – after a fashion. I mean, to *understand* what was being said: of course we never learned to *speak* it – turtle talk being so different.

'But I'm sure if there had been other kinds of animals on our raft, some of them at least would have learned to talk it, as well as to understand it. And then you might have had animal-folk and human-folk talking to one another like friends everywhere – which of course is the way it should have been in the new-born world.

'Soon after the first mountain-top appeared and showed that the Earth was drying again, a visitor turned up. It was a raven. He had been sent out by Noah from the Ark to look for land. He stayed with us for quite a while. He said the Ark smelled like everything; and he wasn't going back to it for the patriarch Noah or anybody else – not to stay.

'He was good company – even if he was an everlasting chatterbox. And he learned the new language of Eber and

Gaza better than any of us. But I heard that later – when his mating season came around and he went off and left us for a while – he soon forgot almost every word of man talk which he'd learned. That's the way with ravens, you know: easy come, easy go. But he was very useful to Belinda and me while he was with us.

'Our mountain-top of course kept growing bigger and bigger with the lowering of the water. But still we could find no food fit to eat. Soon other peaks of mountains began to show here and there, like a chain of islands. I swam over to some of them and hunted for food. But scarcely a thing could I find. And I came back to the raft very discouraged, because I knew how starved that boy and girl were.

'Belinda, the raven and I agreed that Eber and Gaza were getting into poor health for want of something decent to eat; and, although they complained hardly at all, we knew that human-folk couldn't live long without regular meals. Suddenly the raven said,

' "Look here, you two: it's quite likely I can find my way back to the smelly old Ark. There, too, everyone was desperately hungry. But when I left, Old Man Noah had put everybody on strict rations – only so much to a meal, you know – to make the grub last longer. What do you say I go and look for him?"

'My wife and I both agreed readily.

' "When I saw him last," the raven went on, "Noah was just batting around looking for land. Since I didn't go back to him he's probably still waiting for me. There won't be a lot to eat on the Ark; but your boy and girl will certainly be no worse off than they are on this boulder of bare rock – and perhaps much better. I might be able to pinch a few things from the larder for them meanwhile – if Mrs Noah isn't looking. Anyway, it's worth trying, don't you think?"

'We said we were sure it was. And right away the raven took wing – flying up to a great height, so he could look over a good wide stretch of the sea. Then off he went towards the south-west.

'To our great delight he was back again in three hours. And he was all out of breath from excitement.

' "What *do* you think?" he gasped as he landed on the raft. "Noah and his Ark – I tracked 'em down more by smell than anything else – have found land on their own account! – Or rather the land found *them*, I should say. The ship ran ashore on another mountain-top which lay just beneath the level of the water. Very proud, the Noah family is. You'd think they'd found the land by mathematics – when really they only escaped a shipwreck by good luck."

' "Oh, how splendid!" cried Belinda.

' "That was about a week ago – when they ran ashore, I mean. And now there's quite a wide piece of land showing on the mountain – with that smelly old Ark sitting up in the middle on top of it. Looks like an island wearing a cock-eyed hat. Mrs Pigeon told me the mountain is called Ararat – though how they're sure of that, goodness only knows. Myself, I don't think Old Man Noah has any better idea of where in the world he is than you have here."

' "I didn't stop to explore," said the raven. "As soon as I'd made sure of their position, I flew straight back here. – Thought you and Belinda would want to hear the news as soon as possible. There's a full moon tonight. Soon as I've got my breath I'll lead you over there. Gather up those young people and get them on the raft. Hitch on those vine towing-ropes you used before; and let's get started, if you want to come."

' "Don't worry, Raven," said I. "We'll waste no time."

' "And listen," said he: "I'll fly ahead of you – but slow enough so you won't lose me against the night sky. I can see the moonlight flashing on your wet shells as you swim. The two of you, harnessed to that light raft, can make a fair speed. I'll keep an eye on you. – And bring what's left of that fresh rainwater you caught in the last shower we had. The direction we'll travel will be a little south of south-west. If all goes well we ought to sight the Ark by daybreak – and if we don't see it, we'll smell it, believe me."

'My wife and I were very grateful to the raven and we began getting ready at once. We rounded up Eber and Gaza who had gone off exploring somewhere on our island hill-top. We made them understand by signs that we were leaving for a new part of the ocean. And the raven was very proud that he could squawk, *"Ark! Ark!"* Because they understood then where we were going.'

14

THE TIGRESS

'The journey went off very smoothly. A nice steady wind followed behind us and made our job much easier and faster than we'd hoped for.

'As the sun rose next morning it showed another island ahead of us. The raven was right: Noah's ship, which had been so much trouble to build, was perched, all lop-sided, on a high peak in the middle of this island. From afar off it did look like a crazy hat.

'As we pulled the raft in closer, we saw animals of different kinds standing around it on the rock – and Noah's family in twos and threes also. Nobody seemed to be doing anything. And as we drew closer yet, we saw why: there was nothing whatever growing on this island either. All the trees had been killed by the salt-water; and seeds of the grasses and plants had been rotted and spoiled.

'The starving animals, as soon as they saw our raft coming, rushed down to us at the shore, hoping, poor things, that we'd brought food for them. The raven whispered to me, "Look out for that big cat in the front of the gang, the tigress. It's good-bye to Eber and Gaza, once she gets her claws on them. She's a meat-eater – and a fiend."

' "Yes, she looks big and savage enough to eat anything," said Belinda.

' "You bet," said the raven. "Mrs Pigeon told me that the mother-pig had a family of babies while the Ark was at sea – and she wasn't the only one. – The mother-animals kept Noah busy, with the food running short and all. Well, that tigress, when the old man wasn't looking, ate up three of the baby-pigs. Of course there were plenty left in the litter. But Mrs Pig made no end of fuss. – Can't blame her altogether. After that, Noah, who is the only one the tigress

is afraid of, made her promise – with a pitchfork – to leave the piglets alone. But I wouldn't trust her farther than I could carry her in my beak. Keep an eye on her, Mudface. You and your wife are safe against her – with your hard shells. But Eber and Gaza; they're juicy. Remember, a hungry tigress is about the most dangerous beast in the world."

'Belinda and I *did* remember it. We took no chances – for the boy and girl – with Mrs Tiger.

'For the present I left the raft floating a quarter-mile away from the island; only so, I knew, would Eber and Gaza be safe – because the tigress couldn't swim. But, to make double-sure, I asked the raven to stay with them on the raft and bring me word if anything went wrong. Then Belinda and I swam ashore to look for Noah.

'We found the patriarch in an even greater state of puzzlement than he was when building the Ark. Food, food, *food* was his trouble now. All the supplies of hay and such stuff were pretty nearly eaten up; and the animals that lived on meat hadn't had a meal for days. Things looked awful bad. After we had talked to the old man a while we swam back to the raft. And I said to the raven,

' "It's no use our staying around here. There isn't a bite of food to spare – except the fish which the seals are catching; and that's barely enough to feed themselves and their pups."

' "Humph!" said the raven. "If you'll mount guard over the raft here I'll fly across to the Ark presently and see if I can swipe a piece of bacon for you. But I can't carry much you know."

' "Listen," said Belinda: "do you know what I think we should do? – Try to find our way back to Shalba. I've no idea how far Africa is from here. But you remember Mashtu's Royal Botanical Gardens. Every fruit-tree, oranges, olives, bananas, grapes, pineapples – everything was grown there. Surely some of them must be left." '

'Pardon,' said the Doctor. 'But are you sure about the pineapples? Christopher Columbus, you know, was supposed to be the discoverer who first brought them to this side of the world – long after the Deluge.'

'If you'll allow me, Doctor,' said the turtle, 'I'll answer that question too, later on? For the present it may interest you to know that, in the days of Shalba, not only did we have nearly every fruit you can find today, but many more besides. You see, the Flood killed off many delicious fruits and vegetables – with their seeds – so that they never grew in our earth again.'

'Oh quite, quite,' said John Dolittle – 'most interesting. Certainly put off all that till you're ready to tell it. I am most keen now to hear what luck you had in trying to get back to Shalba from the Ark. – Excuse my breaking in, please. What did Belinda say next?'

' "Well," she said, "we've *got* to do something, Mudface. Eber and Gaza are going to starve to death if we stay here."

'That raven was a clever and adventurous bird. (He had already slipped across to the Ark and got a piece of bacon for us.)

' "You're right," he said after thinking a minute. "I'm willing – though I have only a foggy notion which way to go to reach Africa. But I've always trusted my good luck. Maybe we'll fall in with other animals on the way – water-creatures – or what not – who are still alive. For myself, I can probably pick up a thing or two to eat. If it hadn't been for the floating plants, which use no roots – like the water-hyacinth – those two elephants over there would have been dead long ago. Water-hyacinth is all right for vegetable-feeders – if they can find nothing better. But it carries air-balls to keep it floating. And Mrs Pigeon told me the bull-elephant nearly died of colic – gas on the stomach, you know. And when an elephant has gas, he has an awful lot. Like a balloon – very uncomfortable. But he stayed alive."

' "It's those youngsters I'm worried about," said Belinda. "They're just skin and bone. ... Shalba! It's a long trip ahead of us."

' "Well, now," said the raven, "perhaps we can pick up a cormorant – or some other fishing bird – and take him along. If we can, we'll be all right, you know. We'll manage on shrimps, flying-fish and such food. You turtles are too slow for that kind of diving and catching. Myself, being a land bird, I'd be even less use. But a cormorant or a king-fisher could keep us supplied."

'And so it was agreed that all five of us would set out on a very daring journey. I was afraid to keep those youngsters near that fiendish tigress.

'No doubt it's natural that meat-eating animals should

223

kill others, to get food. But Eber and Gaza were now the same to Belinda and me as our own children. I am sure that neither Belinda nor I would have hesitated one second to give our own lives, if it would have saved those youngsters from destruction.

'The animals around the Ark were sorry to have us go. They had seen how I had come through the Flood – leaving the Ark and going off on my own; and how Belinda and I had now returned after rescuing two human beings from drowning. They had hoped I would stay with them for a while to help them with my cunning and wisdom. Seeing their food growing less and less each day, they were losing their faith in Noah as a leader – and they too were afraid of that tigress.

'The deer, giraffes and the rest gathered around, begging us to stay or to take them with us. I felt sorry for them. But the mysterious thought that I might yet be more useful in saving one man and one woman – the very creatures whose kind had imprisoned me and enslaved the world – that thought kept coming back to me: Eber and Gaza must live at all costs. To the hungry animals that clustered around me as I crawled back ashore, I found my heart grow suddenly, strangely hard. All I said was:

' "I must go. I've only returned for a barrel of fresh water to take on the raft. But no one, except my wife, the boy and girl and the raven, come with me on this voyage." '

15

THE RAVEN MEETS WITH ADVENTURES

AFTER we had left the Ark this second time, the clumsy old ship seemed to drop out of sight below the skyline strangely fast. And then only wide empty seas spread all around us again – which gave us a feeling of great loneliness.

'Now an odd thing I'd noticed as we had pulled away from those islands was that some storks and sea-birds seemed to be following us – just drifting here and there, in twos and threes, as if on no particular business.

'Belinda too was uneasy about them. "It looks to me, Mudface," she said, "as if those birds might be trailing us. – Yet why? They're a lot better off, on the Ark back there, than we are – with only a pound of bacon between us. Whatever are they up to? ... I don't like it. – Wish they'd mind their own business."

'I said nothing in answer. But I well knew of what – or of whom – my wife was thinking.

'As for the raven, he gave them only one glance, frowned and then went on with his calculations for the voyage.

' "Let me see," said he: "we are starting about the second hour after sunrise" – though I myself was by no means certain of the time, because –'

'I wish he'd stop trying to remember what time it was,' whispered Polynesia to me in her squawky voice. 'All I want to know is, what *happened*.'

'The raven seemed a little puzzled in his reckoning. "Look here," he said presently, "suppose you keep pulling the raft along this line, changing your course gradually for the position of the sun. I will go ahead of you, flying high; and maybe I'll see something. If I do, I'll come back over this same course and meet you. But, remember: if it gets cloudy and there's no sun to guide you, stop dead where you are and leave it to *me* to find *you*."

'So the raven went off. And we ploughed along through the seas, at an easy pace. After about a couple of hours the sun did cloud over; and remembering our instructions, Belinda and I at once stopped swimming, so as to stay more or less in the same place.

'My wife got sort of anxious. "What would happen," she asked, "if the raven was unable to pick us up again?" A

225

heavy mist lay on the breast of the waters and you couldn't see more than ten feet ahead of you.

' "Don't worry," said I. "That raven, though he's no sea-bird, is clever. He'll get in touch with us again – never fear, if the mist lasts for three days. We've got a whole keg of fresh water, remember – and that piece of bacon he took from Mrs Noah's larder. There's no need to get nervous about the youngsters yet."

'But night settled down upon the ocean with still no sign of the raven. And next morning, I confess, I was very un-easy when I awoke to find the sea mist as thick as ever. Belinda was of course full of worries: what if the mist should last a whole week? The piece of bacon would keep Eber and the girl for only a couple of days. Suppose the raven himself was lost, having no sun to go by? – And a whole lot more.

'But I kept on telling her that I had faith in that chatter-box; and I was quite sure he would turn up any minute, so long as we did as we were told and didn't drag the raft all over the ocean looking for *him*.

'Well, I got the poor old lady quieted down at last – though I never let her know how unhappy I felt myself.

'Somewhere around half past five in the evening – no, maybe later – six or half past, as near as I could judge by the growing dark – '

'Oh, gracious,' sighed Too-Too. 'Now he's worrying about the time again.'

'Well, anyhow, the light was very dim, I remember,' the turtle went on, 'when I thought I heard a sound away off over the stillness of the misty sea.

' "Belinda," I whispered, "did you hear that?"

' "No," she grumbled. "I heard nothing."

' "It's coming from behind you," I said. "Listen again."

'We both strained our ears. And, sure enough, a long way off we could both hear a faint, hoarse sort of cry: *"C-r-a-r-k!* . . . *C-r-a-r-k!"*

' "The *raven*!" I whispered to my wife, nearly falling into the water in my excitement. "I told you he'd never get lost. He's hunting for us somewhere. Let's answer him!"

'Then the two of us let out the most awful noises you ever heard. We waited. A moment passed. And at last we were answered. This time the grating voice came closer still – though the fog was terrible. Soon we felt, rather than saw, dark shapes which swept and circled in the air about us.

'Then, *plop! plop!* – two somethings – the light was too bad to tell what they were yet – landed on the raft between Belinda and myself.

' "Is that you, Raven?" I asked the smaller one.

' "Did you think it was Father Christmas?" growled the scrapy voice. "Gosh! What a night!"

' "And who's that, the dumpy thing over there, you've brought with you?" asked Belinda.

' "Sh!" hissed the raven. – "Not so loud! That's a pelican, the diving bird I said I'd look for. Marvellous to see him work – brings up a pailful of herring in one swoop. But they're very touchy about their looks, pelicans. – Reminds you of a cross between a coal-shovel and a coffee-pot. Stop staring at him, will you? – *He* can't help his shape."

' "Oh, Raven!" sighed Belinda. "What *would* we have done without you?" '

Cheapside woke up with a snap.

'There you are! See what I mean?' he asked.

'Oh, go to sleep!' muttered Becky. – 'Wonderful how you can always pick the wrong time for wakin' up – and the wrong one for goin' to sleep!'

'Now, now!' said the Doctor gently. 'Let Mudface get on.'

'The next day,' said the turtle, 'we were glad to find the fog cleared away and the sun shining brightly. There was no land in sight. But over breakfast the raven told us of his adventures since he had seen us last.

' "I kept straight on, like I told you," said he, "but I couldn't seem to find a piece of land big enough for a

canary to perch on. It was getting dark; so knowing I was
going to have to spend the night at sea, I flew around as best
I could in circles. I was aiming to stay in the same place till
sunrise. But Jiminy! In the morning the fog was worse than
ever.

' "Well, after slapping around a while longer I spied what
might be a barrel, floating a ways off. I was tired from flying
all night. And I needed some place to rest. On my way to
the barrel I picked up an orange. It was pretty rotten; but
I reckoned that if I could get it to the barrel I might be able
to make a breakfast off what good seeds were left inside it.
When I got close I saw there was another bird sitting on the
barrel. I recognized him at once – the last kind of bird in
the world you'd expect to find in a place like that. I know
neither of you will believe me; but it was a *dove* – not
stuffed, mind you – a real one.

' " 'Hulloa!' says I. 'You're a long way from home. How
did you get here?' "

' " 'Noah sent me,' says he.

' " '*Noah* sent you,' I says. 'What for?'

' " 'He said I was to bring back an olive-branch,' sniffed
the dove, water dropping off his nose. His bill chattered so
you could hear it a mile off. Altogether he looked like something they'd used for washing out bottles.

' " 'Noah,' he went on, 'said that the Dove was the Bird
of Peace. And the olive-branch I'd bring back would be a
sign – a sign of the end of the Deluge.'

' " 'Ho, ho!' I says, snickering. 'A *sign*, did he say? – of
the end of the Deluge, eh? Sounds more to me like a sign of
softening of the brain. True, the rain's stopped. But look at
the mess it's left! Now I tell you what you do, old lovey-
dovey: you fly straight back to Old Man Noah, before you
get your death of cold and tell him there aren't any olive-
trees growing round these parts yet.

' " 'He ought to be ashamed of himself, sending a *dove*
out to catch olives – in a wind blowing forty miles an hour!

I wonder he didn't tell you to bring in a gallon of vinegar along with the bottle of olive oil. – Look, here's a couple of good orange-seeds. Toss them down the crop. They'll last you till you reach Noah's ship. And you tell the old man from me that as for you bein' a "Bird of Peace", he's lucky he ain't getting you back *in pieces*.'

' " Well," added the raven thoughtfully, "poor old Dovey was awful glad to be let off duty. And, with his crop full of orange-seeds, he wasted no time flying off to try and sight the Ark from the higher levels. Myself, after tearing what was left of that smelly orange in pieces, I began to work out a plan. The sun was warming up now; and I decided I'd fly as high as the limit and see what I could see.

' "After climbing for more than an hour I ran into a couple of vultures. They were huge, hungry beasts; and had made up their minds I'd be a slick sandwich. But while their speed was better than mine, they were no good at dodging. Still, I knew they could get me in the end; because they had longer wind.

' "But suddenly I remembered the wonderful gift for smelling dead meat at long distances, which vultures are supposed to have. I'll try a bluff, I told myself. Maybe it will work. Then as I looped and ducked around their tails, I said to them, 'What good will a little snack like me do to the hungry stomachs of great creatures like you? You'll be starving again in ten minutes. But listen: not far off from here I've found great lands – not little rocky islands – but huge countries where men once farmed. And there, teams of drowned oxen, flocks of sheep and trains of camels lie dead and rotting in the sun. If you will but leave me alone, I will lead you there and you may eat your fill on the long-dead meat you love so well. Your scent is no good over the sea – *you* know that. Should you kill me now, brothers, you will lose your guide – and likely starve – all for the sake of a little raven.'

' "I could see I'd got them thinking. Myself, I hadn't an

idea of where these great lands lay. But my bluff worked. I saw the vultures start talking to one another in argument. At last they gave in to me.

' " 'So be it, Brother Raven,' said they. 'Lead on – to the big lands where the carcasses of camels lie rotting in the sun.' – I could see that rotten meat stuff had done the business. 'But listen: fulfil your promise – and no monkey-business – or we will snap you up like a field mouse.'

' "Well, my luck was with me. At the end of the first day, when I thought I was going to drop into the water from weariness, I saw a long land-line stretching out ahead of me. It looked like a continent. As soon as the vultures too saw it, I noticed their beaks open and their tongues smear round their dirty faces. They could smell dead camel-meat, the brutes.

' "That did it. They at once forgot all about me. By sheer accident I had led them to an enormous continent with enough rotten camel-meat on it to poison an army. They raced ahead of me at twice my speed and never even looked back."

'My wife, Belinda, sighed heavily as the raven ended the story of his adventures.

' "My goodness, Raven," she said at last, "I think you're wonderful!" '

'What *would* you have done without him?' said Cheapside, mimicking the Doctor, with a yawn. 'Come on, folks – bedtime! I was in the middle of a nice nap; but the smell of them rotten camels woke me up.'

16

THE SEA-BIRDS OVER THE GARDEN

'WHAT land, Mudface, was this continent,' the Doctor asked the following night – 'I mean, where the raven escaped from the vultures?'

'I am pretty sure it was Asia Minor,' said the turtle. 'But I will come back to that too in just a minute, John Dolittle, if you don't mind. It was at first frightfully confusing to turtles of our kind, who often travel great distances by both sea and land. Only a long time after the Earth dried completely were we able to get a true picture of what the new world looked like – and even then we often had to go by guess-work.'

'I can quite understand that,' said the Doctor. 'Excuse my impatience. I am very keen to learn how much the world was changed by the Deluge. But tell me in your own time. We are all ready – when you are – to go on.'

'Well,' said the turtle, 'after we had finished up our piece of bacon, the raven called to the pelican whom he had brought back with him last night.

' "Take a dive, Pel," says he. "We're going to need some grub before we sight the land."

'The pelican grunted and took off. Marvellous it was to see the difference, in that dumpy bird, between his walking and his flying. In the air, he soared most gracefully. He scouted round the raft quite a while before he suddenly shut his wings and dropped like a stone towards the water. His keen eyes had seen fish swimming near the top. What a splash he made! – Reminded me of pitching an anchor into the sea.

'But he knew his business. Disappearing under the water for five minutes, he suddenly pops up again, only a yard away from the raft. We helped him aboard. Then he opens

231

that great shovel-mouth of his and spilled out a load that looked like a fish-market. There were two fine haddock, a mackerel and a lot of little fish besides.

' "Will that do – as a starter?" says the pelican in a gentle grunt. "Light wasn't so good – and many got away from me under water."

' "Brother," says the raven, "that will do elegant. – Enough food to hold us all for quite a while. Boy, you may not hit the water pretty; but you're surely a great fisherman. – Oh, watch that mackerel! He's trying to flip overboard."

'Indeed, Belinda, Eber, Gaza and myself had to get busy keeping the jumping, live fish from hopping back into the sea. Eber had a sharp stone knife he had made. He chopped the heads off the fish, slit them open and – after washing them – set them outside the roof-shelter to dry in the sun. Then the raven says,

' "Now, my hearties, as soon as you're ready, let's go. Your pace – swimming and dragging this crazy raft – will not be fast."

'He spoke the truth. I can only guess how far it really was – close to five or six hundred miles, I'd say. Luckily the wind helped us most of the way. But oh, how sick we got of fish, the only food we had. Yet we never could have made the trip without it.

'At last, on the fifth day, however, we sighted a low line of land ahead of us; and hopes of a new home on dry earth put heart into us. We found a nice harbour or bay, where we anchored the raft. How wonderful it felt to step out on to something dry – which kept still under your feet!

'But oh, the country was desolate! There was nothing growing yet of course – even here. And, although the water had dropped much lower in these parts, the shore was cut by many large rivers. You see, a great deal of water lay on the high plains, many miles inland from the sea; and this was still rushing down to get to the ocean, cutting river-beds on its way.

HUGH LOFTING

'We set about making a home at once – just a hut – out of drift-wood, planks and old wreckage we found along the beaches. Our good friend, the raven, went off searching for seeds of fruits and vegetables. He brought back many kinds that seemed still in good condition. Eber, you will remember, was a very clever gardener, having been chief assistant to King Mashtu's park-keeper – till he was changed over to help Noah in the menagerie. Well, he dug a garden behind the hut and planted seed. But not a single one of them sprouted.

'This puzzled him for some time. But in the end (being a good gardener) he found out the reason. Down here, close to the shore, the salt-water of the ocean – when it had been higher – had so poisoned all the soil that for years it would be useless for plant growth. After that we moved farther inland, hunting for hilly country where the ground might not be as salty. We found what we were looking for only a few miles away. There we built another home, dug a garden and planted more seed.

'This time our luck was better. In a few weeks many of the seeds took root and came up. They grew very slowly and were not much to be proud of; but you've no idea how happy it made us to see anything green sprout out of that bare earth.

'By now, too, the waters at the shore were beginning to settle down; and when rains came we noticed that, in the rivers, it was almost drinkable – though we still did not use it for drinking. We did what we had all along: caught the fresh rain-water in anything we could, and stored it away for drinking and cooking. Off the rocks at the shore, the fishing too was better, as the currents grew calmer. Eber rigged up a kind of spear, or harpoon, and killed sea-otters and the like. So at last we had some fresh meat, instead of that everlasting fish-food which poor Gaza was dreadfully tired of.

'From time to time, when we were working on our garden, we noticed many large sea-birds in the sky above, soaring around in circles. But, at the time, we did not pay much attention to them. We supposed they were just interested to see green plants of any kind coming up for the first time in so long.

'While we were waiting for our vegetables and fruits to get big enough for eating, I went down to the shore and explored under the sea for towns. But I found only a few scattered farmhouses – no towns or villages. Again I got a bottle of wine or two – with a few gardening tools; and these I brought back to our hut. But what I had been hunting for was real solid food, to give the boy and girl a change. They had begun again to look sort of sickly on fish, with only a piece of otter-meat now and then – and no vegetable stuff at all.

'On these trips I was forever hoping to find the old city of Shalba. It had been such a rich and well-fed town, as I knew it before the Flood. I felt sure there must still be plenty of good eatables among the wreckage of its shops – as well as good seeds in its Royal Botanical Gardens.

'But in this too I was disappointed. I could not find Shalba; and nowhere else, it seemed, could I find any solid food for men-folk to eat. I was very unhappy.

'However, on one trip I made a discovery. This time I went farther off than I'd ever done before. I was gone for twelve days and must have travelled several hundreds of miles from the hut.

'I had crossed one deep valley where the current, running through it northward, was terribly strong. I suspected it to be the great River Nile which drains most of Egypt. And, if it was the Nile, that meant I had passed over, under water from Asia Minor to the mainland of Africa. After going on a great distance, I became surer and surer this was true.

'Every once in a while I'd come to deserts and ranges of mountains which I could have sworn I'd seen before.

'Then suddenly I found myself on a long steep slope which stretched downward into much deeper water. Now, in my free days, before I'd been put into King Mashtu's zoo, I had travelled a lot through and around his kingdom – sometimes for big distances. But I couldn't remember ever having seen this steep slope before. I decided to go down to the bottom of it to make sure of where I was.

'Well, I never reached the bottom! For hours and hours I went on, skimming down, lower and lower. The light got so poor that at last it was black as night; and I could see nothing at all. No use to go on: you can't explore where you can't see. I knew, by the terrible cold and great pressure on my shell, that I was now in enormously deep water.

'But I had found out something more. I only guessed at

it then. Years later, when the waters settled still lower, and more shore-line showed, I knew that my guess had been right. This was a *brand-new ocean* I was in, one which had been cut by that wide and mountainous wave we had seen sweeping across the Shalba race-track.

'You see, John Dolittle, the world before the Deluge had been made up of more land than sea; now it is more sea than land.'

'Ah!' murmured the Doctor. 'That explains a whole lot which geographers have been guessing at for thousands of years. – But go on, please.'

'Before the Flood,' said the turtle, 'Africa, Europe and America were all joined – just one large continent. And Mashtu ruled as king over almost the whole of it. This new ocean, into which I had stumbled, was what you call now the *Atlantic*. America was a wild and distant country, with few or no people on it. Between the Old World and the New there was said to be a waterless desert of sand and stones. But later, when the Flood cut through, the ocean was simply full of islands. Most of them were soon washed away by storm and what not.

'And, as you know, today the only big island-groups left are the Canaries, the Cape Verdes, the Madeiras, the Azores – with a few less important ones, like the Bermudas and the Bahamas. The world was changed indeed! Even that little ocean you call the Mediterranean Sea, which used to be a large inland lake, cut the thin neck of land at Gibraltar and poured its waters through, to join the Atlantic.'

'Most interesting,' said the Doctor. – 'Don't miss any of this, Stubbins. It's terribly important to science.'

'Very good, Sir,' said I. 'I've got it all down.'

'Tell me, Mudface,' said the Doctor, turning back to the turtle: 'the climates of the different parts of the Earth must have been changed too by all this, eh?'

'Oh my, yes!' said Mudface. 'In the good old days almost everywhere there seemed to be plenty of sunshine. Many good vegetables grew wild. A man need never starve, even if he wandered without tent or baggage; for almost anywhere the countryside would provide him with the food he needed. For this reason there was very little meat eaten – by civilized people, at all events. It was only after the Flood that Man and Beast had to struggle and fight one another for a living. Ah, yes, it was very different then, keeping yourself alive!

'And it changed the lives of all creatures. Before, Men had spent their days thinking of higher things, singing songs, playing games and inventing poetry. Now everyone had to calculate and work and worry for *one* idea only: getting enough to eat.'

'Do you feel,' asked the Doctor, 'that the world has not yet recovered – got over – that dreadful Flood?'

'No, Doctor,' said the turtle. 'Things got slowly better, of course. But this Earth has never since been the same. What had been warm countries were now cold ones. – Why, palm trees with dates on them used to grow where the North Pole is now placed, in the frozen Arctic Ocean.

'But to get on with my own story: I swam up to the surface and started to go back to the hut. As I said, I had been gone from our home twelve whole days.

'When, after much hard swimming, I at last drew near to it, my heart was filled with fear. Gathered about the hut was a huge crowd of animals of every kind. How had they got here? Cats cannot swim. Then suddenly I remembered the birds who'd watched our gardening: and I knew. Those birds had led them here, over the land which had now grown so much larger with the lowering of the water-line. I cursed my stupidity in staying away so long.

'When I got closer still I saw the tigress, who seemed to be in charge – as usual. For weeks we had felt ourselves quite safe – thinking that, with so much water between us, the cats would never be able to follow. I could see nothing of Eber and Gaza – those children whom my wife and I had

237

grown to think of as our own! ... Were they killed? Had they been eaten?

'Tired as I was from the long swim, I broke into a run towards our home as fast as my legs would carry me.'

17

ANTELOPE AND GRASS-EATERS

'To my surprise, it was the pelican, and not the raven, who came forward to meet me. Without waiting for any questions from me, he hurriedly told me that Eber and Gaza were still alive but in great danger. They had shut themselves in the hut and barred the door; but he feared they would not be safe for long, as the hut was so light and flimsy.

'But by the time I'd reached the edge of the crowd of animals, the bull-elephant had his shoulder against the shack's door. One shove from that great body could, I knew, lay the whole building flat. I cried out to the elephant to stop. Then I spoke to the crowd, asking the animals why they wished to hurt my friends.

' "Your *friends*!" cried the tigress, stepping forward and raising her upper lip in an angry snarl. "Why do you call this man and woman your friends? Have not they and their kind made slaves of us? Did they not take away my cubs and put them in a cage to be looked at?"

' "Aye!" trumpeted the elephant, waving his trunk wildly in the air. "Didn't they make a beast of burden out of me and walk me through the streets in circus-processions? Did they not make slaves of the horses and oxen, setting them to plough the fields in the hot sun?"

' "Let them die!" snarled the tigress. "Elephant, crush in the door and I'll swallow them in two gulps. We want no more Men in the world. *We* are now the masters. This

Earth forever more shall be the Kingdom of the Animals. Smash the door, Elephant. They will make a juicy meal!"

' "Aye, aye!" they all howled. "Break down the door!"

'The elephant drew back his shoulder in readiness, like a battering ram. I saw that this was the moment when I must act – and quickly. I put my head down and pushed my way through that crowd. The sharp edges of my shell knocked the feet out from under animals of all kinds, who fell either side of my path in kicking, struggling heaps. I weighed eight hundred pounds which made my shoving as destructive as the elephant's. I reached the hut; and while the elephant's shoulder was still drawn back, waiting, I slipped in between him and the shack and set my back against the door.

' "Stand aside, Turtle!" yelled the tigress. "Your *friends* must die."

' "Wait!" I cried. "Wait and let me speak. You have told me why you think this man your enemy – that he imprisoned you and gave you hard work to do. Let me tell you that these things were done to me also. I too was a prisoner in a zoo. And yet I call those within this hut my friends. It was not they who made us slaves.

' "It was King Mashtu who did it – he who almost enslaved the whole world, Man and Beast. These two young people you wish to eat were also slaves – like you and me. Yet, in spite of his own slavery, the boy Eber did his best to make life more bearable for me and my companions in prison. And that is why I call him *friend*."

' "What do we care for that?" asked a big black panther working his way forward to the front of the mob. "If these two are allowed to live, they will have cubs, like ourselves, peopling the Earth again with cruel masters. Give them to us, Turtle!"

' "Yes, yes," the crowd yelled. "We would rid the world of Men now and for ever. We want a free Earth. Down with Man! – Let him and the woman be wiped out!"

'Then with ugly howls the crowd rushed forward. Once

239

more the elephant, reaching over my back, put his shoulder against the door. I heard Gaza inside whisper to her companion with a sob, "Good-bye, Eber. This is the end!"

'Then red floated before my eyes and a great anger boiled up in my heart. I shouted to the growling crowd. "If any of you eat them, you're going to have to kill me first."

'And suddenly, rearing up on my hind legs, I bit a piece clean out of the elephant's ear. With a roar of pain he staggered back carrying the others with him. And for a moment the space about the door was clear again.

'But I knew another rush would come. There were too many against me. Belinda, I guessed, was inside the hut, ready to put up a last fight for the youngsters' lives. If only

I had the raven here to help me think out some plan! But he happened to be away seed hunting when that mob of animals arrived. I decided that the best I could do for the present was to keep them talking, hoping against hope that help would come to me from somewhere.

'"What of Noah?" I asked the crowd. "Where is he? Have you eaten him?"

'"No," barked the she-wolf. "He's still back there at the Ark. Only the sheep stayed with him. There are two lambs; and Noah is trying to keep them alive with half a sack of dried rice out of his own stores. We came away and left him in disgust. For *us* he has no food. All he has given us for weeks is just promises. What was the good of saving us, if we are to have nothing to eat to stay alive on?"

'"Maybe that was the only thing the old man could do," said I. "With no more than half a sack of rice left, he chose to save sheep instead of wolves. I'm sure I don't blame him."

'"We would have eaten him and all his family," said the tigress. "But it was he, Noah, who saved us from the waters; so we let him live. But if his sons and their wives have any babies we're going to eat them. And when Noah's grandchildren die, Man shall disappear for good. Stand away from that door, Turtle! You have hindered us long enough."

'"Fools, fools, *fools*!" I cried at the top of my voice – it was the best speech I ever made and that was the way I began it: "Fools, fools fools! Do you suppose this Flood was an accident, like stubbing your foot against a stone? No. Some One – I don't know Who – but Some One *planned* all this. The King of Shalba made himself ruler of almost all the world. But his rule was bad – built on lies, slavery, cheating and broken promises. Still he went on from power to more power. No country had the strength or courage to beat him down."

'I saw that living skeleton, the she-wolf, shift restlessly, impatient at my talk. But many animals were listening with attention. I went on:

' "And had Mashtu become complete ruler of the whole world, nobody can say what bad things would have followed – nor how long that lying King and his children's children would have run the world to suit themselves and their friends.

' "Then this Some One, whose name we do not know, but whose greater power controlled the rains, the tides and the fires in the sleeping volcanoes, made up His mind that the world and its so-called civilization must start again from the bottom of the ladder. And even if some suffered, a new Earth and a better civilization *must* be rebuilt.'

' "Oh twaddle," I heard the tigress mutter. "Words, words! We want food, not talk."

'But most of the animals took no notice of what she said. – Neither did I.

' "Now tell me," I said to the crowd: "do you think you can live without Man? Well, look around at this land which the Deluge has given back to you. Has it grass or fruits or anything to eat on it? No. – And more than half of you live on grass, not meat. When my two poor friends in this hut are killed, when Noah and his family are gone, what then? You'll start eating one another, won't you? – Till there is no life left in a dead world. Look around you. The Earth is naked – nothing but stones and steaming, rotting rubbish. Now go look behind this hut."

'They went. There they saw the seedlings and young plants in the garden. In less than a minute every green shoot had been gobbled up by the hungry deer.

'So much for all of poor Eber's hard work, I thought to myself. But I did not interfere. I slipped back to the front of the hut, put my back to it again and let them finish their meal.

'When they returned and gathered before me again, I said, ' "Now do you understand? It was not planned that Man

242

should pass from the Earth – not in *this* Deluge anyhow. You need Eber's brains and skill if you want to live through this destruction. You need him to farm and plant, so that the Earth may again give you food and pasture and cover."

'Then from the expression in the faces of the deer and antelope – of which there were hundreds of different kinds – I saw that I had got them thinking. They began talking together in low tones. I knew that if I could get all the grass-eaters on my side, my battle was won; for the cats and other meat-eaters – although far more deadly fighters – were fewer than the animals which live on grass and vegetable food.

' "Listen," I shouted, "you who don't eat meat: do you want this man Eber to live and bring the green Earth back to life for you? Or will you give him to these cats to eat?"

'The deer of course were afraid of the tigers and leopards. They whispered together a moment longer, while I saw the scowling tigress talking to the lions a little farther off.

'Then suddenly those hundreds of antelope, deer and chamois sprang to my side and lowered their horns like a row of swords to defend the door – to defend Eber, the gardener, against the meat-eaters of the world.'

PART FOUR

I

MAN BECOMES A SLAVE TO THE ANIMALS

'That, I fancy, was the greatest surprise of Mrs Tiger's life. She was so furious at this unexpected turn that, very foolishly, she got her husband to make another rush at us at once. But the brave antelopes stood their ground. It was a bristling ring of horns that spread around the hut. They did not tremble; they did not give way – though I knew how they feared the Queen of the Jungle. And, within three paces of those spearlike points, the cats changed their minds and slowed down.

'The tigress muttered something – which I could not hear – to her husband. Then they turned and slunk back. Next, I saw her go through the crowd, whispering to each of the meat-eaters in turn. I guessed she was trying to get them all worked up to fighting pitch.

'At any time they were deadly brutes – now made more dangerous by hunger near to starvation. Again I grew afraid for Eber and Gaza; because it was plain the tigress was planning this attack upon the hut from several different points at the same time. Soon I saw the cats getting ready: they were forming up in gangs of six or eight in a bunch.

'But in the nick of time help came to me from a very unexpected quarter. I heard the cow-elephant whisper to the bull-elephant.

' "Husband, this moment is, I'm sure, one of great importance. If the cats should win this battle, much trouble – perhaps death for want of food – may come to us. I am for the turtle – and Eber, the sower of seeds. Where in all this

244

devastated desert of a world are you and I – and our young ones later – going to graze, unless somebody gets the grasses started? The turtle is right. Let us take his part."

'Then (you can imagine my relief!) just as the tigress opened her jaws to give the word for the next rush, those two great elephants tramped forward and stood, shoulder to shoulder, with the antelopes and myself. With them came the two hippos and a pair of rhinoceroses – also grass-eaters. All of them were heavy beasts whose trampling charge could knock a stone wall down. After that, there was no doubt whatever as to which side was the stronger.

' "Get away, you mangy cats!" bellowed the bull-elephant. "Leave the man alone! We want grass. Eber is a good gardener. We need him. He is going to live, I say – to live and work for us. With food, we animals will be the masters of the world and he the slave. When his usefulness is done and the Earth is green again, you may eat him if you wish. But until we have grass, he is under *my* protection. Do you understand? – Good! Let no more be said."

'Well, John Dolittle, that was how a short chapter in the history of the world began – the time when the Animals were the masters: and Man the slave. Alas! I had succeeded in saving Eber and Gaza from being killed, only to see their freedom taken from them a second time.

'When the door of the hut was opened they were set to work at once in the garden, which was made larger yet. They were harnessed to the wooden plough which they had used for their own vegetables. And the elephant drove them like a team of horses along the furrows, cracking a big whip over their heads, the way he had seen the ring-masters do in the circus of Shalba. Many of the animals laughed and jeered at this sight.

'But to me, who remembered how kind Eber had been to the creatures in Mashtu's zoo, there was something terribly unfair and saddening in the whole business.

'However, you could not help noticing, after the

245

HUGH LOFTING.

elephant first defied the cats and took command himself of this new Animal Kingdom, how the creatures of every sort grew less afraid of the tigress. She couldn't boss them around the way she used to. A new leader had taken her place – a leader whose word was law. Many meat-eaters were now doubly dangerous. So near to starvation were they, they often fought, killed and ate one another. Yet they were never allowed to touch Eber and Gaza.

'The birds and the little digging beasts, such as badgers, moles and field mice, were ordered to bring all seed, nuts and acorns to Eber. And these creatures – though they too were ravenously hungry – did as their new elephant-leader told them.

'For they all realized the importance of that first new crop of plants. This crop would of course, in time – as soon as the salt was washed away by the rains – spread its own seed over the world's naked soil. But it must be given a chance to come to full growth. So meanwhile, the grass-eaters were allowed to nibble only enough, here and there, to keep alive. And the leader-elephant – who usually eats an awful lot in a day – he did the same.

'He was, in a way, the new Mashtu of the world – with this difference: *he always kept his word*. And though he worked Eber and Gaza terribly hard, he wasn't cruel or treacherous, like Shalba's king had been. All the animals respected and liked him.

'Those who stayed back with the Ark were treated just as fairly. There, as the islands grew larger with the falling water, Noah's sons, Ham, Shem and Japheth, were put to work, cutting the buds out of old uprooted trees and planting them in the ground to start new orchards. The patriarch Noah was not made to work because he was too old and weak. The elephant sent his own wife over to take charge of this part of his new kingdom – to see that Ham didn't loaf instead of work.

'I have often thought that if the beasts of the world were saved by Noah and his family from the Flood, the animals paid back the debt later. For they kept him and his sons alive by their good sense and planning when starvation – after the land began to dry – seemed to grip all creation with an iron hand.

'And so, for a while at least, things went along pretty well. But they did not suit that savage, selfish tigress. Although she pretended, like the others, to be obedient to the new Elephant Emperor, I – for one – did not trust her.

'She had always wanted to be the boss herself; and something warned me she had never given up hope of some day, somehow, again setting herself up as leader, now that Man had sunk to slavery. Belinda and I talked it over; and we

247

agreed that I was most likely right. So I made up my mind to watch that slant-eyed man-eater. For Eber's and Gaza's sake I did not intend to be caught napping a *second* time.

'I had to be most careful that the tigress should never learn I was keeping an eye on her. At last I became certain that, in spite of all her show of obedience, she was a traitor, jealous of the Elephant Emperor and working secretly for his downfall.

'And this was how I found her out. Eber and Gaza slept in the hut. But every night two animals were posted as sentries at their door, to make sure they did not escape. A short distance away a sort of stable-shelter had been rigged up for the Elephant Emperor to live in. Still farther off I knew the tigress had made a den for herself and her husband, out of a tangle of dead trees.

'It became a habit of mine every night to rest close to Eber's hut. I used to half bury myself near by, so I could see but not be seen. One night, when Eber and Gaza were sleeping inside, tired and worn out with hard work, I saw the dark shape of the tigress lurking around the shack. The sentries on duty that night were two giraffes. But they did not see that great cat. Indeed the beast, in that poor light, sneaking slowly over the ground on her big padded feet, was more like a shadow than a living creature.

'Soon I made a discovery: she had not come to attack my friends tonight. She just wanted to make sure they were still safely locked up. And – what's more – she was, herself, most anxious that the giraffe-sentries should not see *her*. She did not go up to speak with them. But, after sniffing round the hut a bit, she moved off in a direction quite different from that by which she'd come. So, after she'd gone, I followed her, making no more noise than she did herself.

'Now, at the bottom of a big hollow to the south there was a cave in the rocks, where the animals often went to enjoy the cool when the sun was especially hot. Mrs Tiger was headed towards this cave. I reckoned it was about midnight. She came to the mouth of the cave and I saw her glide down into its dark depths without a sound.

'I was about to do the same. But on second thought I decided to hang back a while. – Lucky for me I did! Presently while I watched and waited – crouching low behind a stone – down into that hollow crept more cats: cheetahs, leopards, black panthers, lions and many other kinds. It began to look like a gathering of our old enemies. Still I waited on, to see if there were more to come. After about a quarter of an hour I thought it would now be safe for me to move. I wasn't going down into the cave; but I was going to get as close to the entrance as I could.

'So, first, I went to a mud-hole near by and caked myself all over with mud. When I had finished I looked just like a lump of messy earth. Then I went and placed myself as close as possible to the cave's entrance, drew my head and feet into my shell and kept as still as a stone.

'Well, I heard every word that was said at that meeting – which was what I'd come for. I learned every detail of the great Revolution of the Cats which later overthrew the Elephant Empire.

'The tigress told them she thought the lion should be set up as leader in the elephant's place. The others all noisily agreed to that. But I, at least, was not taken in by her talk. I was still certain the tricky old cat meant herself to be the boss – even while she told the rest of them that in the lion they had chosen a good leader. All she really wanted – for the present – was to set them against the Elephant Emperor.'

2

THE REVOLUTION OF THE CATS

'WELL,' Mudface began, as we sat down next night, 'the tigress told the meeting she had the whole revolution planned out and arranged: tomorrow, Saturday, I think, but – '

'Revolution indeed!' Jip growled in a low and angry voice. 'What that old she-pussy needed was a nip on the ear. – But it certainly sounds exciting!'

'It was,' said the turtle – 'though not exactly as the tigress hoped. Her idea was this: the next night, as soon as the elephant would be fast asleep, she and the lioness, the leopardess and the she-panther were going to surround the leader's shed and force him to give up his empire and go away. If he refused, it was agreed that they would kill him – which they could have done, so long as they attacked him in a band, unexpectedly. In the meantime the lion, the tiger and the leopard would kill Eber. Gaza was to be kept for the women-cats to eat.

'You see, during all this time when the big meat-eaters were short of food they had kept themselves alive by devouring other creatures who were too small and weak to fight back. Noah was not with them now to keep order. And so, John Dolittle – the same as with the trees – we lost many kinds of animals who were completely wiped out and never seen again. And as soon as the tigress spoke to that ravenous pack inside the cave of eating Eber and Gaza, I heard them all lick their chops and grunt with appetite.

'A little later I guessed, from the racket down below, that the meeting was over and the party was breaking up. And before I had time to get away from the mouth of the cave all the big cats came trundling out, talking together in low whispers. For a moment I was scared I would be discovered, spying. But my disguise worked perfectly. With

HUGH LOFTING

my head and feet drawn in and my back all plastered with mud, I looked like a part of the ground itself. Those beasts walked over or around me, never suspecting I'd heard every word of their plot. Many of them actually stepped on me with their large padded feet.

'The last to leave the cave was the tigress. On her face I could see, by the dim moonlight, a grin of cunning conceit. She was thinking of the great plans she had set afoot to make herself Queen of the Animal Kingdom. I watched her long muscular body creep up to the rim of the hollow where she stood for a moment against the sky.

' "All right, you slinky old witch," I whispered to myself.

"It's queen you're going to be, eh? Wait and see. I, Mudface the turtle, know now what you mean to do."

'As she moved off the skyline, towards her den, I brought my head all the way out of my shell and shook off most of the mud in which I had caked myself. At first it seemed to me best to go at once to the Elephant Emperor and warn him of the danger and the Revolution of the Cats.

'But on thinking this over a bit, I could see it wasn't such a good idea. It would only mean that fighting among the animals would break out sooner; for I felt certain at last the tigress would put up a fight to a finish, to be made the leader of the beasts.

'Besides, I myself partly agreed with the animals of the world in their not wanting to become once more the slaves of Man. – That is, I did until I saw how, through their ever-lasting separating and squabbling among themselves, they showed that they had not the sense to rule the Earth – even as well as Man had done. – And that isn't saying much. But anyway, whether the Animal Empire succeeded or not, my mind was made up that neither Eber nor Gaza was going to be eaten.

'So I sat there a while, wondering what was the best thing I could do. And presently I said to myself: "*Tonight!* That's it. Get them out of it – beyond the reach of the cats – before the dawn comes. It's the only way to be sure of saving them. If I wait till morning all sorts of animals will be awake to tell the tigress what I'm doing. I won't stand a chance then. – While now I have only two sentries to deal with – giraffes – and not very bright. Eber and the girl *must* leave tonight."

'I got busy, I can tell you. It was about an hour past midnight. First of all, I followed Her Majesty Mrs Tiger to her den, taking care she shouldn't hear or see me. I lingered near her home till the sounds of a grunting snore told me she was safely asleep. Then I hustled off and woke up my wife, Belinda, who lived not far from Eber's hut. I told her the whole business as fast as I could. When I'd finished, she said,

' "Mudface, you're right about getting those two young people away immediately. But as for the giraffes, the sentries on guard at the hut, you'd better leave them to me. No use trying force, because they'd raise an outcry and we'd have the whole camp around our ears in two seconds. You keep out of sight a minute and let me go talk to the guards. I'll tell them of a place where the wild rice is sprouting."

' "Where's that?" I asked.

' "Nowhere, so far as I know," said Belinda. "Yes, I grant you it's a dirty trick to play on those simple grass-eaters. But the boy and girl come first. The giraffes are hungry enough to believe, and do, anything. I'll offer to lead them to the growing rice. Then, as soon as they and I have left, you burrow in under the wall of the hut and get Eber and Gaza to run off with you!"

' "Humph!" said I. "that may take time, you know."

' "True," she answered. "But we've got some hours before the sun rises. Get as far away as you can and I'll try to pick up your trail as soon as it is safe to give the giraffes the slip. But don't forget that those cats have dreadfully sharp noses for following a scent. You better make for the nearest water. And, again, remember that the nearest water is much farther off than it used to be, now that the seas are dropping lower every day. But once you reach the big water, you'll be safe from the cats – with Eber anyhow. You may not be able to swim with the two on your back. . . . If you can't, hide the girl in a cave or something till I catch up with you. Now I'll go and talk to the guards."

' "All right, Belinda," I said: "Lead them off to the westward for the rice; and I'll take Eber and the girl towards the east. Good luck to you!"

' "Good luck to both of us!" she answered.'

3

THE ESCAPE

'I WATCHED my wife as she crept towards the hut. The long necks of the giraffes stood up like flag-poles before the door. I wanted to hear what was said; but I remembered Belinda's advice and stayed back out of sight.

'Just the same, I knew she must be finding it hard to get them to go away. For minutes and hours passed; and still the low murmur of their talk went on. I began to wonder how much more of darkness I had left to make the escape in.

'At last, to my great relief, the giraffes lowered their long necks and slunk away into the shadows, led by Belinda. Much time had been wasted; and as soon as they were gone I hurried to the door of the hut. I could not undo the latch and was afraid to knock, lest the noise should wake the Elephant Emperor whose sleeping shed was quite near. So I started at once to scratch my way under the door.

'By working like a madman, I soon dug a hole big enough for me to get through into the hut.

'Inside it was pretty dark. – The tiny window was covered with sacks. I moved gently round the little room till I found Eber and Gaza sleeping on the floor. They were scared when I nudged them awake; but the boy's hands, touching my shell as he got up, told him it was I, Mudface – his friend.

'Then came another delay to waste still more of the remaining darkness. *I was unable to tell them what I'd come for!* You see, although I could understand most of their language, I could not of course speak it. I had to use signs and acting. And you've no idea what a time I had getting it into those people's heads that they were in the greatest danger and must fly with me immediately.

'At last, after I'd run back and forth between them and

254

HUGH LOFTING

the hole I'd made under the door, they caught on to what I meant.

' "Eber," the girl whispered, "the turtle is telling us to leave the hut, I think. Perhaps if we follow him we may escape from slavery."

' "What chance is there of that?" asked Eber. 'There are the giraffes outside, on guard. How could we get past them?"

'Then I grabbed hold of him and tried to drag him to the door. He came. He knelt down and peered out through the hole I'd made.

' "Why, Gaza!" he said. – "The sentries are gone! We can escape. ... Good old Mudface!" He patted me gently on the head.

255

'As soon as they fully understood that I had come with a plan – and a chance for them to get away – it was not so hard for me. On all fours, both of them followed me out, scrambling under the door.

'Eber knew as well as I did that their great danger was the big cats (who can follow a trail, when there is meat to kill, better than any animals living).

'And he now did a very bright thing. He told Gaza to wait with me just outside the hut; while he himself ran all around it and went off short distances in every direction. This was to leave his scent all over the place, to confuse the cats when they would try to follow. As soon as he had finished he came back to us. Then we started off.

'I led them to the eastward, as Belinda and I had arranged. But alas! We had scarcely gone more than a mile when I saw the sky ahead of us turning grey with the first show of morning. Most likely, I guessed, the giraffes had already returned to the hut from their wild-rice chase; and any moment now the whole camp would be warned of our escape.

'I was not far wrong. Soon, as we scrambled and tumbled forward, I heard in the distance behind us the howling of wolves and the bark of hyenas. Our flight was discovered.

'I blessed Eber's good sense then in leaving his scent on false trails before we came away from the hut. For, without that extra time, we would have stood a mighty poor chance. I reckon a good hour was spent by Mrs Tiger, shooting off on wrong tracks, before she struck our true trail eastward.

'Now, I had hoped by this time to have found water. But, in spite of Belinda's warning, I had no idea how much more land had been left dry since last I'd gone exploring. The country spread out flat in all directions with not a drop of water in sight.

'Suddenly behind us I heard the first roar of the lion. He had pulled a little ahead of the other cats in the hunt. At

HUGH LOFTING

that terrifying noise, poor Gaza clung to Eber, begging him to find some hiding place.

'Indeed I was beginning to think of that myself – bad though the chance of cover was. Still, I knew there was no hope of outdistancing our enemies in open country, now that they had got our scent.

'I clambered on to a big uprooted tree and looked in every direction for rocks or a cave – anything to put my friends in. There I might at least be able to defend them till Belinda's help arrived – or the elephant caught up with the faster cats and called them off. That would mean going back to slavery at the plough for the boy and girl; but at least it was better than being eaten.

'Suddenly Gaza screamed and pointed to the west. And there, just coming in sight over the skyline, was the whole pack of them – with the tigress now in front – travelling at full speed. Eber picked up a rock and got in front of the girl. But of course for him to stand and fight such enemies as that (there were a good two dozen in the leading gang) was just madness.

'At my wits' end – with no other plan except to get them farther away – I scrambled down from the tree, made a sign to Eber to follow me and stumbled on.'

Mudface stopped a moment; and that same kindly grin passed across his aged face.

'*Stumbled* is the right word,' he said presently. 'I don't believe I ever ran so hard in my life. I tripped and fell and bumped my nose a hundred times. The roaring and the snarling of the cats grew nearer and louder every minute. I really thought it was all over for these human-folk.

'I could hear the elephant now, too, a long way behind the cats, bellowing to them to stop. But the revolution had broken out and they took no notice of the Emperor's orders any more. As I glanced back over my shoulder, I could see that savage tigress leaping towards us at a truly terrific speed. Her husband galloped at her side – with the two lions close behind. And still, because there was nothing else to do, I stumbled on, gasping encouraging words to those two terrified youngsters – but with no real hope left in my heart.

'Soon the tigress, as she now saw her prey almost within grasp of her wicked claws, started jeering and laughing at us – calling me a clumsy fool every time I stumbled or fell.

'But she jeered – and laughed – too soon. The change in my luck was near.'

4

THE FALL OF THE ELEPHANT EMPIRE

'At the last moment, when I was in complete despair – expecting to see the boy and the girl torn to pieces before my very eyes – a miracle happened. The ground suddenly gave way under my feet; and I found myself wallowing in a bog!

'The country, which had looked so flat and dry for miles in all directions, was really one large marsh. I had not reached real water; but I had reached mud, which suited me even better.

'Eber and Gaza were up to their waists already. They scrambled on to my back. With the weight I began to sink – almost out of sight. I could carry one, but not both.

'Eber understood and got off at once, back into the mud. But I knew he couldn't last long there – exhausted as he was. So I signalled to him to take a hold on the shoulder of my shell and cling to it with one hand. In this way I could keep his chin above the mud. So, with the girl on my back and the man in tow, I ploughed on deeper into the bog. Presently I turned my head and shouted to the snarling, disappointed tigress behind us.

' "Come and get them now, you she-devil – from the mud, where *clumsy fools*, like turtles, are at home! Follow us here, if you dare!"

'And, would you believe it, John Dolittle,' (again that half-smile flickered in the eyes of Mudface) 'the tigress was so mad she did try to follow us, as I had challenged her to do? She drew back for a spring and leapt out into the marsh after us, reckoning I suppose, that she'd land on my back in one leap and kill the youngsters before I could get them farther away.

'But, great jumper though she was, she misjudged the

distance that time. And with an awful splash she landed two feet short of me. Down she went in the swampy mire, right up to her ears. It nearly cost her her life, that leap. For in the deep mud she was as helpless as a kitten. Her big paws stuck fast; and the harder she struggled to get them free, the deeper she sank.

'Finally her husband and the other cats formed a living chain from the dry land; and, little by little, they pulled her great body out on to the solid ground. But oh, how she looked! You know cats hate to be wet and dirty. Well, her beautiful striped coat, of which she was so proud, was plastered in slush from head to tail. She reminded me of an enormous drowned rat.

'So now for the present we were safe – but by no means in a pleasant situation for Eber. While I could, even with Gaza on my back, drag him slowly along in the bog, such travelling was dreadfully tiring for him. And I knew that to go any long distance would be quite impossible without the help of Belinda.

'For some time now I had wondered why my wife had not shown up. Where she was I had no idea. Eber, I could see, was already near the end of his strength. I stopped where I was for the moment to rest him.

'Meanwhile I watched the crowd of cats on the shore of the marsh. They were talking together – I suppose about what they could do next.

'Presently the elephant arrived and started storming and scolding the cats for not waiting when he called to them. It was a great surprise to him when the meat-eaters, after they'd whispered to one another some more, suddenly turned on him in open rebellion.

' "We will obey you no longer," snarled the tigress. "You are big, but too stupid to lead the animals of the world. I have been chosen to take your place. Go now – while still you can. You are Emperor no more."

'Then was it seen how that poor, good-natured elephant

was never meant to be a leader. What he should have done of course was to talk pleasantly to these rebels till the rhinos, the hippos and the other big grass-eaters should come to his help. But instead, he gave the tigress such a box on her ear with his trunk that he knocked her over on her back.

'She suddenly turned into a four-legged fire-cracker. From the safety of the mud, I watched her get to her feet. She was positively cross-eyed with rage. She sprang upon the elephant, biting, scratching and tearing like a fury.

'The other cats joined in. And if it had not been for his thick leathery skin he would have been torn to ribbons. As it was, he was soon bleeding badly from many places. He seemed covered in fighting animals – who had tasted blood. Then he suddenly lay down and rolled, killing some of his attackers under the weight of his enormous body. Those who were only wounded by the crushing were immediately eaten by the others, now they could no longer defend themselves. . . . Gaza covered her eyes to shut out the picture. So much, I thought, for a world run by animals alone!

'At last the elephant arose, shook the rest of them off him and, bellowing with pain, galloped across the country as fast as he could. Some moved to follow him; but the tigress bade them stay. The Elephant Empire had fallen; and that strange chapter in the history of the world when Man was the servant of the animals was drawing to a close.'

5

MEETING AN OLD FRIEND AGAIN

'TELL ME, Mudface,' said the doctor: 'after the elephant ran away from the cats, did mankind take hold again and run things?'

'Not exactly – or, I should say, not yet, John Dolittle,'

said the turtle, as he settled down to his storytelling the next evening.

'It is true, of course, that for a while many of the hunting creatures were led by the tigress. But the grass-feeders just kept away from her – out of fear mostly.

'The bull-elephant, for instance, went off and joined his wife in the country where Noah was. From there, later, the pair of them drifted still farther away, seeking better fodder.

'The same thing happened with the meat-eaters, too, in the end. They grew tired of that old she-devil, of her conceit, of her bossiness – as well as of her savage temper. Then another split came. They wanted a chief whom they could respect, who would rule by something more than fear and trickiness.

'The lion was a good fellow. At least he was honest, even if he too was a killer. They elected him. And, as you know, the lion is spoken of to this day as the *King of Beasts*.

'But as for Man's return to the mastery of the world, that did not come about till many years after Eber escaped from the hut.

'And I, the clumsy turtle, did a great deal to make that third big revolution possible. I did not realize this at the time – being only concerned in saving the lives of my human friends from the cruel hunger of a ruined world.

'I will tell you more of that last revolution soon. Just remember for the present, Doctor, that in the story of Eber and Gaza I am going on from where the tigress is still more or less mistress of the Animal Kingdom, determined to destroy mankind altogether. – And we three hunted creatures are waiting out there, in the mud, hoping Belinda will join us any moment. You follow me?'

'Oh, quite, quite,' said John Dolittle. 'And now tell us, please, what happened next.'

'The cats at last,' Mudface went on, 'began to struggle back towards their camp. Anyone could see they were dis-

contented over the tigress's failure to give them meat – as she had boastfully promised.

'As soon as the last of them had disappeared over the sky-line, I got Eber and the girl out of the bog on to solid ground – for a more comfortable rest. But I did not as yet go far from the marsh's edge, lest our enemies return unexpectedly.

'By now I became really worried about Belinda. Surely she must know how much I needed her help! Where *could* she be?

'Well, it was twilight, with a rising moon, before she showed up.

' "What kept you so long, Belinda?" I asked.

' "Oh, dear!" she sighed. "I thought I'd never get free of

those stupid giraffes. I took long enough to coax them away from the hut, but longer still to get rid of them afterwards. I had to keep making up new excuses for not finding that wild rice. But after hours of fooling around, we heard behind us the alarm which meant your escape had been discovered. Then I thought the time was come when I might shake them. Not at all: they stuck to me tighter than ever. Better stay with me, they said, and get some rice out of it, anyway."

'Poor Belinda was almost in tears.

' "Well," I said, "never mind. You got here – that's the main thing. Take the girl on your back: I'll carry the boy. And let's be going. I'm afraid of more trouble from Mrs Tiger any minute. Now that darkness is near, attack will be easier for her."

'As we waded into the marsh with our passengers aboard, I told Belinda about the elephant's downfall and flight.

' "But what on earth is your idea," she asked as I ended, "in taking these young people out into the mud-lands? What are you going to put them on? How are you going to feed them?"

'Belinda nearly always asked her questions in threes – I suppose to make three times sure she'd get *some* answer. I, as usual, picked out the easiest question, knowing she'd likely forget the other two.'

'Huh!' grunted the London sparrow. 'That, my old Mudlark, is somethin' I *really* understand.' Becky pretended not to hear; while the Doctor whispered,

'Hush, Cheapside! – A little more respect, *please*.'

' "Belinda," said I," (the turtle's voice grew tired and I glanced at the watch) ' "my idea is to put them on dry land – when we reach it – the other side of this swamp."

' "But how do you know there *is* any other side?" she asked. "What if this marsh is the end of the land? How can you be sure, husband?"

' "My dear", I said, "I'm not *sure* of anything, except our

264

need to go on. This is the only direction we can take to escape the cats. And if, later, the bog turns into open water, so much the better: our travel will be easier and faster when we can swim. Come along."

'That ended the discussion for the moment. All night long we travelled on in silence, while our weary riders slept on our backs. I took a course, still eastward, by the stars. And as I gazed up from this clinging desert of mud into the free and spangled dome of the sky, I was reminded again of Shalba.

'I thought of the nights when I used to stare into the heavens from the water of our prison-pond. Then those twinkling, distant lights had somehow seemed company for my imprisoned loneliness of heart. And the stars tonight looked exactly as they had above the zoological gardens of Shalba in the Dry Season of the year.

'You see, Doctor, before the Flood we had no Spring, Summer, Autumn and Winter, the way we do now. The year was divided into two halves only: the Dry Season and the Rainy Season. I have met animals who say it was the changing of the Earth's spin at that time – as much as the forty days' rain – which caused the spilling of the oceans, the Great Wave, the rumbling noises underground and all the curious things which happened with the Deluge. But whether this is so or not I cannot tell.

'Anyway, that night as Belinda and I churned our way along, I fell to wondering again what had become of the proud city of Shalba and the spot where it had stood – under water or above.

'As the day was breaking, our flat landscape of swamp showed signs of changing. Wisps of fog appeared ahead. Eber on my back turned and muttered in his sleep, as the chill wind of dawn swept fitfully across the marsh. I sniffed at it and turned to my wife.

' "Belinda," I said, "I think we are coming to a lake. See the wide puddles dotted about in front of us. Look, how queerly the grey light plays on them, between the shifting banks of mist. I wouldn't be surprised if we are near a real big lake."

' "How do you know it's a lake? Why can't it be the sea? What if we've come to the end of everything – but mud?" she asked.

' "Belinda," said I wearily, "whatever it is, I'm going on. We can't go back. *I* think it's a lake we're coming to. . . . *Please*, no more questions!"

'Little by little, the mud gave place to water deep enough for swimming. And by the time the sun was well risen we found ourselves right out in open water, with no land in sight to the eastward. We were on the broad bosom of either a large lake or a sea.

' "This water tastes salt," said Belinda.

' "You can't be certain of that," I snapped back at her.

'I admit I was a bit peeved, after stirring soupy mud all night (and remember, Eber was no light weight to carry). "Not even you can be sure of that, my dear," I repeated. "All water tastes more or less salt now, since the oceans and the rivers got mixed up. I don't suppose this water itself knows whether it's fresh or salt. And as for the rivers, one half of them have forgotten where they're flowing *from*; while the rest are still trying to make up their minds where they'll flow *to*. – Very confusing business, a deluge."

' "That's true, anyway," Belinda grunted. "And *this* Deluge, I believe, husband, has made *you* a little crazy in the head."

' "Maybe so," I said. . . . "Ah – oh, but isn't it a relief to feel your legs free, where it's deep enough for swimming?"

' "I suppose so," was all she answered.

'But even she was cheered out of her grumbling when, in the afternoon, we chanced to meet our old friend the raven. He was flying in the opposite direction, low down over the water. It had been long since we saw him last. He settled down upon my shell. And I told him of the revolution led by the tigress; and the reason for our present flight.

' "Humph!" he grunted. "I'm sorry about the poor old elephant. – A good sort in his way – even if he wasn't a born leader. But, believe me, that big striped pussy will mess things up for the animals far worse than ever he did. . . . Hulloa, Eber! . . . How are you, Gaza?" They smiled at the raven, guessing that this was a greeting from him.

' "Wonderful how they understand me!" he said proudly. – "And me so out of practice in their lingo I can hardly remember a word of it. . . . Well, thank goodness my work's over for this year!"

' "What work?" asked Belinda.

' "You know," said the raven – "the mating season. It used to be easy: hen-bird sits on the eggs and cock-bird sits on a limb near by, singing: *Tra, la – tra, la! – Twiddle-dee – TWEET!* – Oh gracious!" He broke off in a cough. "I declare my voice is getting worse. All this dampness, you know. But if you think you're the only one who's had troubles, Brother Turtle, you ought to try and find enough worms to satisfy a large family of fledgelings. – O' course we *would* have to have one extra egg in a flood year! What beats me, though, is how earth-worms learn to disappear in a deluge. Like looking for needles in a haystack.

' "The wife says it's *my* fault – I've been off gadding instead of attending to my proper job. I'd like to see anybody *gad* since the Big Rain fell! Well, job's over now. The nippers flying around on their own, bumping into everything, bless 'em! . . . But tell me, Mudface, where are you all going now?"

' "Anywhere – to get away from that tigress," I answered.

' "What is this water, Raven?" asked Belinda. "Is it the sea?"

' "Oh, no!" croaked the black bird. "This is only a lake.

267

If you keep on swimming for two or three hours more, the way you are now, you should come in sight of land on the other side."

' "What is the country like on the other side?" I asked.

' "Nothing to boast of," said he – "low-lying and swampy, till you get away back. But then every place is pretty bad now. Got to expect that. I've been trying to catch fish – a fellow must eat something. But I'm no good at the game – never came so near drowning in my life. Wish I had old Shovelface Pelican here to teach me how. Somehow I lost touch with him ages ago."

' "But where *is* the sea then," asked Belinda, "if this is only a lake?"

' "Well," said the raven, "at the farther shore of this lake there's a river running out of it. It flows through a big drowned forest; the trees are all dead – but still standing, like ghosts. It's a gloomy place. If you follow that stream it will bring you out to the sea, a brand-new ocean. I've just come from over there. – Turned back at the shore, because the ocean looked most awful large. But I suppose there must be more land on the other side of it – if anyone had a mind to go and explore. Once there your troubles should be over. No cats ever crossed that piece of water, I'll take a bet."

'Our travelling companion seemed really glad to see us after his lonely wanderings over the sad landscape of a deluged earth. He prattled on a while longer about the things he'd seen; and at last we asked him would he care to come along with us. He thought a moment and then he said,

' "That's not half a bad idea. – Can't see much sense in my going to join the other animals now – so long as that mean-tempered old puss is the boss. I never could stand that sneaky snooper – and she doesn't like me either. . . . Yes, I'll come with you. We always had good luck when we voyaged together before."

'So he joined our party and we went forward again. And somehow on the wide waters of the lake both Belinda and I felt safer and more hopeful, now we had the company of our re-found, chatterbox friend, the raven.'

6

HOW LAKE JUNGANYIKA GOT ITS NAME

'The sun was setting in the west when we reached the farther shore. Here again we found land difficult for travel. But we didn't stop. With the help of the moon and the raven's guidance, we pushed straight on till we came to firm ground, about six miles farther inland.

'Now at last we could let our passengers get off our backs and move around on their own feet. Such a relief for Belinda and myself to be free of our loads! Too weary to bother about a proper camp or anything else, we settled down at once to sleep.

'But next morning the everlasting question of food bothered us once more. Eber and Gaza hadn't had a thing to eat in two days. So I thought I would go back and explore the bottom of the lake. If luck was on our side, who knows? – I might find the homes of men a second time – and food for the youngsters.

'Well, the lake's floor, to my surprise, was gravelly, instead of muddy – at least it was then. And somewhere under the middle of that wide water I ran my nose into – you'd never guess what: the bent and twisted railing of my old prison-pond! I had found the City of Shalba at last! And here before you, John Dolittle, you see the same lake that hid it then and hides it still.

'I knew every scratch, ever chip in the paint on it. It was strange, as I sniffed at that railing beneath the water, how the picture of my bitter, unhappy days of captivity flashed

269

again before my eyes. The smell of the iron reawakened a hatred in my heart for Mashtu, Shalba's cruel king.

'I left the railing, crossed the park and made my way through the crumbling doors of the Royal Palace. And there, among the silent, lofty halls of marble and porphyry, I threw back my head and laughed.

' "So," I said, "Mashtu the King passes! But Mudface the turtle lives on! Now will I go down into the cellars and bring royal food to them who were a king's slaves!"

'My luck was not bad. Dainties and rare things for eating, brought from all over the world, were there in plenty. But only the stuff sealed up in jars and bottles was any good now.

'I picked out one medium-sized jar – with no idea what was inside – swam up to the surface and carried it to the shore. I had a terrible time getting it over the few miles to the camping ground where we had spent the night.

'With hungry cries of delight Eber and Gaza set to work on the cover of the jar and had it open in a moment. Inside there were spiced dates in syrup, a dainty brought from China.

' "Junga!" cried Eber, clapping his hands. You see, that was his native word for dates.

' "Nyika, nyika!" laughed Gaza, shaking her head at him; for such were dates in her language.

' "Junga nyika!" they cried together, cramming the fruit into their starving mouths. So it was that the word passed into their new language, both as the name for dates as well as for the lake in which I found them; and Lake Junganyika men still call it to this day.

'We searched the country about us for fresh food also. But we found nothing, absolutely nothing, for man or beast to eat.

'So I asked the raven how long did he reckon it would take us to go on to the seashore, travelling by the river he had spoken of. And he said we ought to be able to get there in a week.

'For a journey as long as that, Belinda thought we should rest up the young people a little; and it was agreed that I should make several more visits to the palace cellars and get them all the food I could.

'It was hard and slow work, hauling up the stuff, in small quantities, all by myself; for I always left Belinda on guard each time I went down under the water. And so, this way, we spent all of a week, not knowing if we could get them any more food at all, after we should set out on our trip to the sea.

'The motherly Belinda of course pestered the raven and me to death with her fears that, even after reaching the sea, we'd still find nothing for these humans to eat. But the raven said that around a regular ocean-beach we could surely hunt up diving sea-birds, who would at least get fish for us.

'Yet, before we were ready to go, once more the long, threatening arm of danger reached across the desolate starving world to us. One day – I think it was a Sun – '

'Excuse me please,' (this time it was the polite voice of little Chee-Chee, the timid monkey, who interrupted the story) 'but the day of the week makes no never mind. Be so kind as to tell us what happened. – Yes, please?'

'Oh, certainly,' the turtle answered. 'Anyway, it was when our whole party was on a food-hunting trip; and we had come to a place where the dry land around us changed to the mud-swamp of the lake-shore. We were strung out single-file; and this time Gaza happened to be in front. Suddenly we heard the girl give a scream. All of us hurried up to her. We found her pointing with a trembling hand at a mark in the soft ground. It was the foot-print of an enormous cat!

' "The tigress!" whispered Gaza through chattering teeth. "See, she has followed us even here!"

' "How on earth did she get across the lake?" asked Belinda.

' "Never mind how she got across," croaked the raven. "She's here. No mistaking *that* foot-print. We hadn't planned to leave for the seashore before tomorrow. But this changes things. We've got to get on our way *at once*. – And we won't stop even at the seashore to build sand-castles on the beach. We'll go on. We'll cross the sea. – Never mind food or the craft to sail in. We've managed before – somehow; and we'll manage again. But, once you're on that ocean I saw, no cat will follow us any farther. – Step lively and let's get out of here, everybody!" '

7

THE GRAVEYARD OF THE GIANTS

'FROM then on we hustled, and no mistake. No more questions, arguments or worries – even from Belinda. We turtles, who up to this had led the whole escape, were now quite satisfied to leave everything to the raven. It was he who told us what he wanted done: it was we who obeyed. Not one of us went back to the shelter where we'd lived – even for the blankets and the poor bits of things the youngsters owned. At Commander Raven's orders, we just left and raced at once for the river he had spoken of – the one which flowed out of the lake down to the sea.

'We guessed of course that the tigress and most of her man-eating gang would be following us by scent, hoping to cut us off. But they never caught sight of us again, after the raven had seen that big foot-print in the mud. Because his speed didn't give them a chance – either to catch up with us or to cut us off. He knew what danger we were in; he knew of a short cut to that stream; and above all, he knew that once we were travelling in water, no cat could follow us by scent.

'Well, we got to the river. – And *were* we glad to see it? At the spot where we struck the stream it was running wide in flood. We took the youngsters on our backs again, plunged at once into the fast water and headed downstream. Meanwhile the raven flitted back and forth through the dead trees on the banks, keeping a sharp lookout for enemies behind us and troubles ahead.

'Along the first few miles the going was easy, while the powerful current swirled us on our way. But farther down, the river began spreading out into many branches that led nowhere. And if we had not had the raven to lead us, we would surely have been lost.

'That was the last dash which poor Eber and Gaza had to make to escape from the tigress. I told you: we never saw her again. Yet that journey was, I believe, the most terrible one that human beings ever lived through.

'It took us seven days in all. The line of it, from the lake to the ocean, was almost exactly the same as you, John Dolittle, followed in coming here from the ocean to the lake. But oh, how different was the country then!

'As we went forward into the district which the raven had spoken of as a dead forest, the main-stream kept shrinking narrower – and shallower – till it was little more than a muddy dribble that no one could swim in.

'And often it was choked and barred by the big stuff swept down and stuck between the banks. Then we had to set our passengers off, to wait till we found a way for them around, under, over, or through the jam. Truly the raven had been right when he called it the *Land of the Dead Jungle*.

'No words of mine, Doctor, can draw you a picture of the dreary gloom of that drowned forest through which we fought our way to the sea. Some of the trees were of immense size – many still standing upright, but now dead,

HUGH LOFTING

gaunt, leafless and broken. In other places they were fallen
or leaning crisscross in great tangled masses – like walls of
crazy shipmasts as high as heaven.

'And all this dead vegetable growth was steaming, rotting and stinking in the terrible African heat, a Graveyard
of the Giants. While before, it had been lovely greenery;
gay with brilliant parrots; with gorgeous butterflies; with
bright orchids in bloom.

'No birds or creatures of any kind could be seen then. In
the jungle, always so full of life, life had stopped.

'We were unable to find one single scrap of food, in
seven whole days, to feed our human friends – only dirty,
bad-smelling water, half salt and half fresh. In many places

moving forward at even the slowest pace, while keeping track at the same time of that trickle of a stream, was so difficult that Eber and Gaza had to work too – hungry and worn out though they were. The raven stayed aloft in the trees, keeping watch; for he still feared that some prowling band of meat-eaters might by chance cross our path.

'Once Belinda, passing close to me, whispered, "Husband, I fear the youngsters cannot hold out much longer. Don't you think we should rest them a spell, while we send a scouting party forward to seek food?"

'But all I answered was:

' "Leave that to the raven, Belinda. He is a good leader."

'But again, I did not tell her how hopeless I felt myself.

'Yet, sure enough, an hour or so later I came upon the body of Gaza lying in the mud where she had fainted away from exhaustion. While I was trying to bring her to, my wife came up. I sent her to find Eber – who had before shown us he knew how to bring back life into a half-drowned human.

'In less than ten minutes I heard my wife calling to me from the other side of a tangle of fallen trees: "Here he is. I've found him. I'm not sure if he's dead – but unconscious anyhow. Husband, come! *I can't wake him up!*"

'I hurried around to her side. The boy was lying across a fallen log. No amount of shaking brought back any sign of life. I put my ear down against his chest; and heard a regular thump – though very slow and faint.

' "Good boy, Eber!" I muttered. "You're tough, – you're tough, thank goodness! – Belinda, we must get the raven here."

' "He's downstream ahead of us, I think," said my wife. "But what can he do here? Oh, husband," she sobbed, "we'll never get these poor children to the sea! I believe the sun has burnt out and the very Earth itself is dying."

' "Let's find out what the raven says to that," I answered. Then throwing back my head I sent out a parrot's call – a

275

signal we had arranged between us in case of danger – screeching downstream over the leafless tree-tops. It was answered right away by a like call. And two minutes later our guide fluttered down at our feet.

'For once in his life the raven-chatterbox had little to say. As he took a look at each of the youngsters, I could tell very plainly he felt this was a bad business.

' "It's my fault," he croaked solemnly at last. "I've travelled them too fast. But seeing the shortage of food, I thought it best to get this trip over and done with as soon as we could. Besides, having no other birds around, to get news from, made it more difficult – not that I blame anything on wings for staying out of this mess of a country."

' "But what are we going to *do*?" asked my wife, bursting into tears again. "We can't sit by and watch death take them from us, after all they've gone through!"

' "Ah now, wait a minute," said the raven in a kindly voice. "Don't give up yet, old lady. Once we reach the ocean's shore, they'll be all right. Getting them across the sea to the land on the other side may be a longer trip but it will be much easier. This is the bad stretch, the dead jungle.

' "I knew that – but what was the sense in my telling you ahead and getting you down-hearted? The best we can do now is for you to rest them up here while I fly the whole way down to the beach alone. There's bird-life there; and I can likely get some fish. Just how long it will take me to get back here with food, I can't say. Maybe quicker than you think. Because – strange thing – up there in the tree-tops, I've felt the air changing lately: a damp wind off the sea perhaps. Anyway, I've a notion that we can't be *very* far from the river's mouth."

'And then with a flash of his blue-black wings he was on his way, up through the skeleton jungle, to the higher air.

' "Good-bye!" he called. "Don't be down-hearted. We're not beaten yet." '

8

BELINDA CHANGES HER MIND

'WITH uneasy hearts, Belinda and I watched him disappear. We knew we were alone indeed now – with two desperately sick young-folk in our care.

'We found a sort of cave in the river's bank and brought both Eber and Gaza to it. Near by its entrance the stream still flowed sluggishly. Then, with big dry palm-leaves, we scooped the water up, threw it over them and fanned them.

'But after hours and hours of this they still showed no sign of life.

' "It's no use," said my wife. "And what good would it do if the raven did return – with *raw fish*? While they're unconscious, we couldn't make them eat it. True, the heat and the work have been hard on them; but their main trouble is starvation."

'I had to agree with that, of course. But what she said next fairly took my breath away.

' "Mudface," she sobbed, dropping her fan, "you can't ask me to stay and see these brave humans die.... My dear, I – I am going away ... till it's all over."

'Then, when she turned her back on us and slowly moved off, I saw that her mind was made up to desert the task. And of a sudden, something like desperate anger boiled up inside me.

' "Stop, Belinda!" I shouted. "Stay where you are! Did we not despair once before of Gaza's life? Yet we pulled them through, didn't we? Stick on the job: I order you."

' "I *can't* stay and watch them die, husband," she whimpered – "I really can't."

'My heart sank as again she started to go farther into the forest. Never in my life have I felt so hopeless.

' "Belinda," I called after her, "you know I cannot stop

you. But if you leave me alone now, when I need your help so sorely, you will be sorry for it all your living days."

'That halted her. Why, I cannot say. — Women are strange creatures. — Slowly she turned around and came back towards me. And she had not taken more than two steps when a half dozen clams seemed to fall out of the sky upon the muddy ground between us.

'Both of us looked upward. A tall and leafless mahogany tree stood close by the entrance to our cave. In the bare top-most branches of this we saw twenty or thirty pelicans gathered — their great shovel-bills filled with fish to over-flowing.

'Among the queer birds I easily recognized the raven, who wasted no time in coming down to us.

' "What ho, my hearties!" he croaked. "How are the kids?"

' "The same," said I, "as when you left us. We've tried all we know, but no life have they shown yet."

' "Well," said he, "we've *got* to get them awake somehow. No use stuffing unconscious mouths with uncooked fish — it was all I could find. — And we can't afford to be polite: *slap* them awake, if that's the only way."

'So, taking Eber first, I began slapping his face with soft stems of palm-leaves. The raven signalled one of the pelicans to come down with some more clams. Then he explained to Belinda how to crack them up in her mouth till she had a couple of quarts of clam-juice ready.

'Unmercifully I beat and slapped poor Eber for a quarter of an hour. And the treatment must have done something to get his blood circulating again. For presently he mumbled, as if in a dream, about my roughness. At that I put my front legs underneath his arms, lifted him into a sitting position and shook him till his teeth almost fell out. Then he stumbled, all groggy, to his feet and started to fight me back.

' "He'll do," snapped the raven sharply. "Now give the

278

girl the same. Both of them *must* be alive enough to swallow clam-juice."

'With the gentle Gaza I liked this business still less. But I had been given my orders. And after I'd broken six or seven palm-stems over her, she too woke up – and tried to run away! Of course she did not get far before she fell from weakness.

'But things went much easier for us after we had brought both of them to their senses. Belinda trickled the clam-juice into their mouths and they gulped it down hungrily.

'It was wonderful to see how quickly those youngsters changed with food and rest. I watched them talking and smiling together. Once more they had been saved from the very jaws of death. I was happy – happy for them and for myself. But I believe I was happiest of all for Belinda: that she had changed her mind and not deserted us. For had she left me at that terrible moment, I am sure she never could have forgiven herself. Poor, motherly Belinda! She was crying again now – but this time out of gladness and relief.

'In a few days, the raven said, he thought we could be on our way again – as long as we watched how the humans took it.

' "You know, Mudface," said he, "I was delighted to find what a short trip it is. I reckon we should see the ocean within three or four days now – even taking it in easy stages."

'Then he gave orders to the pelicans to fly along with us overhead; and we started off again on our march to the sea.'

9

THE OCEAN AT LAST

ON their way home to bed that night the Doctor's animal family seemed unusually talkative.

'Looks to me, Doc,' said Cheapside, 'as if old Muddy Pants was coming to the end of his story. – Thanks be! ... Just to see dear old London once again! Do you realize, John Dolittle, M.D., 'ow long we've been listenin' to that ante-diluvian yarn-spinner in the middle of this foggy swamp?'

'No,' said the Doctor. 'But anyway it was worth it.'

'Tee, hee, hee!' tittered the white mouse. 'You should know, Cheapside, the Doctor never bothers about time – when he's interested.'

'Ah!' cried Gub-Gub suddenly. 'Home! The thought – the very thought – of a nice large English cauliflower! Um-m-m! I'm terribly tired of these African vegetables.'

'I wonder,' said Jip, 'how old Prince is getting on – teaching those pups to be gun dogs – without losing their tails. I wouldn't want the job.'

'Ah me!' murmured Chee-Chee the monkey. 'Africa *is* a beautiful country, of course. But if you stay away from it long enough, losing touch with your old friends, it's surprising how your taste changes. It'll be wonderful to see dear old Puddleby again.'

'It would be,' muttered Polynesia the parrot, 'if it wasn't for that awful English climate – rain, rain, rain!'

'The truth is, I suppose,' said Too-Too the owl: 'your real home is where your friends are; the Doctor and his stories round the kitchen fire o'nights; the freedom of his home and the rest. Well – '

'And then there's always something new popping up there,' said the white mouse. 'I don't believe I'd *want* to live any other place now. For instance –'

'I'm afraid those kitchen windows,' said Dab-Dab, 'will need new putty. I wonder if Matthew Mugg has kept out of jail. . . . And as for the house-cleaning! Well, as the Doctor says, "Never lift your foot till – " '

And so they all chattered on, mostly about Puddleby and the old home, till we reached the office and I had the note-books safely stowed in the vault under the floor. Then we went to the bunkhouse and turned in.

'You know, Stubbins,' said the Doctor as he lay down and punched his hay pillow into shape. 'I fancy Cheapside's right: Mudface's story of the Flood is coming to an end. I *do* hope Belinda, his wife, shows up before we leave. Mudface shouldn't be alone – with his rheumatism so bad.'

I had been thinking the same thing. 'I suppose he won't take his medicine regularly after we go if she isn't here to see to it,' I said.

'That's what worries me,' said John Dolittle. 'Oh, well, we haven't gone yet. Perhaps she'll return before we have to leave.'

'Do you mean to ask Mudface about those ruined buildings we saw at the lower end of the lake?' I asked.

'Very likely,' he answered, 'very likely. But I have such millions of things I want to learn from him concerning the days of Noah, I'm not sure if I shall get round to it. That's always the way: no matter how many questions you ask – when you have the chance – you always forget the most important, till after it's too late. Oh, well, we'll do the best we can, Stubbins. Good night!'

'We took things much easier now,' Mudface went on the next evening. 'We had to think of the young people's strength. But towards the end of the second day Belinda asked,

' "Isn't the ground sloping all the time? The walking doesn't seem so hard – or is it just my imagination?"

' "No," said the raven, "the going's all downhill, gentle-

like, from here on. This is the ocean slope. We're coming down off a high jungle plain to the beach-level below. Don't you notice that the dead trees are thinning out – growing fewer?"

' "Yes, I do," said Belinda, smiling and brightening up for the first time in seven days.

'And now, soon, the river became wider and deeper. That may not sound much to you. But for me, to feel my feet no longer touch bottom – that I could swim again, instead of that heart-breaking scramble over and around tangled timber, that – well, what's the use? It would be impossible to make anyone understand the joy of it.

'No longer did that dreadful stagnant stench of rotting

woodland-world cling about our weary overheated bodies. The clean smell of an ocean wind blew freshly in our faces.

'Every one of us took new heart, straining his eyes ahead to the promise of a new climate. And presently we saw the river was spreading out more and more, into a regular lovely bay – miles wide.

'I signalled to our passengers to get upon our backs; and with mighty strokes, Belinda and I churned the clean water to cross this natural harbour, the harbour of Fantippo. The raven flew on ahead of us and alighted in a tall tree upon the bank. What a tiny dot he looked! But he was not so small or far that we couldn't hear his bass, croaking voice, as he turned and shouted back to us:

' "Surf ahead! – The beach is just outside the bar. I can see the ocean breaking on the sands. We've done it, my lads! Take your time: we're all right now. – The *sea*, the sea at last!" '

10

BOAT-BUILDING

'OF course,' Mudface went on, 'just for two turtles and a bird, travelling over an ocean would have been easy. But with two weakened people to care for, the crossing was a very different matter – especially since it was a sea no one had ever crossed. The *Atlantic*, you call it now. But at that time, remember, it was newly cut, completely unknown.

'Said the raven, when we were talking over the long trip ahead,

' "This is such a tricky sort of a journey – I think it would be foolish for us to try to get prepared for every little thing. Goodness! No matter what we do, we're bound to run into surprises – things we don't expect."

' "True, Raven," said I – "very true."

' "What we *must* have first," he said, "is good, fresh water, till rains come – and supply us at sea. Next, enough food to get us started. The pelicans tell me there are groups of islands on the way across. And on them we'll hope we can find something more to eat. A few fishing birds have promised me to fly part way with us; so we might be worse off. Then – very important – we must build a boat that will stand storm and rough weather. While you're busy on that here, I'll go ahead and try to find the first islands for you to take a rest on. What do you think?"

' "Sounds like good sense," said I.

' "Very well. Let's waste no time," he said. "I've a feeling speed is going to be important – in spite of my mistake before."

' "We'll keep an eye on the youngsters while you're gone *this* time," said Belinda. – "Don't fear."

'So, taking a couple of pelicans with him, the raven flew off.

'As he disappeared, my wife said, "Husband, let us make sure of the food first. All of us will go hunting. The boat-building will be easier, when we get Eber and Gaza in better health to help us."

'Right away we all went off exploring for food. The young people by now – while they still of course could not talk our language – were much better at catching on to our sign-talk. It took us barely a moment, by acting out what we wanted them to do, to make them understand almost anything.

'Their spirits too were much gayer on this food-searching picnic. They also seemed stronger already – no doubt through the change in air. Truly, I thought, they looked a most handsome couple as they followed behind us, laughing and talking.

' "They don't seem to be hunting very hard for food, now, Belinda," said I, glancing back over my shoulder.

' "My dear Mudface," she whispered, "*eating* is not the

only important thing – except when you're starving. – Sh! That's just a little love-making, stupid! Don't stare at them so! It's *their* business, not ours."

' "Quite, quite," said I. – "Their business, as you say. For truly I never saw turtles make love like that – throwing seaweed at one another. Most peculiar!"

'Along the shore we gathered many kinds of shellfish. These were carried up beyond reach of the tide and stored in marked places, for picking up later.

'A little farther back from the beach, where trees still stood here and there, we discovered the edible tree-mushroom, growing in plenty on the dead trunks. These too we gathered.

'The problem of making something for carrying drinking water in was not so easy. But, luckily the one thing that Eber had brought with him on our last wild flight from the tigress had been his stone knife – which he kept stuck in his belt. With this we were able to kill and skin a seal. Eber spread the skin out on a frame to dry in the sun.

' "I hate to see animals killed," said Belinda, gazing thoughtfully at the spread-out skin. "But this time it had to be done. We can't go without something to carry drinking water. When that hide is sewn up properly, with tough grass-thread, it should hold nearly a hundred gallons. Well let's get to the boat-building. The raven may be back any day now, croaking with impatience to sail."

'This part of our preparations proved the hardest of all. We made many kinds of boats and rafts from the dead poles of trees. But when we came to launch them in the sea they rolled and tossed and cracked us on the head; and they all ended by falling apart in the rough surf. Here we were dealing with water much rougher than the lake.

'It was not till the raven returned that we had any success in our boat-building. Without delay, he explained that there was only one kind of craft for us to use on such a journey.

HUGH
LOFTING

' "It's a sort of faggot-outrigger," he said, "and it is
pretty nearly unsinkable. You make two faggots – out of
long sticks – pointed at their ends, and you lay them side
by side on the beach. Then you get heavier poles to fasten
across the tops of the faggots, binding them firmly over
the faggots to form a deck."

' "What are we going to fasten them with?" asked
Belinda. "We haven't any nails."

' "Why, with ropes made out of bark-strips of course,"
said the raven. "We'll need yards and yards of it – for the
faggots and for fastening the cross-pieces too. Where are
the youngsters? – That will be easy work for them."

' "Well," I said, "last time I saw them they were chasing

one another around the sand-hills – a new game: throwing mud at one another. Belinda says it's a sign – with humans – they're in love, and that I should leave them alone."

' "Throwing mud at one another!" snorted the raven angrily. "Don't they know there's work to be done – and in a hurry too. The sea-birds on the first group of islands told me the wind may change any day at this season. Then it'll be against us instead of with us – cutting our speed in half. It's a long trip – and I've no idea yet what the farther islands may be like. – And these kids are throwing mud at one another !"

' "But they're so young," said Belinda. "The better feeding has made them feel like new people."

' "New fiddlesticks!" snapped the raven. "We've got to be on our way before this wind changes. Go and get them for me at once, please."

'So I went and searched out the boy and girl and brought them back to the job of boat-building.

'The raven, after one glance at their mud-spattered faces, told me to take them off and explain what he wanted about the ropes.

'There was only one kind of tree on the bay-shore whose bark was any good for rope-making. But I found it; and soon we had coils and coils of rope of different thicknesses – twisted, braided and strong. With these on my back and the youngsters clinging to my shell, I swam across the bay again, out to the beach beyond the bar.

' "Good!" said the raven. "I think you've got enough there. Let's go to work."

'Under his directions, I soon saw the shape our raft was going to be. It was a sort of double-keeled canoe. The crosspieces formed a kind of deck; and this was covered over with a shade-cabin in which we were to live and store baggage. It had a window each side, a door at each end – and a roof of thatched grass. By the time it was finished we had stopped referring to it as a raft and had begun to call it a boat: it looked so nearly like one.

' "Now," said the raven, "the paddles are the next thing. Get some soft light wood, you turtles, and bite them into the shape of paddles – with good wide blades and strong shafts. – How about the drinking-water supply? We must have enough for six days at least."

'And Belinda explained how we had made the sealskin waterbag.

' "Fine!" he said. "Then we're all set, as soon as you've made the paddles. Let's launch the boat empty, first, to see how she behaves in rough water. Afterwards we'll bring her back and load her with the stores." '

II

ISLAND OF PEACE

'WHEN our strange boat was loaded up, the young people were delighted with her. The arrangements for paddling were certainly very snug and comfortable. The whole floor inside the cabin was lined with thick soft grass. And the paddlers knelt either side of the boat and paddled out of the windows. When they grew tired, they could just lie down on the cushiony grass and take a rest.

'The deck-house took up only the centre of the boat. – *Amidships* I think you call it?' (The turtle glanced this question at Polynesia, the old sailor – who nodded in agreement.) 'And the ends of the little ship were left unroofed, for storing the food, drinking water, spare rope and so forth.

'We had a rudder – of sorts – a long sweep-paddle: but we meant to steer mostly by watching the raven and his pelicans, who knew the way to the first group of islands. And by night I had the stars to hold a course on.

'At the last moment, the raven said, "By gosh! I almost forgot the sail." And he sent me back into the forest to fetch the bamboo pole. We laced the upper part of this with dry palm-leaves. It looked like an enormous, long-handled fan; and we fastened it in the stern, so it could be turned, and set any way you wished.

' "That'll come in handy – especially if the wind changes," said the raven. "Now, my hearties, say good-bye to Africa. All aboard!" '

The old parrot, Polynesia, had up to this looked bored throughout the whole of Mudface's story. But now she became so interested in the turtle's seafaring talk she suddenly broke out into one of her sailor's songs:

"Sailing, sailing,
Over the bounding main –"

Her voice was very scratchy. And Cheapside growled, 'Oh dry up, me old Pollywog! – Voice needs oiling. – You won't never get back into opera again. – What'll you bet me they don't run into the rocks afore they've gone two miles?'

'Now, now,' said the Doctor. 'We want to hear the story, please.'

'Well,' said Mudface, 'the rest is islands, you might say – islands, islands and more islands. I've told you there were many groups in those times, John Dolittle, which have since disappeared entirely.

'We crossed the Atlantic Ocean at almost its narrowest point. We left from somewhere around what you now call the Bight of Benin, in Africa; and – as near as I can judge – we hit across towards the big bulge of Brazil, in South America.

'In stages the raven led us from one lot of islands to another. They were all different; but practically none had any life on it except sea-birds, shellfish, crabs and the like. One or two islands had high volcanoes still smoking in their centres; and on these islands not even clams or seaweeds were to be seen. Here we anchored offshore, only to get a rest. But underground – or undersea – rumblings kept us awake all night, reminding us of the Deluge earthquakes; and we were glad to get away from them as soon as we could.

'Some of these island-groups were much farther than others. And on one tiresome stretch we crossed about eight hundred miles without seeing land. This was the only stage in the whole trip where our luck seemed to go back on us. First, the wind dropped altogether; and only hard work at the paddles kept us going at all. Then the wind swung about and blew right in our teeth. A storm was gathering.

'Belinda and I got out and swam, towing the craft with ropes. But even that did little more than hold us still, where we were. One blessing was that heavy rains fell which we gathered in palm-leaves – and so partly restocked our drinking supply. But the seas became enormous in size – waves seventy and eighty feet high. And there were times when we thought our outrigger would fall apart.

'But on the third day the dirty weather suddenly cleared; the wind changed in our favour; and, as twilight came on, the setting sun showed us a single lovely island not more than fifteen miles ahead.

'During the storm, which we had come through, our pelicans of course had not been able to catch any fish for us. And even if they had, it is doubtful if Gaza could have eaten it. For she was again in a state of terrible weakness – from the wild tossing of our little ship. In the half-dark we found a bay on the island's south shore where we could anchor in calm shelter.

'Next morning, leaving Eber to act as nurse for Gaza while she rested, we went ashore to hunt up any new sorts of food we might find.

'This island seemed larger than any we had seen so far

And we were very glad – especially the raven – to discover it was a regular homing place for sea-birds. You have no idea how happy we were when they told us that the next lap of our journey would be our last – about three hundred miles, they said. Beyond this there were no more islands to rest on; but if we could make that distance in one trip, we would sight the continent of South America, the country which these birds came from in the early part of the year.

'We had arrived, it seemed, when springtime (a season new since the Flood) was beginning in those latitudes. Nesting was going on at a great pace. In the early sunlight the island's steep sides had sea-birds, in thousands, sitting on nests built on the rocky ledges of the cliffs.

'Remembering that poor Gaza had not tasted an egg in months, we asked the mother-birds to give us some. They refused. Then the raven explained that we were escaping from the cats (old enemies of all birds) and that we had been fighting them half-way across the world. On hearing this, the birds changed their minds and willingly gave us one fresh-laid egg from each nest. This amounted to many dozens.

'And so we were able to make a change in Gaza's diet which got her completely well again in a very short time.

'On this island too we found a good spring of cold drinking water, bubbling up out of the rock. We emptied our water-skin of its last supply – which had grown stale and smelly – and refilled it with this sparkling flow from the spring.

'Fearing more bad weather or other delays, the raven hustled us on again. We stayed only a day and a half on the island while we repaired our boat.

'She had taken an awful battering from that storm. The best we could do was to unbraid the old ropes at the worn places and plait them over again. We had drawn the boat up on the narrow beach at the foot of the cliff, to make working around her easier for us. Said the raven, as we finished rebinding the faggots,

' "Let's hope these lines will hold all right. Mighty important! If we run into tough weather again it'll be pretty near impossible to fix 'em in a rolling sea. Well, we'll hope for the best. Tow her out through the surf, Turtles. – All aboard for the last lap!"

'After we had paddled out from the island and set our patched sail on a westerly course, we were given an unexpected send-off by the sea-birds which I, for one, will never be able to forget. The cliff must have been a good four hundred feet high – with nesting ledges in the rock all the way up. Suddenly those millions of birds rose on to their toes, flapping their wings to us and calling good-bye in their shrill voices. The noise was deafening. And in a flash those fanning wings, like magic, turned the whole island a spotless white, from sea to sky.

'I glanced at Gaza. She was sucking a raw egg at the moment. But when that cry of farewell broke forth, tears ran down her face. And I was near enough to hear her murmur,

' "Good-bye, birds of the sea, good-bye! May your nesting-home stay forever yours – yours alone – an island of peace!" '

12

AMERICA!

'IT turned out that the last lap was to be the easiest of our whole ocean crossing. The wind never again blew against us – though it did sometimes drop altogether.

'We made, I reckon, something between a hundred and a hundred and fifty miles a day. Anyhow, in the middle of the second afternoon, I thought I felt some kind of a change in the air. The wind was now fitful – a sort of gentle breeze, blowing in short spurts from north, south, east or west; sometimes deathly still; sometimes hot; sometimes chilly. There was complete silence in our little ship. To the westward a light haze blotted out the farthest skyline. I was puzzled – expecting almost anything. Suddenly the raven croaked,

' "What are you jerking your head around like that for, Mudface?" (I had no idea he had been watching me.)

' "I don't know," I said. "I've never seen the ocean this way before. It's something new anyhow, and I don't know what. The wind seems to have gone a bit crazy; even coming from the west. I calculate we should now be less than a hundred miles from land – if what they told us at the island is right. But that low mist ahead shuts off the last stretch we should be able to see. – And there's a current too, or rip tide, pushing us along towards the south-west. What do you make of it?"

' "It *is* mysterious, all right," he grunted. "Feels like a new climate to me."

' "And what in heaven's name does *that* feel like?" asked Belinda. "Will you two stop chattering mysteries. – And talk a little sense for a change?"

' "Certainly," said the raven – "as soon as I can make sense of it myself. . . . Oh, look! Look at the girl!"

'Gaza was indeed behaving almost as peculiarly as the wind. She was drawing in deep breaths. She rose slowly from the floor like someone sleep-walking; and, coming over to Eber, grasped him firmly by the shoulder. He gave a startled jump and asked,

' "What is it, Gaza? What's the matter?"

' "Eber, dear," she whispered, "*flowers !* The wind is from the west – from behind that haze. What is it hiding, that mist on the skyline?" And again she breathed deeply. Her eyes sparkled. She seemed almost in a trance; and we could barely hear her words:

' "Jasmine," she murmured at length, "violets and sweetbrier ... lilies of the valley ... lilacs – all the flowers the Queen loved – and, above all, magnolias. I had almost forgotten that they ever bloomed!"

'Then once more the wind's mood changed – not steadily blowing in any direction now, but swirling round in gentle cyclones. And the far-off mist began to lift and roll away.

'At last we saw it – *land!* But none of us spoke: we were struck too breathless by the picture slowly getting clear before our eyes. Land growing higher and higher, and as we crept nearer the curtain of haze lifted. From the level of the sea, upward and upward, to where the mountains sloped into the white clouds, it was all colours. – Land, fertile land in blossom – land as it had been before the coming of the Flood!

'Still not one of us said a word – just gazed and gazed. Then suddenly Gaza sprang forward and, grasping the mast at the head of the boat, she began singing. . . . And oh, *how* she sang!

'King Mashtu had boasted that this slave, whom he had brought from foreign lands to entertain the ladies of his queen's court, had the loveliest voice in all the world.

'She began very, very softly – little more than a murmuring hum. I had not heard her sing since we turtles listened from our prison-pond across the zoological park of Shalba. Now, as the mist kept fading and the strengthening wind blew us closer to America, we saw that this great land stretched to the right and left of our course as far as the eye could reach. And slowly Gaza's voice grew and grew to its full glory. Eber moved forward and put his arm gently about her waist.

'Presently the raven (who always wanted to be a singer himself) was so carried away by the beauty of her voice that he joined in. But his croaking was so dreadfully out of tune that we all, Gaza included, broke into laughter. Then we all sang, just anyhow. Gaza came back from the bow and threw her arms around my neck while Eber did

HUGH LOFTING

the same to Belinda. The spell was broken and there was general hubbub.

'And so, laughing, singing and joking, we landed in America.'

13

THE RAVEN EXPLORES A NEW WORLD

THERE was complete quiet while Mudface stopped and took a drink of muddy water from his dish on the floor. I rested my wiggling pencil and stretched my hand to get the cramp out of it; meanwhile I glanced round the faces of the audience.

They were not an easy crowd to talk to, by any means. (Those hundreds of monkey-carpenters were a restless lot.) But it was clear that the turtle had got them all interested now – no matter what they might have been before. Even the rowdy sparrow, Cheapside – still of course pretending to be asleep – had, I noticed, one eye open and was listening with all his attention. As for the rest of them, they were clearly impatient for the turtle to go on.

'My, oh my!' the Doctor sighed as the turtle was finishing his drink. 'What a thrill *that* must have been for you! To discover a new world. While we, with our little page of history, have always given honour to Columbus.'

'Oh, well, Doctor,' said Mudface, wiping his mouth with the back of his right claw, 'you must remember that what I am telling you came just after the Deluge. – Also don't forget Christopher Columbus had no raven to fly ahead and guide him.

'We had barely landed before the raven took me aside and said, "I'm off on a big trip, old-timer. You and your wife must take care of the youngsters for a while; because someone has got to find out if they've any enemies here, same as they had at home. Sure, we've seen no people as yet. But that doesn't mean there aren't any. There was supposed to be a desert where the ocean is now, eh? And Mashtu always claimed that America belonged to him. But very few travellers, I think, got as far as this. And no one who set out to cross the Atlantic Desert *ever returned to Shalba*. . . . Sounds queer, what? Anyway it's got to be looked into."

'Well, he was gone some months.

'Before he got back to us I was beginning to be homesick for the countries I'd left behind. Can't say just why. But I suppose home is always home. I found myself wondering how everyone was getting on back there. . . . Yes, maybe that was it: age. I belonged to the Old World – while these young people were interested only in building a new one.

'I talked it over with Belinda; and I found that she agreed with me – for once – completely.

' "Why, of course we can't stay here – for keeps," she said. "I too want to know how my friends are getting on. Gaza and Eber are doing splendidly here. Whenever you're ready, Mudface."

'So, we turtles had it all planned to say good-bye as soon as the raven showed up. We made no preparations at all. Sea-going turtles, when they decide to take a journey, just get up and go. It is only Men who pack a lot of bags and things and lie awake nights before, trying to remember what they have forgotten. All *we* want is water and – or – mud.

'The raven came. And I have never known him to have so much to chatter about. You should have been there, Doctor. He was chock-full of science.

'Of course we *were* interested. But we were also anxious to tell him the news that we were going back home. However, he jabbered on and on. Why was this country, he asked, so much further recovered than the ruined land we'd left behind? – Because, he answered himself, the Big Wave (when the poles of the Earth shifted and the Mediterranean burst through the mountains at Gibraltar) cut the new Atlantic Ocean on its way. It didn't come straight across west. The Gulf Stream had something to do with that. And by the time the Wave had cut right across the Atlantic Desert it had, it seemed, spent most of its strength. Never got far inland this side, on account of the big mountains – the Andes and the Rockies – but just footled along on a more or less north-south line and washed the poisonous sea salt *off* the land instead of pushing it on inland and westward.'

297

Mudface paused a moment, smiling. 'Oh, that raven and his science! I couldn't get a word in edgewise.'

'Well, well,' said the Doctor, 'I suppose it *was* exciting for him to have discovered why the land was undamaged by the Flood.'

'Yes,' said Mudface, 'but he wasn't through yet. I asked him if he'd seen any cats.'

' "There are a few native ones – like the lynx in the north and the jaguar in the south. But none of the deadly fellows, like Bengal tigers and African lions – no real man-eaters. Still it surprised me there were any at all."

' "That's good," I said. "Now, there's something my wife and I would like to talk over with you. . . . Belinda, Belinda! – I'd swear she was here a minute ago. That's strange. . . . Belinda, Belinda! . . . Where are you?"

'No answer.

' "Wait here," I said. "I'll go to the beach-shack and see if I can find her."

'Half-way to the shack I met Belinda – in a great state of excitement.

' "Oh, husband," she gasped. "She's going *to have a baby* – Gaza! Isn't that simply lovely? I just found out. – Ah, I'm not saying I didn't suspect it before. But now it's certain. You remember I told you that when human beings started throwing mud at one another, it's a sure sign they're in love. . . . Oh," (she gasped again) "I'm all of a twitter! – Glad I could give you the wonderful news alone, without the raven hearing it yet. Because of course we can't leave now – not before the baby's born, can we?"

' "Why not?" I asked.

' "Good gracious!" she cried. "Who's going to look after the child, if I'm not here? Gaza never had one before. And besides, it will be the first *American* baby. Men-folk don't know anything about raising children. What if anything should happen to it – colic, foot-and-mouth disease . . .?"

'I thought heavily a while before answering. For me, it

298

had always been only Eber who must be saved from the Deluge, from the tigress – from the meat-eaters. The girl, well, she was only necessary to keep him company.

'I was still in favour of a peopleless Earth. Man, with his wars and all, had made such a mess of the world! And now my wife was asking *me* to help build a new race of Men!

'Belinda must have read my thoughts. For presently she said very gently,

' "Husband, have you forgotten your words to Noah? You promised we'd rescue Eber so that he could start a world of his own, a world of happiness. Tell me, how can that be done if Gaza has no sons. Have you forgotten that we risked our lives over and over again to keep these two young people safe from that she-devil tigress and a hundred other dangers?"

'But still, for a moment, I gave her no answer.

'And suddenly a picture glowed before my eyes: the picture of all we turtles had suffered that those two might live. What use would it be now if new dangers destroyed their sons as soon as we left. And I said,

' "Belinda, we'll see it through. Whatever may come of it, as your brother, Wag, warned us, none can tell. But, homesick as I am, I'll stay with you till the first American is born in his own land. . . . You're sure it will be a boy?"

' "Bless you, Mudface!" said she. "What *else* could it be?" '

14

THE FARM

'WELL, the great day came, the day when the first new human arrived in the New World. When I say *first* human, I mean of course, the first as far as we knew. Because who can tell, with all the history books swept away, how many deluges there were before the one I saw?'

'Quite so,' the Doctor muttered thoughtfully. – 'A very interesting consideration.'

'Nor can we say, John Dolittle, how many more world-floods yet may come – to start Earth's life all over again.

'Anyhow, this baby was no ordinary child. Yes, it was a boy, all right; a most charming young person. He was tough and strong from the start – like his father. And he had a smile that would charm the birds off the trees – like his mother. He was named Aden.

'We all fell madly in love with him – you couldn't help it. Even the raven, who said that children to him were nothing but a nuisance – even he, when he thought no one was listening, used to sing lullabies in that cracked voice of his over the cradle. And he did clownish antics to amuse the little one – who enjoyed the performance with no end of giggles and gurgles.

'And, I have to confess, I was nearly as bad, myself. The baby seemed to take as great a liking to me as I did to him. When he was grown large enough to crawl, he tried to climb up on to my back.

'So, I told them how, by making a little fenced play-yard with a sunshade over it, and tying it firmly on top of me the baby could be set safely inside it. This was done. And I would take him for rides around the country.

'Secretly, once in a while, I even paddled him out into the shallower water; and took him on little exploring

cruises round the lagoons and lakes that lay inland from the beach. He loved these water-trips most of all. And he came to feel that I was his personal property and slave – a sort of mixture of nursemaid, play-yard, perambulator and his own private boat.

'But it was Belinda herself who was the worst of all. The way she fussed over that child from morning to night, you'd think it was *her* baby instead of Gaza's.

'And it was really my wife's fault that we stayed in America for so long, instead of only the week or two which we had planned.

'At last the raven said to me in private:

' "Listen, I know how hard it is for you to leave all this. –

I mean, for instance, Gaza over there: a picture of content-
ment – calm and happy eh? . . . But I'll bet you one thing."

' "What's that?" I asked.

' "She's going to have another – and soon."

' "Going to have another what?"

' "Another baby of course."

' "What makes you think that?"

' "Oh, I'm not talking any highfalutin stuff like Belinda,"
said the raven. "But I've just noticed that folks on farms
always has lots of kids – maybe it's the fresh air or something. It stands to reason she'll have another. And when
she does, Brother Turtle, where will *we* be with Aunt
Belinda? I tell you, when Gaza has *two* babies to look after;
well, we're here for life, if you don't put your foot down.
Two years we've been loafing round here like nursemaids.
The Old World may have changed a lot in two whole years.
– Have you spoken to Belinda yet?"

' "Oh yes, Raven. But I got nothing but the old excuses.
I've argued and argued with her."

' "Well, *don't* argue with her. – She's a woman. Y'ought
to know better, at your age. Bound to lose. *Don't* argue
with her: talk to her. Just say: the party is leaving for
Shalba on Wednesday at eight in the morning. That's all."

' "Yes, I know you're right," I said. "I better speak to my
wife tonight – firmly. Maybe it'll be too late if I – by the
way, will you help me to – er – persuade her?"

' "Bless your heart!" he laughed. "Of course I will. Myself, I'm getting a little sick of the roses round the door in
America. . . . If it wasn't for that kid –"

'Well, poor Belinda! I fancy she'd been having some of
those *suspicions* about Gaza again. In any case, I've no
doubt that if I hadn't had my friend to back me up, I'd have
given in once more. But the raven just said off-hand-like –
after we had talked a while of this and that –

' "Heigh ho! It's my bedtime. – Oh, I almost forgot :

Mudface and I are leaving for Africa day after tomorrow, Wednesday. You care to come along with us? – Oh, my Sunday tail-feathers, just look at the way that baby sleeps over there! My, but he's a healthy one! – Good night."

'And before Belinda had a chance to answer him at all, he was on his way down the stairs. I went with him to see him out at the farm-house door. But before he left we stopped in at the kitchen to tell Eber and Gaza.

'It took me only a minute or so to make them understand in our sign-language that we were leaving for Africa. Gaza cried a little. But Eber told me that, although they would both miss us terribly, our news was not a surprise to him. He had told his wife many times that, sooner or later, we would want to go back to our old home. It was only natural.

'And that was that! I felt a great weight lifted from my mind as I bade the raven good night and arranged with him to meet again the following day.

'The time went quickly. A grand feast was prepared at the farm to celebrate our going away. Eber asked if we would come back sometime to visit them – and we said we hoped so. However, I'm afraid that no one at the party was very gay – except little Aden, who was hardly old enough yet to know what was going on.

'The next day we went down to the shore. My wife and I waded out into the swirling blue-green water of the sea, while the raven took to the air above. Eber and his family waved to us from the sands. I do not like good-byes. And I was especially glad that this looked like being a short one. I think everyone, including even the raven, felt the same way about that farewell.

'But it was little Aden – barely big enough to talk at all – who changed it into something different. Suddenly he realized at last that we were leaving him, that he was losing his old animal friends. He burst into tears and stretched his chubby hands out towards us.

303

'"Linda!" he called. "Do not go! Aden wants you, Linda."

'Then I noticed that my wife was crying silently as, beside me, she breasted the heaving swell of the ocean in a desperate kind of way. But she did not look back at little Aden – I think she was afraid to.

'And then, after all, I found myself wondering: *why* did she weep? Suddenly, in the way she often did, she answered my thoughts aloud:

'"Oh husband, husband," she sobbed, "they're so helpless – really! Even if they have more brains than we have, and so can run a world in what seems a better way, they have not our animal sense to know when danger is near – though it's true we cannot tell *how* we know. They're helpless against the stormy seas – which we can cross like stepping over a log; they're helpless against starvation, when we can go without food for weeks; they're helpless against the wild beasts of the jungle. And because, sooner or later, my Aden will go down – fighting – where you or I would come through alive, I am crying, husband – crying because I know we'll no longer be there to protect him with our – our animal sense."

'It broke my heart to see the way she half turned to look back at the human family on the beach – then thought better of it and firmly ploughed on, eastward, towards the Old World.

'"Somehow I feel certain," she said, "that we'll never see them again. Other men are bound to come and discover this great land. And what then? Some new Mashtu will arise and crush the little world of peace and friendliness they're building – crush all the kindly faith in justice and honesty which Gaza is teaching the little one. . . . Tell me, even if we came back, who could find my Aden for me then . . . my baby?"

'For the moment I had no answer, no word of comfort to give her. But presently I said,

' "Belinda, my dear, I know we have never spoken openly of these things before. But perhaps it was all planned this way. Maybe the Some One, whose power was greater than Mashtu's, never intended that Man should die out in this Deluge; and He sent you and me, the peaceful turtles, across the path to save Man from complete destruction. If that's so, we succeeded, didn't we? ... Look forward to seeing Shalba's lovely countryside again. All's well, they say, that ends well. Come, come! Cheer up!"

'But she just swam on, giving me no answer – trying only to hide her tears. I too felt very gloomy.

'Our feelings – indeed the whole business – was strange, making no sense. The ocean, wide-spread before us, looked unhomelike now, bleak and dull. Could it be, I asked myself, that living with a human family had changed us? Yet was it not ourselves who had made possible the busy happiness of life for those people we were leaving behind? Had we, the independent turtles, become a little like the warmblooded menfolk – through years of living with them? We had grown homesick for the Old World; yet this parting now seemed like leaving our own family.

'Suddenly a little cheerfulness reached us from above, from the after-sunset sky – where you could hardly pick out anything but the Evening Star. It was the hoarse bawling voice of the raven; but it made us feel less lonely.

' "Hulloa, down there, Turtles! Set the course south-east by east. – Should be a fine night, by the look of it. You'll hear from me again in the morning."

'And that, John Dolittle, is the end of my history of the Deluge.'

No one spoke for nearly five minutes after the turtle came to a stop. The Doctor himself just stared at the floor, far away in thought, as though, it seemed, all the questions he had meant to ask had gone clean from his mind.

At last, with a sort of start, he pulled himself together and spoke.

'Pray excuse me, Mudface,' said he, 'for not even thanking you for the most interesting story I've ever listened to. There are many questions I would like to ask but I will have to run through all the note-books with Stubbins to recall them. That would keep you up too late now. You have already talked longer than usual tonight. Please take your medicine and go to bed right away. You know, I am sure, how grateful I am to you.'

'I was glad to tell it, Doctor,' was all the turtle answered. 'Good night!'

15

WE PADDLE DOWN THE SECRET LAKE

TURTLETOWN, as Cheapside had called it, was closing up. Great quantities of medicine for Mudface had been mixed and stored in the bunkhouse. John Dolittle had asked our visiting monkey-carpenters to pull down most of the smaller shacks, because he feared that with bad weather they would most likely fall apart and become unsightly wrecks after we had gone. But the turtle's big shelter-shed had been strengthened to last a long time.

The monkeys then became the street-cleaning squad, cleared away the rubbish of the old buildings, swept the trash from the roadways and tidied up generally.

'I can't see the use of going to all this trouble, Doc,' said Cheapside. 'There certainly ain't goin' to be no visitors coming up to see old Mudpie's Castle-in-the-Fog for quite a while yet.'

'Never mind,' said John Dolittle. 'The turtle may be muddy; but he likes to have things orderly and neat. I know, because when I got my post-office birds to build the island for him long ago, he was delighted with the way they finished it off before they left.'

'Yes, and the blinkin' earthquake nearly finished it off too,' grunted the sparrow. 'This may be the top of the world, all right. But in my 'umble hopinion, the Deluge ain't over yet in these 'ere parts. The Earth still seems rollin' around, 'avin' tummy-aches, you might say. Remember them ruins of the old 'ouses we saw, comin' up 'ere? Why, what's the matter, Doc?'

'My goodness, I nearly forgot!' said the Doctor.

'Forgot what?' asked Cheapside.

'Why, his garden,' said the Doctor. 'Mudface loves nothing better than a nice garden – the same as I do. I must attend to it right away. . . . Excuse me a moment, please.'

The Doctor hustled off and questioned many of the monkey-leaders. Well, they not only brought kernels which would grow into fine shady palms – and bulbs that would become plants – but they actually got all the seeds from which the turtle's medicine was made. So, when these were planted, John Dolittle did not have to worry about his patient ever running short of what he had ordered for him.

While all this was going on I was digging down into our fire-proof safe under the office-floor. I was trying to sort out, from all those note-books, the questions which the Doctor wanted to ask the turtle. But what a job! Were there *ever* so many notebooks – filled from cover to cover?

After three hours of work I hadn't got very far; and Polynesia went to fetch the Doctor himself. He glanced through my work and said,

'The whole record does you great credit as a secretary, Stubbins.' He sat on the floor almost buried in note-books. 'But great heavens, to weed all the questions I want out of this library would take weeks, maybe months! Let's just pick out the most important – and hope for the best, shall we? I really don't see what else we can do.'

So that evening, when we gathered once more in the turtle's shelter, John Dolittle fired off question after question; and Mudface, if he could, shot the answers back just as fast – or shook his head – if he couldn't answer.

It was nearly all about science – about what changes the Deluge had made in the world. Some of the audience were deeply interested: others not at all. But we all stayed up till long past midnight. And everyone, by the end of it, was so weary that there was no talking whatever, after we bade the turtle good night and made our way home to bed.

In the bunkhouse we found a visitor waiting for us. It was one of those wild ducks that so often carried messages between the Doctor and his family in Puddleby. This duck had come to tell him that the old horse in the stable near the 'zoo' had complained that his roof was leaking badly.

'All right,' said John Dolittle. 'We are leaving here for Puddleby right away. Thank you very much for your trouble. Remember me to the birds in my garden, please – if you get back before we do.'

The next day, when all was in readiness for our leaving, Mudface asked the Doctor if he might swim down to the lower end of the lake to see us off. John Dolittle was delighted with the compliment and readily said yes.

'Who knows?' he laughed – 'on the way I may remember a few more questions which I forgot last night. I may not get another chance after this for a long time.'

So, late in the afternoon we all left the landing at the foot of the long road which led down from what was left of Turtletown at the island's top and started off. The fog over the Secret Lake was not bad; though once in a while it would roll up thick and heavy, close to the canoe and we were glad to have a guide with us. Mudface knew his way across this lake (hundreds of miles wide at the centre) in the pitch-dark. He took no notice of the cloak of mist about us, just staying close enough to the Doctor's stern-paddle, so that we should not lose touch with one another.

'Tell me, Mudface,' said the Doctor after we had gone about a mile, 'how did King Mashtu come to get all this power you spoke of?'

'Through the children – mostly,' said the turtle quietly.

'The *children*?' cried the Doctor in surprise. 'I don't understand.'

'Well,' Mudface answered, 'King Mashtu was all in favour of education. But instead of educating the children in the right way, in honesty and fairness, this king saw that an easier way to power for himself was to educate them the *wrong* way.

'Oh, Mashtu was clever. He taught those youngsters never to doubt his word. Then, when they were old enough to vote for him, he slyly put over his scheme for a one-man government for Shalba. – That is, a government run really by a single person. He knew that even though many were allowed to take part in running the country, one and one only should be the head, *His* word must be the law. And he lived and dreamed of one plan alone: that he, Mashtu, should be that head. He counted the days till he should be elected not only the head of the government, but King of Shalba.'

'Mudface,' asked the Doctor through the clammy fog – 'I believe of course every word that you are telling me – but how did *you* come to learn all this yourself? You were a prisoner in a zoo.'

'Well, Doctor,' said the turtle, 'Noah spoke often of the times before the Deluge. You remember he was the only one, besides yourself, to learn animal language. He too was a prisoner; though, as the head zoo-keeper, he was treated well. The old man had a habit of talking to himself. But, being afraid of spies, he always spoke in animal language – even in his sleep. So of course no one understood him, except the animals. . . . He did not like Mashtu or anything about him.'

309

'Ah, I see,' said the Doctor.

'Also,' Mudface went on, 'much of what I've told you I learned long after it happened – from Eber and Gaza, when they were building up their new language. Belinda and I got to understand it quite well. And we would enjoy, by the hour, hearing Eber and Gaza chat over past times.'

'Of course, of course,' the Doctor answered. 'I just wondered how turtles who always – and sensibly – mind their own business, I wondered – naturally – how you came to know so much about public affairs in bygone days: government, politics and all that, you know. Your memory is marvellous. Thank you. Pray go on.'

'King Mashtu!' sighed Mudface. 'He could have done so much good had he wished. But he was a puzzle no one ever understood. . . . Ah, well, he's gone now. Yet while he lived I don't suppose any man was more admired – or more hated.'

And of a sudden, just as I had expected, this strange story broke off; the turtle was silent; the fog, in true Lake Junganyika fashion, had lifted without warning. And there, quite close on our port bow, lay the ruined buildings we had seen before.

'There they are, Doc!' cried Cheapside. – 'The half-drowned slums we saw on our way in. . . . Jiminy crickets! I've run across some ramshackle waterfronts in me day: but never nothing like this. . . . Lumme, what a mess!'

I saw the Doctor in the stern (up to this he had been nothing more than an occasional voice behind a wall) look down at Mudface who swam near by. The turtle, treading water with his hind feet, stretched his neck up as high as he could to see the buildings better.

'Shalba!' he gasped. 'I know every alley, every stone in it. But how comes it here at the surface of the lake? Last time I trod its streets it lay beneath two hundred feet of water – at the bottom of Junganyika! This is magic John Dolittle.'

'No,' said the Doctor gently. – 'No, no magic, old friend. I'm sure it's just the earthquake, the same one that buried you. They do these queer things sometimes. It has heaved the floor of the lake up, at this end, in almost one piece, so the buildings show above the water. That is all.'

'Shalba!' muttered the turtle again. 'Shalba arisen from the past, arisen from the Deluge. . . . Shalba arisen from the dead!'

16

THE TREASURE VAULT

'I WOULD be grateful, Mudface,' said the Doctor presently, 'if you could show us something of the city before we leave. – But I don't want you to overtire yourself, you understand.'

'Certainly,' said the turtle. 'Come!' And he led the way.

On the poorer alleyways leading us into the town, the buildings were no different from those we had seen on our first and hasty visit. The streets were really canals, full of water, which lapped in and out of broken windows. The houses – small shops and the like – were nearly all of them partly ruined at least.

We did notice, however, as we paddled on, how many of them were at the same level. This, as the Doctor had said, must have been because the lower end of the lake's floor had been pushed up in one piece – without splitting the town in halves.

After winding through many side-streets and narrow lanes, Mudface presently led us out upon a wide open space. At first sight, it might have been a market, a public park or something of the kind. The buildings surrounding it were in a much better state.

'This was called Victory Square,' said the turtle. 'Once

the middle of it was filled with lovely flowering-trees, fountains and park benches.

'All the buildings you see around it now were put up when Mashtu came back from his last great war – against the Dardellians. It was built to commemorate that famous victory. Every house in this square was a part of the King's home. These on the left were the Royal Stables. Next to them were the quarters for the King's Guard; and beyond, you see what is left of the Royal Kitchens – they were almost as big as a town in themselves. Most of the rest were offices and government buildings.

'And that big place, with the crumbled towers, facing us, was the Royal Palace itself, where King Mashtu lived in a splendour such as the world had never seen before.'

I find it hard to give anyone a picture in writing of what the turtle was showing us. Certainly the man who laid it out was a true artist, a great architect. The square was unbelievably large – certainly, I would say, a mile from end to end; and more than half a mile wide. The stone used must have been granite or some other very hard form of rock, to have lasted all those thousands of years.

Even now (though there were gaps of ruins here and there in the close, even rows of buildings which surrounded the pleasure-park) enough of the vast planning still showed a beauty and magnificence which simply took our breath away.

The Doctor knew a good deal about ancient architecture; but, he told me later, the style of these buildings was like none he had ever seen – and gave him no idea of their age. The palace at the far end of the Square of Victory particularly held our attention. The outside of it, at least, seemed perfect – except for one of the high slender towers which had crumbled away a little, near the top. It still looked what it had been: the proud and splendid home of a king long dead.

'Stubbins,' said the Doctor at last in a voice strangely

hushed, 'just *look* at that huge main doorway! Did you *ever* see such carved stonework?'

The palace seemed to stand slightly higher than the rest of the square. For, even at that distance, we could see a half-dry strip of ground, showing in the front – and, above that, a wide terrace which ran completely round the palace.

Suddenly Mudface spoke again; and the way his voice startled us both, made us realize how long we had stared, almost in a trance, at this enchanted monument of the Past.

'That piece of dry land,' said he, 'in front of the palace should mean that its ground-floor will be all right for us to get in. Would you like me – if it's possible – to guide you through Mashtu's home, John Dolittle?'

'You took the words right out of my mouth,' laughed the Doctor. 'I'd like nothing better. Who would miss a chance of seeing the palace of a king who lived before the Flood?'

So the turtle swam across the square while we, very interested and all excited, paddled close behind him. Reaching the strip of land before the big door, we got out and tied up our canoe. A wide flight of steps led to the top of the terrace and the main entrance.

Mudface's great body (it looked like some big, mud-spattered van) was already scrambling up the royal steps – even before we had the canoe made safe by its painter-rope. As we hurried to follow him into the palace, I noticed that all our company were very grave and silent. They reminded me – for some reason – of a company of children being taken into church for an extra special service.

Inside, the light was very dim; and it took our eyes a moment or two to get used to the gloom – though we had by no means come from full sunshine outside. Presently, however, our surroundings began to take shape in the half-dark.

We seemed to be in a sort of passage. The confusion of the furniture and such was dreadful. A film of mud or slime covered everything.

The great turtle lumbered his way down the corridor. John Dolittle and I stuck close to his heels. Mudface, with his great muscles, shoved everything aside, no matter how heavy, making a pathway for the rest of us to follow.

We came out presently into a high, enormous room. The dim ceiling must have been a hundred feet above the floor-level. The clutter and confusion were not so bad here — though in places a rafter or beam had fallen from the roof. At the end of this tremendous chamber a high-backed chair stood all alone upon a low, raised platform.

This time the Doctor went ahead of our guide. He took his penknife from his pocket and gently scraped the slime from the arm of the big chair. Beautiful green stone was at once uncovered beneath the thin coating of mud.

I was close enough behind John Dolittle to hear him whisper, 'Good heavens. It's pure jade! I suspected, from the shape, it wasn't wood. – Must have cost a fortune. Solid jade, the whole chair! And the polish and colour are just as good as when it was first carved. . . . This seat, Mudface, was of course the Royal Throne?'

'Yes,' said the turtle. 'This room was called the Throne Room of the Royal Hall of Audience. It was here that King Mashtu sat in council and in judgement. And often – but – oh my gracious! Look, Doctor – over there – the Treasure Vault! . . . Why – why, *it's open!*'

Mudface was usually a very calm animal. It took a lot to upset or disturb him. That was why both the Doctor and I turned quickly at the excited tone of his voice. He was staring across the big hall at a door which led into another smaller room. The wall above it had a crack running from the Audience Hall's high ceiling right down to the top of this door's frame. Plainly the door itself had been damaged, instead of left open by chance. For we could see that the frame, into which it had fitted, had broken down at the top; it was this that had burst it open, inward. The door was enormously thick and strong. Six heavy hinges had once held it in place; but now, all askew, it hung by only one.

'Come, John Dolittle,' said the turtle. 'I think you will wish to see what lies within that broken door.'

17

CROWN OF THE WORLD

AGAIN, much too thrilled with expectation to talk, we followed our guide. He made light work of the rafters that lay in our way. Some of the stuff was terrific in weight. But, as Cheapside used to say, once Mudface pulled his head inside his shell and shoved, well, even if it was St Paul's Cathedral, it *had* to move. And as he worked forward, the turtle talked to us about the little room we were making for:

'King Mashtu kept the crown jewels in there. That's why it was called the Treasure Vault. Ten soldiers of the Royal Guard kept watch here every hour of the day and night. Mashtu had sent searchers all over the countries he had conquered to get the best locksmith in the world. He was found; and brought to Shalba, after the messengers had hunted for two whole years. He did a grand job for the King – made the vault – and its doors – the strongest ever built.'

'Yes,' the Doctor put in, peering ahead, 'I'd say he certainly did.'

'No thieves could get in,' the turtle went on – 'even supposing they could go to work with ten soldiers on guard. This locksmith was an old man. The King promised him all sorts of pay and presents for his work – a fine house of his own to live in, in his old age and all that. But when the work was finished Mashtu had him killed instead. You see, Mashtu was afraid the locksmith might give away the secrets of the vault, or keep an extra key to the locks, so his friends could help themselves to the treasure and money stored there.'

'But,' asked the Doctor, 'where – how – did Mashtu get all this money and treasure? For a vault, that room should be fairly large, judging by the size of the door.'

'Well,' the turtle answered, 'some came through taxing his own people. But most of it he took from the kings and princes he captured or killed on the battlefield. He was crazy about money – not for itself so much – but he needed it to make war – more and more wars. And he didn't care how he got it.'

We were standing before the door itself.

'Here we are, Doctor,' said Mudface. 'The boy can crawl in under at the left-hand lower corner. I'll have to stay behind a moment till I can push the whole door down flat. – Even then the entrance will be only just wide enough for my shell to pass through.'

I got down on my knees and started to creep in under the door, the animals waiting in line behind to follow me. To say that I was 'thrilled' would give you no idea of the tingle that ran down my spine. I was Captain Kidd and all the buccaneers of history rolled in one. For me it was the moment of a lifetime.

The light was poorer still inside; and I called back for Too-Too (the owl who could see in the dark) to come forward and help my groping steps. The Doctor, also crawling on his knees, took hold of my left foot so we should not lose touch with one another.

But here again it was only a minute or so before we got used to the darker room – or at least could see well enough to make out most things pretty plainly. Against the four walls, all around, stood heavy chests. But within the vault – except for the broken door – everything seemed orderly, in place and neat. Of course there was that thin coating of mud everywhere which told the story of long, long neglect. – Ghosts seemed moving and whispering everywhere.

Soon the Doctor rose from his knees and examined the whole room with great care.

'My goodness, Stubbins,' he murmured presently – 'King Mashtu's Treasure Vault! Almost gives you the creeps, doesn't it? There must be no end to the secrets that have laid hidden within these four walls – for no one knows how many thousands of years. Because every paper that was important or valuable to the State would have been brought down here for safe-keeping. . . . Er – er, I wonder what *that* is.'

His gaze had shifted now from the strong-boxes round the walls to the centre of the room.

There, about the height of a man's chest, it stood all by itself; and it looked like a cabinet of some kind. It wasn't large; but its sides were solid, so you could see nothing through them. But the top was grated; and through this you could look down inside.

For the first time the Doctor took a box of matches from his pocket and struck a light, Cheapside was perched upon my shoulder. Silently the three of us peered in through the grating. The bottom of the cabinet was partly filled with sand which had sifted in. But, in a circle, points of some half buried metal were sticking up. I wondered was my imagination working overhard in this spooky room; but I felt almost sure that that half-hidden thing down there might be a crown!

'Huh!' chirped Cheapside. 'Looks like old King Mashtu's top-hat, if you ask me, Doc. – Heaven defend us!' he added as the match burned out in the Doctor's fingers and a thunderous crash filled the room. – 'What's that noise? Sounds as if the roof was fallin' in.'

We turned quickly. But it was only Mudface. Dimly we could see he had pushed the heavy door right down and was now trampling slowly over it into the vault.

Said he, as he came up to the Doctor,

'That old locksmith's work was better even than I'd calculated. I thought I'd never break that last hinge.'

'Well now, old Muddy-puddy,' said Cheapside, 'how about tryin' yer muskles on one of these 'ere treasure-chests? They look as though they might 'ave somethin' in 'em better than dried apricots.'

At that, without a word, the turtle put the shoulder of his shell against one of the big chests. He took a good grip on the floor with his hind feet. And then he shoved. He was squeezing the heavy metal box against the wall.

Soon we heard a sharp *crack*. The lock gave way; the chest simply fell apart. And a great pile of gorgeous jewels and gold coins flowed over him upon the floor.

'Crikey!' muttered the sparrow. 'Would you look at that? Golden sovereigns the size of saucers. Why, with just one of these 'ere trunks a bloke could buy out the Bank of England! – And look at the pearls, diamonds – rubies like hens' eggs – enough jools to give you the drools. Hold me up, Tommy, I feels a faintin' spell comin' on. Now, Doc, you can live on Easy Street for the rest of your life.'

'But it's papers I'm looking for, Cheapside,' said John Dolittle – 'documents, you know, which will tell me about the world in Noah's time. What would I do with pearls and rubies?'

'Oh, I wasn't digesting you should wear 'em round yer neck, Doc,' said the sparrow. 'But this is *real money*! There's a fortune lyin' at your feet.'

Dab-Dab waddled forward across the room.

'Now, Doctor,' said she, as though she were talking to a naughty boy, 'I know I've been through all this with you before. But do try – for once – to be sensible. Have we *ever* had enough money for the housekeeping in Puddleby? You're always going broke. Now tie up a handkerchief full of those large rubies. The weight will be nothing in the canoe. Then we'll never have to worry about money again. *Please!*'

'No, no,' said the Doctor quickly. 'You don't know what you're asking me. All this treasure has been stolen, taken from conquered kings and murdered princes. These gold coins cry out with the voice of suffering – of innocent men, of women and even children slaughtered in war. Money! Bah, it is the curse of the world!'

319

His voice rose almost to a shout as he pointed to a string of glistening diamonds near his foot.

'No, no, Dab-Dab!' he repeated. 'This treasure stays where I found it. These precious stones have *blood* on them!'

The white mouse crept forward and examined the diamonds with his microscopic eyes. Then he looked up at Dab-Dab and gravely shook his head.

'I don't see any blood on them.'

The duck shrugged her wing-shoulders helplessly and turned away; while Polynesia the parrot, who was standing near, raised her old eyebrows and murmured wearily, 'What else did you expect?'

'Too bad, too bad, Dab-Dab, me old darling,' chirped the ever-cheerful Cheapside. 'But this little pile would sure have bought you a nice lot of sardines. – Well, well, easy comes, easy goes.'

'Mudface,' asked the Doctor, 'do you know what this is in the stand over here in the middle of the room?'

'Ah, that?' said the turtle. 'Yes, it was called the Crown of the World. After the King's last victory – over the Dardellians – many false-hearted men came to Mashtu with a very gorgeous gold crown and asked could they crown him King of the World. They said he now owned pretty much the whole of the Earth and therefore he deserved it.

'But there was still one people left unconquered. They were called the Zonabites; and their country – which wasn't large – was a long way off from Shalba. They were mountain-folk and tough fighters. Mashtu had had a try at them before; and found them a hard nut to crack. They had thrown his troops back – almost the first time that a Shalbian army had been beaten.

'Mashtu was a villain: but he was no fool. He knew that to make war on the Zonabites, so far from Shalba, would cost a terrible lot of money. Also, being no fool, he guessed that these men wanting to crown him King of the World were only trying to flatter him – to get themselves made generals, or something of the kind. So he spoke his mind to them in plain language.

' "No," he said, "I will not be crowned King of the World till the Zonabites are conquered and the whole world is truly mine." (That was what he had always wanted.) "Till the country of the Zonabites is under the rule of Shalba," said he, "what you offer me is nothing but a sham and a mockery. And you know it.

' "What's more," he added, "when I am crowned as ruler of the universe, I don't want any fancy gaudy thing like *that* put upon my head. I will have a simple crown, costing nothing, made of bronze, with no jewels in it! Thus, when I am truly Master of Mankind, when the Zonabites are crushed, I will show how little I thought of them – these last miserable enemies who keep Shalba from our dearest desire."

'All this, Doctor, is written, I believe, in the Shalbian language, around the head-band of the crown in that cabinet.

'Then King Mashtu began to get ready for his war. In spite of the sneering way in which he'd spoke of the Zonabites, his preparations for *this* war were the greatest in all his history. He spent money like water, fitting out his armies with all the latest deviltries his inventors could think up.

'He built great fleets of ships, down at the mouths of the rivers, to carry his soldiers across the seas to the distant land of the enemy. He meant to take no chances. He had the biggest army gathered together that mankind had ever seen. For this time, he boasted, he was going to wipe the Zonabites out, man, woman and child, so they could never rise again.'

The turtle sighed and stopped speaking a moment. And even in the poor light I thought I saw that half-smile play again around the corners of his wrinkled mouth.

'But five days,' he said presently, 'before the Shalbian army was to sail, the Flood came. It began, as I told you, with a gentle rain only. The King ordered the ships to put out to sea anyway; and the captains obeyed and sailed. But every single ship was smashed and sunk by that great wave we'd seen roaring across the Shalba race-track.'

Once more Mudface hesitated, deep in thought and memories. And soon the silence that hung over us there in the dim-lit vault was broken by the voice of John Dolittle.

'And so,' he said slowly, 'Mashtu did *not* become complete master of the Earth? He never lived to wear this,' (the Doctor laid his hand on top of the cabinet) 'the Crown of the World? But it took a deluge to stop him – from gaining his dearest wish. . . . I wonder what kind of a world we'd be living in now if there had been no Flood and – and he had succeeded.'

The Doctor's voice dropped and slowed down so we could only just hear him. It seemed almost as if he were in a dream, talking softly to himself, his eyes half closed.

'Thanks to you, brave Zonabites! – And, despite all the suffering the Deluge brought, thanks be to heaven for the Flood too! Mashtu all but wore it, the Crown of the World! . . . Could you get it out of this case for me?'

'Certainly,' said Mudface. He threw his front legs around the slender cabinet and squeezed. The grating in the top popped off and clattered to the floor like a tin plate. The Doctor put his arm down inside and fished up the bronze crown. He cleaned it off a little with his sleeve and examined the strange writing cut into the head-band.

'Dab-Dab,' he said quietly, 'we will take *this* back with us to Puddleby. It is worth nothing, as King Mashtu himself said – just bronze. So I do not feel I am taking stolen goods.'

Without another word he turned and moved towards the door.

Cheapside was still perched upon my shoulder.

'Tommy,' he whispered in my ear as we all started to follow John Dolittle from the room, 'that's the Doc all over, ain't it? – Look at 'im: knee-deep in diamonds – and all 'e carries home out of a royal treasure vault is an *old brass hat*! Swap me pink, that I should ever see the day!'

Outside upon the palace terrace we found the sun shining gaily; but it was getting low down, for evening was coming on. We had no idea that we had stayed so long within King Mashtu's gorgeous home. Remembering the wild duck's message from the old lame horse in Puddleby, we wasted no time in unhitching the canoe.

The Doctor stowed away the bronze crown with care. He fastened it, like the precious packages of note-books, to the canoe's bottom.

'That, Stubbins,' said he, 'is in case we have an upset. If the rest of the baggage is lost, the floating, wooden canoe will still save the most precious things for us, as long as they are tied in. – No, no, Gub-Gub, we can't go back to the palace cellars for your preserved dates, now. – Sorry, no time.'

Then the Doctor, before saying good-bye, gave the turtle his last instructions about the medicine; the foods he should, or shouldn't eat; and all the things he should do to keep well.

'You *will* take care of yourself, Mudface, won't you?' said he. 'Don't forget that the wild birds will always bring your messages to me, if you fall sick again or anything. As for your story, old friend, I don't know how to thank you enough.'

'I am only too glad that I had the chance to tell it to you, John Dolittle,' said the turtle. 'As for thanks, you have done far more for me than I did for you. My heart is sad indeed to see you go. But I know you must.'

The Doctor nodded. 'Alas, old friend, I must,' he agreed.

Mudface gazed down into the lake where the evening shadows of the palace towers were beginning to stretch out into the gloom of coming night.

'And yet, Doctor,' he added, 'if you do write what I have told you in a book, for all the peoples of today to read – who

323

knows? – maybe war may stop altogether and no leaders like King Mashtu ever arise again.'

The Doctor, silent, thought a moment before he answered.

'Indeed I hope so,' he sighed at last. 'At least I promise you the book shall be written and I will do my best to write it well. How many will take any notice of it: that is another matter. For men are deaf, mind you, Mudface – deaf when they do not wish to hear and to remember – and deafest of all when their close danger is ended with a short peace, and they *want* to believe that war will not come back.'

He turned suddenly and looked down into the canoe. Everyone was in his place, waiting. The Doctor slipped into the stern and took up the long paddle.

'All right, Stubbins,' he called. 'The painter's free. Shove off!'

And, as I pushed the canoe's bow out from the steps, I saw Mudface start lumbering down towards the corner of the terrace, where there was a grand view of all the south end of Junganyika. The old fellow meant to see the last of us from the best place.

Hereabouts, where the Secret Lake began draining itself into the river, a strong current swept us on our way. Once clear of the stonework, we let the canoe drift pretty much, saving our strength for the harder work which would come later.

As the lake narrowed still more we saw a sharp bend ahead of us. We knew that, after we had passed that bend, we would no longer be able to see the palace, or the waiting turtle. The Doctor and I turned and looked back.

There he was still, his giant shape standing up on the terrace-corner, black and clear against the evening sky. He waved a right foreclaw at us in farewell. We waved back.

'Good-bye, Mudface!' muttered the Doctor. 'Who knows how much you changed the history of the world – in gratitude for the kindness of one man, Eber. ... Good-bye to you, good health and good luck!'

I glanced at the mangrove-covered shores; they were nearer. We had rounded the bend. I looked back no more. I knew the turtle was now out of sight.

'You're right, Doctor,' said Cheapside suddenly. 'May – may good luck stay with 'im for – for the rest of his days.'

I glanced quickly at the sparrow. It was not what he had said that made me look at him. But I heard a queer, choking catch come into his voice. And I knew that this vulgar little rowdy of London's streets – Cheapside, who always made a joke out of everything – was, for perhaps the first time in his life, very close to tears.

In fact, we all had that 'let down' feeling which so often follows great excitement. The twilight had become almost real darkness now. A few big stars had appeared and their light made shimmering paths on the gloomy water. We still rested our paddles, knowing that the powerful current must carry us into the river without the help of any guide.

So this was the end of the 'lucky voyage'. We had done what we came to do. By rights, everyone in that canoe should have been talking gaily of a well-done job behind us and a well-loved home ahead. But, instead, we were thinking, glumly – all of us, about the same thing: our leaving Mudface behind and alone.

It made no difference that we couldn't take the great beast with us. In any case the English climate would have been too cold for him. But he had been sick here in his native Africa. . . . No, it was impossible to feel happy about our lucky voyage when we were leaving him this way.

The mangroves on either hand were closing in now, as we drifted nearer to the river. I knew without him telling me, that John Dolittle felt the most uneasy of us all. Suddenly he spoke,

'Stubbins, what's that ahead of us, near the opening to the stream? Seems to be coming towards us. Watch, you'll see the starlight glint on its wet body every once in a while.'

I had long since given up being surprised at his truly marvellous eyesight for long distances. All I answered was:

'Yes, Doctor, there's *something* there – and moving. But goodness knows what. – Hard for me to make out anything in this light.'

A moment later he gasped: 'By jingo! It looks like a turtle. . . . But what a size! I'd swear it was Mudface himself, if we hadn't just left him behind us on the terrace.'

It was plain soon that the creature could see us. It was making straight for our canoe with no shyness or fear at all. It swam swiftly, but so low in the water that little more than its head showed.

Motionless, we all gaped over the side till this strange thing out of the night was practically alongside our bow.

Then I saw that it was indeed so like Mudface I could easily have mistaken it for him in full sunlight. It raised its dripping head slowly out of the water and said in turtle language,

'Could you, by any chance, be John Dolittle?'

'Why, yes,' the Doctor answered. 'But –'

'Thank goodness!' the turtle interrupted. 'I hardly dared to hope that I would find you. Is it true that Mudface met with some accident? Is he still alive? Can you tell me where to find him, please?'

'Yes, Belinda,' said the Doctor, 'he is still alive – and very well, too.'

'Bless you, John Dolittle,' said the turtle. 'When the sea-birds told me you were here, I prayed I'd be in time to meet you. – But, tell me, how did you know I was Belinda?'

'Well,' said the Doctor smiling, 'you always ask your questions in threes – your husband told me so. I've never been so happy to meet anyone in my whole life.'

At that, the turtle looked aside, down into the black water. 'I'm so ashamed, Doctor,' she whispered.

'But, why?' asked the Doctor.

'For leaving my husband,' she said. 'I meant to be gone only a few weeks instead of all this everlasting time. You see, even after years and years away from Gaza and Eber and my baby Aden, I still longed for the human friends I'd left. And when news reached us that wars had started again, even in that beautiful America, I got so upset that, well, I couldn't sleep.

'I kept thinking of my baby Aden – or his children's descendants, as it would be by now. Still they were mine. They were fighting the foreigners from Asia. Eber and Gaza must have died of old age. Would the Eberites be beaten and wiped out after all? That tribe, too, was mine and Mudface's.

'My husband was too sick for such a journey. I thought it over a long while. Would my animal sense be of any help in saving the tribe – as it had in the past, rescuing Gaza and her husband? At last I made up my mind I'd go and see.'

She started to cry a little.

'And so,' she went on through her tears, 'when poor Mudface was asleep one night I sneaked away and crossed the ocean once more. I left a message with the snipe who lived near us to tell my husband why I simply *had* to go.'

'I understand. Cheer up,' said the Doctor.

Belinda went on: 'When the sea-birds told me that the giant turtle had disappeared I was almost frantic with worry: I had left the kindest husband in the world alone, when he was sick! ... I came back here as fast as I could possibly swim.'

As the turtle stopped for breath I could see she was almost too weary to stay afloat. 'But,' she asked the Doctor, 'you're sure he's all right? He wasn't injured by this earthquake or whatever it was the sea-birds told me about? Which way did you say I should go to get to him?'

'Straight ahead, Belinda,' said the Doctor. 'We left him a few miles back. I imagine, by now, he is on his way to the island my post-office birds built for him a few years ago.'

'Thank you,' said she. 'I'll hurry on now, if you'll excuse me. I seem to be the only creature living that never met you, John Dolittle. Even in America every bird, beast and fish still speaks of you and your kindness. I hope I'll see you again soon.'

Mrs Mudface was already churning the water like a steamboat, away from the canoe's side – headed for the island.

'Thank goodness for that,' sighed the Doctor. 'I feel better now. Somehow I hated leaving him all alone this time. But Belinda will take good care of him.'

And of a sudden all our own family brightened up. Cheerful chatter broke loose fore and aft and amidships. Cheapside even popped up to the mast head and shouted after the fast disappearing swimmer.

'Three cheers for Belinda! – Hooray!' He was joined in his noisy outburst by all of us. And at the end of the cheering Polynesia's voice could be heard singing alone:

> "For she's a jolly good fellow.
> Yes, she's a jolly good fell – Hello!
> Oh, Belinda's a jolly good fell – Hello!"

The Doctor and I broke into outright laughter. For the parrot had set the words to the tune of a sailor's hornpipe.

Then, like one man with one thought, John Dolittle and I plunged our paddles into the starlit water at the same moment. The canoe shot forward into the river like an arrow (upsetting most of the merry-makers in a laughing heap on top of the baggage). We were on our way downstream, towards the west, towards Puddleby and home.

THE DOLITTLE BOOKS

THE STORY OF DR DOLITTLE. 'A work of genius. It is the first real children's classic since *Alice*.' *Hugh Walpole*

THE VOYAGES OF DR DOLITTLE. 'Children will delight in this book. Dr Dolittle wins all hearts.' *The Times Literary Supplement*

DR DOLITTLE'S POST OFFICE. 'Incomparably the best new book for children of the year.' *Spectator*

DR DOLITTLE'S CIRCUS. 'The purest delight ... as good as the rest of the books dealing with that immortal and delightful person.' *Observer*

DR DOLITTLE'S ZOO. 'It is with genuine regret that we once more say good-bye to the little man who manages to combine Franciscan heroism and charm with homely sanity.' *Nation*

DR DOLITTLE'S CARAVAN. 'A lively and ingenious "Dolittle", and although at the end of the book he has retired to Puddleby, we cannot believe that he is anywhere near the end of his activities.' *The Times Literary Supplement*

DR DOLITTLE'S GARDEN. 'No books of our time can compare with these for communicating to youthful readers those constant glows of appreciation that make them gurgle with joy.' *Daily Telegraph*

DR DOLITTLE IN THE MOON. 'Each generation cries for the moon in turn, and the very newest one will find in these pages not something to cry for, but something to completely satisfy their fleeting fancy.' *Spectator*

DR DOLITTLE'S RETURN. 'It is, indeed, good news that this most lovable man has returned from the moon.' *Lady Cynthia Asquith* in the *Daily Telegraph*

DR DOLITTLE AND THE SECRET LAKE. Humorous, eventful, and never condescending in tone.' *Irish Times*

DR DOLITTLE AND THE GREEN CANARY. 'Dr Dolittle long ago joined the small band of those chosen by children as worthy of more than casual notice.' *Manchester Guardian*

DR DOLITTLE'S PUDDLEBY ADVENTURES. 'Hugh Lofting will take his place among the immortal humorists who have given pleasure to countless millions of readers.' *Children's Newspaper*

JONATHAN CAPE
THIRTY BEDFORD SQUARE, LONDON

And all now available in Puffins

BAGTHORPES UNLIMITED

Helen Cresswell

'I wish to see my children, and my children's children, gathered together so that I can feel my life has not been in vain. I want a Family Reunion.'

This announcement by Grandma Bagthorpe produced a long silence while everyone digested the horrors of what lay in store. But anything was better than being reunited with Uncle Claud and his family, so William, Tess, Rosie and Ordinary Jack knew there was only one course open to them – to drive the Dogcollar Brigade from the house at the earliest opportunity! More monumental mix-ups and mishaps which follow the other books in the Bagthorpe Saga – *Ordinary Jack* and *Absolute Zero*.

SUPER GRAN

Forrest Wilson

Super Gran Smith hurled herself at young Willard's football in a sliding tackle. 'Come on, laddie, give us a wee kick at your ball,' she cried. Willard stared, amazed. Only a minute ago she had been just a little old lady sitting on a park bench. But that was before the strange beam of blue light shot through her – the start of being Super Gran, with incredible speed, strength and X-ray eyes. But it was Edison who knew that Gran's miracle powers had come from a machine invented by her father, now stolen by the Inventor for his own plans to take over the world. Daunted by nothing, and gathering a force of Super Oldies, Super Gran goes forward to battle with the Inventor and his Super Toughies.

NED KELLY AND THE CITY OF THE BEES

Thomas Keneally

What would you do if you were lying in hospital, and a sympathetic bee offered you the chance of visiting her hive? Ned Kelly didn't hesitate for long. Apis's hive was an extraordinary place – a great dim cave full of mysterious doorways, and workers doing jobs he didn't understand. Luckily Miss Nancy Clancy was there to show him around – she'd been living in the hive for more than a hundred years and knew it pretty well. Ned didn't mean to stay a whole summer with the bees, but he hung on to find out what would happen next. Would the revolt the drones were planning for the autumn be successful? Was the Queen growing too old? If so, who would be her successor? With questions like these, it would be hard for Ned to tear himself away.

THE SNOW HOUSE

Nora Wilkinson

If a deputation of excessively nice and polite mice told you they were in danger of starvation and death from fearful traps, wouldn't you want to help? Well, Fred certainly did, and he invited them to go and live in the Snow House (an enormous snowball) which was just the right size for them. There were difficulties, of course, and the actual journey across the snowy Square at midnight was fraught with peril. But eventually they were all safely installed and living happily, until something even worse happened – they were kidnapped, and seemed destined for a fate worse than death. This is the story of the biggest and most daring rescue in Mouse History, and it will be enjoyed by everyone who feels friendly towards mice.